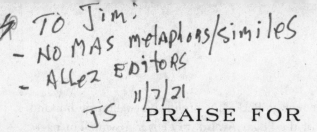

PRAISE FOR

A PRIVATE CATHEDRAL

"An imaginative blend of crime and other genres, Burke's existential drama is both exquisitely executed and profoundly moving."

—*Publishers Weekly* (starred review)

"Burke has concocted his usual gumbo of thrills and chills, stirred it with gusto and seasoned it with plenty of local superstition and rumor. What makes these books so enduring (this is the 23rd Robicheaux novel) and the storytelling so seductive is that Burke has the voice to do justice to the region's ancient curses and its modern crimes."

—Marilyn Stasio, for *The New York Times Book Review*

"[A]ll-enveloping mix of horror and crime."

—*Booklist* (starred review)

ALSO BY JAMES LEE BURKE

DAVE ROBICHEAUX NOVELS

A Private Cathedral
The New Iberia Blues
Robicheaux
Light of the World
Creole Belle
The Glass Rainbow
Swan Peak
The Tin Roof Blowdown
Pegasus Descending
Crusader's Cross
Last Car to Elysian Fields
Jolie Blon's Bounce

Purple Cane Road
Sunset Limited
Cadillac Jukebox
Burning Angel
Dixie City Jam
In the Electric Mist with
Confederate Dead
A Stained White Radiance
A Morning for Flamingos
Black Cherry Blues
Heaven's Prisoners
The Neon Rain

THE HOLLAND NOVELS

Another Kind of Eden
The Jealous Kind
House of the Rising Sun
Wayfaring Stranger
Feast Day of Fools
Rain Gods

In the Moon of Red Ponies
Bitterroot
Heartwood
Cimarron Rose
Two for Texas
Lay Down My Sword and Shield

OTHER FICTION

Jesus Out to Sea
White Doves at Morning
The Lost Get-Back Boogie

The Convict and Other Stories
To the Bright and Shining Sun
Half of Paradise

A
PRIVATE
CATHEDRAL

JAMES LEE BURKE

Simon & Schuster Paperbacks

New York   London   Toronto   Sydney   New Delhi

Simon & Schuster Paperbacks
An Imprint of Simon & Schuster, Inc.
1230 Avenue of the Americas
New York, NY 10020

First Simon & Schuster trade paperback edition June 2021

SIMON & SCHUSTER PAPERBACKS and colophon are registered trademarks of Simon & Schuster, Inc.

For information about special discounts for bulk purchases, please contact Simon & Schuster Special Sales at 1-866-506-1949 or business@simonandschuster.com.

The Simon & Schuster Speakers Bureau can bring authors to your live event. For more information or to book an event, contact the Simon & Schuster Speakers Bureau at 1-866-248-3049 or visit our website at www.simonspeakers.com.

Interior design by A. Kathryn Barrett

Manufactured in the United States of America

1   3   5   7   9   10   8   6   4   2

Library of Congress Cataloging-in-Publication Data

Names: Burke, James Lee, 1936- author.
Title: A private cathedral / James Lee Burke.
Description: First Simon & Schuster hardcover edition. | New York : Simon and Schuster, 2020. | Series: The Dave Robicheaux novels |
Subjects: GSAFD: Mystery fiction.
Classification: LCC PS3552.U723 P75 2020 (print) |
LCC PS3552.U723 (ebook) | DDC 813/.54--dc23
LC record available at https://lccn.loc.gov/2019058582
LC ebook record available at https://lccn.loc.gov/2019058583

ISBN 978-1-9821-5168-3
ISBN 978-1-9821-5169-0 (pbk)
ISBN 978-1-9821-5170-6 (ebook)

For James Joseph Hogan
One of the good guys
who has walked the walk with us
for over thirty years

"Going down in Lou'sana, gonna git me a mojo hand."
—Muddy Waters

Chapter One

You know how it is when you've kicked around the globe too long and scorched your grits too many times with four fingers of Jack in a mug and a beer back, or with any other kind of flak juice that was handy. And if that wasn't enough, maybe doubling down in the morning with a half-dozen tall glasses of crushed ice and cherries and sliced oranges and vodka to drive the snakes and the spiders back into the basement.

Wow, what a gas. Who thought we'd ever die?

But why get into all that jazz? I'll tell you why. I'm talking about those moments when you strip your gears, whether you're chemically loaded or not, and get lost inside the immensity of creation and see too deeply into our ephemerality and our penchant for greed and war and willingness to destroy the Big Blue Marble, and for a brief moment you scare yourself so badly you wonder why you didn't park your porridge on the ceiling a long time ago.

That kind of moment came to me once when I was standing on a Texas dock in the sunset while the waves rolled below me and thudded as hard as lead against the pilings, an incandescent spray blowing as cool as refrigeration on my clothes and skin, a green-gold light as bright as an acetylene torch in the clouds, the amusement pier ringing with calliope music and the popping of shooting galleries. It was one of the moments when you hang between life and death and ache to hold on to the earth and eternity at the same time, regretting all those days and nights you pitched over the gunwales while you deconstructed your life.

I'm talking about the acknowledgment of mortality, and not the kind that slips up on you in a hospice or on a battlefield filled with the cawing of carrion birds or by way of a drunk driver bouncing over a curb into a playground. I'm talking about seeing the Seventh Seal at work and a string of medieval serfs and liege lords and virginal maidens wending their way across a hilltop to a valley dark as oil, their silhouettes blowing like pieces of carbon in the wind.

The people who have these moments of metaphysical clarity are what I call members of the Three Percent Club, because in my opinion that's approximately the percentage of people who fry a couple of their lobes and are able to talk about it later. You can pay your dues in lots of ways: on a night trail sprinkled with Chinese toe-poppers and booby-trapped 105 duds; or stacking time on the hard road; or kneeling on a hard floor in a convent with a rosary twisted around your knuckles; or listening to voices in your head that are as loud as megaphones. The surroundings don't matter. You're in a black box for the duration, Jason. You literally sweat blood, bud. To say it's a motherfucker doesn't come close.

After you're through with the long night of the soul, or after it's through with you, you're never the same. Earthly fears disappear like a great weight removed from a scale. You have no inclination to argue or hold grudges; reticence becomes a way of life; it's hard to stay awake during an average conversation.

The downside is you're on your own, the only occupant in a cathedral in which you can hear your heartbeat echoing off the walls.

What does all this have to do with Johnny Shondell? I'll tell you. He was out of another era, even though he was more symbolic of it than part of it, an era we always want to resurrect, whether we admit it or not. Jesus talked about people who are made different in the womb. I'll take that a step further. Maybe some people were never in the womb. They arrive inside a golden bubble and somehow become the icon for the rest of us. At least that's how I thought of Johnny and Isolde. Call it a scam or a sham or the stupidity of the herd, who cares? The only reality you have is the one you believe in. I say eighty-six the rest of it.

Back in that other era, America was still America, for good or bad. Men such as Harry Truman and Dwight Eisenhower were president; we didn't have the daily arrival of the clown car. People can say that's just nostalgia talking. They're wrong. For us in Louisiana it was a time of music and drive-in movies and starry skies and two-lane roads that meandered for miles through meadows and oak trees hung with Spanish moss. If you don't believe me, ask my friend Clete Purcel. He'll tell you all about it. I can almost hear him now: "It was deeply copacetic, noble mon. You can take that to the shack, Jack. I wouldn't give you the slide, Clyde."

BUT LET'S GO back to that summer evening on the dock many years ago. I had an appointment the next day at Huntsville Pen, one I didn't want to think about, so I walked onto the amusement pier and saw Johnny Shondell up on the bandstand, belting it out to a crowd of teenage girls whose faces glowed not only with adoration but with a vulnerability that made you ache to hold and protect them.

Johnny's parents had been killed in an airplane accident when he was very young, and he had been raised by his uncle Mark. I had watched him grow up around New Iberia the way you watch kids grow up in a small town: You see them at a church service, playing a pinball machine in a café, smacking a baseball, quarterbacking at the state finals, rocking at the senior hop, boxing in the Golden Gloves, or boosting cars or getting involved in cruel and hateful behavior such as nigger-knocking and the abuse of the poorest of the poor. Johnny didn't fit in a category. His musical talent was one step short of cosmic, and the first time you heard him play and sing, you knew he'd hooked on to the tail of a comet and would defy both mortality and improbability. Yeah, that's right, in his journey across the heavens he'd sprinkle the rest of us with stardust, even if he was a member of the Shondell family, millionaire liars and bums that they were.

You bet, the Shondells had money, tons of it, but like most wealthy people in our Caribbean culture, they made it off the backs of others and had family secrets that involved miscegenation and exploitation of the out-of-wedlock children they sired. Don't be shocked. In Louisiana we don't have Confederates in the attic. We have them everywhere, including the basement and the outbuildings, the cistern and sometimes couched in the forks of our emblematic live oaks.

Johnny wore white slacks and a maroon silk shirt that puffed with wind. His physique was as lithe as a whip, his black hair combed in ducktails, thick and glistening; the stars were white and cold overhead, as though the backdrop had been created for that particular moment, one that was Homeric, as foolish as that sounds. Hey, even the waves had turned wine-dark under the moon, as though I were watching either the beginning or the end of an era.

"I know you," a voice said behind me.

I turned around. The girl who had spoken couldn't have been over seventeen. Her hair was whitish-blond, her skin the color of chalk, her cheeks pink like a doll's. A tattoo of roses and orchids dripped off her left shoulder (this was at a time when nice girls in New Iberia were not allowed to leave home with bare arms). "You don't remember me?"

"I'm sorry, I don't have my glasses," I lied.

"I'm Isolde Balangie. You know my family."

Oh, yes, I thought.

"You're a police officer," she said. "You used to come in my father's restaurant in the French Quarter. But you're from New Iberia. That's where my family is from, too. After Italy, I mean."

"I *used* to be a police officer."

"You're not one anymore?"

"Sometimes I am."

She had hazel eyes that went away from you in a sleepy fashion, then came back as though she were waking from a dream. "What does 'sometimes' mean?"

"I was fired from NOPD. Getting fired is my modus operandi."

"Fired for what?"

"I was a drunk."

"You're not now, are you?"

"A drunk is a drunk." I tried to smile.

Her gaze remained fixed on Johnny Shondell, her lips parting, and I knew she was no longer listening to me. I also knew my problems weren't worth talking about and were part of the chemically induced narcissism that every boozer carries with him like a sacred flame.

"It was nice seeing you, Miss Isolde," I said.

"You believe in kismet?"

"Where'd you hear of kismet?"

"At the movies. Do you believe in it?"

"I think it's Arabic for 'God's will.' I'm no expert about things like that."

"My family has hated the Shondells for four hundred years."

"That's a little unusual."

Her face sharpened. "They burned my ancestor."

"Pardon?"

"At the stake. In chains. They put nails through his mouth so he couldn't talk. Then they made him suffer as much as they could."

I stared at her.

"You don't believe me?" she said.

"Sure."

"That's why I think the Shondells should be killed."

"Killed?"

"Or blown up or something."

"So why are you here watching Johnny?"

"He's delivering me to his uncle Mark."

I didn't want to hear any more. The Balangie family was trouble, their ways arcane and, some said, incestuous. "Take care of yourself, kid."

"That's all you have to say?"

"Yeah," I replied.

"Then fuck you."

There is no human being who can become angrier than an injured teenage girl. I winked at her and walked away. That night I slept with the windows open in a salt-eaten, wood-framed 1940s motel room. I heard the waves pounding on the beach, devouring the sand, as though the tide were sliding backward in mockery of itself.

Chapter Two

I WAS SCHEDULED TO visit a convict in Huntsville at eleven A.M. But I didn't show up until four in the afternoon because I idled away the morning in Hermann Park Zoo and also watched some boys play softball. I wasn't looking forward to my visit with an inmate named Marcel LaForchette, and I was tired of evil and all its manifestations and our attempts to explain its existence. If you've ever dealt with evil, the real deal, up close and personal, you know what I mean.

How do you explain the Hillside Strangler or Ted Bundy? Childhood trauma? Maybe. When you read the details of what they did, you feel a sadness and a sense of revulsion that makes you wonder if we all descend from the same tree.

I don't mean Marcel was a ghoul or he would sexually torture and murder a woman or girl the way Bundy did. Marcel was made out of different clay, I just didn't know what. He was from the little town of Jeanerette, down the bayou from New Iberia, and came from a background not much different than mine, poor illiterate Cajuns like my mother, who worked in a laundry, and my father, who trapped and fished and racked pipe on the monkey board of an offshore drilling rig.

I graduated high school when I was seventeen. At the same age, in the same year, Marcel started a three-to-five bit in an adult prison for grand auto. When he was still a fish, he was cannibalized and made the punk of a half-dozen degenerates. You know what was oddest about Marcel? He never got tattooed, and this was in an environment where men wear sleeves from the wrist to the armpit as an indicator of their jailhouse mileage.

The other peculiarity about Marcel was his eyes. They were turquoise, the radiance trapped inside them so intense you couldn't read them. His thoughts could have been ethereal in nature or straight from the Marquis de Sade, but few people wanted to find out. Marcel was a button man. When Marcel pushed the "off" button, the target hit the floor like a sack of early potatoes.

Twenty miles from the pen, on the two-lane back road, I saw a purple Oldsmobile make the curve behind me. I thought I remembered seeing it at the zoo in Houston, but I couldn't be sure. I pulled in to a roadside park inside a grove of slash pines. The Olds passed me; its windows were tinted, the license plate caked with mud. Then a phenomenon occurred that I had seen twice before: A wide column of tarantulas crossed the road like a stream of wet tar in a creek bed. Years ago the tarantulas had come to the Texas coast on banana boats and spread inland, hence their presence on a state highway far from Galveston. Nonetheless, I wondered if I was watching an omen, one that meant no good would come from my visit with Marcel, a man whom I could have become or perhaps who could have dressed in my skin.

MY RELATIONSHIP WITH the assistant warden got me in, but it didn't get me liked. Back then I didn't have a good reputation, and I was late on top of it, and to make it worse, at least in terms of my conscience, I had lied and told an administrative officer I was investigating a crime in Louisiana and hoped to get some help from Marcel.

Two gun bulls brought him from the field in waist and ankle chains, and sat him down in a small concrete-floored room with two chairs and a wood table and a window that looked out on the Walls, the huge redbrick complex of buildings and ramparts that were an architectural emanation of the original 1848 structure. Both gun bulls were big men with big hands and wore coned cowboy hats, their armpits dark and looped with sweat, their thoughts hidden behind their shades.

"Sorry to make a problem for you guys," I said.

One of them sucked a tooth. "We don't have anything else to do," he said. The door was constructed of both bars and heavy steel plates. He slammed it into the jamb and twisted a tiny key in the lock, a drop of sweat leaking from his hairline.

Marcel was wearing work boots that looked as stiff and uncomfortable as iron, and a dirty white pullover and white pants stained at the knees. He had a Gallic nose and a high forehead and sweaty salt-and-pepper hair; his body was taut as whipcord. He gave me a lopsided grin but did not speak. His eyes were unblinking, the pupils no more than small black dots, as though he were staring at a bright light.

"Why the chains?" I said.

"This is Texas, second only to Arkansas when it comes to the milk of human kindness," Marcel answered.

"In your postcard you said you had a gift for me."

"Information."

"But you want something first?"

"Know what it's like here when the lights go out? Show a li'l respect."

I looked at my watch. "I want to get back to New Iberia this evening."

He worked a crick out of his neck, his chains tinkling. "I'm doing eleven months and twenty-nine days, two jolts back to back. Follow me?"

"No."

"The judge gave me one day less than a year so I'd have to serve my sentences in a county bag that's making money off the head count. Except somebody screwed up and sent me to Huntsville. My lawyer is getting me paroled. But I'll have to do my parole time in Texas."

"What does this have to do with me?"

"I want to go back to Louisiana. I want to go straight."

"You?"

"Maybe I could do security work. Or be a PI."

"You were a mechanic, Marcel."

"No, I got caught up in a gang war in Brooklyn. Then there was a li'l trouble in New Orleans. But I never clipped nobody for hire."

"Why are you in chains?"

"A Mexican got shanked in the chow line. I was in the vicinity."

"You didn't do it?"

"I'd joog a guy when I'm about to go home?"

"Yeah, if he got in your face, you would," I said.

The sun was a dull red in the west, and I could see dust devils spinning out of a cotton field, breaking apart in the wind. Six mounted gun bulls were silhouetted like black cutouts against a horizon that could have been the lip of the Abyss. "Didn't you work for the Balangie family?"

"Briefly."

"I ran into Isolde Balangie last night. At an amusement pier. She was there to see Johnny Shondell."

"Get the fuck outta here."

"Teenage girls aren't drawn to guys like Johnny Shondell?"

"The Balangie and the Shondell families get along like shit on ice cream."

"What if I told you Isolde Balangie was being delivered to Mark Shondell?"

"'Delivered,' like to be deflowered?"

"I don't think she'll be working in the kitchen," I said.

I stood up and rattled the door for the screw. Marcel blew out his breath. "I need a sponsor if I'm gonna get out-of-state parole."

"I have a serious character defect, Marcel," I said. "I don't like people using me."

"Your mother probably got knocked up by a whiskey bottle, but you're on the square. You know the people on the parole board."

"You need to rethink how you talk to other people, Marcel," I said.

"Come on, Dave. I'm telling you the troot'. I want to go straight."

"What's the information?"

"Sit down."

"No."

The room was growing hotter. I could smell his odor, the dirt and cotton poison, the sweaty socks that probably hung on a line in his cell and never dried, the fermented pruno that was a constant cause of inmate incontinence.

"I ain't asking much," he said.

I haven't been honest. I wasn't there out of humanity or duty. I was there because I wanted to believe that evil has an explainable origin, one that has nothing to do with unseen forces or even a cancerous flaw in the midst of Creation, and that even the worst of men could reclaim the light they had banished from their souls. I retook my seat. His eyes resembled hundreds of tiny blue-green chips of glass.

"New Orleans was the staging area for the hit on John Kennedy," he said.

"Old news," I said. "No, not just old. Ancient."

"I knew one of the guys in on it. He was an enforcer for the Mob in Brooklyn. His street name was Chicken Cacciatore. I ain't putting you on. He got mixed up with the CIA and some blackmail schemes in Miami."

I knew the name of the man he was talking about. He worked for the Miami Better Business Bureau and received paychecks from one of our national political parties as well. He also ran a car-theft ring. I knew that no one could have cared less.

"You just gonna look at me like that?" he said.

"I'll see if I can help out with the interstate parole situation."

"No kidding?"

"Why not? You said you're going straight."

"Like maybe you can get me a job?"

"Got any car wash experience?"

He lowered his eyes. He shrugged. "I'm up for whatever it takes."

"That was a joke. You'd better not burn me, Marcel."

"You still tight with Clete Purcel?" he said.

"He's my best friend."

"That's like saying clap is my favorite shade of pink."

I rattled the door again and this time called for the screw. "Don't get your expectations up."

"Come here," he said.

There it was, the dictatorial command, the smugness and condescension that constitute the tone of every narcissist. I stepped toward him. "Change your tone," I replied.

"I tole you I had some information. I was working your crank. I cain't do time no more. I got too many bad things in my head. Maybe I got to get something off my conscience."

I didn't want to become his confessor. But neither was I an admirer of the Texas prison system. I propped my arms on the table, my back to the door, blocking the screw's view of Marcel. His face was narrow and furrowed, his cheeks unshaved, dirty-looking, as though rubbed with soot.

"I was the driver on a whack for the Balangie family," he said. "The guy was a child molester. He's in the swamp on the north side of Lake Pontchartrain. There's people in New Iberia who want to know where he's at."

"I don't."

"Are you serious?" he said.

Like most recidivists, Marcel had spent much of his life inside the system, and his knowledge of the outside world was like a collection of old postcards someone had to explain to him.

"Hey, you listening?" he said. "There's no statute of limitations on homicide."

"Put it in your memoir," I said.

"Why'd you come here?"

"I wondered if you were born without a conscience or if you made yourself that way."

"You cocksucker."

"I'll see what I can do about the parole."

"I don't want your help. Stay away from me. Don't use my name."

"A deal is a deal," I said. "You're stuck with me, Marcel. Disrespect my mother again and I'll break your jaw."

Ten minutes later, as I walked outside through the redbrick complex, I wondered which building had housed the electric chair, called Old Sparky by people who thought shaving the hair off a human being and strapping him to a chair and affixing a metal cap to his scalp and frying him alive was the stuff of humor. I also wondered again if the entirety of our species descended from the same antediluvian soup. My guess is that our origins are far more diverse; I also believe that the truth would terrify most of us. What if we had to accept the fact that we pass on the seed of the lizard in our most loving and romantic moments? That the scales of the serpent are at the corners of our eyes, that bloodlust can have its first awakening when the infant's mouth finds the mother's nipple?

Chapter Three

I RETURNED TO NEW Iberia and my shotgun house on East Main, not far from the famed antebellum home called the Shadows. I was living the life of a widower back then, in the days before 9/11, a recluse trying to hide from my most destructive addictions, Jack on the rocks with a beer back and my love affair with the state of Louisiana, also known as the Great Whore of Babylon. For me she has always been the embodiment of every vice on the menu, starting with racetracks and bourré tables and casinos and lakes of gin and vodka and sour mash and hookup joints with a honky-tonk special on every stool aching to get it on in four/four time.

Think I'm giving you a shuck? People of color have a saying: If you're black on Saturday night, you'll never want to be white again. The same kind of thinking applies in Louisiana, but on a wider scale and not on a basis of race or the day of the week. The southern half of the state is the cultural equivalent of the Baths of Caracalla; the only difference is the coon-ass accents and the fact the slop chutes never close. I knew a famous country musician who moved to a farmhouse in Carencro to get sober, even surrendering his car keys to his wife. Yeah, I know, with the help of A.A, miracles happen and you can get sober anywhere. That's what the musician's wife thought until Mardi Gras kicked into gear and her husband drove the lawn mower eight miles down the highway to Lafayette so he could march in the parade and get soused out of his mind.

I fished in the evening with a cane pole among people of color, and watched the August light drain out of the sky and gather inside the oaks and disappear on the bayou's surface in a long brassy band that, as a child, I believed was a conduit to infinity. It was a strange way to be, I guess. I had been suspended or fired from three law enforcement agencies, and even though I was relatively young, I felt the tug of the earth at eveningtide and a gnawing hole in my stomach that told me the great mysteries would always remain the great mysteries, and that the war between good and evil was so vast and unknowable in nature and origin that my ephemeral efforts meant absolutely nothing.

The weeks passed without any contact from Marcel LaForchette. Then on a Sunday afternoon, when I was walking in City Park, I saw two men in a purple Oldsmobile pull onto the grass and park under the oaks and get out and remove a golf bag from the trunk. They were stout men in their prime, tanned perhaps as much by chemicals as sun, dressed in sport clothes, the kind of men who probably played college football one or two semesters and later sold debit insurance, ex-jocks you felt sorry for.

Until you looked at the scar tissue in the hairline, or the big hands with too many rings on them, or the white teeth that were too wet, the smile like that of a hungry man staring at a roast.

They teed up on the grass and whocked two balls down the bayou, watching them arch and splash in the distance.

"Excuse me," I said behind them.

They turned around, resting their clubs, their faces full of sunshine.

"This isn't a driving range," I said.

"Didn't think anyone would mind," the shorter man said. He had thick lips and hair that was long and hung in ringlets and was as bright as gold, like a professional wrestler's, his biceps as solid as croquet balls. "Did you think anyone would mind, Timmy?"

"Not unless we hit a fish in the head," Timmy said.

"A lot of people seem to think Louisiana is a garbage dump," I said. "We've got trash all over the state."

"Yeah," the shorter man said. "It's a shame, isn't it?"

"He's talking about us," Timmy said. "Right? You're saying we're trash?" His brown hair was soft-looking and dry and cut in a 1950s flattop and looked like an upturned shoe brush. His smile never left his face.

"I'm a police officer," I said. "I'd appreciate y'all not using the bayou as a golf course. That's all."

"We're not troublemakers," Timmy said. "The opposite. We're problem solvers."

The man with gold hair that hung in ringlets licked his lip. "That's right. We wouldn't jump you over the hurdles, sir."

"I look like an old man?" I said.

"A show of respect," he said.

"You guys like zoos?" I said.

"Yeah," Timmy said. "You got one here?"

"No, but there's a nice one in Houston," I said. "In Hermann Park, off South Main."

"Without much work, this town could be a zoo," the shorter man said. "Circle it with some chicken wire, then charge people admission."

"Yeah, our man here could probably run it," Timmy said. "What do you say about that, slick?"

The oak tree above us swelled with wind. A white speedboat sliced down the middle of the bayou, its wake washing organic detritus over the cypress knees and bamboo roots that grew like half-buried knuckles along the mudflats. "I think you boys passed me on the highway when I was driving up to Huntsville," I said. "Tarantulas were crossing the road, hundreds of them. It's quite a phenomenon to witness."

The speedboat engine whined in the distance like a Skilsaw cutting through a nail.

"We passed you?" Timmy said. "I think you got us mixed up with somebody else."

"I'm not real popular these days," I said. "Why do you want to bird-dog a guy like me?"

"Because Marcel LaForchette is a button man for the Jersey Mob," said the man with the gold hair. "Because he made the street four days ago. Because you had something to do with getting him out."

"I don't have that kind of juice," I said.

"Call me Ray," the man with gold hair said. He twisted one of his ringlets around his finger. His eyes were out of alignment, one deeper and higher than the other. "We're private investigators. LaForchette is an animal. Our client is a man who has reason to worry about a guy who worked with Jimmy the Gent. You know who that is, right?"

"Yeah, Jimmy Burke," I said. "He's doing life in New York."

"He *was* doing life," Timmy said. "Now he's sleeping with the worms. But LaForchette is still around. So why don't you tell us what you had to say to him in Huntsville?"

"You didn't start your surveillance of me at Hermann Park Zoo," I said. "You were at the amusement pier the night before."

"You think you saw us on an amusement pier?" Ray said.

"Maybe you were looking at me through binoculars. But you saw me talking to Isolde Balangie. That's what this is about, isn't it?"

Ray brushed at his nose and huffed through one nostril. "Sometimes it's not smart to show you're smart."

"I never claimed to be smart," I said.

"You lose your badge for drinking or being on a pad?" Ray said.

"Call it a sabbatical," I said.

"So you won't mind?" he said.

"Mind what?"

"This." He slid a driver from the golf bag and dropped three balls on the grass. He whocked the balls one after another, then watched the last one splash in the bayou and offered me the club. "I got some more balls in the car. Smack a few. We don't mean to offend. A young girl is missing. If she isn't found, some people are gonna be swinging by their colons."

The only sound was the wind in the trees. Timmy's eyes lit up as they settled on mine. He nodded as though confirming his friend's statement, one finger bouncing in the air. "I've seen it. Meat hooks. Fucking A, man."

"Y'all know where I live?" I said.

"Right across the bayou," Ray said. "A shotgun house. You got four-o'clocks and caladiums around the trees in your yard."

"Don't come around," I said.

"Hold still," Timmy said. He popped a leaf off my hair with his fingers. "I hear you got a daughter. One in college. I got one, too."

I stepped back from him. I could feel my hands opening and closing at my sides. "I'm going to walk away now."

"He's walking away," Timmy said.

"Yeah, that's the way they do it here," Ray said. "They walk away. They don't want trouble in Dog Fuck. So they walk away."

I cut through the shadows of the trees, light-headed, my ears ringing, and walked down the single-lane road that wound through the park. I heard their engine start behind me, then the Oldsmobile inching by, the gravel in the tire treads clicking on the asphalt. Ray was humped behind the wheel, his hands tapping a beat to the music on the radio, and Timmy was in the passenger seat, smoking a cigarette with lavender paper and a gold filter tip, blowing smoke rings like a man at peace with the world.

The Oldsmobile passed a group of black children kicking a big blue rubber ball on the grass. Autumn was just around the corner. The strips of orange fire in the clouds and the shadows in the live oaks and the coolness of the wind and the tannic odor of blackened leaves comprised a perfect ending to the day or, better yet, a perfect entryway into Indian summer and a stay against the coming of winter.

But if the evening was so grand and the riparian scene so tranquil, and the presence of the children such an obvious testimony to the goodness and innocence of man, and if I were indeed above the taunts of misanthropes, why was my thirst as big as the Sahara and my heart wrapped with thorns?

THE NEXT DAY at a New Orleans saloon on Magazine, I gave Clete Purcel a short version of the events on the pier and at the prison and on Bayou Teche. Magazine was where Clete had grown up. The saloon had a stamped-tin ceiling and a grainy wood floor and a long bar with a brass rail, and the owner kept the beer mugs refrigerated so they were sheathed with ice when he filled them, and for all those reasons Clete used the saloon as his office away from his office.

He listened while I spoke, his quiet green eyes staring at nothing, then chalked his cue and split a nine-ball rack and gazed at a solitary ball dropping into a pocket. It was dark and raining outside, and the shadows of the rain running down the window made his face look like he was crying.

"When the two guys drove past the black kids, you thought they might be planning to hurt them?" he asked.

"I don't know what I thought," I said. "Sometimes I think too much."

"Tell me about it."

"What's that mean?"

He shook off the question. "Marcel LaForchette was sprung five days ago and is in New Iberia?"

"In all probability."

"Stay clear of this, Streak. Starting with LaForchette. He was the iceman for the Balangie family."

"He admits to being the driver on a hit they ordered."

"Driver, my ass. He was one of the guys who sawed up Tommy Fig and froze the parts and strung them from a ceiling fan. You got the tag on the Olds?"

"I couldn't get a good look at it."

"Who's the missing girl?"

"They didn't say."

He was bareheaded and wearing a Confederate-gray suit and a Hawaiian shirt and oxblood loafers. His blond hair was cut short and neatly wet-combed, his cheeks freshly shaved. A scar like a flat pink worm ran through one eyebrow to the bridge of his nose. He picked up a longneck and tilted it against the light, drinking the bottle empty, the foam sliding into his mouth. "You want a soda with lime and cherries?"

"I'll let you know when I do."

"I was being courteous. You're getting played by LaForchette. Why'd you visit a geek like that, anyway?"

"He got a bad break as a kid."

"So did Thomas Edison. A train conductor slapped him upside the head and broke his eardrum. He invented the lightbulb instead of killing people."

"Edison provided the electricity for the original electric chair. He did it to drive his competitor out of business."

"Only you would know something like that, Dave."

"Why would the two guys in the Olds follow me to the joint? Why are they interested in me at all?"

"Back it up. They saw you talking to the Balangie girl on the pier. Right?"

"That's my guess. Why else would they be bird-dogging me?"

"Who knows? They sound like ex-cops with bubble gum for brains," he said.

"The Balangie girl said she was being delivered."

"You mean like white slavery?"

"Yeah, exactly."

"This has the smell of greaseballs all over it. Don't go near it. Don't give me that look, either. 'Greaseball' is not a racial slur. It's a state of mind. The only guy who ever got the upper hand on the Balangie family was Mussolini. He tore their fingernails out."

I went to the bar and ordered a po'boy sandwich loaded with fried catfish. I got an extra paper plate and cut the sandwich in half and went back to the pool table. I put Clete's plate on the chair next to his empty beer bottle. "You want a refill?"

"Why do you always make me feel guilty, Dave?"

"It's a talent I have."

"You want me to see what I can find out?"

Clete knew almost every street dip, hooker, Murphy artist, button man, crack dealer, low-rent PI, car booster, and dirty vice detective or cop on a pad in Orleans and St. Bernard Parish.

"No," I said. "You're right. It's not worth fooling with."

He racked his cue on the wall, picked up the po'boy, took a big bite, and chewed slowly, gazing through the front windows at the rain and the headlights on the asphalt and the fog puffing out of an alleyway. "I don't like those two pricks in the Oldsmobile bracing you."

"They didn't brace me," I said.

"Call it what you want. The lowlifes aren't allowed to disrespect the Bobbsey Twins from Homicide. I'll show restraint. I'm completely copacetic and mellow these days, and think only about serene subjects. It's part of a yogi program I'm in."

"Clete—"

"Did I ever tell you I once played nine-ball with Jackie Gleason? Minnesota Fats and Paul Newman were there. So was Jake LaMotta. Rack 'em up, big mon. We don't care what people say, rock and roll is here to stay."

Chapter Four

Two nights later, Clete pulled up in front of a line of cottages outside Broussard, midway between Lafayette and New Iberia. Most of the cottages were unoccupied. Fireflies flickered among the live oaks, then disappeared like pieces of burnt string. Balls of electricity rolled through the clouds and burst silently over the Gulf. He could smell rain blowing across the wetlands, like the smell of broken watermelons or freshly mowed hay. It was part of the Louisiana he loved, a hallowed memory he'd taken with him to Vietnam and into which he'd crawled when the rain clicked on his poncho and steel pot at the bottom of a hole or when an offshore battery lit the sky like heat lightning and the shells arched overhead and exploded with a dull thump in the jungle, the air suddenly bright with the smell of wet dirt and leaves and water that had been full of amphibian life.

A purple Oldsmobile was parked in front of the last cottage on the row. Clete tapped lightly on the door. He was wearing a porkpie hat tilted over his brow, his coat open, a lead-weighted blackjack in his right coat pocket, a manila folder rolled in a cone and stuffed in the other.

A bare-chested man with peroxided, coiled hair that hung in his face opened the door. His lips looked made of rubber, his torso a stump tapering to a thirty-inch waist. He wore sharkskin slacks and suspenders and flip-flops. One eye looked punched back in his skull. He took out a comb and began combing his hair, exposing his shaved pits. "What do you want?"

"Ray Haskell?" Clete said.

"Maybe. Who are you?"

"Clete Purcel. I called your office in New Orleans."

"About what?"

"Dave Robicheaux. Can I come in?"

"Who told you where I was?"

"I asked around the Quarter. I'm a PI. Like you. You got a beer?"

"I look like a liquor store? What's with you, man?"

"What I just said. Hey, I dig those sharkskin drapes. That's fifties-style, right? Can I come in or not? It's about to rain."

"I'm a little occupied. Get my drift? Make an appointment."

"Just want to know why you followed my podjo Dave to Huntsville, then dissed him on the bayou with that routine about driving golf balls. See, you diss Dave, you diss me. *Diggez-vous* on that, noble mon?"

Ray Haskell replaced his comb in his back pocket. "I got a friend due here you don't want to meet. So I'm gonna do you a favor and close the door. Then I'm going to bolt it and put the night chain on and check on my lady. You reading me on this?"

"Sure," Clete said. "But I got these printouts and photos of you and a guy named Timothy Riordan. It looks like you're both former flatfeet now doing scut work for the Shondell family and maybe a few people in Miami. I'm talking about political nutcases who speak Cuban and like to feed body parts to the gators in the glades."

"You read too many comic books. Regardless of that, we got the message. So I'm saying good night. Tell Robicheaux and tell yourself no foul, no harm. Now get the fuck out of here."

The bathroom door opened. Clete heard sniffling, then saw a slight, pretty black woman step out into the light of a bed lamp. He had known her when she turned tricks for a pimp named Zipper, who got his name from the scars he left on girls who tried to go independent. Her name was Li'l Face Dautrieve. Her hair was shiny and thick and looked like a wig that was too large for her head. Her eyes and nose and mouth were concentrated in the center of her face, not unlike sprinkles on a cookie. Her upper lip was split and her left eye swollen behind a bloody Kleenex she held against it. One cheek looked like she had swallowed a mouthful of bumblebees.

"This guy did that to you, Li'l Face?" Clete said.

"Ain't your bidness, Fat Man," she said. "Don't be messing in it."

"You did that, asshole?" Clete said to Ray.

"You'd better beat feet, pal," Ray said. "If you—"

Clete's fist was almost the size of a cantaloupe. He drove it into the center of Ray's face and sent him crashing into a breakfast table and chair. Then he kicked the door shut and picked up the chair and broke it on Ray's head.

"I ax for it, Fat Man," Li'l Face said. "I got a baby. He know where I stay at."

"Why'd he hit you?"

She shook her head.

"Answer me, Li'l Face."

"He wanted me to do things like Zipper made me do. He tried to put his—"

"I got the picture," Clete said.

He ripped the sheet off the bed and wrapped it around Ray's throat, then dragged him squirming and twisting into the bathroom, spittle running from the corners of his mouth. Clete drove his head into the toilet bowl and slammed down the seat, then mounted it and began jumping up and down on it like a giant white ape, crushing Ray's head into the shape of a football, blood stippling the bowl.

"He's strangling, Fat Man," Li'l Face said.

"Get his wallet and take whatever you want, then go home," Clete said.

She pulled the wallet from Ray's back pocket. Clete thought he felt a whoosh of air in the room, then he smelled the odor of rain and wet trees. He turned and saw Li'l Face squeeze past a tall man by the bed. She dropped the wallet and ran for the front door. The man pointed a nine-millimeter at Clete's chest. "Get down."

"You're Timothy Riordan," Clete said. "I got your photo."

"My friends call me Timmy. You can call me the guy who's about to print your brains on the wall."

Clete held up one hand. "I'm coming." He stepped down, balancing himself. "Things got out of control. We can work this out."

"You wish, blimpo."

Clete entered what he sometimes called "the moment." Someone points a gun at you and lets it wander over your body as arbitrarily as the red dot on a laser sight. Eternity and what it holds or may not hold is one blink away. The round in the chamber will probably tear through your sternum or heart or lungs, carrying bits of you into the wall. The pain will be like a firecracker exploding inside your chest. You will not be blown backward or spin in a circle, as shooting victims are portrayed in motion pictures. You will drop straight to the floor, like a collapsed puppet, and lie in a fetal position and feel your blood pool around you. If you are lucky, your tormentor will not try to increase your pain and fear. All because you made the wrong choice during "the moment."

So what do you do?

"You're quite a guy," Clete said. "I've seen your jacket. You worked vice. You were getting freebies up on Airline. You liked to knock around Vietnamese girls. Where'd you get your piece? Off a crippled newsy? You like movies? I do. Humphry Bogart says something like that in *The Maltese Falcon*."

Timothy Riordan blinked. Clete grabbed the frame of the nine-millimeter and twisted and simultaneously kicked him in the shin. Then he twisted some more, until Timothy's face folded in upon itself and a simpering voice rose from his mouth and tears slid from his eyes.

It should have been over. The gun was on the floor. Clete had his blackjack halfway out of his coat pocket. Then it caught on the flap, and in two seconds Timothy had a stiletto in his hand, the blade oiled and rippling with light and streaked with the whisker-like marks of a whetstone. He sank it in Clete's arm.

Clete felt the blade strike bone. A wave of nausea swept through his body. His loins turned to water; his sphincter started to cave.

He tried to speak, but his mouth wouldn't work. His fist landed in the middle of Timothy's face, slinging blood on a lamp shade, probably breaking his nose and front teeth, bouncing him off the wall. Clete pulled the stiletto from his arm and flung it across the room, then stomped Timothy's head with the flat of his shoe and dragged him to a side window and crashed him headfirst through the venetian blinds and glass. He left him hanging half outside, like a giant clothespin.

Ray was trying to get up from the bathroom floor, propping himself with one arm on the toilet. Clete kicked his feet out from under him. "This has been a lot of fun," he said. "I really dig your threads. Keep a cool stool. But if you even look at Li'l Face, I'll pull your teeth, Keith. Or make you real dead, Fred. Have a nice night."

Two DAYS LATER, Clete sat with me on the back steps of the shotgun house I owned on Bayou Teche, deep in the shadows of oak trees that were two hundred years old. He was perhaps the most complex man I ever knew. His addictions and gargantuan appetites and thespian displays were utilized by his enemies to demean and trivialize and dismiss him. His vulnerability with women—or, rather, his adoration of them—led him again and again into disastrous affairs. The ferocity of his violence put the fear of God into child abusers and rapists and misogynists, but it was also used against him by insurance companies and law enforcement agencies that wanted him buried in Angola.

He was the trickster of folklore, a modern Sancho Panza, a quasi-psychotic jarhead who did two tours in Vietnam and came home with the Navy Cross and two Purple Hearts and memories he shared with no one. Few people knew the real Clete Purcel or the little boy who lived inside him, the lonely child of an alcoholic milkman who made his son kneel all night on rice grains and whipped him regularly with a razor strop. Nor did they know the man who served tea on his fire escape to a mamasan he accidently killed. Nor did they know the NOPD patrolman who wept when he couldn't save the child he wrapped in a blanket, ran through flames, and crashed through a second-story window with, landing on top of a Dumpster.

Maybe his collective experience was responsible for an even more bizarre aspect of his personality. Years ago he tore a black-and-white photograph from a pictorial history of World War II and carried it inside a celluloid pouch in his wallet. The photograph showed a stooped woman walking up a dirt road with her three small daughters. The woman and the children wore rags tied on their heads and cheap coats on their backs. The smallest child was little more than a toddler. The viewer could not see what was at the end of the road. There were no trees or grass in the background, only an electric fence. The photograph was taken at Auschwitz. The cutline in the photo stated that the woman and her children were on their way to the gas chamber.

Once, when Clete and I were hammered in Sharkey Bonano's Dream Room, I asked him why he would want to carry such a gruesome photo on his person.

"So I don't forget," he said.

"The Holocaust?"

"No, the guys who ran those places. I'd like to get my hands on some guys like that. Maybe some of those neo-Nazis marching around with the Confederate flag."

I don't think Clete was talking just about Nazis. He hated evil and waged war against it everywhere he found it. I sometimes wondered if he was an archangel in disguise, one with strings of dirty smoke rising from his wings, a full-fledged participant in fighting the good fight of Saint Paul. Maybe that was a foolish way to think, but I never knew anyone else like him. Trying to explain his origins was a waste of time. The way I saw it, if Clete Purcel didn't have biblical dimensions, who did?

His left arm was in a sling; his right hand was curved around a sixteen-ounce Styrofoam cup of coffee. The trees were dripping, the bayou swollen and yellow and carpeted with rain rings.

"Those two guys didn't dime you?" I said.

"They don't want to lose their meal ticket. Down the line, they'll hire a third party to come after me."

"What's Li'l Face doing around here?"

"She lives with her aunt in the Loreauville quarters. Dave?"

I knew what was coming.

"The two guys I bounced around?" he said. "The word is they work for Mark Shondell. We need to chat him up."

"Noooo," I said, making the word as round as I could.

"You know the big problem you got here in New Iberia? Shintoism. You should get rid of all your churches and start building Japanese temples."

"Leave Mr. Shondell alone."

His face was serene, the part in his little-boy haircut as straight as a ruler. "*Mr.* Shondell? Wow."

I stared at the bayou, my hands hanging between my knees.

"I'm not letting you off the hook, Streak. What about the girl, what's-her-name, Isolde Balangie?"

"What about her?" I said.

"Is she missing or not?"

"Not officially."

"You checked with the locals?"

"I got my badge pulled. I'm not renewing old relationships these days."

He wagged his finger in my face. "See? The Balangies and the Shondells are making a deal of some kind, and they're using a teenage girl to do it. You're going to leave her twisting in the wind?"

"That knife wound could have been in your neck."

"Let me worry about that."

I took a breath. "You have to promise me something: I talk, you listen."

"I'm a fly on the wall. I wouldn't have it any other way." He pressed one hand on my shoulder and stood up, his posture erect, his face lit by the sun. "Beautiful, isn't it?"

"What is?" I said.

"The world. It's beautiful. Sometimes you got to stop and take inventory and appreciate the good deal you've got."

I had no idea what he meant. But that was Clete—a man with Janis Joplin and the full-tilt boogie in his head and a black-and-white photo in his wallet that most people would try to acid-rinse from their memory. "Coming?" he said.

MARK SHONDELL LIVED up the bayou among live oaks hung with Spanish moss in a glass-and-steel home of his own design, one that was as alien to our plantation culture as a spaceship. When he was much younger, he had been a co-producer of eighteen Hollywood B movies and had lost a fortune. When he left Los Angeles for the last time, he supposedly said, "One day I will destroy Hollywood. And the Jews who run it."

He was an eccentric, a scholar, a technocrat, a graduate of the Sorbonne, and a recluse. Some said his ancestors were nobility from the Italian Piedmont and allies of the Borgias; others said the Shondells descended from Huguenots who delighted in smashing Catholic icons; at least one Shondell had been a member of the Vichy government after France's surrender to Hitler.

Mark Shondell was forty and certainly handsome and distinguished in his bearing and carriage. Externally, he was kind and deferential and reticent, never given to offense. But he dined alone in our restaurants and did not entertain. His contributions to charity were given without ceremony. His gentility and the solipsistic distance in his eyes were such that people of humble origins were intimidated by him and often could not speak to him without a catch in the throat.

Unlike many in our state, he did not earn his wealth from the petroleum and chemical industry and the culture that produced Cancer Alley, a study in environmental degradation. The Shondells owned freighters and sailing yachts and plantations in Chile and Costa Rica and Colombia. Latin American dictators whose military uniforms tinkled with medals visited his home with regularity.

His genteel affectations and his cosmopolitan education aside, he had peculiarities that I didn't understand. He wore multiple rings, as though some flaw in his lineage made him blind to ostentation. His eye wandered when a girl too young for him walked by. In a restaurant, he often bent to his food and scooped it into his mouth. Or he might use a toothpick while still at the table, shielding it with one hand, then leave it on the plate like a statement of contempt.

Clete and I turned in to his driveway and parked in front of the porch. His gardens were blazing with rosebushes and hibiscus and bougainvillea, the shady areas soft with blue and pink hydrangea, the base of the tree trunks ringed with four-o'clocks and caladiums. The steel and glass in his three-story home seemed to pull the sunlight out of the sky. I went to the porch and pushed the doorbell with my thumb. Shondell answered as though he'd expected us, although I had not called in advance.

"Come on in, Dave," he said. "Your friend also. I have to be going shortly, but it's always good to see you."

"I'm Clete Purcel," Clete said, stepping inside, his gaze sweeping the spacious rooms. "Dave and I both worked Homicide at NOPD."

Shondell was dressed in a blue suit and a French-vanilla shirt with ruby cuff links. His face looked older than his years, but in a mature way, as though his wisdom were a gift and not an acquisition that takes a toll on the spirit. He waved at the white leather furniture in the living room. "Please sit down. Tell me what I can do for you."

"We're worried about a teenage girl named Isolde Balangie," Clete said before I could reply. "Last time anybody saw her, she was watching your nephew Johnny on an amusement pier over in Texas."

I wanted to kill him.

"I have no knowledge about that," Shondell said.

"Then I had trouble with a couple of PIs who were bird-dogging her and Dave," Clete said. "That's how I got this hole in my arm."

This was Clete's idea of a fly-on-the-wall methodology.

Shondell was seated across from us. He folded his hands. "Dave, can you clarify this for me? I'm truly lost."

"It's as Clete says. I saw Isolde Balangie at the pier. She claimed your nephew was delivering her to you." I had to cough when I finished the last sentence.

"There's a misunderstanding here," he said. "Tell you what. I was preparing a brunch for some friends. Let's have a bite and talk this thing out. I don't like what I'm hearing."

"That's not necessary," I said.

"It certainly is. I'll be right back."

You didn't argue with Mark Shondell. He gave an order or lifted a finger and robbed people of their words before they could speak. Are the very rich very different from you and me? What an absurdity.

How about this as a better question: In what way are they similar to us?

Through the sliding glass doors, I could see a man weeding a flower bed on his knees, his back to us, a frayed wide-brim straw hat shading his features. I heard wheels squeaking on the carpet, then saw a white-jacketed black man pushing a serving cart out of the kitchen. It carried trays of bacon and ham and scrambled eggs and a pitcher of orange juice and one of tomato juice; it also carried bottles of rum, brandy, and vodka, clinking with the motion of the cart.

I saw the cautionary look on Clete's face. "Mr. Shondell, we're taking up too much of your time. We just need to get that girl's situation behind us. Do you know where she is?"

"No, I do not," Shondell replied. "Frankly, I don't appreciate your tone or implication, either."

"How about your nephew, the rock-and-roll singer?" Clete said. "Is he here'bouts?"

"No, he is not."

"I heard he lived with you?" Clete said.

"He does. I raised him." Shondell's gaze went away from us, then came back, as though he had gotten control of his emotions and refocused his thoughts. His profile was as sharp as tin. He poured orange juice into two glasses, then added brandy in both and handed me one, his chest rising and falling. "Please help yourself, Mr. Purcel. Cheers, Dave. You were always a good fellow. You whipped the best of the best in the Golden Gloves."

I wasn't sure if he knew I was trying to live a sober life or not. Maybe he was one of those who thought alcoholics sought control of their drinking rather than abstinence. However, there was no question about his anger toward Clete. Nor was there doubt about how Mark Shondell dealt with his enemies. I set down the glass. "Mr. Shondell, I can't believe you don't know where your nephew is. I also can't believe you're not disturbed by the disappearance of the Balangie girl, particularly if she was being delivered to you."

He drank his glass empty and wiped his mouth with a white napkin, then dropped it on the cart. His face was gray, his eyes furious. "Have you talked to the Balangie family? Please tell me you have."

"No," I said.

"I see. You were honoring me by coming to me first about the 'delivery' of a seventeen-year-old girl? To me personally." His voice started to climb. "To my home."

"I didn't mention her age," I said. "But you're correct. She's seventeen. Or at least that's what I've been told."

His jaw tightened. He paused as though counting to three in his head. He cleared his throat. "It was good of you to come by. Johnny and I had an argument. I want him to attend Tulane and study to be a physician. He wants to gyrate on a stage. So he went off in a huff. I think he has a flirtation with the Balangie girl. That's all I know about any of this."

His explanation seemed plausible. Or at least that was what I wanted to believe. I was about to write off our visit when the gardener got to his feet from the flower bed and turned around. He removed his straw hat and wiped his face on his sleeve, then saw me staring at him and grinned. Shondell followed my gaze. "You know Marcel?"

"Who does not know Marcel LaForchette in New Iberia?" I said.

"The man needed a job and a little help with the parole board," Shondell said.

The room was quiet. Shondell looked at Clete. "Sir, do you have a reason for staring at me?"

"LaForchette is a button man," Clete said.

"He's a what?" Shondell said.

Clete picked up the orange juice and brandy I had set down, then widened his eyes and said, "Bombs away," and drank the glass to the bottom, letting the ice slide down his throat, his cheeks filling with color. He suppressed a burp. "I'll be out in the car, Dave. Mr. Shondell, you've got quite a place here. It puts me in mind of an Erector Set. In the best way."

He went out the door. Shondell let his eyes rest on mine. "You need to leave my home, Dave."

"Sir?"

"I won't suffer your rudeness or your bringing that man in my home."

"I had a problem of conscience about the girl. That shouldn't be hard for you to understand."

"Get out."

I rose from the leather softness of the sofa I was sitting on. Maybe I had reached an age when I was tired of restraint and being deferential to people I secretly loathed. If you have not lived in a hierarchal culture, one that reeks of hypocrisy and arrogance and entitlement, you will probably not understand a society in which you daily give homage to people whose ancestors kept your ancestors poor, uneducated, and terrified.

"Marcel LaForchette worked for the Balangie family, who are supposedly your enemies," I said. "Why would you bring him across the moat and into the castle? You're too smart a man for that."

"Do you want me to take a quirt to you?" he said. "I'll do it."

"I believe you," I replied. "See you around. You put your foot in it, sir."

Inside the darkness of his eyes, I saw a flare like the ignition of a kitchen match.

Chapter Five

CLETE HAD A PI office in both New Iberia and the French Quarter. We drove in his pink Caddy to the motor court on East Main where he stayed when he was in New Iberia. If you wonder why we didn't ask the Balangie family first about Isolde's safety rather than Shondell, I'll try to explain. The Balangies were people you didn't get involved with, not on any level, no more than you would wish to submerge your arm in a saltwater tank loaded with jellyfish.

Governor Huey Long, the prototype for all American demagogues, past and present, literally gave the state of Louisiana to Frank Costello. In turn, Costello gave the management of our statewide vice to an immigrant leg-breaker named Pietro Balangie, who put slot machines in every drugstore, grocery, nightclub, and saloon in South Louisiana. Did anyone object? In South Louisiana? Are you kidding?

Some suspected that Pietro was involved in the murder of John Kennedy. His level of rage toward the Kennedys was legendary, and Robert in particular made life miserable for him. But Pietro was old-school and took his secrets to the grave.

Clete sat on the bed in his cottage and gazed out the window at a dredge boat working its way up the bayou. "Want to take a drive?"

"To see Adonis Balangie?" That was the son of Pietro Balangie. He was also somebody I didn't want in my life or my head or anywhere in my vicinity.

"We should have slipped the punch with these guys," Clete said. "But we're stuck with the situation now. Or at least I am."

"I'm not?"

"All right, we're both in it," he said. "Adonis isn't such a bad guy. I mean in terms of greaseball standards. He went to college. He doesn't blow his nose on his napkins or anything like that."

Did Clete know how to say it?

But secretly, I wondered if I was afraid of Adonis. I don't mean in a physical way. He bothered me for other reasons. I never knew who Adonis really was. Nobody did. He had qualities. He had been a champion swimmer in high school and college and a paratrooper in the service. Like most mobsters, he was a womanizer, but he never used profanity or was vulgar or lowered himself to the level of his enemies. It was the unreadability of his eyes and his lack of emotion that gave him power. Adonis didn't rattle.

THE GROUNDS OF the Balangie estate were comparatively enormous for an urban area, particularly on Lake Pontchartrain, and surrounded by brick walls and piked gates. The grass was chemical-green and without shade trees, spiked with artless statuary that had no visual unity or theme, the mansion itself a parody of Greek revival that could have been transported from Disney World. The concrete pillars on the porch were swollen in the center and resembled giant beer kegs painted with strings of English ivy. The veranda contained a refrigerator and an exercise cycle and a bed frame with a rubber-encased mattress, where the father used to lie in the afternoon with a glass of lemonade propped on his stomach, his body hair oily and slick against his sun-bronzed skin.

The most attractive aspect of the compound was the view of the lake and the yacht club to the south and the sailboats tacking in the chop, and I wondered if Pietro, the Balangie patriarch, believed he was part of it, reborn in the New Country, safe from poverty, forgiven for the sins he committed out of necessity in the service of a capitalistic God.

I had Adonis's unlisted number from years ago, and I had called before we arrived. Adonis walked out on the porch before we could exit the car, wearing white slacks and sandals and a long-sleeve

black shirt with red flowers on it. His hair was the color of dark ma-
hogany, combed straight back, his complexion as smooth and flaw-
less as the skin on an olive. "Please come in," he said.

"What's the haps?" Clete said.

I thought I saw a flicker of goodwill in Adonis's expression, but
I suspected I was erring on the side of charity. Adonis weaponized
silence, and this moment was not an exception. At the entranceway,
Clete removed his hat and offered to take off his shoes.

"No," Adonis said. "Come in as you are."

"How have you been, Adonis?" I said.

"My home is yours," he said, stepping aside, letting my question
hang.

The upholstery and curtains and wallpaper were a mixture of
lavender and pink and pale green, a combination I would normally
associate with seasickness, all of it printed with flowers, creating the
affect of a villa in southern Italy. An oil painting of Pietro Balangie
and his wife hung over the mantelpiece. She wore a royal-purple
brocaded coat with a white brooch on the chest and had beautiful
gray-swept hair and a placid expression that could be interpreted as
one of either fortitude or acceptance. Pietro wore a three-piece suit
and a boutonniere and a plum-colored tie, his neck like a stump protruding from his shirt, his hair combed neatly. Pietro might have had
the body of a hod carrier, but in the painting and in real life, there
was no denying the regal aspect in his classical Roman features and
the quiet confidence that could make ordinary businessmen tremble.

Three bear rugs lay in a semicircle around a stone fireplace, their
mouths propped open, their glass eyes staring as though in anticipa-
tion of the gas logs igniting. A half-dozen cats were lying or walking
on the furniture.

"You giving my home the once-over?" Adonis said.

"Sorry?" I replied.

"The decor in my home. It doesn't meet your standards? Or
maybe you don't like cats?"

"It's a fine place," I said.

"I'm glad you approve."

"You asked me a question and I'm answering it," I said. "It's a fine home."

His eyes held mine. "My mother and father were proud of it. So am I. That's why I don't change anything about it, or invite just anybody inside it."

I let my eyes slip off his.

"We appreciate your invitation," Clete said, breaking the silence. "See, we heard maybe your daughter is missing, and we tried to help out. A couple of guys who work for Mark Shondell started a beef with us, and I ended up in the hospital. We thought you could give us a little information."

"Isolde is my stepdaughter," he said. "Her father died on a mercy mission to Rwanda."

"Whatever," Clete said. "She told Dave on this amusement pier over in Texas that she was being delivered to the Shondells. That's a little weird, right? I mean the word 'delivered.' That's what I would call deeply weird."

Adonis's gaze was focused in neutral space. His eyes seemed to change color, as though either a great sadness or a great darkness were having its way with his soul. "Why do you feel compelled to speak of things like this to me? Are you telling me I'm irresponsible as a parent? That's why you've come into my home?"

"We treated your father with respect when we were at NOPD, Adonis," I said. "We wouldn't disrespect either you or your family."

There was a pause, a silence in which I could only guess at his thoughts, the kind of moment you remember from high school when you stepped on the wrong kid's foot and you felt an elevator drop to the bottom of your stomach.

"Walk with me," he said. "I have to feed my animals. Do you know my wife?"

"No," I said, letting out my breath. "We need to get the issue of your stepdaughter out of the way, Adonis."

"You don't wish to meet my wife?" he said.

Clete signaled me with his eyes. "Yes, sir, I'd love to meet Ms. Balangie," I said.

"Call her 'Mrs.' She's a little traditional. That stuff about my step-daughter? I don't want to hear about it. Not on any level. Are we understood?"

I should have known better than to come to his house. Involvement in the arcane culture of the Shondell and Balangie families was like walking through cobwebs. You never got it off your skin.

"We came here out of goodwill," I said. "I think we need to have an understanding about that."

He paused again, his eyes searching my face, as though I were an object of idle curiosity. "All the courtesies of my home will be extended to you, but after you leave, I ask that you not interfere in my family's affairs again."

I didn't answer. He opened the French doors onto a patio and looked back at me. "I asked you if we're clear on that."

"No, we're not clear on anything," I said. "Not at all."

He stepped out on the flagstones. The patio was canopied by a grape trellis thick with vines. Adonis's face was patched with sunshine and shadow. "My wife insisted that she meet both of you. After I introduce her to you, our visit will be over."

I stepped toward him. "I'll take one more run at it, Adonis. If somebody tried to do to my daughter what someone is doing to your stepdaughter, I'd blow him out of his socks. That means I can't wait to get out of here. That also means I will not be rude to your wife. Would you like me to write that out in longhand? Or would you like to walk off in a more private place where we can raise the ante, got my drift?"

"Wait here," he said. He turned his back on me and walked down a gravel path and entered through another set of French doors.

"Why don't you spit in the punch bowl, Streak?" Clete said.

"I can't take that bastard," I said.

"Gee, you could have fooled me."

The wind shifted and a cloud moved across the sun, and the temperature seemed to drop ten degrees. I smelled the salt spray from the lake and heard a sail flapping. A boat with two black sails was in trouble, the captain trying to gather up one that had torn from the mast.

"Think that guy is all right?" Clete asked.

"The lake isn't that deep there," I replied.

"You ever see a boat with black sails?"

"Not that I remember," I said.

I was bothered by the black sails, although I didn't know why. Have you ever seen van Gogh's last painting, the one in which the crows invade the perfection of the wheat field, the one that he was painting when he either shot himself or was shot accidentally by boys playing with a pistol? The boat with the black sails tipping in the wind gave me the same sense of desolation. "You okay, Dave?" Clete said.

"Yeah," I said. I heard footsteps behind me.

"This is Penelope, gentlemen," Adonis said.

When I turned around, I saw the woman I'd heard about but never seen. She was less than medium height and kept her chin tilted up the way short people do. Her eyes were warm and attentive; a strand of auburn hair lay on her cheek. She wore a white mantilla on her head and gripped a rosary with scarlet glass beads in her pale hand. Her mouth made me think of a small purple rose, with a black mole next to it.

I tried to remember what I had read about her. Her maiden name was Di Betto. She was from Sicily or Corsica; her family owned farmland and canneries and fishing fleets, things associated with the earth and sea. She was one of those women a photographer aches to get inside his lens, because no matter when or where he clicks the shutter, he knows he's captured an artwork.

She extended her hand when Adonis introduced us. "It's so nice to meet you," she said. "Adonis says you're among his oldest friends."

That was a stretch.

"Yeah, we go back," Clete said. "I mean to the old days."

"I know what it means, Mr. Purcel," she said.

"Sure," he said. "I meant . . . I don't know what I meant."

"Adonis says you're a kind man."

"Me?" Clete said.

"And Mr. Robicheaux, too," she said.

I nodded uncommittedly and then took a chance, one I knew would cause Adonis to veil his eyes, lest we see the wrath that was the Balangie family heirloom. "We're a bit concerned about Isolde."

"I don't understand," she said.

"We were under the impression that she disappeared," I said.

"Isolde is on a trip. I spoke to her on the telephone today."

"I see." I kept my gaze on her to the point of being rude. Her hand tightened on her rosary. "I guess our worries are misplaced."

"I hope I have set you at ease," she said.

"You have a chapel inside?" I said.

"How would you know that?"

"The mantilla," I said, knowing I was getting too personal, turning dials on Adonis that were better left alone.

"Penelope and I are expected in Baton Rouge," he said. "I'm afraid we have to say goodbye."

"I thought the Church got rid of head-covering a long time ago," Clete said.

"I didn't," she said. She smiled, then looked up into my face, not Clete's. "I'm very pleased to have met both of you."

"We're running late," Adonis said, his words flat, his eyes lowered. "Y'all don't mind walking around the side of the house, do you?"

"Not at all," I said. "One more thing?"

"Yes?" he said.

"Did you know Marcel LaForchette was working for Mark Shondell?" I asked.

"Excuse me?"

"LaForchette just got out of Huntsville. Shondell got his parole transferred to Louisiana. Actually, I was going to do that, but Shondell beat me to it."

"What's your point?" Adonis said.

"I always thought LaForchette worked for the Balangie family. Why would he go to work for the Shondells?"

"Because LaForchette is for sale," Adonis replied.

"Marcel is lots of things, but a rat isn't among them," I said.

Adonis puckered his mouth. "Don't trip on the hose. The things

that hurt us are usually lying in the weeds, where we can't see them.
That's an old Sicilian proverb."

WE DROVE TO the French Quarter and parked Clete's Caddy at his
office and ate an early dinner at the Acme Oyster House on Iberville.
We had spoken little after leaving the Balangie estate, in part because
of anger and shame, whether we were willing to admit it or not. People
whose wealth came from narcotics, prostitution, pornography, loan
sharking, labor racketeering, and murder had eighty-sixed us as though
we were low-rent ignorant flatfeet unworthy to be in their home.

The other problem we had was figuring out Penelope Balangie's
attitude about the missing girl. I had no doubt Isolde was her daughter; they had the same mysterious eyes, and they both seemed to float
on their own wind stream.

While we waited for our oysters on the half shell, Clete kept tearing off bits of French bread and dropping them in a saucer of oil and
vinegar.

"What are you thinking about?" I asked.

"Penelope Balangie's tom-toms. For a minute or two I thought my
magic twanger was shifting into overdrive."

"Will you stop that?"

"No normal guy can see a set of bongos like that without his pole
going on autopilot, so stop pretending. Before it's over, she'll have
Adonis sticking a gun in his mouth. She's the kind that promises you
a ride, then ties your schlong to a car bumper."

"Do you have to say everything through a bullhorn?"

"Adonis isn't going to let anything happen to the girl. Time for us
to bow out."

"You're right."

He raised his eyebrows, surprised at my reaction, and adjusted the
sling on his left arm. He bit his lip.

"You still have pain?" I said.

"No," he said, obviously lying. "By the way, you got to Adonis
when you told him LaForchette was working for Shondell."

"I don't feel too good about that," I said.

"Quit it. He treated us like shit. What I don't get is why a broad with money and education and tatas like that would marry a grease-ball notorious for following his stiff one-eye."

"Earlier you said he wasn't a greaseball."

"I said he went to college. You're always twisting things around. You know your problem? I mean your *real* problem?"

"No, tell me."

"You think you can save people from themselves. That's why you went to see LaForchette in Huntsville."

"That's not why I went to see him."

"So why did you?"

"I'll tell you one day," I said.

He put a chunk of bread in his mouth and chewed. "Know what?"

"What?"

"The Bobbsey Twins from Homicide are forever."

"Until one of us gets shot."

"So don't make the wrong choices with the wrong broad and get us into trouble. Face it, big mon. If I wasn't around, your life would be a toilet. Am I right or wrong? It's not an easy job, either. Show a little gratitude."

When we got back to the Caddy, all four tires were slashed, the taillights in the fins broken by a brick that lay on the asphalt. A note under the windshield wiper read, "This is for openers, queer-bait. I hope your arm hurts like a motherfucker. If you need a wrecker service this time of day, dial 1-800-EAT-SHIT."

"Shondell's PIs? I said.

"Who else?" Clete said. He crushed the note in his palm and tossed it at a sewer grate. "I should have popped both of them. How'd we get into this?"

I pretended not to hear him.

I was exhausted when I got home. My daughter, Alafair, was away, and the house creaked with wind and emptiness when I opened the bedroom window and lay down in the dark. I could hear tree frogs singing on the bayou and see the lights of the sugar mill reflected in the clouds. I closed my eyes and was soon asleep, hoping that in the morning I would free myself of the Shondells and the Balangies. But rather than find a degree of nocturnal peace, I dreamed of a dark sea on which galleons with either black or white sails slid down waves twenty feet high, the oars manned by half-naked convicts chained to the handles, foam exploding on the bows. The ships pitched with such ferocity that sometimes the oar blades struck in empty air. The expressions on the faces of the convicts could have been taken from paintings depicting the souls of the damned.

I was awakened by the phone on the kitchen counter at 2:14 A.M. I put on my slippers and went into the kitchen without turning on the light; I looked at the caller ID. I didn't recognize the number. I answered anyway. "Hello?"

"Mr. Robicheaux?"

"Yes."

"You're a good man. I could see it in your face."

There was no mistaking the voice and accent. There was also no mistaking a thread of manipulation. "Ms. Balangie?"

"I'm sorry to call. I need your help to get my daughter back."

I don't know if my next question showed more concern for her or for me. "Are you at home?"

"No. I'm at a—"

"I don't need to know." I was so tired I thought my knees were about to give out. I sat in a chair and took a pencil and notepad from a drawer. "Are you safe?"

"Yes."

"Give me a number I can call tomorrow."

"You're not going to contact Adonis, are you?"

I thought again of the dream I'd just had. What did it mean? I had no idea. "No promises about anything, Ms. Balangie. Not about your daughter. Not about you. Not about your husband. Not about anything."

Chapter Six

MY CALL TO her at midmorning went immediately to voicemail. I left the following message: "Miss Penelope, regarding your daughter's situation, my advice is you contact the FBI. You should also contact the state police and the sheriff's department in New Orleans. I don't believe I can be of any other service to you."

I was sitting in the backyard with my cell phone, which I believed symbolized humankind's latest attempt to control our lives and our fate. But I didn't feel any control at all. The leaves were turning gold and red in the oak trees, rustling each time the wind scudded across the bayou's surface. Robins that had just arrived from the north pecked in the grass, and the Teche was flowing at high tide through the pilings of the drawbridge at Burke Street. It was one of those Indian summer days in South Louisiana that is cold and warm simultaneously and makes you feel that the earth will abide forever. But on this day I felt there was a hole in my life I would never fill, an ache that had no source. Death is not a transitory or incremental presence. It swallows you whole.

I went inside and began fixing breakfast. Fifteen minutes later, I heard an automobile turn in to my gravel driveway, the tires clicking. I looked through the window and saw Penelope Balangie behind the wheel of a maroon Ferrari convertible, the top down. She wore black sunglasses and a white silk scarf on her head. I went out the door and walked across the lawn, my unraked leaves crackling under my shoes.

"How did you know where I live?" I said.

"Asked."

"I left a message. You didn't retrieve it?"

"No," she said. "What did you wish to tell me?"

"I appreciate your situation, but I don't want to have any more to do with it. Call the FBI or a state or parish agency."

"Adonis says 'FBI' stands for 'Forever Bothering Italians.'"

"That's what most of the wiseguys say. That's because they're dumb. And because they're dumb, and I mean stupid-to-the-core incapable of thought, most of them end up in jail."

She removed her sunglasses. She wasn't wearing makeup, and her skin was pale and puckered around the eyes. "What made you change your mind?" she said.

"Change my mind about what?"

"You tried to help Isolde. Now you regret it."

"You've got it wrong, Miss Penelope. I talked to her on an amusement pier, then got harassed by a couple of bird dogs who work for Mark Shondell. That's when Clete Purcel stepped in and got a stiletto stuck in his arm. The same guys slashed all four of his tires after we left your home."

"You're Catholic, aren't you?"

"What's that got to do with anything?"

"I thought you'd understand."

"Understand what? That you gave away your daughter in some kind of political deal with the Shondells?"

"We made peace with them. My family subsidizes charities all over the Third World. Mark Shondell has a chance to do a great deal of good rather than harm."

"It sounds more like human trafficking."

She got out of the car as though she'd been slapped. "Don't you dare speak to me like that."

"Sorry, I have my own problems. Your husband is a gangster. So were his father and grandfather. I don't like your husband, and I didn't like his father or his grandfather. They give your people a bad name. Why don't y'all wise up?"

"Excuse me, Mr. Robicheaux, but that's a ridiculous statement." She stepped closer to me. She seemed small and absolutely determined and unafraid; she looked up at my face. "Your government doesn't run a gulag of torture chambers? It doesn't make deals with the Saudis and the junta in Argentina? Stop embarrassing yourself.

You have no idea how many people are dependent on us for their survival, both in Italy and in this country. My family has been loyal to the unfortunate for five hundred years."

Her eyes were burning. I could hear myself breathing. "Take a stroll with me."

"Where?"

"Down the street. I'll give you a history lesson."

We walked down East Main through the tunnel of live oaks that led to the Shadows, a two-story pillared brick home built in the early 1830s, galleried and hung with floor-to-ceiling storm shutters, now a tourist stop surrounded by a piked fence and a bamboo border. We walked onto the grounds, in deep shade, and around back where the lawn sloped down to the bayou. The drawbridge at Burke Street was on our left; people of color were fishing under it, all of them sitting on inverted buckets, as their ancestors had probably sat there 150 years ago. The tide was in, and the tops of the elephant ears on the mudbank were almost underwater, rippling like a green carpet on the current.

"It's a fine-looking place, isn't it?" I said. "William Faulkner and Henry Miller were friends of the owner and used to visit here. Tourists love it. But here's the real story. Three hundred slaves did the work. You see their graves anywhere? They're fertilizer in a field or under a dry-goods store. The wife of the owner was known as a good person who refused to flee the Yankees in 1863 for fear the black people who were sick would have no one to care for them. But that doesn't change the fact that slavery was evil."

"I think that is the most insulting thing anyone has ever said to me. You're saying this about my relationship to Isolde?"

"People aren't chattel. There's nothing noble about controlling the lives of other people, Miss Penelope. You're an intelligent and educated woman. What in the name of suffering God are you and Adonis doing?"

"If I were a man, I would knock you down."

"The question still stands."

The wind was wimpling the bayou, bending the cattails, swelling inside the live oaks. She took the scarf from her head and shook out her hair. She tilted up her chin. "I can pay you."

"Nope."

"I think Isolde and the Shondell boy may have gone to a recording studio in Alabama. The Rolling Stones recorded there."

"Then let them have some fun. Get Isolde away from Mark Shondell. He's the scum of the earth."

"Do you know how many people have died in the feud between our families?"

"Not interested."

"I thought better of you."

"Think what you wish. I don't like cleaning up other people's mess. Particularly your husband's."

"You keep your mouth off him."

"Gladly," I said.

Her eyes were wet. I had thoughts and feelings about her that I don't want to admit. Tingling in the hands, dryness in the throat, desires that hide in the subconscious. She had a strong and solid figure and clear skin and a bold stare that was both intelligent and principled, and she carried herself like a princess; she was obviously not an ordinary woman and not a follower of fashion and was lovely to look at and yet somehow vulnerable at the same time. For most men, this is a combo that turns into a sure bear trap, but it's one that's hard to resist and, let's face it, often worth the trouble. There was only one problem: She was another man's wife.

"Why do you have that funny look on your face?" she said.

"I think you're an admirable lady, Miss Penelope."

"But you won't help?"

"No, ma'am."

"Then I'll walk myself back to my car."

"No, you won't."

"I beg your pardon?"

I cupped my hand on her elbow. "The sprinklers are on. I'll walk you along the slope to my house. Things will work out for you. I'm sure they will."

Her forearm felt as light as air in my palm as I stepped over the gnarled roots of the bamboo that grew wild along the bayou. I wondered if my gentlemanly conduct was a sham and a way to deceive myself and take me across the wrong Rubicon, a feat that in the past I achieved only by getting drunk.

TWO DAYS LATER, I got a call from the sheriff of Vermilion Parish. "We've got a couple of guys in a weighted barrel, Dave. Or rather, I think it's a couple. One of them had a picture of your house in his phone."

"Say again?"

"I'm a little bit southeast of Henry. I could use your he'p."

A half hour later, I drove my truck up on a levee that overlooked the northern tip of Vermilion Bay. Two cruisers were already there, as well as an ambulance and a state police boat. The sun on the bay looked like a flame on a bronze shield. A polyethylene tarp had been pulled over a large metal barrel lying on its side. The sheriff walked toward me. He was a fat man named Eli Guidry. He wore rubber boots that were slick with mud, the trouser legs stuffed inside. The coroner had not arrived.

"Take a deep breath," Eli said. "I think these poor bastards were ripe befo' they went into the water."

He peeled back the tarp, first off the barrel, then off the contents that had been piled outside it. I stepped back from the stench and the cloud of bottle flies and the crabs skittering on the sand.

"A fisherman hung his anchor on the cinder blocks," he said. "You ever work one like this?"

"No, sir," I said.

"Think it was a chain saw?"

"That'd be my guess."

"One has gold hair," Eli said. "Know who that might be?"

"Ray Haskell."

"Who is he?"

"An ex-cop. A hard case. Called himself a PI. I think he was just a dirty cop."

"How about this other guy?"

"Timothy Riordan. Same history."

"Why would a picture of your house be in the phone?" Eli said.

"Which guy was carrying it?"

"The one still got part of a suit coat on."

"That's Haskell. He was the one with the brains."

"You ain't answered my question."

"They were bird-dogging me. I got in their face about it. They probably wanted to square it."

"Bird-dogging you why?"

"You got me," I said, avoiding his eyes. "Neither one of them was real bright."

"Don't know anyone who might want to do this to them?"

I shook my head and looked out at the bay.

"Wish you had your shield back, Dave."

"I'm not a big loss to the department."

"You're not holding back on me, are you?"

"No, sir," I said.

Eli was a good guy but not someone you talked with about the realities of the system we served and the corruption that hovered on its edges. I moved upwind from the body parts that had been poured from the barrel. I tried not to think about how these men had died. Were they alive when they were cut up? Did they weep? Did they betray each other? I had seen men cry out for their mothers in a battalion aid station. Did these men do the same?

"What are you thinking about?" Eli asked.

"Nothing worth talking about."

"What are you not telling me, podna?"

"These guys worked for Mark Shondell. Talk to him if you like."

There was a beat. "Mr. Shondell is involved in this?"

I didn't answer. Eli's face had gone empty. "Dave, I'm axing you again. We're talking about the Mr. Shondell that lives in New Iberia?"

"The one and only."

He looked past me at the levee. His eyes were dead. Then he saw an automobile coming on the levee. "There's the coroner now. You been real he'pful. Coming out and all. I'll be checking wit' you later."

THE NEXT EVENING Clete called me from New Orleans. It was dark outside, the rain drumming so hard on the roof I could hardly hear his voice. "Hey!" he said.

"Hey, what?"

"A musician on Bourbon told me Johnny Shondell and Isolde Balangie were recording for three days in Muscle Shoals, Alabama. A place called Fame Studios."

"Yeah, I know."

"How?" he asked.

"Penelope Balangie told me."

"She called you?"

"She was in New Iberia."

"What's going on, big mon?"

"Nothing. End of subject," I said. "You heard about those two PIs?"

"Yeah, I was all broke up."

"Has anybody tried to question you?"

"Because I had a run-in with them?"

"Because one of them put a knife in you," I said.

"I'm keeping myself unavailable. Let's get back to Penelope Balangie. You're not letting those lovely tatas get to you, are you?"

"Will you lay off that?"

"I know what you mean. My Jolly Roger never gets out of control, either."

"I'm not going to have this kind of discussion with you, Clete."

"I know you, Streak. You run into a broad with her heart on your sleeve, and suddenly, it's boom-boom time on the bayou. They're in Bay St. Louis."

"I can't keep up with what you're saying. Who's in Bay St. Louis?"

"Johnny Shondell and Isolde Balangie. This musician friend of mine says they're in a rich guy's place on the beach. The guy is some kind of geek who's big stuff in the music world."

"I told Penelope Balangie I'm out. I meant it."

"Regarding the two fuckheads who ended up Vienna sausage? Somebody wrote down my license number after I busted them up in the motel. NOPD has been knocking on doors and asking around. A couple of them still want to do some payback for a few things I did back in the eighties."

"Get out of town for a while." I could hear static on the line but no voice. "Clete?"

"You advise me to hide?" he said. "That's the best you can do?"

"We need to sit this one out."

"Stop pretending."

"About *what*?"

"We both know what happened to those guys. That was a grease-ball hit. It's the same way Johnny Roselli went out. They cut off his legs and put an ice pick in his stomach so his barrel wouldn't float up. I bet both those guys took one in the stomach. Right or wrong?"

I didn't answer.

"Told you," he said.

"And?" I said disingenuously.

"And nothing," he said. "See you around."

"Where are you now?"

"A dump in Holy Cross."

"Give me the address."

"I'll hump my own pack on this one, Dave."

"You're really making me mad, Clete."

He gave me the address of the hotel where he was staying. I knew the place well. He was right: It was a dump, the kind where you paid cash and slept off hangovers when you couldn't afford a detox unit. "Bring some eats, will you?" he said. "It's pouring here."

There was something I wanted to tell him real bad. But I was too embarrassed. It's funny how Clete could read my mind. "You want to get something off your chest, Streak?" he said.

"I'm having 'warning dreams.' Stormy seas, a galleon with convicts chained to the oars. They look like they're in hell."

"You just scared the shit out of me."

"How?"

"I've had the same dream."

I felt like he had kicked me in the stomach.

Chapter Seven

IT WAS STILL raining hard when we drove into Mississippi the next morning. The house that Clete's musician friend had told him about was a sun-faded pink art deco place stuck back in a cove where a desiccated shrimp boat lay on its side in a slough overgrown with vines and palm and persimmon trees. A half-dozen vehicles were parked in the driveway or partially on the grass. I thought I could hear music playing.

Clete parked the Caddy and cut the engine, the rain hitting like drops of lead on the convertible's top. Out of a clear sky on the southern horizon, jagged bolts of lightning struck the water without making a sound. "Something keeps eating on me," Clete said.

"We got ourselves in the cook pot," I said. "What's new about that?"

"This is different. Everything we're doing. The way the world looks. Like we're going in and out of time."

Somehow I knew what he meant, although the right words wouldn't form in my mouth and the right image wouldn't come clear in my mind. The rain, the defused light, the storm debris in the waves, our visits to the homes of the Balangie and Shondell families, vicious deeds out of the past, the rip-sawed bodies packed in an oil barrel, all these things seemed part of a fantasy but one that had become real. Let me put it differently. It was like waking from a bad dream as a child only to find, as the sunlight crept into the room and drove away the shadows, that your nocturnal fears were justified and that the creatures you couldn't flee in your sleep waited for you in the blooming of the day.

"We've seen the worst of the worst, Clete," I said. "Let's get on it."

"I got it."

"Got what?"

"The feeling I couldn't explain. When I woke up this morning, it was like I'd walked off a cliff and was standing on air. What's a dream like that mean?"

"It means take it easy on the flak juice."

"I wish I had all the answers," he said. "Like knowing the mind of God. I'd love to get in on that."

I made a mental note to write that one down.

We ran splashing across the yard to the front door and rang the bell, the wind blowing the rain in our faces. A thin, deeply tanned man in a white linen suit and a black silk shirt unbuttoned at the collar opened the door. His hair was copper-colored and streaked with gray and worn like a matador's, pulled back in a pigtail; a gold cross and chain gleamed on his chest hair. "What can I do for you fellows?"

"We're looking for Johnny and Isolde," I said.

He looked over his shoulder, then back at us. People were drinking at a wet bar, and a couple of long-haired young guys with pipe-cleaner arms covered with all-blue tats were tuning their guitars on a platform. All of them looked half-wrecked. The house had a cathedral ceiling, the blond wood in the walls glowing against the darkness outside.

"Sorry, but who are you?" the man said.

"Friends," I said.

"This is kind of a private gig, fellows."

"We're friends of Adonis Balangie," I said.

"That's cool. But that don't cut no ice here. You got an invitation from one of the musicians?"

"Yeah," Clete said.

"So *who* invited you?" the man said. He tried to smile.

"Guy who plays on Bourbon Street," Clete said.

"The guy with no name on Bourbon?" the man in the white suit said. "Know him well. Come see us another time."

A girl in a bikini leaned down and sniffed a line off the bar. The man with the pigtail followed my eyes. He started to shut the door.

Then I saw Isolde. She was wearing jeans low on her hips and flowers in her hair and a halter top over her breasts. The roses and orchids tattooed on her shoulder looked real rather than made of ink, as though they had been pressed flat and pasted on her skin. Her mouth opened with surprise when she saw me. She had changed since I'd seen her on the pier in a way I couldn't explain. Her complexion glowed; her whitish-blond hair seemed thicker, her mouth waiting to be kissed. She walked over to us. "Let him in, Eddy," she said. "That's Mr. Robicheaux. He's a friend of ours."

"It's an invitation-only party, baby doll," Eddy said.

Baby doll?

"Come on, Mr. Robicheaux is one of the gang," she said.

"What can I say? Come in, fellows. Don't steal my ashtrays."

Then we were inside, the door closed behind us. Through the picture windows, I could see the bay striped with foam, electricity dancing on the horizon, which was growing darker by the minute. At the bar, I saw two men who didn't fit with the others. They wore green cargo pants and black T-shirts emblazoned with crossed white M-16s and military-style boots that were part leather and part canvas. Their stomachs were as flat as boards inside their belt buckles, their heads shaved.

Isolde gripped my upper arm with both hands. "I want to apologize for saying 'fuck you' on the pier," she said.

"I considered it a compliment," I said. "This is Clete Purcel."

She touched his arm, too, as though sharing a secret message. I had the feeling Johnny Shondell wouldn't be delivering Isolde to his uncle's home. "It's all so wonderful," she said.

"What is?" Clete said.

"Everything," she said. "We recorded an album at Muscle Shoals. I sing on three of the songs. Eddy's company is going to sell them all over the country. Isn't that right, Eddy? We're signing the contract today."

"Yeah, we better get on that," Eddy said. "You fellows get yourself a drink."

"You from the Bronx?" I said, smiling.

"Miami," he said.

"Nothing for me," I said.

"Same here," Clete said.

Eddy circled his fingers around Isolde's wrist as though he were picking up a dog leash. "Let's get on it, doll. I got to get back to Fort Lauderdale tonight."

Johnny Shondell waved at us from the bar, then headed toward us. He was sure a good-looking kid, the kind who seemed to float through a crowd of his peers rather than walk. It was no wonder the girls loved him, but I had a feeling he was a one-woman man. His eyes never left Isolde, even when he was shaking hands with us. Eddy was trying to get his attention. "Johnny, I got a business to run, here. Hey, what am I, a fire hydrant waiting for somebody to piss on? Look at me."

"I got you covered, Eddy," Johnny said. "We're about to play a couple of numbers. Get the marimbas. You can play along."

"The marimbas can wait," Eddy said. "These guys can wait. The whole fucking world can wait. But the banks in the Islands do not wait. You hearing me, here?"

"Calm down, Eddy," Isolde said.

"I'm telling you, I don't got time for this," he said.

"Put an ice cube in your mouth," she said. "It'll help you think." Then she saw the look on his face. "You're adorable, Eddy. Don't be sensitive." She kissed him on the cheek. His eyes were lumps of coal focused on nothing, his nostrils dilating.

"You own a record company?" Clete said to him.

"Do I own a record company?" Eddy said. He turned up his palms, as though he couldn't fathom the question. "My house looks like I drive a bread truck?"

"Johnny, don't you need a lawyer when you sign contracts?" I said.

"I'm the lawyer," Eddy said.

"You?" I said.

"I don't look or talk like a lawyer?" he said.

"Ole Miss?" Clete said.

"I went to law school in the Dominican Republic," Eddy said.

"Can I use your bathroom?" Clete said.

"Through the hallway," Eddy said. "Make sure you flush."

But I knew the bathroom wasn't on Clete's mind. He had been glancing at the two men in cargo pants at the bar. He walked down the hallway and into the bathroom, then came back out and stood at the bar next to the two men, studying the bay through a picture window, his back to the men.

Johnny rejoined his musician friends and hung a Gibson Super Jumbo acoustic guitar from his neck, then went into Larry Finnegan's "Dear One." The keyboard and the rumble of the drums and the resonance of the Gibson and the four/four beat created a throbbing combination reminiscent of Phil Spector's Wall of Sound. When Johnny finished singing, the room went wild. Johnny was way beyond good. He was painted with magic. His voice, his lack of pretense, his obvious love of music for its own sake, and his appreciation of Larry Finnegan's tribute to the 1950s were like an invitation into a cathedral you never wanted to leave.

Isolde's eyes were damp. Eddy had gone into the back of the house. Isolde and I were alone.

"You okay?" I said.

"I don't want it to ever end," she replied.

"The song?"

"All of it. I don't want it to end."

"Why should it end, Isolde?"

"Because we're not meant to be."

"Not meant to be? Who's not meant to be?"

"We're supposed to live our lives for others. Me and Johnny."

"This is still the United States," I said. "You can be whatever you want and tell other people to kiss your foot."

"I'm scared, Mr. Robicheaux."

"Call me Dave. Scared of what? Of whom?"

"The people who are going to take it away from us."

"Nobody is going to take anything away from you. Not if Clete and I have anything to do with it."

She wasn't buying it. In the meantime, something had happened at the bar. I should have known it. William Blake called it the canker in the rose.

CLETE HAD OBVIOUSLY changed his mind about having a drink. He was leaning against the bar, wearing his Panama hat, a bottle of tequila and a shot glass and a salt shaker and a saucer with sliced limes in front of him. As I walked toward him, he poured a shot and knocked it back, then sucked on a salted lime. He wiped his fingers and began talking to two men in paramilitary drag as though continuing a lecture he'd had to interrupt in order to put some more fuel in the tank. "See, I know a little Vietnamese and a little Japanese, but I never took up the study of European languages. So you got to tell me what those words on your medallions mean. They look like artworks. I might want to join your organization."

"What's happening, Cletus?" I said.

"No haps," he said. "I just dig these guys and their medallions. There's a torch on them, like at the Olympics. What looks like German writing, too. I'm correct, aren't I? It's German?"

One man stared at me boldly, then went back to his beer. He was either a pro who knew when to disengage or a man who didn't like even odds. The second man's body was as stiff as coat-hanger wire. A tiny swastika was tattooed at the corner of one eye. His face had the angularity of an ax blade, like he was wired on meth or fear.

"You guys mercs?" I said.

"Security," said the man with the ink.

"Let's get some food, Cletus," I said.

"Absolutely not," Clete said. He poured into the shot glass until it brimmed, then knocked half of it back. He sucked on the lime, then set down the glass and wiped his mouth. "Come on, buddy, don't leave me in the dark. I know what *Juden* means. How about the rest of it? You guys work for the Israeli government?"

The man drinking beer laughed to himself, looking out the window at the rain. He was unshaved and had a cleft chin with a scar across it, like a piece of white twine. I put my arm across Clete's shoulders. "Time to dee-dee."

He shook off my arm. "There's coke and weed all over this place," he said to the two men. "These kids don't need that. If you guys are doing security, it really blows."

"We do what Eddy tells us," said the man with the swastika. His pupils were tiny dots. He touched Clete as though they were brothers-in-arms. "Look around. This is a Caucasians-only environment. That's because we do our job. If a little product gets in, we keep it under control."

"I want to know what the German writing means," Clete said.

"It means whatever you want it to mean," said the man with the scar on his chin, gazing out the window at the squall. "It could mean haul your fat ass out of here, Bluto."

"Bluto?" Clete said. "Like the guy in *Popeye*? That's probably a compliment, right? Just tell me what the German writing means."

"Or what?" said the same man, twisting his head.

"I could use a job. Maybe you guys could help me out. I was in the service."

"Ou-rah," said the same man.

"Say that again?" Clete said.

"I get sick of you assholes," the same man said, sipping at his beer, not bothering to turn around.

"Let's go over in a quiet corner," said the man with the swastika. "Just us three." He kept his gaze off me.

"I hate to be obsessive here," Clete said, fishing in his coat pocket. "I want a translation."

"Why?" asked the man with the swastika. His mouth moved slowly when he spoke, as though he were afraid to grin and afraid not to.

Clete removed a pack of cigarettes from his pocket. He shook one loose and stuck it between his lips. "You might be Jews. You know, undercover."

The man with the swastika flexed his mouth, almost like rictus. "Us?"

"Maybe you're with the FBI," Clete said.

The man with the swastika took a long swig from a beer mug that had been filled with Jack poured on crushed ice. He lowered the mug and looked sideways at Clete, his pulse fluttering visibly in his throat. "We're trying to be nice, man. We're a brotherhood. We ain't out to hurt nobody. Unless we get pushed. My friend Klute here is pretty well known in the movement. He's not a man you mess with."

"I'll keep that in mind," Clete said. He tossed his unlit cigarette at a trash can behind the bar. "What's *tod* mean?"

"That's German for 'death,'" said the man with the swastika.

"How about *für*?"

"Come on, man."

"What's it mean?" Clete said.

"It means 'to.'"

"And *Alle*?"

"Like it sounds. It means 'all.'"

"What's the whole thing mean?" Clete said.

"There's a couple of people over there probably don't need to hear this," said the same man. "We got no beef with them. We're for Aryan people. That don't mean we're necessarily against other kinds of people."

"Don't make me ask again," Clete said.

"It means death to all Jews," said the man with the swastika.

The man named Klute drained the foam out of the bottle and lay the bottle flat on the bar. He spun it in a circle with one finger, then glanced at Clete. His mouth was small, his teeth tiny, spaced apart. "You're not gonna do something silly, are you?"

"Dave and I are going to eat, then we're leaving. I shouldn't have been preaching about weed and such. I've got addiction issues myself. I just don't like to see you screwing up these kids, because if there's any product in this room, you brought it here."

"Hang around and see what they're doing later," said the man playing with the bottle. "Ever hear of a Crisco party?"

"I think you're full of it, Jack," Clete said.

"You're a familiar kind of guy," the man said. "You did something in 'Nam you can't forgive yourself for, so you go around playing the good guy and sucking up to any titty-baby bunch of knee-jerk liberals that'll let you clean their toilets."

Clete's eyes were green marbles, devoid of expression, as though he had floated away into a serene environment no one else could see. He seemed to gaze out the window like a man about to fall asleep. He blinked and rested one hand on top of the bar. He picked up his cigarette lighter and dropped it into his pocket. The crow's-feet at the corners of his eyes had flattened and turned into tiny green threads, the skin white and as smooth as clay. He pursed his lips and breathed slowly through his nose, then smiled at the two men.

The man named Klute seemed bewitched by Clete's tranquility and appeared to have no idea what was occurring. Clete fitted his hand around the man's neck and drove his face into the oak bib of the bar, smashing it again and again into the wood. Then he elbowed the other man in the face, kicked his feet out from under him, and proceeded to stomp both men into pulp, coating the brass rail, balancing himself with one hand, breaking bone or teeth or cartilage or anything he could find with the flat of his shoe.

I grabbed him by the shoulders and tried to pull him back. I could smell the heat and funk and rage and trapped beer-sweat in his clothes, see the acne scars and flame on the back of his neck, the grease in his pores, the moisture glistening on the tips of his little-boy haircut, and I knew there was no way I could restrain him, any more than I could save a drowning man who would take down his rescuer if necessary.

Then he went to one knee, fumbling his wallet from his back pocket, spilling the contents, digging out the photo of the Jewish woman and her three children on their way to the gas chamber, sticking it in the unrecognizable faces of the two mercenaries. "See that?" he said. "Look at it! That's what you're responsible for. I'd shove this down your mouths, but you're not worthy to touch these people's picture."

He stood up, steadying himself on the bar, and wiped the picture on his shirt and folded it carefully and put it in his shirt pocket. A rivulet of blood slid from the bandaged knife wound in his left arm.

The people in the room had become statues, unable to speak, avoiding eye contact with us or each other. Isolde held her hands over her mouth. The only person who reacted was Johnny Shondell. He laid his Gibson on a couch and picked up a bar towel and knelt by the two men on the floor, then looked up at Clete and me. "Jesus Christ," he said. "What'd these guys do? Mr. Clete, this isn't you." He paused. "Is it?"

I gathered up the contents of Clete's wallet, and the two of us walked outside and left the door open behind us, the rain sweeping inside, the wind shredding the palm trees. In seconds our clothes were drenched, and Clete's Panama hat was torn off his head and flying end over end down the beach, where it was sucked into the surf. Clete stared at it blankly, his swollen, blood-streaked fists hanging at his sides, seemingly bewildered by the storm taking place around him.

Chapter Eight

Cops from both Mississippi and New Iberia were at my house the next day. I denied any knowledge of Clete's whereabouts. I didn't have to lie, either. I had told Clete to get lost and not tell me where. A Mississippi plainclothes told me the man who took the worst hits looked like a volleyball wrapped with barbed wire.

"Sorry to hear that," I said. "Does he have a sheet?"

"He was up on a rape charge in the army. The nurse was afraid to testify."

"How about the other guy?"

"Pretty much a wannabe. A couple of domestic-abuse charges. He went to a phony merc school in the Everglades."

We were standing in my front yard, the trees aglow with red and gold leaves. "Anything else?" I said.

"I grew up in Mississippi. My father was in the Klan. He was un-educated and poor and thought they could offer him a better life."

I kept my face empty and gazed at some children riding their bicycles over the concrete sidewalk that was cracked and peaked by the huge oak roots in front of my house.

"My father was at the liberation of Dachau," the plainclothes said. "When he came back home, he burned his robes in the back-yard. You know where I'd like to be in weather like this?"

"No, sir, I don't."

"Palm Beach. I hear the kingfish are running night and day. A couple of weeks in a place like that and a man could forget all his troubles."

Four days later, Clete called me on my cell phone. "Where are you?" I said.

"Down by Cocodrie. Anybody been around?"

"What do you think?"

"How bad is it going to be?"

"Just stay off the radar awhile," I said.

"I checked out the guy with the house in Bay St. Louis. His name is Eddy Firpo. He screws every musician he gets his hands on."

"Forget about Eddy Firpo. Just stay out of town. Here as well as New Orleans."

"What's going on with the Balangie girl?" Clete asked.

"How should I know?"

"That's where all this stuff started."

"It started because you sent four people to the hospital," I said, and immediately regretted my words.

"You're right," he said.

"No, I'm not. I should have stayed away from Marcel LaForchette. I should have forgotten my conversation on the pier with Isolde Balangie and never made contact with her family or Mark Shondell."

"You're a cop, Dave. Whether you've got your shield or not. What were we supposed to do? Leave a seventeen-year-old girl on the auction block? I feel like we're in the Middle Ages."

"There was a detective here from Bay St. Louis. He said the kingfish were running in Palm Beach and that's where he'd be for a couple of weeks if he had his druthers. I think he was telling me to tell you to cool it and you'll be all right."

"They're going to cold-case it?"

"That's my guess."

He was silent. I thought I had lost the connection. "You there?" I said.

"Don't get mad at me, but I got to say this: You're not having the wrong kind of thoughts, are you?"

"Thoughts about what?" I asked.

"I saw the look on your face when Penelope Balangie came out of the chapel with a rosary in her hand."

"We've already been through this, Clete. Give it a rest."

"You saw a woman with a rainbow around her. Get real, Streak. She's Adonis's wife. She knows Adonis has ordered people killed or done it himself, but she probably gets it on with him every other night anyway. Look at that image in your head and tell me you want to get mixed up with a broad like that."

"You're all wrong," I said.

"Do you know why we drink? So we can do the things our conscience won't let us do when we're sober."

If you're a souse, try to refute a statement like that.

THE FOLLOWING WEEK, in the late afternoon, I saw a restored 1956 Bel Air parked under a live oak in front of Veazey's ice-cream store on West Main. The trunk of the tree was painted white up to the fork, and in the fork was a loudspeaker blaring out a song by the Chordettes. I parked and went inside and saw Johnny Shondell seated on a stool, wearing gray drapes and a sky-blue cowboy shirt sewn with roses and tasseled loafers hooked on the rungs, his knees so elevated they were higher than his waist. The Wurlitzer against the wall was loaded with Swamp Pop and 1950s rock, the plastic casing swimming with liquid balls of color. Johnny's mouth was bent to the straw in a chrome milk-shake container. His face lifted to mine. "Hey, Mr. Dave. What's shaking?"

"No haps," I said, and sat down next to him. "You doing all right?"

"Right as rain," he said, his eyes drifting away, as though he were trying to wish himself out the door.

"Sorry we messed up your gig."

"Yeah, I'd rather forget about that, Mr. Dave."

"I know what you mean. But something was going on there that really bothers me. Stuff you and Isolde don't need in your lives."

"You're thinking about some of the drugstore products that were floating around?"

"Blow and weed aren't drugstore products."

"Yeah, I dig what you're saying, Mr. Dave," he said, looking out the window where an orange sun glowed behind the trees. "Why'd your friend bust up those guys?"

"Those 'guys' are Nazis. A better question is why are you hanging with a fraud like Eddy Firpo?"

"Eddy's not a bad guy."

"So why would he have Nazis around?"

"Takes all kinds?"

"You're a good kid, Johnny. Don't degrade yourself."

"That hurts my feelings, Mr. Dave."

A shaft of sunlight shone on one side of his face; the other side was buried in shadow.

"How's Isolde?" I asked.

"All right." He set down the chrome container and looked at the marks his fingers had left on the coldness of its surface. "I mean I'm guessing she's all right."

"She's back in New Orleans?" I asked.

"I didn't say that."

"So where is she?"

"Can I order you an ice cream soda or a malt?"

"Did you take her to your uncle's house?" I said.

"Ask Uncle Mark."

"I don't get along with him. So I'm asking you."

Three teenage girls came in, the bell ringing above their heads. They began giggling as soon as they saw Johnny. He folded his hands tightly and put them between his legs. "There's lots of secrets in my family, Mr. Dave. Maybe our ways are strange to others, but that's the way it is."

"Whoever taught you that is an idiot, Johnny. Where's Isolde?"

"I'm staying at the house alone. My uncle Mark is gone. That's all I can tell you." Half his face remained in shadow.

"You'll have to do better than that. Look at me."

"No."

"Who hit you?"

"It wasn't his fault."

"Your uncle struck your face? For what? You sassed him?"

"A little more serious than that."

"It doesn't matter. No adult of conscience would strike a young person in the face."

"A guy gave me some purple acid. I'd never done it before. I took some and gave the rest to Isolde."

"You gave her LSD?"

His face reddened, causing the welt on his cheek to stand out like a piece of white bone. "I didn't think."

"What happened?" I asked.

"I don't want to talk about it, Mr. Dave."

"You want me to ask your uncle?"

"I ran away with her. I wanted her for myself. She wanted me, too. It was like that for five days, in a motel on the beach in Biloxi. But not because of the acid. It was like she was my sister and my girlfriend and my lover and my wife and the person I never wanted to let go of."

"It's called falling in love."

"It was wrong. I owe my uncle."

"Get this in your head," I said. "You and Isolde aren't the problem. The problem is your uncle and the fact that nobody has shoved a gun in his mouth and put his brains on the wall."

The three teenage girls were in a corner booth. One of them caught my tone or saw my face and looked away, the blood draining from around her mouth.

"Uncle Mark agreed to be her guardian and godfather," Johnny said. "It's a tradition that goes way back in our families."

"White slavery isn't a tradition," I said. "You heard about the two guys who got stuffed in a barrel piece by piece?"

"Down by Vermilion Bay?"

"They worked for your uncle."

"A lot of people do."

"Wake up," I said.

"I'm leaving my uncle's house. I'm leaving Louisiana."

"Where you headed?"

"Florida."

"Fort Lauderdale?"

"How'd you know?"

"That's where Eddy Firpo has his studio. He's a bucket of shit, Johnny. He'll ruin your career, then your life."

"I don't care about my career anymore. I lost Isolde. I'll never get her back. I want to do something awful."

He was nineteen. I remembered the degree of judgment I had at that age and shuddered.

IT WAS TIME to up the ante. Marcel LaForchette, the button man I visited in Huntsville, had been getting a free pass, largely because he was one of those undefined and marginal creatures who lived in the murk at the bottom of the aquarium, then one day you discovered he'd eaten everything in the tank.

Marcel hung in places that weren't good for me. I wasn't simply an alcoholic; I was a drunkard. What's the difference? An alcoholic has a deep-seated, armor-plated neurosis buried in the unconscious that keeps him constantly at war with himself. The drunkard cuts to the chase. A chemical form of sackcloth and ashes becomes his coat of arms. He drinks until he passes out, gets up and pours down another fifth, chases it with a case of Tuborg or a half-gallon of dago red and repeats the process until he enters what is called alcoholic psychosis and slides the muzzle of a double-barrel twelve-gauge over his teeth, the way Ernest Hemingway did it, and lets his family clean up the room.

My wife Annie was murdered and my wife Bootsie died of lupus, and my daughter, Alafair, was a student on an academic scholarship at Reed College in Portland, Oregon. I didn't handle solitude or mortality well. I don't guess anyone does. Here's the strange thing about death. At a certain age it's always with you, lurking in the shade, pulling at your ankles, whispering in your ear when you pass a crypt. But it doesn't get your real attention until you find yourself alone at home and the wind swells inside the rooms and stresses the joists and lets you know what silence and solitude are all about. That's why most drunks become believers, no matter how long they've been atheists or agnostics, and often preface the Lord's Prayer with the rhetorical question "Who made the stars and keeps us out of bars?"

But on that particular night I went to a low-rent pickup dive on the edge of the black district nine miles up the bayou in St. Martinville. The walls were bright red, the pool table unbalanced, the felt faded and patched with tape, the race of the customers hardly definable, most of the women unhinged and often dangerous. Marcel was by himself at a table in back, playing solitaire, a Coca-Cola bottle by his elbow. The restrooms were ten feet away, hung with red-bead curtains, the light golden behind them, the ammonia smell of urinated beer blowing in the breeze from the electric fans.

He had obviously seen me when I came in, but he kept his gaze on his cards. When my shadow broke across his face, he said, "Doing research on the other half?"

"Just you," I said, sitting down without being asked. "Your PO doesn't mind you coming here?"

"Long as I drink Coca-Cola."

The bottle was half empty. The liquid at the top was diluted, brownish. "I got a beef with you, podna."

His pupils were as small as match heads. "What'd I ever do to you, Dave?"

"Waltz me around, jerk my chain, try to fuck me over?"

He looked at the bar. Several women, their arms heavy with fat, were drinking there, standing up, talking to each other. "You use that kind of language because of the environment you're in? Like it's something to wipe yourself with?"

"I agreed to help you with your parole transfer. But you cut a deal with Mark Shondell."

"He gave me an apartment over his carriage house. He gave me a good salary. You were gonna do that?"

"Stop lying. You gave him information about the Balangie family."

"What, that the Balangies are gangsters?"

"You said you were the driver on a whack that would interest some people in New Iberia."

"Yeah, I guess I was a little too forthcoming on that."

"Who was the whack?"

"Long time ago, Dave."

"You said he was a child molester."

"'Pitiful' is a better word."

"About fifteen years ago a member of the Shondell family disappeared," I said. "He was a sidewalk painter in Jackson Square."

"Here's what I remember. The guy was a serial offender. He was on the floor of the backseat. He was crying and begging and shit." He glanced at the bar. "Pardon my language, ladies."

I leaned forward. "Cut the act. Who was the hit?"

"It came down from Pietro Balangie, the old man. He didn't allow jackrollers in the Quarter, he didn't allow child molesters anywhere."

"You're testing my patience, Marcel."

"That's *your* problem," he replied. "I thought they were gonna knock him around and run him out of town. That's not what happened. After we got back from the lake, I shot up in my apartment. China white with a half teaspoon of Jack. I couldn't get the screams out of my head."

I didn't know if I bought his story or not. Or better put, I didn't know if I bought his tale about his suddenly acquired abhorrence of human cruelty. I kept my eyes on his.

"They took Polaroids for the old man," he said. "Not the kind of stuff a guy like you wants to see, Dave."

"Save the dog shit. What was his name?"

"One of the guys said something about him being an artist. He looked like a marshmallow. He started making baby sounds when he knew what was gonna happen."

"So you told Mark Shondell you were part of the hit team that killed one of his relatives? For that, he helped you with a parole transfer and gave you a job and an apartment?"

"I didn't say nothing about the hit." He scratched an eyebrow and looked at the bar, where two black women were talking loudly; their mouths were full of gold teeth.

"Go on," I said.

"Mr. Mark talked about me changing my life. The only other person who ever talked to me like that was you."

"Mark Shondell is the soul of goodness?"

"What do I know? I went to the nint' grade." He took a drink from his Coke and set it down. "Want one?"

I picked up the bottle and smelled it. I set it back down and clinked a fingernail on the bottle neck. "You trying to go back inside?"

"That's probably where I'll end up anyway. Next time down, I'm looking at 'the bitch.' "

"Habitual offender?"

"I've been working on it since I was seventeen. That's the year I got turned out."

"You were raped?"

"For starters. Look at it this way. Adonis Balangie isn't his father or grandfather. Mr. Mark is trying to work a truce. So maybe he looks at me as some kind of window into the Balangie family. What's the harm in that? Bottom line, I ain't done nothing wrong."

"Maybe you're right," I said. "Can I ask you another question?"

He touched at his nose and sniffed. "If I don't got to answer it."

"We're sitting in front of a fan, but you've got a tic in your eye, and there's perspiration on your upper lip."

"Something happened at Mr. Mark's place I cain't put together." He looked again at the bar. "Somebody ought to shut up them women."

"Tell me what happened, Marcel."

"A tree limb went down on the power line a few nights ago. I went into the main house to he'p Mr. Mark light some candles. While we were walking around in the dark, he says to me, 'Bet you never thought you'd meet Pluto before your time.' "

He waited for me to respond. I kept my eyes on his and didn't speak. He cleared his throat. "I axed him if he was talking about Mickey Mouse's dog. He laughed his head off. Not in a nice way. I felt stupid and didn't know what to say."

"Yeah, that's a bit strange," I said.

"I looked up who Pluto was. The Roman god of the underworld."

"Maybe Shondell was just making a joke."

"That ain't all that happened. Mr. Mark's candles melted down. I went to the Walmart and bought some more. When I got back to the house, it was still raining and lightning. He didn't answer the door, even when I banged. I went around the side and looked through the French doors. The power was still out, and the inside of the house was black. He was sitting at his desk in front of his computer. There wasn't no battery power, no generator backup, nothing like that anywhere near his desk."

"I'm not following you."

"Lights were flashing in his face. But there wasn't any source. Just big blades of yellow light all over his face." He squeezed at his stomach, then drank from the bottle. "I think I got an ulcer. Jesus Christ, Dave, don't just sit there. How do you explain that?"

"It was probably a flash of lightning reflecting off a surface on Shondell's desk."

He jabbed his finger in the air, shaking it for emphasis. "That's right! That's probably what it was! You got it, man!" He hit me in the chest. "You're a smart man, you."

But his description of Shondell's face during the storm made me think of a figure in the works of Dante and Milton. His name meant "the light bringer." The name was Lucifer.

Chapter Nine

I'VE ALWAYS BELIEVED that normalcy is highly overrated and not to be confused with virtue. With that in mind, I can say in a charitable way that Father Julian Hebert (pronounced a-bear) was the most eccentric Catholic priest I've ever known. He went by his first name and never wore a Roman collar or a black suit, and he encouraged people to call him by his first name and not his title, which was hard for most Cajuns to do. He was socially tone-deaf and often a disaster at public gatherings. Last and most important, he had no filter between his brain and his vocal cords.

His mother was Irish and his father hard-core coon-ass. Clete Purcel called him "Goody Two-shoes Meets Chuck Norris." With his incongruous athletic physique and short blond hair and egg-shaped face and baby-blue eyes and complexion that resembled the skin of a pinkish-white balloon, he floated around the community and anchored himself in various venues where, without speaking a word, he made everyone either uncomfortable, puzzled, afraid, or willing to throttle him. These venues included dog- and cockfights, drive-through daiquiri windows, cage fights, strip bars, porn theaters, and casinos that gave free drinks around the clock to pensioners and functionally illiterate people who often lost everything they owned.

On a national Sunday-morning television show, when the other guests were discussing homosexual, bisexual, transgender, lesbian, and restroom issues as though there were no other terms for human beings and no other noteworthy subjects on earth, Julian said, "How about we just drop it? Who cares how people use their equipment? In your world, I'd probably have to introduce myself as a premature ejaculator. At least if I had a love life. Anyway, give it an effing break, will you?"

Whenever the bishop sent him a letter of reprimand or correction, Father Julian would report back that he had taken care of the problem. He always told the truth. He took care of the problem by dropping the letter in the wastebasket, not even bothering to wad it up.

He went bowling by himself at three A.M. in an all-night bowling alley in Lafayette and line-danced at a nightclub. He gave most of his money away and was arrested twice at Fort Benning in the protest against the School of the Americas. His tiny church down the bayou was the poorest in the diocese, and his parishioners were mostly people of color. The only toilet in the building was always stopping up with either roots or mud that seeped into the drainpipe whenever it rained. But Julian never lost faith and was beloved by his parishioners. His greatest oddity was his similarity to Clete Purcel. He recognized virtue in others but did not see it in himself.

The morning after I spoke to Marcel LaForchette, I drove to Jeanerette and parked by Father Julian's cottage and knocked on the door. The sky was blue, a crusty sliver of moon still visible above the trees, the sugarcane bending in the fields. Down by the bayou was a cemetery with crypts that were green with lichen and scattered down the slope like huge decayed teeth. I wanted to wander by the water and let go of all my troubles and try to remember the admonition that the race is not to the swift nor the battle to the strong. I wanted to throw bread crumbs on the edge of the lily pads and watch the bream and sunfish rise to the surface like wobbling green and gold air sacs of sunshine. I wanted these simple pleasures and a world free of death, a place where evil men do not break in and steal. Maybe that was the world Father Julian sought, too, I thought. Maybe that's why I was a cop. If so, both of us were probably headed for a huge disappointment.

You might wonder why I sought out the counsel of an iconoclast like Julian Hebert. There were several reasons. He was originally from New Iberia and knew Marcel LaForchette, but he had also known the Balangie family in New Orleans and supposedly attended

Pietro Balangie on his deathbed. In fact, there was a legend about it. Julian congratulated the old man for owning up to his sins, then said, "There's one other thing we should think about, Pietro. Maybe you can reach out to a few of your enemies and ask their forgiveness."

"I can't do that, Father," Pietro said.

"Why not?" Julian asked.

"I killed them all," Pietro replied.

But I'd heard the same story told about Frank Costello, so maybe this was another urban legend lending a degree of humor to the evil that can dwell in the human heart. Regardless, my recount is probably an attempt to hide the real reason for my visit to Julian's cottage. I was still bothered by Marcel LaForchette's tale about the power outage at Mark Shondell's house. I may have had other things on my mind as well, namely, the wife of Adonis Balangie.

Julian and I took a stroll by the graveyard. He was wearing Levi's and sandals with white socks and a T-shirt that had been washed from purple to lavender, with Mike the Tiger's head emblazoned on the front.

"Marcel saw lights flashing on Mark Shondell's face?" he asked.

"That's what he said."

"Marcel is a superstitious man."

"Why would Shondell make a joke about a pagan god? Marcel thought he was talking about Mickey Mouse's dog."

An alligator gar was rolling among the lily pads, its armored back slick and serpentine, sliding down into the root system where the bream hid. "Who knows why Mark Shondell does anything?" Julian said.

"You're not a fan?"

His blue irises were the size of nickels. He picked up a pecan that was still in the husk and tossed it at the gar. "I think you should stay away from Shondell."

"Do you know something about him that I don't?"

"I also think you should get your badge back," he replied.

"You can't talk to me about him on a personal basis? He confided something to you in the confessional?"

"That's a laugh."

I had told him only part of the story about the Shondells and the Balangies, and I didn't know if I should say more. Why burden a good man with a problem neither of us could solve? Anyway, he beat me to it. "What's really on your mind, Dave?"

I told him about Isolde being used as a pawn by Adonis and Penelope Balangie.

"They gave away their daughter?" he said.

"That's the way it looks."

"Have you reported this?"

"There's nothing to report. There's no evidence of a crime."

"Does Adonis Balangie know?"

"He's behind it," I said.

"What about Penelope?"

"I'm not sure. She's hard to read."

He was looking at the trees across the bayou. His eyes cut to mine. "In what way?"

"She came to see me in New Iberia. She said she wanted help."

"You believed her?"

"I'm not sure."

He stared at the water. The gar was gone. The wind was cold and damp and gusting on the bayou's surface, shriveling it like old skin. "She's a beautiful woman."

"I noticed."

"They're murderous people, Dave."

"The Balangies?"

"They claim to be descendants of Giordano Di Betto. Maybe they are. But Giordano Di Betto was not a killer. He was a victim, tortured and burned alive."

"Why would Penelope Balangie give her daughter to a lecherous man like Shondell?"

"That's the question she'll use to draw you into her life."

"Say again?"

"When you went to her house with Clete Purcel, did she make an appearance with a rosary?"

I stared at him, dumbfounded.

"Yep, that's Penelope," he said. "Be careful what you touch, Dave. Roses have thorns."

I WENT HOME. I wanted my badge back. In Louisiana the most powerful people in the parish are the sheriff and the tax accessor. If you're smart, you treat the former with caution and send a Christmas card to the latter. At the time the events I describe took place, the sheriff's department was involved in a disputed election that in effect had crippled the department, and my career rested in the hands of Internal Affairs, headed by Carroll LeBlanc, a former vice cop in New Orleans and an enemy of Clete Purcel.

Vice cops, male and female, have their own culture, one that is raw, depraved, and predatory. Many of the players are closet degenerates. Narcs and Treasury agents take enormous risks. Down on the border, they can suffer the fate of the damned if they fall into the wrong hands. Controlling the sex trade and human trafficking is another matter. Some undercover cops who work sex stings are mean to the bone and take a sadistic pleasure in their work. They set up drunks outside bars and gays in restrooms and ensure that the story makes the newspaper and the six o'clock news. Shorter version, they ruin careers and break up families. I knew one female vice cop who loved her role as a hooker and always made the same statement to the john when she busted him in the hotel room: "You came here to get fucked. Congratulations."

LeBlanc had thick facial skin, like pork rind, and recessed dark eyes that could be attentive one moment and then listless or vaguely lascivious. There was a string of black moles under his left eye, like cinders that had blown from a fire. To my knowledge, he had never married. His interest in others was fleeting, as was his concentration. His sanctuary lay in his computer and his file drawers. He dressed like a bookie or a horse tout or a sharper in a card game. But there was nothing of Damon Runyon in Carroll LeBlanc. He was as nasty as they came.

We were in the old office in the courthouse. Through the window, I could see the crypts in St. Peter's Cemetery. A freight train was creaking down the tracks, wobbling on the rails that traversed New Iberia's old red-light district. LeBlanc had stretched out his legs and crossed his ankles and opened a manila folder and propped it on his crotch. He glanced up and followed my line of sight out the window. His shirt was an immaculate white, his blue silk necktie draped on his stomach. "What are you looking at?"

"It's funny how whorehouses and graveyards seem to go together," I said. "Sometimes I wonder if South Louisiana isn't a giant necropolis."

"A what?"

I shrugged off my own comment; I regretted cluttering up the conversation. He was reviewing the charges that had cost me my badge. He made a sucking sound with his teeth. "Without authorization, you took Purcel to a crime scene on the St. Martin Parish line?"

"I needed his help," I said.

"The St. Martin cops say Purcel left his shit-prints all over it."

"He did six weeks in their stockade," I said. "They have a long memory."

"Maybe so. But I got to go with what's in the file. There's another problem here. You hid a confidential informant at your house. A black woman. There was a warrant on her."

"A federal judge was going to expose her and confine her to a halfway house. Remember what happened to Barry Seal?"

"You weren't dipping your wick, were you?"

"I'm going to forget you said that, Carroll."

"So the federal court system is your enemy?" he said.

"Are you going to cut me some slack or not?"

"I thought you told everybody you were done with the department."

"You know about those guys who got stuffed in a barrel?" I said.

"Down in Vermilion?"

"They braced me on the bayou."

"From what I hear, Clete Purcel might have been mixed up in this."

"That's a lie, and you know it."

"A cop who killed a federal witness and was a hump for the Mob in Reno and Vegas? Yeah, I can't imagine him going astray."

LeBlanc closed the folder and placed it on his desk. His jaw went slack, the way an old man's does when his thought processes take him into blind alleys. He scratched the row of moles that seemed to leak from his eye. "I can recommend you for temporary reinstatement until we get our administrative problems straightened out. In other words, you'll be on probation and treated as such. You will also report to me, no one else. You copy?"

I stared into space.

"You got a bug up your ass about something?" he said.

"No."

"I asked if you copy."

"I'm extremely copacetic with everything you've said, Carroll. I appreciate your oversight. Thanks for being here."

I could see an incisor whitening his lip. He waited for me to leave, but I didn't. I let my eyes stay on his. "*What?*" he said.

"I think there may be an instance of human trafficking going on in Iberia Parish."

"You're talking about illegal immigrants?"

"I'm talking about Mark Shondell."

He tossed my IA folder on the desk. "I knew it. You can't keep your nose out of trouble."

"Call the home of Adonis Balangie and ask him where his stepdaughter is."

"You know the feeling I have about you, Robo?"

"No clue."

"You think your shit doesn't stink. You never had to work vice. You never had to clean AIDS puke off your clothes. You never had to let a perv go for your joint."

"I didn't know that went with the job. *AIDS* puke?"

"Get out of my office."

"Nice to be back working with you, Carroll. Keep fighting the good fight."

Through the ceiling, I heard a toilet flush, the water powering through the drain pipe, shaking the walls.

I HAD PROMISED CLETE Purcel that one day I would tell him why I'd visited Marcel LaForchette in Huntsville Pen. It was the same reason I'd visited my priest friend Julian Hebert. I wanted to know the origins of human cruelty. Please notice I did not say "evil." The latter is a generic term; the former is not. Evil can encompass addiction, greed, sloth, bad sexual behavior or just imperfection, and all the other doodah that goes along with the cardinal sins, depending on who the speaker is. Cruelty is different. It has no limits and no bottom. Often it has no motivation. It's usually fiendish and more often is done collectively than by individuals.

In the year 1600, at the end of the Renaissance and the beginning of the Age of Reason, Giordano Di Betto was stripped naked and hanged upside down over a fire with his lips pinned together so he couldn't speak or scream. Jump forward 365 years to an Asian country where I called in Puff the Magic Dragon on a ville after the enemy trapped us in a rice paddy and let loose with RPGs and a captured blooker and a fifty-caliber with tracer rounds just before bagging ass into the jungle.

I still remember the sparks twisting into the evening sky, the glow of the hooches, the screams of children. I tell myself I had no alternative. Am I telling the truth? To this day, I hate people who assure me I did nothing wrong. I hate them most for their sophistry and the hand they place on my shoulder as they talk about things of which they have no understanding. And finally, I hate myself.

I'm really saying I visited Marcel LaForchette in Huntsville Pen and Father Julian in Jeanerette to prove I'm not guilty of the behavior I have seen in others. But I know the level of rage I took with me to Southeast Asia, and I know the number of men I killed as surrogates for the man who cuckolded my father and destroyed my family. I would fire all eight rounds in my .45 auto at an Asian man's face as though I were sleepwalking. Sometimes I had to be shaken awake by my sergeant when it was over. I received several medals for wounds and acts of bravery and felt I deserved none of them. The only true symbols of my war experience were malaria and scar tissue from jungle ulcers and the abiding conviction that the Beast had left his imprint on me.

ON AN EARLY Friday afternoon, Clete Purcel got off the plane in Fort Lauderdale and took a cab up to Pompano Beach. The two-lane street bordering the beach was cluttered with coconut palms and neon signs and stucco motels painted with pastel colors. He checked in to a ten-story hotel that looked over the water, then he showered and shaved and put on fresh clothes, including a Panama hat and a Hawaiian shirt. Then he rented a car and drove down to Lauderdale-by-the-Sea, where Eddy Firpo kept his recording studio, one half block from the ocean.

When Clete opened the door and went inside, an electronic chime rang in back and the clock over the counter said 4:49. No one was up front. Through a door behind the counter, he could see chairs and musical instruments and guitars and microphones and a glassed-in sound engineer's booth. He flipped through a collection of celluloid-encased photos in a folder on the counter. The photos went back into the 1950s—working-class Italian kids from the Jersey Shore, R&B singers, a shot of Muddy Waters and Etta James together, Swamp Poppers who created what was called "the New Orleans sound." The last photo was of Jerry Lee Lewis seated in front of a piano at the Apollo Theater, one two-tone shoe propped on the keys.

Clete heard someone from the inner doorway. A man in white slacks and a silk shirt as black and wet-looking as oil was staring at him, a gold cross hanging on his chest, his skin as brown as leather. "The fuck?" the man said as he realized who Clete was.

"I dig these photos," Clete said. "But why is it a lot of these people don't seem to have anything to do with your studio?"

"Take your greasy hands off my book. You wrecked my house

and put my security guys in the emergency room. Three of my guests got busted for possession. I checked you out, asshole. You belong in a cage."

"There's a lot of agreement on that. Johnny Shondell back there?"

"Are you hearing me?"

"You might have kidnapping charges filed against you, Eddy. That's a federal rap."

"Who got kidnapped?"

"Isolde Balangie. Know where she is?"

"I'm a lawyer and promotor. I don't kidnap people."

"Did you know Jerry Lee Lewis is from Ferriday, Louisiana?"

Eddy looked from side to side, as though someone else were in the room. "What do I care about Jerry Lee Lewis?"

"He's in your book."

Eddy stuck fingers into both his temples as though they were drills. "You need to get yourself lobotomized. You got some kind of brain disease. Like you figured out a way to piss on it."

"Not a time to be cute."

"I'll give you cute. This is South Florida. All I need to do is make one call."

"You work with Nazis?"

"Keep talking, wisenheimer."

"Where's Johnny Shondell?" Clete said.

Eddy began punching in a number on the counter phone. Clete jerked the receiver from Eddy's hand and wrapped the cord around his neck and pulled it tight, cutting off the carotid. Eddy's eyes popped and his face darkened, as though someone had lowered a shade on it.

"Answer the question, Eddy," Clete said.

Eddy's fingernails were hooked inside the cord, spittle draining from his mouth. Clete tightened the cord. Eddy was making gurgling sounds, his face purple now. He swatted helplessly at the air. Clete unwrapped the cord and let Eddy drop to the floor. "I'm sorry," Clete said. "You okay down there?"

Eddy made a sound like water being sucked through a water hose.

He staggered to his feet, hardly able to speak. "You almost pinched off my head."

"You dealt it, Eddy."

"You're nuts. You should be taken to a hospital and killed."

"I know everything about you, Eddy. You're paying three points a week to some shylocks in Miami, which means they own your soul. Your father was a hump for Joey Gallo. You do legal work for the Klan and some neo-Nazis up in the Panhandle. Bottom line, a guy like me is the least of your problems. Where is Johnny Shondell?"

Eddy huffed a spray of blood out of one nostril and wiped it on the back of his hand. "Rick's, on Duval Street in Key West. How you know that stuff about me?"

"I do investigations. I got to say, I don't see the upside of the connection with the Klan and the Nazis."

"You're already up to your bottom lip in Shit's Creek, douche brain," Eddy said. "You just don't get it yet."

"I'd better not have a reception waiting for me in Key West, Eddy."

Eddy took a Kleenex from a box and blew his nose. "You got no idea what's out there. Call me in a few days and tell me how you like it."

Chapter Ten

CLETE DROVE HIS rental down to the Keys. On the western horizon, trapped under a black lid of storm clouds, was an eye-watering band of blue brilliance and a pinkish-yellow sun that the rain could not diminish and the Gulf of Mexico could not sink. He opened his windows when he drove across Seven Mile Bridge, the salty denseness of the wind like an immersion into a warm pool that could magically restore his youth. For just a moment he felt a sense of comfort so great that he dozed off and hit a rumble strip that jarred his teeth.

He righted the steering wheel and glanced down through the steel grid and saw a patch of color in the water that looked exactly like india ink floating under the surface. He wondered if he was dreaming or witnessing a sign. By the time he reached Key West, the sun was only a spark on the horizon, the moon was rising, and Duval Street was filled with music and celebrants who were innocently happy and hilariously drunk, forming conga lines on the curbs, perhaps certain that death would pass them by or perhaps accepting it for what it was.

In Clete's mind, for good or bad, Key West had always been a hole in the dimension that took him back to his childhood in old New Orleans. Rick's Bar was a two-story white frame building with a big veranda and numerous windows and doors, similar to the nineteenth-century residences in the Irish Channel. Clete went inside, sat at the bar, and ordered a vodka Collins and two dozen oysters on the half shell.

The stage was small and bare and framed with different-colored

86 JAMES LEE BURKE

lightbulbs. Johnny Shondell came out from behind a curtain with his Super Jumbo Gibson slung from his shoulder, the belly and neck pointed down. Hardly anyone took notice of him. He was grinning as he bent to the microphone and adjusted it to his height. A thick dark blue cloud of smoke sagged from the ceiling. Clete took a long swallow from his glass, letting the crushed ice and cherries and orange slices and the coldness of the vodka have their way.

Johnny looked up and momentarily seemed to recognize him, then dropped his gaze and began tuning his guitar. The bartender set a napkin and a tiny fork in front of Clete, then went back to the bin and opened an oyster and slid it down the bar trailing ice. "Curbside service," he said. "I shuck 'em, you chuck 'em."

"How's the kid doing with your customers?" Clete asked.

The bartender's arms were huge and tanned and wrapped with black hair. "It's Key West. People see UFOs under the water. How do you compete with an act like that?"

Johnny made a chord up on the neck of his Gibson, ran his thumb over the strings, then went into Doc Watson's "Freight Train Boogie." The speed of his fingers was stunning. Clete once saw Robbie Robertson and Eric Clapton perform together: It was the only time he had seen anyone faster and more graceful than Johnny. Four other musicians joined Johnny, and he played and sang six traditional numbers in a row. The applause was more courteous than passionate. A man shouted for an Elvis song as though Johnny were a reenactor. Johnny sang "Heartbreak Hotel," then left the stage and ordered a drink at the end of the bar.

Clete picked up his glass and moved down the bar and sat on the stool next to him. "I really dug your songs," he said.

Johnny was shaking his head negatively before Clete could continue. "We shouldn't be talking, Mr. Clete."

"Eddy Firpo told you I was coming?"

"He's still in shock from what you did to his house in Bay St. Louis."

Clete signaled the bartender for another Collins. "Dave Robicheaux and I are trying to do you a solid, kid. How about getting with the program?"

Johnny looked at Clete's left arm. "You're out of the sling, huh?"

"Forget about me. You got a lot of talent. You can go somewhere."

"I'm heading out to Los Angeles with Eddy. I know you don't like Eddy, but he's on my side. Now lay off us."

"Eddy Firpo is not a person. He's a disease. Time to take off the blinders. You going to see Isolde in L.A.?"

Johnny looked into his drink. "That's all over."

"I heard y'all sing together. You remind me of Dale and Grace. Maybe even better."

"You got to leave this alone, Mr. Clete."

"If Adonis Balangie or your uncle is behind this, we can do something about it," Clete said. "This isn't 1861."

Johnny looked over his shoulder and scanned the street. "Have you talked to Isolde or seen her?"

"No," Clete said.

"I don't know what to do."

"Start telling the truth. Stop covering up for greaseballs. What the hell is the matter with you?"

"Nobody would believe it."

"*I* believe it. I look like I just got off the boat with a spear in my hand and a bone in my nose?"

"You said it's not 1861. You got that right."

"What's that supposed to mean?"

"Try four hundred years earlier."

Clete finished his first drink and started on the fresh one. He leaned closer to Johnny. "Here's the truth about the Mob. Most of them skipped toilet training. They smell like salami and hair tonic and BO. They were either lazy or too stupid to hold honest jobs, so they terrorized their fellow immigrants and thought up a bunch of crap about burning pictures of their patron saints and slicing their hands and smearing blood on each other and swearing themselves to secrecy and calling themselves men of honor. You think Adonis Balangie does shit like that? He wouldn't let those guys lick his toilet."

"I got to get back to work."

"I'm not good with words," Clete said. "Hey, kid, this is what it is. You make other people see the glass rings on the bar, the honky-tonk angels, Dallas at night from a DC-9. Don't let these bums destroy your life."

Johnny looked at Clete, then at Clete's drink, then at Clete again. "You talk pretty good for a guy who—"

"A guy who what?"

"Nothing."

"A guy who drinks too much? You're right. My head glows in the dark. At night I don't have to use a reading lamp," Clete said. "After you get through here, let's grab a steak. I knew Louis Prima and Sam Butera when they played at Sharkey Bonano's Dream Room on Bourbon. My favorite lyric from Louis was 'I'll be standing on the corner plastered when they bring your body by.'"

"No more sermons, Mr. Clete."

"Me?" Clete said.

AT TWO-FIFTEEN A.M. Clete picked up Johnny Shondell at the curb. They ate at an all-night diner and drove down to Johnny's motel on the southern tip of the island. Clete had put away half of a large bottle of Champale while he drove, the cold bottle swishing between his thighs. His arm ached from the knife wound that had not yet healed; his eyelids felt like lead, and his vision was starting to go out of focus. He looked at Johnny's profile in the glow of the dash and wanted to speak but couldn't remember what he'd planned to say.

"You're not going to drive back to Lauderdale tonight, are you?" Johnny said, getting out of the car.

"I'll find a rest stop," Clete said.

"You don't want to get arrested in Key West, Mr. Clete." Johnny was leaning down, the car door still open, the breeze puffing his shirt on his wide shoulders. There was an unnatural shine in his eyes. "I get weirded out sometimes at night. You know that expression 'the night has a thousand eyes'? That's the way I feel."

"We'll sit on the dock," Clete said.

The motel had been built on the southernmost tip of the key. The water was dark green under the moon, a small boat bumping against a piling beneath the dock. Johnny and Clete sat down in a pair of recliners. Clete felt two hundred years old. He offered the Champale bottle to Johnny. "No, thanks," Johnny said.

"You're not big on alcohol?"

"Not much."

"It's better if a guy can do without it."

"So why don't you?" Johnny said.

"I never think about it. That's what happens when you're on the juice most of your life. You don't think about it."

Johnny sniffed and pulled his cuffs down on his wrists. "It's getting cold."

"Want to tell me why you're putting up with your uncle's bullshit?"

"About Isolde?"

"Yeah, what do you think I'm talking about?"

Johnny flinched as though someone had touched him with a hot cigarette. "You don't know how it is at my uncle Mark's house."

"I'll take a wild guess. He's a prick?"

Johnny picked at his nails and rubbed his nose with his wrist. "I think something happened when I was real little. Something I'm not supposed to remember. I have dreams about it. In the dream, I run away so I don't see something that's in a room with a closed door."

"Marcel LaForchette told Dave Robicheaux a story about your uncle sitting in front of his desk while the power was out. There were lights flashing on his face."

"Marcel said that?"

"According to Dave. Your uncle's in a cult or he's got magical powers or something?"

"Marcel better be careful."

"Or?" Clete asked.

Johnny looked at the waves. "I got to go inside."

"What's wrong?"

"I catch colds easy."

"You're going to give up your girlfriend to a man like your uncle? You don't seem like that kind of kid."

"I'm not a kid." Johnny stood up, his shirt flattening in the wind. A wave full of bioluminescent organisms that lit like green fireflies slid into the pilings. "We're not in the place you think we are, Mr. Clete. It's not the date you think it is, either."

"Run that by me again?"

"What I said. You don't have any idea what you're involved in."

"In my next life, I'm coming back as a swizzle stick so I won't have to listen to this kind of stuff anymore."

"It's not funny," Johnny said.

Clete stood up and corked the Champale bottle and dropped it on the chair. He thought he saw, three hundred yards to the south, a large wood boat with two masts and many oars. He wiped at his eyes and looked again. The boat was gone. "I'm going to head back to Fort Lauderdale," he said.

"I meant it when I said watch out for the cops in Key West."

"Yeah, yeah, yeah," Clete said. "I got to tell you something about your girlfriend. If I don't, I'll resent myself in the morning."

"Say it."

"I fathered a daughter out of wedlock. Her mother was a stripper and a junkie. I never learned what happened to my daughter. A pimp is probably banging her now or a guy is shooting her up or giving her AIDS or herpes. You can't walk off from an innocent girl like Isolde and expect her to land on her feet. Now clean up your act."

"I can't handle this, Mr. Clete."

"Evidently not," Clete said. "I'll see you around, kid. I hope you have a good life. Right now you're genuinely pissing me off."

Clete walked to his car, the dock tilting as though he were aboard a ship dipping into waves higher than the gunwales.

HE MADE IT to Seven Mile Bridge, then pulled onto the shoulder, zoned and shit-blown, a stench rising from his armpits even with the air conditioner on. Voices in his head were arguing with each other, his ears whirring with noises like malarial mosquitoes. Twice Florida Highway Patrol cruisers had gone flying past him, buffeting his rental, their lights flashing. He knew he would be immediately arrested if he were stopped. He also knew the only way to downshift the situation was to park the rental, pull the keys, get in the backseat, drop the keys on the floor, and go to sleep. No reasonable cop would take him in.

But back there on the dock, Johnny's biggest problem had been on full display. What do you do? Tell the kid not to sweat it, mainlining skag is groovy and the Abyss is probably a blast?

Clete swung off the shoulder, bounced over a divider, scraping the steel frame on the concrete, and headed back for the motel.

Chapter Eleven

THE YOUNG CLERK at the night desk looked at the badge in Clete's hand. "That says you're a private investigator."

"Right," Clete said.

"I can't give out a room number unless you're a real cop."

"Thanks for the compliment. Walk me to the room."

"I can't do that, either."

"Call the room."

The clerk punched in a number on the console of his phone. "No answer," he said.

"Call 911 and ask for an ambulance."

"What for?"

"There's a medical emergency in that room."

"What if the guest is just asleep?"

"We'll tell the ambulance to beat it. If there's any charge, they can bill the motel. Your boss won't mind."

The clerk walked Clete to a room at the back of the motel and tapped on the door. When there was no answer, he stuck the key in the lock and twisted the knob and let the door swing open. The television was on, the sound off. Johnny was sitting in a chair, silhouetted against the screen, head on one shoulder. Clete stepped between Johnny and the clerk. "I'll take it from here," he said.

"Is he all right?"

"I'll tell you if he's not." He put a ten-dollar bill in the clerk's shirt pocket. "Thanks for your help."

After the clerk was gone, Clete shook Johnny by the shoulder. His eyes were half lidded and his mouth hung open. A syringe and the rubber tubing he'd used for a tourniquet lay on the carpet. His skin was pale blue, as though it had been refrigerated.

Clete shook him again, harder. "Wake up," he said.

Johnny's head sagged forward. Clete went to the phone. "No," Johnny said.

Clete replaced the receiver. "Look at me," he said.

Johnny raised his head and tried to speak. His words were in slow motion and seemed to break like bubbles on his lips.

"How many times a day you shoot up?" Clete said.

Johnny didn't reply. Clete made sure the curtains were secure, then clicked on the overhead light. He pulled up Johnny's sleeves and turned up his forearms.

"You're a pincushion, kid," he said.

"Not a kid," Johnny said. "Need to sleep now."

"Where's your stash?"

Johnny closed and opened his eyes. "I don't have any."

"I'm calling for an ambulance. I need to flush your stash."

Johnny bent over, then tried to roll himself out of the chair but obviously didn't have the strength. "Narcan," he said.

"Where?"

"The suitcase."

Clete took the suitcase off the baggage stand and dumped it on the bed. He picked through the folded shirts and trousers and underwear and socks and swim trunks and snorkel gear.

"You can't find it?" Johnny said.

"Yeah, I can't find it because it's not there."

"Must have used it up."

"I hate dropping the dime on you," Clete said, "but I don't want to go to your funeral."

Johnny looked at Clete as though he were having a dream and Clete was not real. "I'll go to Raiford."

"They don't put people in Raiford for holding."

"I'm already on probation."

"Get up!" Clete said.

"No."

"I'm taking you to the hospital. While you're there, you're D, D, and D. Got that?"

"What?"

"Deaf, dumb, and don't know."

"Whatever you say."

"Ready?" Clete said. He worked his arms under Johnny's and lifted him from the chair. He could smell Johnny's body odor, the funk in his breath, the cigarette smoke in his hair and clothes. Johnny's tongue had turned gray. Clete lost his balance, and Johnny hit the floor on the base of his spine.

"I'm sorry, kid," Clete said. "I'm as fucked up as you are."

"No, you're not. You're a good guy," Johnny said. "I got to get Isolde back, Mr. Clete."

Clete went to the phone and rang the desk. "Call an ambulance and tell them you got a code red."

He found Johnny's stash of China white on the closet shelf. It was the size of a baseball and double-bagged in a Ziploc. Clete gathered up the syringe and the rubber tubing and a burned spoon he found on the lavatory, wrapped them in a towel and went outside and dropped them in a trash barrel, then walked out on the dock and shook the Ziploc empty over a passing wave. The white granules dissolved like snow on a woodstove. He looked at the horizon and thought he saw the Southern Cross pulsing in the heavens, but he knew it was impossible to see the Cross from this latitude and he wondered if he was becoming delusional. The wind was as warm as a wet kiss on his skin. Inside the hiss of the waves sliding through the pilings, he thought he heard wood knocking against wood, then the sound thinned and stopped when a wave smacked against a piling.

He walked back to Johnny's room. In the distance he saw the heavy, boxlike shape of an emergency vehicle coming down the two-lane, its flashers floating through the darkness as silently as tracer rounds. Why was the siren off? Why did he seem trapped under a black-green starlit Plexiglas dome, one that could suck the oxygen from his lungs? His father had died a wet-brain. Was it now his turn?

Ten minutes passed. Clete kept going to the window, trying to catch sight of the emergency vehicle he had seen. He had pulled back the covers on the bed, laid Johnny down and covered him up, then put his hand on Johnny's forehead. His temperature felt normal and the color had started to come back in his face. *Maybe I should cancel the 911,* Clete thought. It was the kind of decision that nobody wants, but one that is forced regularly on the friends and families of addict-alcoholics. Every minute in an addict-alcoholic's life is a roll of the dice: a blood clot in the brain, a seizure that leaves him frothing at the mouth on the floor, a handful of downers that reduces the heart to marmalade, an eruption in the stomach that causes him to strangle to death on his own vomit.

Fuck it, Clete said to himself. *Maybe the night clerk didn't make the call.* Clete picked up the phone and rang the desk. No answer. Great. He left the door cracked so he could get back in the room, and headed up the outside walkway. The wind was stronger now, sweet with the promise of rain, the streets empty and shiny with night damp. Directly overhead, a cloud bloomed with lightning that flickered and died.

No one was at the counter. Clete patted the bell. "Hey, you back there? Where's the meat wagon?"

No response. Clete went behind the counter and into a back office. The bathroom door was ajar. "Hey!" he said.

He pushed the door wider. The bathroom was clean, the seat up, the toilet bowl flushed. He went back through the office and saw a Styrofoam cup on the floor behind the desk, a thread of coffee leaking into the carpet.

He went back to the counter and picked up the desk phone. Just as he began punching in the 911, he saw a black police cruiser turn off the street and drive through the porte cochere and circle to the back of the motel. Clete went outside and followed the cruiser to Johnny's room. A large man in a fedora cut the cruiser's headlights and engine but did not get out. Clete heard the squawk of a handheld radio. Clete walked to the driver's window. It was already rolled down. The driver had a round, fleshy face with small eyes and gaps in his teeth like the carved mouth on a jack-o'-lantern. "You called in the 911?"

"The clerk did," Clete said, glancing at the emblem on the door. It was a dull bronze color, the kind that was hard to read against the black background and was used to nail speeders. "Where's the ambulance?"

"Ambulance?" the man said. "We got a disturbing-the-peace complaint."

"A kid overdosed," Clete said. "He's coming around. Maybe I can handle it."

"OD-ed on what?"

"Unknown," Clete said.

The man got out of the cruiser and shut the door. His suit fit him like a tent. "What's your name?"

"Clete Purcel. I'm a PI from New Orleans."

"I'm Detective Bell. Let's take a look at your friend."

"Can I see your shield?" Clete said.

Bell wore a clip-on holster; there was a sag on the right side of his coat. "What's this cruiser look like, a school bus?"

"You're a plainclothes responding to a disturbance report?"

"A gas line blew up about a mile from here. I just got off my shift and volunteered to fill in. You smell like a cross between a beer vat and a rendering plant, sport. Want to drive your friend to the hospital or let me do my job?"

"Sport?"

Bell laughed to himself and studied his note pad. "I got a bad habit of giving people names. Your friend is in room 136?"

Clete nodded.

"Stay behind me," Bell said. He looked at the sky. "Strange weather, huh? One minute it's balmy, then coconuts are coming down on your car. Purcel? Where did I hear that name? You haven't been inside, have you?"

"You mean in the joint?" Clete said.

Bell kept walking and didn't reply.

"Hello?" Clete said at his back.

"You look a little woozy. I hope you're not planning on driving anywhere tonight. This is Monroe County. Heavy on family values. Kind of place that's not DUI or spear-chunker friendly."

"What was that last part?"

"I was pulling your leg. Had you going, didn't I?"

Chapter Twelve

JOHNNY HAD FALLEN on the floor of his room. "Help me get him on the bed," Clete said.

"Put a pillow under his head and leave him where he is," Bell said, his eyes roving around the room. "Did you get rid of his works?"

"No," Clete replied. "Why'd you ask me if I was inside?"

Bell grinned. "You look like you've been around. No insult intended. Anyway, I don't know what to tell you, Mr. Purcel. This kid has tracks on both arms. It's your decision."

"I'll take care of him."

Bell nodded contemplatively. "Tell me the truth. You've been up the road?"

"A navy brig and a few local slams. I was in the Crotch."

"Semper Fi," Bell said.

"You were in the Corps?"

"Is it Semper Fi or Semper Cry?" Bell said.

"That's pretty clever. How about cleaning the potato salad out of your mouth?"

Bell went to the front door and opened it partway. "Come here a second, will you?"

"What for?"

"To show you something," Bell said. He clicked off the light and opened the door wide. The salt air ballooned into the room. "See all that blackness out there? That's the world, sport. That's what I serve. I don't make the rules or get a vote."

"What are you talking about?" Clete said.

"You're probably a PI because you were once a cop who got in trouble. Which means you understand how the system works."

"Tell you what, bub," Clete said. "I'll take care of my friend, and you can roll it up and head on down the road. You know, *hasta lumbago* or whatever."

"I was First Cav. Know what the Marines used to tell us about our insignia? 'The horse they couldn't ride, the line they couldn't cross, the color that speaks for itself.' A piece of shit like you is a gift."

From his right-hand pocket, he pulled a blackjack and swung it across Clete's temple. Clete went down like a sandbag, his arms at his sides, his jaw locked open, his face bouncing off the floor.

HE WOKE DRESSED only in his skivvies, suspended upside down, bound hand and foot, his head perhaps four feet above the ground, in a place where he could see buttonwood and gumbo-limbo trees and sandspits humped like the backs of sand sharks and mangroves and stacks of crab traps and a huge expanse of water and clouds as black as cannon smoke on the horizon.

His feet were attached to a cable that hung from the boom of a giant tow truck. His head felt as though all the blood in his body had settled in the top of his skull; his skin was frigid in the wind.

He remembered nothing after hitting the floor of the motel. One eye was swollen the size of an egg, with only a slit he could see through. For a second he thought he was going to vomit. The water sliding past the mangroves was green and frothy and phosphorescent, as though filled with electric eels. A few hundred yards from shore, he saw a tiered wooden ship, like an ancient prison vessel, its sails furled, its oars dead in the water.

Clete heard someone walking toward him. The steps were measured and heavy, like those of a man wearing boots, the soles crunching grittily, the sound of a man walking with a purpose. Clete thought he smelled gasoline. He felt his colon pucker, his skin shrink, his breath seize in his throat. A man in a cowl stepped into his line of sight. The man was wearing steel-toed boots and leather gloves and tight riveted trousers that were stiff with dirt and grease and hitched high on the hips and tight around the scrotum. Inside the cowl was a narrow face that had the iridescence of the bodies Clete had seen washed from their graves during the monsoon season in Vietnam.

"Know who I am?" the man said.

The voice was guttural, as though the speaker had sand in his throat. Clete had no doubt about the voice's origins. It lived in his dreams and sometimes in the middle of the day. He'd carried it with him to El Salvador and to the brothels of Bangkok and Saigon's Bring Cash Alley. The voice was one of ridicule and debasement and often came with a slap on the ear or a razor strop biting into his buttocks or grains of rice he was forced to kneel upon. He had no doubt someone had injected him with a hallucinogen or dropped it in his mouth.

"How you doin', Pop?" he said. "Long time no see."

"Know why we're doing what we're doing to you?" said the voice inside the cowl.

"I don't care," Clete said. "It's not real."

"Tell me that five minutes from now."

Clete squeezed his eyes shut, then opened them again. "Pop, I know that's you. Don't tease me."

"You've become a believer?"

"If that's you, Pop, tell me about the greenhouse on St. Charles."

"Still thinking about that, are you? You should. You were a bad boy."

"Tell me."

The man reached out and spun Clete around. "A rich lady asked you to come to her ice-cream party. You put on your Easter suit and knocked on her front door, but you got sent around back. The yard was full of raggedy-ass colored children. You went back that night with a bag of rocks and broke all the glass in her greenhouse. You cost me a customer."

"Screw you, Jack."

"I'm glad you said that. It makes me feel better about my duties."

"Screw you twice," Clete said, struggling to keep the anguish from his voice.

The man in the cowl walked away, then returned with a jerry can hanging from his hand, the cap dangling from a chain, the contents sloshing inside. "You shouldn't have used that language to me. I've told you about using profanity."

"This isn't happening."

"When we're done, your ashes will go into the water. Then you'll be part of history. Think of it as an honor."

"Why is that ship out there?"

"You don't need to worry about that."

"Why not?"

"You'll soon join them. Forever."

"Who is 'them'?"

"You'll find out. The galleon culture can be quite intimate. Have you heard about the crews on the Middle Passage?"

"I'll get you, you cocksucker."

"They all say that. But I'm still here, and they're not."

Then the man began breaking up orange crates and piling the pieces below Clete's head. He added a box full of wood shavings and wads of newspaper and rotted boards spiked with nails. He began pouring the jerry can on the pile and then on Clete, starting with the soles of his feet, soaking his skivvies, drenching his face and hair.

"If you're familiar with the procedure, you're probably aware that I'm showing you a degree of mercy," the man said. "You'll go faster than some of the others. Burning from the feet up is no treat."

"This is a dream. I know it's a dream. I'll wait you out."

"Want to tell me anything? You look like you're crying."

"Lean close. I can hardly talk."

Clete thought he saw the man smile inside the cowl. "You wouldn't try to spit on me, would you?"

"No," Clete replied.

The man leaned forward, his right hand behind his thigh. For a second Clete saw a pair of elongated eyes, a harelip, and a nose that resembled the nostrils on a snake. Clete gathered all the phlegm in his throat and tried to spit. The man laughed and threw a tin can filled with gasoline in his face.

"Bad boy," he said. He rolled a piece of newspaper to use as an igniter and thumbed a Zippo from his watch pocket. "I'm going to step back from the flash. Any last words I can give to your father?"

"Yeah. He never got a break," Clete said. "When he wasn't drinking, he was a good guy. You're a lousy imitator of him. One other thing: If I had a face like yours, I'd be pissed off, too."

Clete closed his eyes and waited to join the dead who, for decades, in one fashion or another, had been his constant companions. Then he realized he *was* crying, but he didn't care. His tears were not for himself. They were for his poor father and mother and the unhappiness to which they woke every day of their lives, and for the wretched childhood of his sisters and for all the suffering he had seen in El Salvador and for the people in a line of hooches he had seen engulfed like haystacks by one snake-and-nape flyover.

He heard the man clink the top off the cigarette lighter and flick the wheel, then smelled the flame crawl up the piece of rolled newspaper. He prayed that his death would come quickly, and no sooner had he finished his prayer than he felt his head begin to swell as though all the blood remaining in his body had filled his cranium and was beginning to boil, squeezing his eyes from their sockets, bursting his eardrums, setting his brain alight.

But something was happening that had nothing to do with the realities of a violent death, particularly one that involved death by burning. He opened his eyes. Instead of flames, he saw a dense white fog puffing off the water, swallowing his body, anointing his brow and eyes, like the cool fingers of a woman stroking his skin, assuring him he would never be abandoned.

He could hear thunder crackling in the clouds and feel rain hitting his body as hard as marbles. The gasoline had been washed from his skin. Hailstones bounced on the ground and pattered on the buttonwoods; waves swollen with organic matter were coursing like a tidal surge through the mangroves. A tree of lightning lit up the clouds from the southern horizon to the top of the sky. The ship with the furled sails and giant oars was gone. In its place, dolphins were leaping from the swells, arching as sleek and hard and sculpted as mythic monsters, reentering the rings of foam they had created.

He felt the winch jerk, then lower him to the ground. He wondered if a deliverance was at hand or if another trick was about to be played upon him. The fog was so white and thick that he wanted to stay inside it forever and float out to sea, far beyond the horizon, and stay in the company of whoever had touched his eyes and brow. He wondered if that had been his mother. Who else could it have been? He was curled like a broken worm on the ground. He could hear feet crunching on the sand and shale, walking toward him, as loud and metronomic and heavy as the blood drumming inside his head.

Don't do this to me, he said to someone. *Please.*

The words did not sound like his.

Chapter Thirteen

JOHNNY SHONDELL SET down the fire extinguisher he was carrying and took out a pocketknife and knelt on one knee and sliced the ligatures on Clete's wrists. The butt of a small semi-automatic protruded from the pocket of his jeans. He looked into Clete's face. "You all right, Mr. Clete?" he said.

"No," Clete said. "I don't think I'm ever going to be all right. What happened?"

"I know some of the places they use. So I came here."

"Who's 'they'?"

"You don't want to find out."

Clete shook his head. "This isn't real."

Johnny put his hand under Clete's big arm and helped him to his feet. "Get all these memories out of your mind. There's a world around us other people can't see. You and Mr. Robicheaux found your way into it. That was a mistake. You got to undo the mistake. You hear me, Mr. Clete?"

"I'm not going to put up with this greaseball craziness, Johnny."

"What day is it?"

Clete had to think. He had flown into Lauderdale on Friday. "Saturday morning."

"It's Monday," Johnny said.

"It can't be."

"It is," Johnny said.

"How'd I lose two days?"

"Maybe they used drugs on you. Maybe they didn't need drugs. They have powers we don't understand. The only thing they fear is discovery."

"What?"

"They're always out there. They don't want people to know they exist. There's good ones and bad ones."

"Cut that out. What's this place we're in?"

"A junkyard."

Clete started to shiver. The sky was still black, the rain still falling, twisting like drops of crystal. "You got a car?"

"A rental."

"What about the cop who hit me with a blackjack?"

"I don't know anything about a cop."

"He was plainclothes," Clete said. "He came to your motel room."

"I don't remember that," Johnny said.

"We're going to hunt down this guy and find out who he's working for."

"No, we're not."

Clete felt his legs going weak. His head began to spin, as though he were still suspended from the cable. His throat had never been so dry, even after weekend benders. Johnny steadied him with one hand. "My car is over here, Mr. Clete. I'm going to take you back to the hotel."

Clete looked at the southern horizon. The waves were rolling out of the Straits, dark green and capping and glazed with the moon's reflection. "What happened to the ship? The one with the masts and oars."

"You're not making sense. Oars on a sailboat? That doesn't sound right."

"It looked like it was out of medieval times."

"Don't think about these things anymore, Mr. Clete. You can't talk about this to others, either. The more you do, the more people will not believe you. You see any of their faces?"

"Yeah, the cop and the guy in a hood."

"What'd the guy in the hood look like?" Johnny asked.

"Not human."

"That's what I'm saying. Don't talk about any of this. People will try to put you away. Most people don't want the truth."

Clete wiped the rain out of his eyes. His skivvies were translucent, his skin blue. He let Johnny help him to the rental car. For the first time in his life, he believed that madness might be the norm and that his own mind might become his greatest enemy.

CLETE SPENT THE next two days in Fort Lauderdale, then flew back to New Orleans and drove to New Iberia in his Caddy. In the meantime I had gotten my badge back and was hoping to put to rest my involvement with the Shondell and Balangie families.

Of course, that's not the way things worked out. Clete hit town a nervous wreck. We were sitting at the redwood picnic table in my backyard when he told me what happened in the Keys. The cicadas were droning in the trees. But I could hardly hear them because of the popping sounds Clete's words left in my ears. I thought he had finally lost his mind.

"Johnny Shondell showed up in the junkyard with a semi-auto?" I asked.

"He said he carried it in his guitar case."

"Like that's what all musicians do?" I said.

He didn't answer. He stared at a blue heron that was standing in the lily pads on the edge of the bayou, pecking at its feathers.

"You couldn't find the plainclothes who sapped you?" I said.

"The city and county guys said there was no one fitting that description in their departments."

"How about the motel clerk who made the 911 call?"

"He blew town." Clete gazed at the shadows under the trees as though the light were shrinking from the world.

"Stay here," I said.

"Where you going?"

"You need something in the tank."

"You got a shot of Dr. Jack stashed away?"

Sometimes I kept booze in the house. Or guests left it there. That might seem a funny admission from a recovering drunk, but the problem is in the man, not the bottle. If a drunk wants booze, he'll burn down the liquor store to get it. For guys like Clete or me or anyone who shares our metabolism, alcohol and heroin are chemically synonymous, and the temptations are everywhere. A normal person cannot understand the longing a drunk feels for his glass. It is stronger and worse than any sexual desire, any fear of hell, any allegiance to family, country, or church.

I fixed a glass of iced tea and a ham-and-onion-and-avocado sandwich and brought them to him on a tray. I thought he'd be irritable because I didn't bring him four fingers of Jack on the rocks or at least a beer. But he didn't complain. I think Clete knew he was teetering on the edge of a breakdown. You've heard of the thousand-yard stare? His hands were shaking on his sandwich as though he had a chill.

"We've been in rougher spots," I said.

"When?"

"Where's Johnny now?"

"Back in town. Probably at his uncle's. I can't trust my own thoughts. I think I'm going crazy, Dave."

"You saw the ship out on the water, the one with the oars?"

"The one we've both had dreams about. Explain that to me." He grasped his stomach. "I feel sick."

"I need to make a phone call," I said. "Don't go anywhere."

The air smelled cold and tannic, and the sun was red yet gave no heat. I went inside the house and called Father Julian.

WE DROVE IN my pickup to Julian's cottage down Bayou Teche just outside of Jeanerette. The sun was barely a spark in the west, the sky the color of a bruise. The lights were on in the cottage, the church dark. Clete and I got out of the truck and started toward the cottage. Someone was banging on the church roof. Clete stared at a figure silhouetted against the sunset. "What's *he* doing here?"

"Good question," I said. I walked to the base of a ladder propped against the church's eave, then climbed far enough to see a man with a face like a dehydrated prune hammering nails in a sheet of corrugated tin, his knees spread like a jockey's on the roof's spine.

"Hey, Marcel," I said. "You helping out Father Julian?"

"No, I'm vandalizing the roof of his church," he replied.

"You're doing a good deed. You're a stand-up guy."

"If that's Pork Butt Purcel I see down there, tell him I said eat shit."

"What do you have against Clete?"

"He's on the planet. That's enough."

"You never disappoint, Marcel," I said, climbing back down the ladder. I rejoined Clete.

"What did LaForchette have to say?" he asked, still staring at Marcel's silhouette, an unlit cigarette hanging from his mouth.

"He's at war with the world," I said.

"What a joke," he said.

"Pardon?"

"That crazy fuck *is* the world, Dave."

Father Julian opened the screen door onto his small gallery. He was wearing sandals and elastic-belted khakis and a yellow T-shirt with Mickey Mouse's face on it. In his hand he had a magnifying glass, the one he used when he worked on his stamp collection, which was extensive and the secular love of his life. "Come in and tell me what all this is about," he said.

"I don't know if you're going to be up to it, Julian," I said.

"It can't be that bad, can it?"

"Wait and see," I replied.

CLETE NARRATED EVERYTHING that had happened in Key West, starting with Johnny Shondell's overdose in the motel room and the plainclothes cop who'd clocked him with a blackjack. Up to that point, there was nothing surprising about the narrative, considering the source. In fact, Father Julian seemed to be nodding out. Then Clete told of awakening upside down in his skivvies and discovering that he was about to be burned alive by a figure whose face seemed less than human while, offshore, a multitiered vessel that resembled a medieval prison ship lay at anchor.

"This guy had on a cowl, you say?" Julian asked.

"Yeah," Clete said.

"So maybe the shadows created an effect you can't be sure about?" Julian said.

"No, that's not it," Clete replied. "He looked exactly like I said. Here's the rest of it. He could see into my head. He knew about an incident in my childhood I never talk about. I busted up a greenhouse behind a lady's house in the Garden District. He taunted me with it like he was my father talking to me."

"I don't have an explanation, Clete."

"The guy was going to burn me upside down. Dave says that means something."

Julian's eyes looked haunted. "It's the way Giordano Di Betto died."

"Penelope Balangie's ancestor?" Clete said.

"Yes," Julian said, his voice solemn and dry.

"Then this fog blew in, with hail and thunder and rain," Clete said. "It saved my life. I felt like a woman was stroking my eyes and brow."

"I've got to stop you here," Julian said.

"What'd I say?" Clete said.

"You said nothing wrong. But I have no knowledge about these things. They're frightening in their aspect. They're frightening in what they suggest."

"How you mean?" Clete said.

"It's too easy to get lost in the images you describe. How do people explain Auschwitz? They blame it on the devil. I don't buy that. There's enough evil in the human heart to incinerate the earth." His cheeks were pooled with color, his nostrils white around the edges, as though he had been breathing the air in a subzero locker.

"I'm not getting you," Clete said.

"There's a good chance you were drugged," Julian said. "Don't give supernatural powers to these men. They have none. They live under logs."

Clete looked away, obviously disappointed in the way the conversation was going. "I think you're slipping the punch, Father," he said.

"You're probably right," Julian said. "I hate the cruelty that lives in us. I think about Joan of Arc and the way she suffered, and I want to weep." He picked up his magnifying glass and looked through it, one eye swelling to bulbous proportions. "I get carried away. I mentioned Auschwitz. I went on a tour there. I thought I heard people crying in one of the rooms. There was a vice president of a midwestern university in our tour group. He said, 'I know this sounds bad, but what a masterpiece of administration.' I wanted to beat him with my fists." Julian set down his magnifying glass and stared at the rug.

"We saw Marcel LaForchette up on the roof," I said.

"Yeah," Clete said. "He's quite a guy. You might keep a high-tech lock on the poor box."

"He's a sad man," Julian said.

"His victims might argue with that," Clete said.

"You're a tough sell, Clete," Julian said. "I wish I could be of more help. The truth is I don't have answers to much of anything."

"You've been very helpful, Julian," I said.

"Good try," he said.

We said good night and went outside into the dark. It wasn't a good moment. There are situations for which no one has a solution, and it's unfair to push the burden upon people who are unprepared to deal with it. I looked up at the church roof. Marcel LaForchette was gone. I felt awful about Julian. I suspected he would not sleep that night.

I heard the screen door open again. I turned around and saw Julian silhouetted in the doorway. "Dave, could I speak to you a minute?" he said.

"Go on. I'll be in the truck," Clete said.

I walked back to the gallery.

"There are times when I fail," Julian said. "This is one of them."

"None of this is your fault. Clete and I got into this on our own."

"There's something I need to tell you. It has nothing to do with anything Marcel told me inside a confessional. He says Mark Shondell is part of a group that plans to stir up hatred toward minority people on a national scale."

"I never thought Shondell was political."

"For Mark Shondell, politics and money are interchangeable. He's the lowest form of humanity I've ever known."

I had never heard Julian speak of someone in that way.

"Shondell is going to undo the Civil Rights Act?" I said, trying to smile.

"Do you know how many people secretly wish that were the case?" he said. "I'm going to have a drink now. Probably more than one. Take care of yourself, Dave. And take care of Clete most of all." He latched the screen but continued to look through it as we turned around in the yard and headed back to New Iberia. Moths were clustered like wet chicken feathers on the electric light above his gallery.

ONE WEEK LATER, the sheriff's department merged with the Iberia City Department and moved into City Hall, a lovely two-story building on the Teche with a reflecting pool in front and a long semicircular driveway shaded by live oaks. The driveway stayed in deep shadow and led past the library and a grotto dedicated to Jesus' mother. On the other side of the grotto was a canebrake and a Victorian home that once was the residence of Joel Chandler Harris, the former Confederate officer best known for his Uncle Remus and Brer Rabbit stories and his passionate concern for people of color.

My office was on the second floor of the building on the Teche. I loved walking down East Main to work, in the shadows of the massive oaks up and down the street, and picking up my mail and pouring a big cup of coffee and taking the stairs to my office and sitting behind my desk, and gazing out the window at the camellias blooming on the far side of the bayou and the urban forest that comprised City Park.

Clete had gone back to New Orleans to take care of his office on St. Louis Street in the Quarter, and I tried to concentrate on the good things in my life and let go of the things I couldn't control. Our recent election of a sheriff was still in chaos, but in the state of Louisiana, chaos is more the norm than an anomaly. In the meantime, we were stuck with a pro tem sheriff. Guess who that was?

Carroll LeBlanc came into my office on a sun-spangled morning when God seemed in His heaven and all was right with the world. "Tell me your secret," he said.

"About what?"

"Uptown cooze on the hoof."

"Sorry, that went right past me."

"This particular uptown cooze drives a maroon Ferrari. My hat is off to you, Robo, but I don't want you dragging your private shit into the department."

I tilted back in my chair and swiveled it so I could gaze at the bayou and the park and not look at LeBlanc. "It's a bluebird day," I said. "You could strike a match on the sky."

"Do you have a hearing problem?"

"Nope, I hear just fine."

He walked behind my desk and interdicted my line of sight. "I'm talking about Penelope Balangie, who happens to be the wife of Adonis Balangie."

"What's the news on Ms. Balangie?"

"She was here yesterday afternoon. Looking for you."

That one got to me. But I kept my face empty. "You took a message?"

"I don't take messages. I'm the sheriff."

"I don't know what to tell you about Penelope Balangie, Carroll. Why don't you talk to her? Talk to Mark Shondell also. The issue is human trafficking."

"You got something going with that bitch?"

I stood up and looked down on the bayou and the sun's reflection wobbling under the surface. "You got a problem, bub."

"What did you call me?"

I looked him in the face. The line of moles under his left eye resembled a string of black insects; there was dried mucus at the corner of his mouth. I could smell his deodorant. "You have sex on the brain," I said. "Either get your ass out of my sight or get your ashes hauled. I don't care which."

"I can have you up on insubordination."

"Do it."

He wore a polyester navy blue suit that looked like it had grease in it, and a gold tie and a white dress shirt with tiny silver fleurs-de-lis. His right hand was clenching at his side. "Maybe I should pop you right here."

"I like your shirt," I said. "What was that about popping me?"

"I gave you a break because you're a recovering drunk and twice a widower. When the wife of a notorious mobster comes into my department and asks about one of my detectives, I get curious."

"I can't blame you, Carroll. I don't know what Ms. Balangie wants."

"This isn't the first time. You were seen walking with her at the Shadows."

"You're following me around?"

"Right or wrong, you were at the Shadows with her?"

"Yes."

He tapped his finger on the air. "When I was in vice, I never took juice. But you hang with Clete Purcel, a guy who made a living out of it. Tell me who has the problem. I catch you playing sticky finger while you're on the job, I'll have you cleaning toilets."

"You're a heck of a guy, Carroll," I said.

After he left the room, my head was a Mixmaster. Yes, Carroll LeBlanc was a misogynist, a homophobe, and a racist, but he saw a weakness in me that I could not deny. The mention of Penelope Balangie had caused a quickening in my heart, the kind every man remembers from his youth. For me it happened when I was seventeen and I pitched a perfect game against Lafayette in the American Legion finals at the old Brahman Bull Stadium. Fans and players alike were jumping up and down and pounding me on the back as we walked off the field, the electric lights iridescent in the sunset. But the only person in my ken was a girl from Spanish Lake waiting for me by the dugout, her heart-shaped face glowing with the lights of love and adoration, her mouth aching to be kissed.

A moment of that kind never goes away. You take it to the grave. Tell me I'm blowing smoke.

Chapter Fourteen

THAT SAME DAY, at 6:47 exactly, I returned to my house from Winn-Dixie and saw a Ferrari by the curb, the left rear tire on the rim, Penelope Balangie struggling with the spare. I pulled in behind her. She dropped the tire and dusted off her hands. Her face looked hot, her hair damp on her cheek. "I just discovered you have no Triple A," she said.

"We're purists in that regard," I said. "As few services as possible. Let's see if I can help."

It seemed too much of a coincidence that her tire would go completely flat in front of my home. The air loss was the kind you associate with a sliced valve. I squatted down and ran my hand over the casing. A two-inch piece of angle iron, its edges knife-sharp, was embedded in one of the grooves.

"I had to special-order the spare," she said. "I just noticed it's smaller than the others. Is that going to be a problem?"

Yeah, it is. In more ways than one.

"There's a guy in Lafayette who sells used Ferraris," I said. "You can give him a call."

"I can't get service on my cell phone here."

"Yeah, that's another problem we have," I said. "Miss Penelope . . ."

"What?" she said.

"A very nasty plainclothes named Carroll LeBlanc says you were looking for me at the department. LeBlanc would like to take my skin off. I wish you wouldn't help him do that."

"Would you please explain how I'm impairing your career?"

"You're the wife of a notorious gangster. Your father-in-law may have been involved with the assassination of John Kennedy."

"These things are not true."

"The Balangies made their money peddling bananas?"

"There are many things you think you know about me, Mr. Robicheaux. Most of them are wrong."

"You want me to put on your spare?"

The light was dying in the trees. Down the street, flocks of swallows were descending on the Shadows.

"If you would be so kind," she said.

Her lipstick was purple, the mole by her mouth sensuous in a way I didn't understand. I wanted to reach out and touch it.

"After I change your tire, I have to be somewhere else," I said.

"As you like."

I saw the disappointment in her face. I did not think it was feigned. "What is it you want to talk to me about?"

"Everything. That is, everything I am and everything I am not. But if you're busy, I understand."

FIFTEEN MINUTES LATER, I had the spare tire on. Because of the spare's small size, the Ferrari was canted on one side. Our best hotels and motels were out by the four-lane, several miles away. The Ferrari would probably have problems all the way there.

The streetlamps clicked on. A car went by, blowing leaves and carbon monoxide in its wake.

"There's a bed-and-breakfast on the next block, but they're probably full up," I said.

"I'll manage," she said.

"Why don't you call your husband and ask him what he wants you to do?"

"Adonis is not my husband," she said.

"Did I just hear you right, or is one of us crazy?"

She looked at my humble house, with its boxcar-like design and peaked tin roof that was stained with lichen and rust, the gutters impacted with Spanish moss. "I promise I'll only take a few minutes of your time. Then, if you tell me you never want to see me again, I'll abide by your wishes."

"Come in," I said. I parked my truck in the porte cochere and carried my groceries through the back door and placed them on the drain board, refusing to accept that I was trying to hide her presence on my property. "You want a Dr Pepper or a glass of lemonade?" I said.

"Nothing, thank you."

"What was that about Adonis not being your old man?"

"Why are you using that kind of language?"

"I didn't give it any thought."

"Don't lie. You're trying to be someone you're not. You're a gentleman, Mr. Robicheaux, so act like one. Don't let fear turn you into a dolt."

I felt my face shrink. "Miss Penelope, I'm a widower and a drunkard. My relationship with the sheriff's department is tenuous. My stepdaughter and a half brother are my only family. Clete Purcel is my best friend. That is the sum of my time on earth. There's a shorter version. I'm bad news, and I don't have answers for myself, much less others."

"Adonis and I were never married," she said. "I was part of a business deal. Or at least that's what you would call it here. The custom goes back five hundred years in our families. I'm talking about the Shondells and the Balangies."

"So how about eighty-sixing tradition and living your own life?" I said.

"In my way, I try to do that." She was standing closer to me than was proper in the culture of New Iberia. "When I say I'm not married to Adonis, I mean I'm not married on any level and never have been. Do you understand?"

"Yeah, I'd say that's clear enough. But this isn't information I necessarily want or need."

"Faux marriages have existed since the beginnings of civilization. So just stop it, Mr. Robicheaux."

"Stop what?"

"Acting like you're shocked. It doesn't become you."

I took an ice tray and two cans of Dr Pepper from the refrigerator and knocked the ice against the sink and began filling two glasses with it, my hands uncoordinated, even shaking. She stepped closer so I could see her at the corner of my vision. "Don't be so emotional."

I propped my arms on the sink's rim. "I don't care if you're married or not," I lied. "You cannot deny the source of your wealth, Miss Penelope."

"Would you please not use that servile form of address to me?" she replied. "Where are your pets?"

"My pets?"

"You have pet bowls inside and outside. There's a rabbit hutch under your tree."

"I have a pet coon and a number of cats. In fact, the lady next door and I feed most of the cats in the neighborhood."

"See? You're a kind man. Why do you try to hide your qualities?"

I dried my hands. I turned and looked down at her. I thought of that twilight evening when I'd pitched the only perfect game in my baseball career. "I'm not your guy, Ms. Balangie."

She circled my wrist with her thumb and forefinger. "Look at me."

"Nope. No more gamesmanship."

Her eyes jittered as they searched mine. "You think I'm immoral? You think I'm a liar. You think I don't weep for my daughter? You look me in the eye and say that."

"No, ma'am, I don't think any of that."

"Then maybe think of someone other than yourself."

"Pardon?" I said.

"Damn you," she said. "Damn you to hell."

Then she beat my face with her little fists, cutting and bruising my lip and cheek and the edge of my eye. I stood with my hands at my sides and let her do it and never blinked. I stood like that until her fingers knitted themselves in my hair and tears leaked from her eyes, and I did not move even when she pulled my face down to hers and kissed my eyelids and my mouth and smeared my blood on her hair. Nor did I defend myself when she stood on top of my shoes and opened my shirt and kissed and bit my chest.

"I'm sorry for the pain you feel, Ms. Balangie," I said. "I just don't know what I can do about it."

She pressed the side of her face against my heart. I placed both hands between her shoulder blades. Her hair smelled like the Caribbean. I felt a throbbing inside me I could barely restrain, and I could think of no words to say to my Higher Power other than *I'm sorry for this.*

FOUR DAYS LATER, Clete Purcel was back from New Orleans. He called in the early morning and asked me to meet him for breakfast at Victor's Cafeteria on Main. "Something happen in the Big Sleazy?" I said.

"I'm feeling a lot better, that's all," he replied. "I'll tell you about it."

Victor's was right across the street from Clete's office, not far from the drawbridge. He was waiting for me by the front entrance. The air was cool and damp, the pavement still in shadow, the buildings dripping with moisture. He was wearing a soft wool suit with a crisp dark brown shirt and a shiny thin brown belt and brown alligator loafers. His eyes were clear, his cheeks rosy. "You look sharp," I said.

"Let's get some eats," he said.

Inside, he stacked his tray with ham and scrambled eggs and grits and gravy and laid in to it, bending forward each time he put a forkload in his mouth. "What'd you get into while I was gone?" he said.

"I'm back at the department."

"Your face."

"A lady got emotional. It wasn't a big deal."

"What's the lady's name?"

"I already forgot. You said you were feeling better and you were going to tell me about it."

He glanced up at the stamped tin ceiling, his eyelids fluttering. I could hear his shoes tapping up and down under the table. "Okay,

here it is," he said. "I figured out some of those things that happened
in the Keys."

I should have been happy about his resilience. But I wasn't. I
knew the syndrome too well. Denial, as we call it today, is the brain's
anodyne and far less harmful in most situations than the booze that
people like me soak their heads in. In this instance, I believed my
best friend was not only lying to himself but setting himself up for
another disastrous fall.

"See, I was hitting the sauce as soon as I got to Lauderdale, then
I really turned on the spigot down in Key West and got sapped by
that cop who was probably working for Eddy Firpo. They dosed me
up with purple acid, and I started having hallucinations about my
childhood, and I imagined this guy in the hoodie was my father or
something like that."

"How do you explain the galleon out on the salt?"

"I told you, I had a dream about a galleon earlier."

"Right, the same dream I had," I said. "What are the chances of
that?"

"Dave, think about it. You're always talking about slave ships and
the Middle Passage. How about that place on the bayou where you
say Jean Lafitte used to moor his boat and sell slaves and loot to the
locals? The mooring chains are still in the tree, right up the bayou
from the old Burke house, right or wrong? How many times have
you told me those stories about digging for Lafitte's treasure when
you were a kid?"

"You're right," I said.

"See?" he said, pointing his fork at me. "There's always an answer
to these things."

"I've got another question for you," I said. "How does a kid like
Johnny Shondell run off the guy in the hoodie as well as the guy's
friends?"

"Maybe the guy in the hoodie was by himself. Maybe the guy is
a freak and a meltdown and a sack of shit and didn't want to cap
Mark Shondell's nephew and decided to get lost."

I gave up. But in so doing, I knew what was coming next. "So what happened when I was gone?" he said, gazing at the cut on my lip and the scratch and bruise next to my eye.

"Nothing."

"Penelope Balangie came to town?"

"That's one way to put it."

He stopped eating. "I don't believe this. You're telling me y'all got it on?"

"I don't ask you questions like that. Why don't you show me the same respect?"

"You plowed the wife of Adonis Balangie?"

"Why don't you write it on the wall?"

"Did you or didn't you?"

"They're not married. They've never had marital relations, either." I could feel my voice starting to break. "Or at least that's what she said. And I didn't say I did anything."

"Are you out of your mind? You cuckold a greaseball and he'll come at you with a blowtorch. It doesn't matter if the wife looks like the bride of Frankenstein."

People were starting to look at us. "I'll see you outside."

"Sit down," he said, lowering his voice. "Just tell me the truth. Your plunger took over your brain or it didn't. It happens. Just don't lie about it."

"I'm not going to talk about her on that level," I said.

"She says she lives with a gash hound like Adonis but she doesn't come across? Dave, you're not that stupid."

"I believe what she said."

"I'm going back to my office and see if I can get you admitted to the state asylum. I thought I had problems."

"She had a flat in front of my house and an inadequate spare. She stayed over."

"An inadequate spare? That's great. Anything else inadequate? Did the neighbors get an eyeful?"

My scalp felt tight, my face hot. He got up and put his hand on my shoulder and squeezed it. "Don't answer that. I didn't mean to be hard on you. But you've gotten us into a pile of it, big mon, and you know it."

He went out the door, the sunlight from outside splintering through the room, most of his breakfast uneaten.

That night the weather was rainy and cold in New Orleans, with few tourists on the sidewalks by the French Market and the Café du Monde, and no one paid particular attention to the tall, slender man in a hooded slicker crossing Jackson Square. He paused in front of St. Louis Cathedral and looked up at the towering spires and the rain spinning out of the sky, his mouth open like a supplicant's. He continued his journey down Pirate's Alley, past the small bookstore that was once the residence of William Faulkner, past the piked iron fence and live-oak trees behind the cathedral, and finally to a walled courtyard where the man had rented a room in a guesthouse.

He entered the courtyard but was studying the philodendron and elephant ears and caladiums and rosebushes and banana plants in the flower beds when a couple with children passed him with umbrellas over their heads. After they were gone, he unlocked the door to his room and went inside. Down the block, a band was blaring from a strip club, the front doors open, while topless women danced on a stage.

The man removed his raincoat and hung it on the showerhead in the bathroom, then sat on the bed and looked at himself in the mirror. His head was shaped like a snake's and his skin was the pale green of latex, his nose little more than a bump. He stared at the floor with his hands pinched between his knees.

He opened a small address book and dialed a number on the telephone by the night lamp. "Sea Breeze Escort Service," a woman's voice said.

"I need a girl," the man said.

"Where are you located?"

The man gave her the address of the guesthouse.

"Is that in the Quarter?" the woman asked.

"Yes."

"The Sea Breeze doesn't serve the Quarter anymore."

"Give me the number of somebody who does."

There was a pause. "Tell them Dora gave it to you. They owe me one."

Twenty minutes later, there was a knock on the door. He put on the night chain and eased open the door and looked at the profile of a young black woman who was staring through the gate at a taxi parked by the curb, its headlights tunneling in the rain. He turned off the lights inside the room, unhooked the night chain, and pulled the black woman inside.

"Hello," he said. "I'm Gideon. I hope you'll forgive me for bringing you out on such a bad night."

Chapter Fifteen

SHE WAS SHORT, probably not more than twenty-five, her black hair flowing like paint, her skin smooth and dark and free of scars. She wore a white blouse and a pink wool jacket and a skirt that exposed her knees. Her hands were locked on top of her purse; her eyes were bright with fear as she stared into Gideon's face.

He took a plate of beignets from the refrigerator and set them on the table. "I got these at the Café du Monde. I thought you might like some."

"I ain't hungry."

"I have a bottle of wine, too."

"The man in the cab needs seventy-five dol'ars. That's for one hour. More than that, you pay it to me."

"I see," Gideon said. "I'll be right back."

He draped his raincoat over his head and went through the court-yard and jumped into the front seat of the cab, slamming the door before the driver could react. In seconds, the driver started the cab and drove down the street and turned a corner. Ten minutes later, Gideon returned to the room on foot, out of breath, his face peppered with rain. "Well, we have that out of the way," he said.

"What out of the way?" she said. "You went somewhere wit' Beaumont?"

"Sit down," he said. "You didn't tell me your name."

"Sarah."

"You're pretty."

"Where you gone wit' Beaumont?"

"Don't worry about it. You look frightened. Do I scare you?"

Her face jerked. She fastened her gaze on the wall, the red and purple bedspread, an ancient suitcase on top of it, a belt holding the suitcase together. "What you wanna do?" she said.

"Talk."

She closed her eyes and opened them again, as though the room were swaying. "What you did wit' Beaumont?"

"Are you a little obsessive?" he said. She didn't answer. "He showed me a couple of historical buildings. He seems to know the Quarter."

"That don't sound like him. What kind of game you playing?"

"No game," he said. "Sit down. Please."

Her brow furrowed. She sat down slowly at a small breakfast table. He removed a shoebox from the dresser and sat down across from her. "How long have you been in the life, Sarah?"

"What you mean 'the life'? I don't know nothing about no life. I don't like what's going on here. You give Beaumont the seventy-five dol'ars?"

"You have a child? I suspect you do."

She reached in her bag.

"It's not a good time to do that," he said.

"I'm calling Beaumont."

"I told him you're in good hands. The most important moment in your life is taking place right now. You need to be aware of that."

"I ain't up to this. Beaumont's all right, ain't he?"

"A man like that is never all right."

Her gaze seemed to take apart his face, as though her fear had been replaced by curiosity. "You got freckles under your eyes."

"You think that's funny?"

"My li'l boy watches a cartoon about a friendly snake. It's got freckles under its eyes, like yours."

"Sarah, you may have depths that have never been plumbed."

Her mouth formed a cone, but no words came out.

"Forget it," he said. He removed the lid from the shoebox and emptied the box. Bundles of fifty-dollar bills fell on the table. The bills were crisp and stiff, as though fresh from the mint. He thumbed their edges like decks of cards. "There's thirty thousand dollars here," he said. "It's yours. But you have to change your ways."

"You're setting me up for something," she said. "Maybe a snuff film. I ain't putting up wit' it."

"It's not a trick." He was smiling now.

"Why you wanna do this? You don't know me."

"Maybe I can come see you sometime. Maybe we can be friends. Maybe I can help you get a job or go to school."

"If I take that money, I ain't gonna be around here."

"Send me a postcard."

Her eyes swam with confusion.

"That's a joke. Go wherever you want."

She picked up one of the bundles, then set it down. "Beaumont's gonna take over half of this."

He shook his head slowly.

"Why ain't he?" she said.

"His circumstances have changed."

"What happened out there?"

"You really want to know?"

She looked at him uncertainly.

"We talked a minute or two. That's all," he said.

Her eyes dropped to the bundles of money. She touched one as though it were a forbidden object. "This ain't counterfeit?"

"Counterfeiters don't give away the product of their labor. Show some trust in people, Sarah."

She let out her breath as though a long day had caught up with her. "People don't never tell me the troot', not about anything. Why should you be different?"

"Because I'm a revelator."

"A what?"

He put the bundles back in the box and replaced the top. He pushed the box toward her. "I'll call a cab for you."

"I ain't taking this money. I ain't taking this box. I ain't taking nothing out of this room."

"You have to take it."

"No."

He stood up, towering over her. He opened her purse and shook the bundles into it, then zipped it shut. The purse looked as big and round as a small watermelon. "Do as I say." He raised a finger in her face when she tried to speak. "Don't argue, and don't disappoint me."

She seemed to shrink, like a flower exposed to intense heat. "I ain't meant to argue or make you mad."

"Now go be a good girl."

"Beaumont tole you where I stay?"

"Maybe."

"What you done to him?"

He placed his hand on her head. His fingers resembled the tentacles of a small octopus threaded through her hair. "You're a nice lady. The world has hurt you. I've tried to make up for that. It's that simple."

She waited a long time before she spoke. "If I walk out of here, you ain't gonna do nothing to me? You're sure about that?"

"You've done a good deed for me," he said. "You just don't know it."

She looked at him, her eyes out of focus. Then she picked up the purse and put it inside her pink jacket and opened the door and hurried through the courtyard, the soles of her shoes clattering on the sidewalk. The rainwater on her hair looked like tinsel on a Christmas tree.

Down the street, two drunks stumbled from the topless bar. "Where you goin', mama?" one yelled. "I got yo' candy cane hangin'."

Both men laughed so hard they could hardly hold each other up, then they followed her, bumping into each other, rounding the corner behind her and disappearing into the dark.

THE NEXT DAY, Tuesday, Carroll LeBlanc called me into his office. He was sitting in a swivel chair, dressed in a suit that was as bright as tin, his booted feet propped on the desk. The boots were

Luccheses, the shafts hand-tooled with blue flower petals, the soles hardly scratched, the toes buffed. I had never seen him show any interest in horses or racetracks. A yellow legal pad covered with swirls of blue ballpoint ink and elaborate capital letters lay on his desk. He stared at me. "How'd your face get marked up?"

"A household accident."

"Somebody close her legs?"

"Why'd you call me into your office, Carroll?"

"Got a call from NOPD this morning," he said. He picked up the legal pad and stared at it, scratching the rim of a nostril with one fingernail. "Have a seat."

I sat down and didn't reply. I knew that whatever he planned on saying would come a teaspoon at a time. With LeBlanc, the issue was always control.

"A taxi driver was found in his cab with his neck broken," he said. "The cab was parked in an alley in the Quarter one block from North Rampart."

I nodded.

"Did you hear what I said?" he asked.

"Got it," I said.

"The cab was wedged in the alley. Whoever killed the driver couldn't open the door and had to kick out the windshield."

"This was a robbery?" I said.

"That's what NOPD thought. Except the driver had over eight hundred dollars in his pocket." LeBlanc looked down at his legal pad again. "A guy named Beaumont Melancon. Ring a bell?"

"No."

"He was a Murphy artist."

A Murphy artist is a pimp who lets his hooker set up the john, then bursts in on the tryst, claiming to be the outraged husband or boyfriend, thereby terrifying and subsequently extorting the john.

"What does this have to do with us?" I said.

"A little later the same night, two guys in the same general area claimed a guy with an ugly face beat the living shit out of them."

"Why'd the guy attack them?"

"They said they didn't know. They said he just came out of nowhere and started ripping ass."

"What's the rest of it, Carroll?"

"A homicide cop started checking bars and guesthouses from Burgundy down to Jackson Square. The night clerk at one guesthouse said he saw a black woman leave one of the rooms and walk toward North Rampart. The two guys who got their asses kicked started making fun of her. Then a guy from the guesthouse came out of the same room the black woman did and followed her and the two white guys."

"The beating victims were white and baiting a black woman?"

"That's what I said."

"No, you didn't," I replied. "Was the guy with the ugly face white or black?"

"They didn't say."

"Who is 'they'?"

"NOPD. Did you get drunk last night?"

"I have no idea why you're telling me all this," I said.

"I'm trying to give you a heads-up."

"I see. I appreciate that. But I'm going back to my office."

He swung his feet off the desk. "The night clerk at the guesthouse said the black broad was probably a hooker he'd seen around. She'd been in the room of a guest. He left the guesthouse at midnight; he was carrying a beat-up suitcase with a belt around it. The homicide cop found a piece of paper in the trash can with an address on it. Guess what? It's on East Main in New Iberia."

LeBlanc read the address aloud. It was mine.

"Thanks for the tip," I said. I got up to leave.

"That's it?"

"What's the name of the homicide cop at NOPD?"

"Magelli."

"Thank you."

"I've got more."

"I think I've got the big picture. One of these days we'll have a talk after hours, Carroll."

"Feeling a little irritated, are we? If so, maybe you should go back to New Orleans and get your old job back. Oh, I forgot. You got fired twice there."

I HAD KNOWN DANA MAGELLI at NOPD since Clete and I came back from Vietnam and walked a beat on Canal and in the Quarter. The three of us had made detective grade at the same time and were close friends, although Dana was a family man and didn't succumb to the occupational legacy of violence and wasted days and nights the way Clete and I did. Dana was also the bane of the Balangie family, whom he despised for the damage they did to the Italians who were decent and hardworking and paid the price for scum like Adonis.

I called Dana Magelli from my office.

"Hey, Dave, how you doin'?" he said. "Carroll LeBlanc gave you all the information on the taxi driver homicide?"

"More or less," I said. "You found my address in the wastebasket at the guesthouse?"

"Yeah, but the guy at the guesthouse paid with cash and registered as G. Smith, and we got no idea who the black woman was or why somebody would break the cabbie's neck, unless he tried to run a Murphy scam on the wrong guy."

"Murphy artists in the Quarter?"

"No, Adonis Balangie runs New Orleans vice like his old man did. No jackrollers or Murphy scammers are allowed between Esplanade and Canal, Decatur and Rampart."

"Can you give me a detailed description of the man who tore up the drunks?"

"The victims say he was big and had a head like a snake's. That's about all they'll say. I think they're afraid they'll have to identify him."

"No mention of a harelip or a tiny nose?"

"Negative. You know something about this guy?"

"Clete had some trouble in the Keys."

"With a guy who looks like this?"

"Clete got abducted. He woke up suspended from a wrecker hook. A guy with a harelip and a bump for a nose was going to light him up."

There was a long silence. "What are we dealing with here?"

"I don't like to think about it."

"I want to talk to Clete."

"Good luck," I said.

"Look, I'm working on another lead. We've pulled a bunch of surveillance cameras that show our guy leaving the guesthouse in a hooded raincoat and walking with his suitcase up Pirate's Alley and trying to get in the back door of the cathedral. Then he walks out of the Quarter and shows up on three cameras on St. Claude Avenue and disappears in the Ninth Ward. Get this. Somebody broke into a colored church down there and slept under the altar."

"You get any prints at the church?"

"Yeah, same as inside the cab, so many we might as well be doing the Superdome. I haven't slept in over thirty hours."

"You're a good cop, Dana."

"Tell Clete he can get in touch with me or see how he likes one of our new holding cells. I've got a question for you."

"Go ahead."

"Your colleague LeBlanc says Penelope Balangie came to your department looking for you. He also says she was seen at your house. Please tell me it's not what I think."

DANA HAD BROUGHT up a major problem of conscience for me. Celibacy and I had never been very compatible. I tried, certainly, but at best usually ended up with a C-minus. Through my encounter with Penelope Balangie, I had managed to involve myself with people whose thinking powers were probably locked inside the sixteenth century. On top of it, I had trouble keeping her out of my thoughts.

Also, I was worried about Clete Purcel, and the innocence and naïveté and false optimism that often blinded him to the pernicious nature of the people with whom he surrounded himself. And if that sounds like an indictment of myself as well, you're right.

What are your choices in a situation such as this? What would a great philosopher of ethics such as Jeremy Bentham probably say? I suspect something like "Search me, pal."

Anyway, I knew where to find Adonis Balangie on midweek nights and Sunday mornings. I checked an unmarked car out of the department Wednesday afternoon and headed for New Orleans.

His tennis club had the best clay courts in the city. At sunset the lights clicked on with a loud *swatch,* glowing with humidity against a sky that was the color of torn plums, tall palm trees with slender trunks creating an additional ambiance that could have come from *The Arabian Nights.*

I parked my car in the shadows and wandered over to a court where Adonis was playing doubles with three women, the metal eyelets on the nylon screens clinking softly in the breeze. A woman at the net swung her backhand four feet from his face and almost took off his head. Gentleman that he was, Adonis grinned and said, "Fine shot, Leslie. My God, you could rip off a man's head."

She seemed to beam in response, although I wasn't altogether convinced of her sincerity. I watched them walk off the court and sit at a table under the palms. In the center of the table, a magnum of champagne was nestled in an ice bucket sweating with frost. I knew Adonis had seen me approach, but he gave no sign, instead listening keenly to one of the women. It was hard to tell them apart. They seemed designed the way a brand-name product was, each with coarse bleached yellow hair pulled straight back, each suntanned, each with a lean and hungry look. I walked into the light.

"What's the haps, Adonis?" I said.

"Didn't know you were a member, Detective Robicheaux," he replied, his gaze resting playfully on the three women as though I were part of a humorous script.

"Can we take a walk?" I asked.

"I think not," he said. He removed the foil from the champagne bottle and twisted the key on the wire cage and dropped it on the table, then gripped the cork and twisted the bottle from it without spilling a drop. "Like to join us? Here, I'll pour you a glass."

I pulled up an iron chair and sat down. I was pretty sure Adonis knew I was in the program, and I believed he was taunting me. My feelings were strange, though. I wasn't angry with him; I felt disappointed.

Then I saw a thought swim into his eyes. He tapped himself on the forehead. "Sorry, Dave. I forgot you have a problem with sugar or something. You want some hot tea?"

"No, thanks," I said. "How are you ladies tonight?"

They smiled but didn't speak. Their eyes didn't seem to match their faces, as though each was wearing tinted contact lenses.

"Y'all don't mind giving me five minutes, do you?" Adonis said.

As the women walked toward the clubhouse, the one named Leslie turned and looked at me and put one finger in her mouth and sucked it while crossing her eyes. There was a scar on her cheek she had covered with makeup. I had seen her before, but I couldn't remember where. Adonis followed my line of sight. "Leslie has a rough edge or two, but live and let live, right?" he said. "What brings you to my club?"

"Know a guy with a harelip and no nose who likes to hurt people?"

"Haven't had the pleasure." He poured into a champagne glass and drank from it. The tips of his hair were sun-bleached and glistening with moisture. "He's somebody I should be concerned about?"

"You tell me. I hear Johnny Shondell is in a treatment center in Baton Rouge."

"I wouldn't know."

"How about your stepdaughter? Where is she?"

"With Mark Shondell."

"That's a fucking disgrace," I said.

I had taken it to the edge. It wasn't wise. His eyes drifted onto my face. "This is my club. We don't use that kind of language here. We don't speak about family matters, either."

"I don't get you," I said. "You were in the airborne. You're educated and smart. Cops may not like you, but they respect you."

"So?"

"You're playing tennis while your stepdaughter is in the hands of a molester."

He watched the shadows of the palm trees swaying on the clay courts, which were a soft pink and seemed to have absorbed the afterglow of the sun. "You know who Bill Tilden was?"

"A national tennis champion during the twenties?"

"He made two famous statements about tennis: 'Doubles is a game of angles' and 'Women emasculate genius.' I like the former more than the latter."

"What does that have to do with criminality?" I said.

"It has to do with everything. And 'criminality' is a relative term."

I knew the argument and the rhetoric. The Mafia was no different than corporations. Prostitutes were sex workers and prostitution was a consensual and victimless activity. Marijuana was harmless. Sado-porn was protected by the First Amendment. Legalized gambling helped the poor. Blah-blah-blah.

"Sell your lies to someone else, Adonis."

"I think you're here for another reason."

I felt my stomach clench. I cleared my throat. I held my eyes on his. "Ms. Balangie came to New Iberia because she was terrified about her daughter."

"And you helped her out at your office?"

Then I knew he knew. "She had a flat in front of my house. I changed her tire and asked her inside. I talked to her a long time. Then she left."

My mouth was dry, the wind cold on my face. A black man wearing a white jacket and white gloves put a tray of stuffed shrimp on the table. Adonis thanked him. The sprinkler system for the grounds came on. I could hear a jet of water striking the trunk of a palm tree.

"Are you listening?" I said.

"She told me. I'm not sure what I should do with you."

"Say that again?"

"You may not have done anything wrong, but you thought about it. And the next time out, you will. It's a matter of time, isn't it?"

I stood up. I wanted to pull him out of his chair. He bit into a shrimp and wiped his fingers on a napkin. "You've come uninvited to my table," he said. "You've tried to embarrass me in front of my friends, and you've sullied my wife's name in public. I'm going to let these things pass. But only once."

I could feel a tremble in my right hand, sense a flicker behind my eyes, a sound like a hummingbird in my ear. "The guy with the hare-lip tried to burn Clete Purcel to death, in his skivvies, hanging upside down from a steel hook. That same guy was carrying my address. I think you know who he is."

"You look a little tense. You're not going to do something you'll regret, are you?"

"If I told you what I want to do, you'd be on your way home."

"Should I call security?"

"Penelope is a nice lady. She did nothing wrong. That's what I came here to say."

"You refer to my wife by her first name?"

"She's not your wife," I said.

The redness of the sun seemed to dance on his face, then he looked at me in the way a man does when he knows that one day he will have his revenge and that his victim in the meantime will be powerless to defend himself or to guess the moment when the blade will fall. This was what I had done to myself.

The women returned from the clubhouse. Adonis picked up his racquet and walked onto the court. "Sorry to have kept you, ladies," he said. "Let's have at it, shall we? What a beautiful evening it is."

Chapter Sixteen

I DROVE OUT BY the golf course and parked under a tree and waited until the woman named Leslie emerged from the clubhouse and got in her car, an old Honda. She had changed into jeans and a snap-button denim shirt. It started to rain. I followed her up to Metairie into a 1950s subdivision lined with two-bedroom houses, all of them with the same gravel roofs and faux brick walls and lawns that resembled Astroturf.

I waited at the end of the street while she parked in her driveway and went into the house. Before I could pull up, the front door opened again and I saw her give money to a teenage girl under the porch light. The girl got into a car and drove away. I waited until Leslie went back in the house, then I parked in front and stepped across a rain ditch and rang the bell. She opened the door, a sandwich in one hand. "My," she said.

"Could I talk with you a few minutes?"

"What's on your mind, cowboy?"

I glanced at my slacks and shoes. "I look like a cowboy?"

"Yeah, one who thinks he's gonna get an easy ride."

"Wrong," I said.

"You probably don't remember me," she said.

I felt the rain blowing on my neck. "You look familiar."

"I used to see you in the Quarter. You were a souse back then."

"Yeah, I remember now. You were a dancer in a joint on Bourbon."

"I didn't dance. I just took it off."

"I remember," I said. "Vividly."

She took a bite out of the sandwich. "Cute, but no can do, sweetie."

"No can do what?"

"Let you pump me in multiple ways."

"You cut to it, don't you?" I said. "Why'd you make a face at me with your finger in your mouth?"

"I like to give limp-dicks a throb or two."

I couldn't help but laugh.

"What, you think I'm a comedian?" she said.

"No," I said. "Where'd you get the scar?" It looked like a flattened worm on her jawbone.

"A pimp named Zipper Clum was in a bad mood."

"If it's any consolation, a psychopath took Zipper's arm off with a machete."

She combed back her hair with her fingers, her eyes still on mine. Her hair looked sprayed and stiff as wire. "Okay, honey bunny, let's make it fast. I have a daughter to take care of."

She let me inside. I sat on the sofa while she went in back. She returned with a young girl in a reclining wheelchair. The girl rested on her side as though she were sleeping. "This is Elizabeth," Leslie said. "Elizabeth, this is Mr. Robicheaux. He's a friend of ours."

"Hello, Miss Elizabeth," I said.

The girl had her mother's good looks and eyes that were as innocent and empty as blue water. Leslie turned on the television and inserted a video underneath. SpongeBob sprang to life on the screen. The girl made a mewing sound.

"Come into the kitchen," Leslie said.

"I never got your last name."

"Rosenberg."

The house was old, but all the furniture, rugs, curtains, and appliances seemed new. I sat at the breakfast table. She opened the refrigerator. "I make Elizabeth a snack before bedtime. While I do that, you can tell me why you're here. Then you leave."

"You know anything about Adonis's stepdaughter? Her name is Isolde."

"I don't ask him questions about his family."

"That's convenient."

She gave me a look.

"You're just a tennis partner?" I said.

"You're about to get yourself invited back out the door."

She cut a piece of pie and put it on a plate with a spoon, then went into the living room. I knew I probably couldn't imagine the amount of care she had to give her daughter, which I was sure involved changing diapers and bathing and feeding and dressing her, never having enough asleep, and ultimately accepting exhaustion as a way of life. In other words, I believed Leslie Rosenberg had her own Golgotha. She came back in the kitchen and washed the plate and spoon in the sink.

"I'm not out to nail Adonis, Miss Leslie. I need to find Isolde. I think she's a victim of human trafficking."

"What's with the 'miss' routine?"

"It's a leftover courtesy from a gentler time."

"A little of that Aunt Jemima stuff goes a long way. Isolde Balangie is a victim of human trafficking? One of the richest teenage girls in New Orleans? Where do you get this stuff?"

I had the feeling Leslie Rosenberg didn't take prisoners. She sat down across from me. "You see all this? The house, everything that's in it? It comes from the Balangie family."

"You work for them?"

"I'm a cashier in one of their restaurants. They're not white slavers."

"You and the other two ladies at the tennis courts bear a lot of similarities."

There was a beat. "You're saying we're collectibles?"

"Adonis doesn't do anything for free."

"How'd you like a slap across the face, cop or not?"

"I think you're heck on wheels, Ms. Rosenberg."

She rolled her fingertips against the heel of one hand. "You're not going to be a problem, are you?"

"No, ma'am."

She paused. "Want a piece of pie?"

"Sure," I said.

She got up and took the pie from the oven and set in on the counter, then sliced it with a knife, her back to me. She had the physicality of a working-class woman, as well as the confidence. She handed me a piece of pie on a plate.

"Did you ever speak at the Work the Steps or Die, Motherfucker meeting?" I said.

"Oh, yeah," she said.

"'Oh, yeah' what?"

"I knew that one would catch up with me one day."

I remembered her in a much more detailed way now. She had been heavier, probably from a jailhouse diet, her hair much longer, partially dyed; she was just beginning the steps of the program. But I remembered her most for her candor. Women speakers are the most honest at A.A. meetings and often give histories about themselves that men do not want to hear, because they fear the same level of honesty will be required of them. Leslie Rosenberg went the extra mile and left nothing out. Had there been a parole officer at the meeting, she could have violated herself back to the Orleans Parish Prison.

She ran away from home at age seventeen and hooked up with three outlaw bikers who gang-raped her on the way to Sturgis. She had an abortion in Memphis and spent three months in jail for soliciting at a truck stop on I-40. The next two stops were Big D and New Orleans and runway gigs with a G-string and pasties, then Acapulco and Vegas with oilmen who could buy Third World countries with their credit cards.

Miami was even more lucrative. She went to work for a former CIA agent turned political operative who set up cameras in hotel rooms and blackmailed corporate executives and Washington insiders. She helped destroy careers and lives and woke up one morning next to the corpse of a married man who died from an overdose in his sleep and whose family she had to face at the police station. One week later, she swallowed half a bottle of downers, turned on the gas in the oven, and stuck her head in. Three weeks later, she slashed her wrists. One month after that, she helped a pimp roll a blind man.

It's not the kind of personal history you forget.

"Something wrong with the pie?" she asked.

"It's good. Do you still go to meetings?"

"Mostly to N.A. I was into drugs more than alcohol."

"Who's the father of your little girl?"

"The dead guy I woke up with. I think I said that at the meeting."

She waited for me to speak, but I didn't.

"You're wondering why I had one abortion but not another one?" she said. "I figured I owed the guy something. Or his family. Shit if I know. Anyway, I love Elizabeth."

"Where does the Balangie family come in?" I said.

"I moved back to New Orleans, and Penelope saw me at the clinic where I take Elizabeth. I told her my story. She introduced me to Adonis. That was it."

"That doesn't sound like Adonis."

"Try getting to know him."

"No strings attached?"

"I'm going to say this only once," she said, "and that's because I don't want you walking out of here with the wrong story. Adonis is a gentleman. He asks. You get my meaning?"

"He *asks*?"

"Yeah, fill in the blanks."

"You're an intelligent woman. There's something weird going on with the Balangies, and I have a feeling it bothers you."

She tried to stare me down.

"You ever hear of a guy who has a face like a reptile?" I said.

"No."

"A guy who enjoys breaking the necks of pimps?"

"I don't know anything about that."

I was tired and the rain was blowing hard, the banana fronds outside pressing wetly against the glass. I knew I would probably hit high winds around Morgan City. I put on my coat.

"Adonis told me something I didn't understand," she said.

I waited.

"He said to watch out for a guy who calls himself a revelator. I asked him what a revelator was. He said a guy with leather wings and a torture chamber for a brain."

"That's all he would say?" I asked.

"Then he said he was kidding and tried to shine me on."

"That's the Adonis I know," I said. "A guy who scares people to death, then refuses to explain himself."

"You don't know anything about a revelator?"

"Latter-day Saints use the term," I said. "But I doubt Adonis hangs out with the Mormon Tabernacle crowd. Want my advice, Ms. Rosenberg?"

"Drop the 'miz' crap."

"If Adonis gives away something, it's for a reason. His father was the same way. The Balangies never forget a debt, an injury, or a favor. But the one they remember the most is the injury. Ask any prostitute from New Orleans to Galveston who tries to go independent."

"Boy, you're the light of the world," she said.

"More like a dead bulb," I replied. "Good night, Miss Leslie. Excuse me. Leslie. I think you're probably a fine lady."

For just a moment her face softened and showed a vulnerability that didn't go with anything she had told me.

"Hey," she said.

"What?"

"If you're in the neighborhood."

"You mean drop by?"

"Elizabeth likes you."

I said good night and ran through the rain to my unmarked car just as lightning leaped through the clouds and lit up the entire neighborhood. The tiny boxlike houses trembled like a cardboard replica of Levittown, then the darkness folded over them. It was one of those rare moments when the ephemerality of the human condition becomes inescapable and you want to smash your watch and shed your mortal fastenings and embrace the rain and the wind and rise into the storm and become one with its destructive magnificence.

DANA MAGELLI CALLED me from NOPD the next day. "Trying to get yourself smoked?" he said.

"Don't know what you're talking about," I replied.

"My sister-in-law plays tennis at the same courts as Adonis Balangie."

"I tried to force his hand."

"How'd that work?"

"Guess," I replied.

"I'd go easy on that, Dave. But that's not why I called," he said. "A black woman named Sarah Gooding got stopped on St. Charles for a broken taillight. The patrolman ran her tag and found she had three bench warrants for traffic violations and one for soliciting. He also smelled weed inside the car. She had a little boy in the backseat and said she was leaving town. The officer searched her vehicle and found thirty thousand dollars in the trunk."

"Why are you telling me this?"

"I talked to her. She tried to lie her way out of it. She said she'd saved the money over the years, and she and her son were moving to Mississippi. I explained to her that the bills had purple dye on them and were probably from a robbery. I also told her the prints on her sheet for the solicitation pinch matched prints we found in the taxi driven by the pimp who got his neck broken. That's when she broke down."

"Wait a minute. You found her prints in the taxi driven by Melancon?"

"No, I was lying to her."

"How about the dye on the money?"

"That's true. It's not much, but it's there. The serial numbers are not in the FBI database, so maybe the money is from a source that can't report the loss."

"Go on," I said.

"She said Melancon would take her to hookups in the Quarter, in-and-out deals that didn't have the approval of Adonis. The night Melancon got killed, the john was a guy with a face like a snake. He said his name was Gideon. He gave her the thirty grand."

"For what reason?"

"Try to process this: She has to get out of the life. The john is a combo of Billy Graham and Reinhard Heydrich."

"It's funny you used Heydrich's name."

"What about it?" Dana said.

"His middle name was Tristan."

"So what? Look, there's something else. The black hooker says the john called himself a revelator. You ever hear anything like that?"

"Yeah, last night, from a woman with ties to Adonis Balangie."

"What'd she say?"

"She said Adonis warned her about a guy calling himself that."

"Who's the woman?"

"She's not a player."

"Like Penelope Balangie is not a player?"

I didn't reply.

"A ghoul was carrying your address," he said. "While you're busy inserting yourself into the Balangie family's inner workings. Notice my choice of words."

"I appreciate your concern, Dana. But you're mischaracterizing the situation."

"I tried."

"You ever deal with Mark Shondell?"

"Shondell wouldn't take the time to piss on us if we were burning to death," he replied. "You never cease to astound me, Dave. Have a nice day."

The line went dead. In all the years I had known him, Dana Magelli had never hung up on me.

THAT EVENING I drove to the treatment center in North Baton Rouge where Johnny Shondell had checked in for a minimum stay of a month. I suspected one month would be for openers. You don't have to die to visit Dante's Ninth Circle. Junk is a culture unto itself. The body, the brain, and the soul are the property of the dealer. Street addicts knowingly inject themselves with AIDS and hepatitis rather than face withdrawal. When it comes to satisfying the addiction, no form of depravity is off the table. How does anyone get himself in that kind of shape? It's easy. You've got snakes in your head, the rattling of Gatling guns in your ears, and a sense of despair as bottomless as the Grand Canyon, and voilà, here comes the candy man, who offers you a ride on the big white horse, and with just a little poke in the arm, you're galloping through a field of flowers.

Johnny's cottage was nestled among azalea bushes under a gnarled oak with limbs so big and heavy they touched the ground like giant elbows. By the tree was a stone bench green with lichen and age and the coldness that seemed to live permanently in the layer of leaves that had turned black and yellow and slick on the ground. The surroundings reminded me of the graveyard behind Father Julian Hebert's church in Jeanerette, and I wondered if this was not perhaps a reminder of the tenuous grasp we have on our lives.

I sat with Johnny on the bench. He was wearing an Australian infantry hat and a brown wool jacket zipped up to the throat, and in the dim light, he could have been one of the poor fellows in the trenches at Gallipoli waiting to go over the top into Turkish machine-gun fire, with the same dread of the grave, with the same heart-draining sense of abandonment.

"How are they treating you, Johnny?" I said.

"Fine," he said, looking at the shadows.

"When did you go on the spike?"

"A year ago," he said.

"Why'd you do it?"

"Probably the same reason people climb in a bottle."

"You wanted to?" I said.

"Nobody held a gun on me."

"You're looking good," I lied.

"Think so?"

"Sure," I said. "Where'd you get the digger hat?" He didn't understand what I meant. "The Aussies call those 'digger hats' because the prospectors in the Outback wore them."

He took off the hat and brushed a strand of Spanish moss off the brim, then put it back on. "Maybe don't tell anybody about this, huh?"

"Your hat?"

"Isolde sent it to me. There wasn't a return address, but I know it was from her. She knew I wanted one."

"I'm at a loss about something, Johnny. Your uncle Mark has no feelings about others. Why cover for a man who has done such harm to you and Isolde?"

"Uncle Mark is a man of destiny."

"What kind of destiny?"

"He won't say. Something big."

"Marcel LaForchette was a button man for the Balangie family; more specifically, he helped whack a child molester from New Iberia. I had the impression the molester might have been an employee or a member of your family."

"I don't want you talking about the Shondells like that, Mr. Dave. Besides, why would Uncle Mark hire a guy who had killed one of his relatives?"

Because Marcel LaForchette might end up a sack of fertilizer in your rose garden, I thought.

"Know any revelators?" I asked.

His face drained. "Where'd you hear about revelators?"

"Know a guy named Gideon?"

"Gideon Richetti?"

"Yeah, that might be the guy." I had no idea what Gideon's last name was. "You're buds with this character?"

"Don't do this to me, Mr. Dave. I'm already falling apart."

"My address was found in his room in the French Quarter."

Johnny's lips were gray and chapped, his eyes lustrous, as though he had a fever. I could smell an odor rising from inside his shirt. "You have to get away from Gideon," he said.

"He's a killer?"

"He travels through time. He's the guy who hung up Mr. Clete."

"Gideon is the guy who almost burned Clete to death?"

"Yeah, what does it take to get that across?" Johnny said. He caught the tone in his voice and wiped his mouth. "I've been trying to tell you, Mr. Dave, but you don't listen. Don't mess with things you can't understand. The same goes for Mr. Clete."

"Do you know how unhinged all this sounds?" I said.

He lowered his head, his hands balled in his lap. I had made a mistake, one that in my case was inexcusable. Many people do not understand that drug and alcohol addiction are joined at the hip with clinical depression and psychoneurotic anxiety. The combination of the two is devastating. An outsider has no comprehension of the misery that a clinically depressed person carries. The pain is like dealing with an infected gland. One touch and the entire system tries to shut down, because the next stop might be the garden of Gethsemane.

"You working the steps?" I said.

"I'm trying to."

"You feel like you have broken glass in your head?"

"I don't know what I feel. I don't feel anything."

"Here's how recovery works, Johnny. When you dry out or get clean, you have memories that are like scars on the soul. You accept the things you did when you were high or drunk, so you feel like you're living in a nightmare that belongs to someone else. In some ways, it's like a soldier returning from war. He finds himself a stranger in the land he fought to protect. Except a drunk or drug addict gets no medals and has no honorable memories."

Johnny stared at the brick cottage he had been assigned. It was in deep shadow now, the windowpanes dark, faintly luminescent, like obsidian. "I brought my Gibson."

"Why don't you get it?"

He went inside and returned with his Super Jumbo acoustic guitar hanging from his neck. He sat down on the bench and made an E chord and rippled the plectrum across the strings. Then he sang "Born to Be with You" by the Chordettes. The driving rhythm of the music and the content of the lyrics were like a wind sweeping across a sandy beach. I don't know how he did it. It was stunning to listen to Johnny sing it, because his voice, his lungs, and his heart seemed disconnected from the hollow look in his eyes. As I listened, I wanted to tear Mark Shondell apart.

"That's wonderful," I said when he was done.

"Think so?"

"I don't know if I've done you much good coming here," I said. "But I want to leave you with a thought: Don't be the dumb bastard I was."

"I don't know what you mean, Mr. Dave."

"Don't let anyone take your first love from you. You'll never forgive yourself. Steal her away or give up your life if you have to."

"Is that what happened to you?"

"Mine to know and grieve on. I got to go," I said. I stood up and placed my hand on his shoulder. "Watch your ass, kid."

Chapter Seventeen

ONE WEEK LATER, Mark Shondell was back in town, perhaps with Isolde or perhaps not. People were afraid to ask. If you have not lived in a small Southern town or city, you will probably find this strange. But the greatest fear in our culture has always been deprivation. It trumps all the other sources of our discontent, including the racism that has been with us since Reconstruction. So maybe it seemed almost appropriate, considering the times in which we find ourselves, that Mark Shondell returned to New Iberia with a former Klan leader and neo-Nazi by the name of Bobby Earl.

I do not mean to impugn Bobby. He had been with us a long time. He was not the problem. We were. He was the aggregate for everything that was wrong in us. Unfortunately, he was a master at making use of his perverse gifts to mesmerize a crowd and validate their barely concealed desire to do great physical injury to Jews and people of color. Women loved him, ignoring the fact that most of his facial features were the product of plastic surgery. Men did, too. He was a womanizer, an LSU graduate, and he attended all their home games. Invariably, he was interviewed in front of Tiger Stadium before the game, exuding an almost rapturous adoration of the Southeastern Conference because it was comprised entirely of Southerners, concluding for the television audience that no matter the numbers on the scoreboard, both teams were victorious. Bobby was a pioneer in the conflation of militarism, football, and evangelical Christianity. I wonder sometimes why his constituency has not raised a statue in his honor.

His lies, his disingenuousness, the way he could create a tragic profile before a camera, like Jefferson Davis gazing upon the ruins of Richmond, were seldom if ever challenged, even by the media, because Bobby Earl was impervious to insult and, in reality, thrived upon it, floating above the fray like a phoenix above the ash.

He wore tailored three-piece gray suits like the one worn by Robert Lee during the surrender at Appomattox, although I doubted that Bobby had any grasp on the meaning of Lee's last words when the old general suddenly woke on his deathbed and cried out, "Strike the tent and tell Hill he must come up." I also doubted that Bobby Earl would enjoy marching up the slope at Cemetery Ridge with the boys in butternut, many of them barefoot and emaciated, tearing down fences in ninety-degree heat as they went, while Yankee grapeshot and canister and chain whistled in their midst and air bursts blew off the tops of their best friends' skulls.

Clete had been in New Orleans for five days. When he returned to New Iberia, I asked him to go to lunch with me at Bon Creole out on Old Spanish Trail. We ordered po'boy sandwiches and shrimp and sausage gumbo and iced tea, and while we waited for our order, I told him everything Johnny had said about the man named Gideon Richetti.

"Johnny says that's the guy who hung me upside down?" Clete said.

"Yeah, but I came up with blanks," I said. "There doesn't seem to be any such guy anywhere. No sheet, no prints, nothing."

"He travels through time? What the fuck is that?"

"Will you lower your voice?"

"You went through NCIC?" he said.

"Everywhere. The FBI, the state police, the state attorney's office in Florida, John Walsh."

"Why him?"

"He finds people nobody else can."

I could see Clete's frustration. I was giving him information that was not information while calling to mind one of the worst experiences of his life.

His gaze wandered around the room. There were antlers and deer heads and a marlin mounted on the walls. Then he looked out the window at a black Mercury with tinted windows that had just parked under a live oak. The waiter put our food on the table. Clete went to the window and came back. "If that guy comes in here, I'm calling the health department."

"What guy?"

"Bobby Earl."

"Clete, if you get us kicked out of here—"

"Don't start," he replied, popping open a napkin on his lap.

"I mean it."

"The passenger window is down," he said. "The Balangie girl is in the front seat. They don't have the decency to bring her inside."

Bobby Earl and Mark Shondell came through the front door and got in the service line. All faces in the restaurant turned toward them. But in one second, with no change of expression, the same people looked quickly at their food or at their hands or at the deer heads and the marlin on the wall. Mark Shondell looked across the room at us and smiled, but I didn't acknowledge him. He left the line and came to our table. His tan was darker than the last time I had seen him, his expensive clothes immaculate, not one hair out of place on his head. The jeweled rings on his fingers glinted under the ceiling lights. "It's nice to see you, Dave," he said, ignoring Clete.

I didn't answer.

"Sir, did you hear me?" he said.

"Yeah, I did," I replied, looking through the window at the Mercury.

"Then what seems to be your problem?"

"Your treatment of Isolde Balangie," I said.

He looked over his shoulder, then back at me. "Her stomach is upset. She didn't want to come inside."

"You're molesting her, you son of a bitch."

The waiter and waitress and patrons became motionless, as though they were painted on the air. You could not hear a fork or spoon scrape against a plate or saucer.

"How dare you," he said.

"Get away from our table," I said.

I doubted that Mark Shondell had ever been called to task in public. A single blue vein was throbbing in his left temple. "You will not speak to me like this."

"Don't embarrass yourself any worse than you have," I said.

"Walk outside with me," he said.

"No, we'll end this right here," I said. I stood up, and with my open hand, I slapped him across the face as hard as I could, so hard his chin hit his shoulder.

"Oh, shit, Dave," I heard Clete whisper.

I cannot tell you with exactitude what happened next. I felt as though I were standing in the middle of a dream from which I couldn't wake. The other patrons were staring at their uneaten food. Bobby Earl slipped his arm inside Shondell's. "Let's go, Mark," he said. "It's all right. He'll never be your equal."

He led Shondell outside in the silence.

"How about those Saints?" Clete said to everyone in the room.

No one laughed.

IT WASN'T OVER. I followed Bobby and Shondell into the parking lot. The sky was blue, the live oak above us full of wind. It was a grand day and should have been one of celebration, but I knew a couple of cruisers were probably on their way and that I didn't have long before someone else took over the situation. Shondell was already in the backseat, and Bobby Earl was getting behind the wheel. I opened the passenger door. Isolde Balangie looked up at me. Her cheeks were pooled with color, her whitish-blond hair sifting on her face. She made me think of an abandoned doll.

"Come with us, Isolde," I said.

"I'm with Uncle Mark," she replied.

"He's not your uncle. He's a pervert."

Shondell leaned forward so that his head was right behind Isolde's. His features looked like an inverted triangle, one that was full of hate. "Be gone, you evil man."

"I'm going to get you, Shondell," I said.

"Your career is over," he said. "You've slept with this poor girl's mother, and you accuse me of moral turpitude? I'm going to expose you for the trash you are."

"Let's go, Dave," I heard Clete say behind me.

"No," I said. I picked up Isolde's hand and held it in mine. "I visited Johnny at the treatment center. He was wearing the digger's hat. He played his guitar for me. He loves you, Isolde."

Tears formed in her eyes. "I have to be with Uncle Mark," she said.

"Your mother doesn't want you to do this," I said.

"She brought me here."

"I'll have a talk with her about that," I said.

"Let go, Mr. Dave," she said.

I felt Clete's hand on my arm. I stepped back and closed the door. Bobby Earl scoured gravel out of the parking lot onto the highway, the dust and exhaust and stench of the tires drifting into our faces.

At two p.m. that same day, Carroll LeBlanc called me into his office. I suspected I had put my badge in jeopardy again, and I prepared myself for another onslaught of LeBlanc's disdain and sarcasm. But I was about to learn again that people are more complex than we think. "What started it?" he said.

"At Bon Creole?"

"Oh, yes, could it be that?"

"Mark Shondell is molesting a kid in plain sight," I said. "That doesn't bother you?"

"Yeah, it does, so sit down and shut up a minute." He propped his foot on the trash can and looked out the window at the grotto dedicated to Jesus' mother. He glanced at his ever-present legal pad. "You popped Shondell in the face?"

"I think that's what happened. I had a blackout."

"You were drunk?"

"I have blackouts without drinking. It keeps my bar tab down."

"What's the deal with the Balangie girl? Don't tell me human trafficking, either."

"That's what this is about—human bondage."

He rubbed his mouth. "Yeah, there's predation involved, but it's in-house stuff between the greaseballs. I just don't get the trade-off."

"What do you mean, trade-off?"

"What is Adonis Balangie getting out of this? How about the mother? You're getting in her bread, right? What does she have to say about her daughter?"

"Carroll, I believe you come from another planet. Maybe another galaxy."

"Stop being so sensitive. If I had my way, I'd be up her dress, too. Does Adonis Balangie know what y'all are doing?"

"I'm not doing anything."

"I got to give it to you, that broad's ass ought to have its own zip code."

"I'm about to leave your office, Carroll."

He dropped his foot from the trash basket and held up his hands. "All right, that's a little crude. What's really going on between the Balangie family and the Shondells?"

"I think it's about money."

"That simple, huh?"

"Not quite," I said.

"What's the rest of it?" he said.

"Johnny Shondell says there's a player who travels through time."

"Anyone local?"

"Talk to Clete Purcel."

"In your dreams."

"I'll see you later, Carroll."

"Unfortunately," he said.

I started to leave.

"Hold up," he said.

"What is it?" I said irritably.

"You really smacked Shondell across the face? Not just a tap? You let that prissy cocksucker have it?"

"Afraid so."

He looked at me as though seeing me for the first time. "You're a motherfucker, Robo."

THAT EVENING I sat at the picnic table in the backyard and fed my cats and two raccoons and a possum who carried her babies on her back and invited herself to a free meal whenever she had the opportunity. If you're given to depression, the fading of the day can seep into your soul and bind your heart and shut the light from your eyes. During those moments when I'm tempted to let my thoughts be drawn into the great shade, I seek out the company of animals and try to take joy in the transfiguration of the earth as the sun's afterglow is absorbed into the roots and trunks of the trees and the clumps of four-o'clocks and the Teche itself at high tide, when the light is sealed beneath the water and shines like rippling gold coins in the current.

I walked down to the bank to a spot where I could see the drawbridge at Burke Street and the black people who fished under it with cane poles and cut liver. Another storm was rolling in from the Gulf, already chaining the water's surface with rain rings. In one fashion or another, our history was written on Bayou Teche. Spanish and French explorers had used it to invade and steal the Indians' land. Pirates like Jean Laffite had sold slaves from the West Indies on its banks in violation of Thomas Jefferson's embargo of 1807. (One of Lafitte's partners was James Bowie, who would later die in the Alamo.) In 1863 an entire Yankee flotilla came up the Teche loaded with soldiers who got deliberately turned loose on the civilian population, particularly on women of color, who were raped at random. Our history was not a benign one.

But rather than dwelling on iniquitous deeds, I wanted to remember the Cajuns who lived on houseboats and went up and down the bayou in their pirogues back in the 1940s, and the paddle wheeler that one night a week came by at dusk, a sculpted replica of Charlie McCarthy on the prow, the decks as brightly lit as a wedding cake, a Dixieland band blaring on the fantail. Even today I sometimes see a pirogue in the fog, with my mother and father on board, beckoning at me, and the experience is not a bad one at all.

The rain began clicking on my hat, and I went inside and ate a cold sandwich at the kitchen table, then fell asleep in a chair in the living room. When I woke, the rain was thundering on the roof, the trees thrashing outside in the darkness, sometimes flickering whitely as though a giant strobe had flashed from the clouds. The phone rang, but when I picked it up, I heard only static. The caller's name was blocked. I replaced the receiver and went to bed. An hour later, the phone rang again. I looked at the caller ID. This time it was completely blank, something it had never done before. I picked up the receiver and placed it to my ear but said nothing.

"You—" a voice rasped.

"Who is this?" I said.

"Need to pay."

"Pay what?"

"Come outside," the voice said. "It's your time. Nothing you can do will change it."

"Time for what? Who is this?"

"You have intervened in things that are not your concern. Now you must pay."

"I'm about to hang up. You'd better get yourself a better scriptwriter, bud."

"Walk to the water's edge."

"What for?"

I was in the kitchen and the lights were off; I believed I could not be seen. I could see the driveway and my pickup and the porte cochere and the backyard. I was convinced no one was there.

"You and your friend are going on a journey from which you will not return," the voice said.

"Tell you what, podna. How'd you like to eat a bullet?"

"Bravely said. But in each man is a child. They whimper like children. They beg and soil themselves."

"I'm going to hang up now," I said.

"I thought you were a more dignified and modest man."

"Say again?"

"You're dressed in your underwear. That's both unclean and immodest."

High in the sky, lightning jumped between the clouds. There was no one in the yard. I could hear myself breathing. "Your first name is Gideon. Your last name is Richetti. You broke a pimp's neck in the Quarter, and you gave a hooker thirty grand to start a new life. Who knows, maybe you're not all bad. But how about losing the time-traveler charade? It's a drag."

"You say time traveler?" the voice said, each word coated with phlegm. "Look out the back window again, my friend."

Then I saw the galleon slide into view in the middle of the Teche, its wood sides and oars glistening with rain, a muscular man in a brass helmet and leather vest and leather skirt beating cadence on a drum.

"Do you deny what your eyes tell you?" the voice asked.

"Yes," I said.

"How so?"

"Because you're a fraud of some kind. Because maybe you're—"

"I'm what?"

"Evil," I said. "A magician of the mind, someone who knows how to use hallucinogens on others. But ultimately a hoaxer."

"You lie," the voice said. "Never speak to me that way again."

I fumbled the phone onto its cradle, my hand shaking. Then the phone fell into the sink. I jerked the cord from the base unit. The phone was completely disconnected now. But the caller's voice rose from it, disembodied, floating in the air around me, laughing.

I went to the window. The galleon was gone. The room was tilting and spinning around as though I were caught in a vortex. I tried to walk into the bedroom, then stumbled and fell, taking a chair down with me. I woke at two in the morning, trembling as though the malaria that lived in my blood was giving me a free ride back to Vietnam, my ears filled with hissing sounds like automobile tires on a wet highway, like 105 artillery rounds arching out of their trajectory, like snakes writhing upon one another in a basket.

Chapter Eighteen

At 4:23 A.M. I was admitted to Iberia General. The diagnosis was food poisoning. I have been wounded four times, twice in Vietnam (the second time by a Bouncing Betty) and twice on the job. I have never experienced any pain, however, as bad as that produced by the botulism that attacked my system that morning. It was the kind of pain that is so bad you cannot remember how bad it was.

By nine A.M. it was gone. My first visitor was Clete Purcel, whom I called as soon as I was able. The second person I called was Carroll LeBlanc, who said, "You didn't shag that Italian broad again, did you? Hit it and git it, Robo."

Clete pulled a chair up to the bed, his porkpie hat on his knee. Clete never wore a hat inside a building, never walked in front of a woman through a doorway, and never failed to rise from a chair when he shook hands or when a woman entered a room. "What did you eat?" he asked.

"That's not the problem."

"Then what is?"

"I thought I told you on the phone."

"You didn't tell me anything. You kept saying, 'We can't get the slick in. They're coming through the wire.'"

"The guy who hung you up in the Keys called me," I said. "I saw the galleon out on the bayou."

Clete was waving off the image before I could finish. "Don't tell me that."

"Okay, maybe I was out of my head."

Clete's right leg was pumping up and down. "The guy who called, he told you he was Gideon Richetti?"

"I addressed him by that name. He didn't correct me."

"Dave, I can't take this."

"I hit the deck minutes after his call. My memory is suspect. Nothing I say is reliable. But I'm telling you what I think I heard and saw."

Why burden an already burdened man? I asked myself. But in truth, I wanted a rational explanation for the phone call, for the voice that rose from the disconnected receiver, for the prison ship that had wended its way out of history and up Bayou Teche. The sound of Richetti's voice was like spittle in my ear.

"What are we going to do, Streak?" Clete said.

"Take it to them with tongs."

"You can't cowboy a guy like Mark Shondell."

"I didn't say anything about Shondell."

"Then who are you talking about?" Clete asked.

Anyone and everyone, I thought.

"What'd you say?" Clete asked.

"Nothing," I said. "Rhetoric is cheap. I don't know where to start on this."

"It's got to be about money," Clete said.

"Richetti gave thirty grand to a hooker."

"Yeah, and it probably came from a robbery," he said. "Maybe he's trying to buy his way into heaven."

That wasn't a bad speculation.

I SPENT THE REST of the day researching all disappearances and homicides in the greater New Orleans area from fifteen years before. I also talked with Dana Magelli at NOPD. The following day, Saturday, I found Marcel LaForchette in the same dump on the edge of St. Martinville's black district where I'd found him before. He was at the end of the bar, eating fried crawfish and dirty rice with a spoon from a paper plate. A fat woman with gold hair and skin the color of paste was sitting next to him. I remembered her from somewhere. Maybe a motel raid, a drug bust, a domestic shooting, the kind of events that happen most often on the first weekend of the month.

The red paint lacquered on the walls looked smoked, darker, as though it were being consumed by its own garishness.

"Lose your way to your A.A. meet again?" Marcel said.

"Your PO told me to check you out," I replied.

"Funny man."

"You don't have a parole officer anymore?"

"Mr. Mark got me cut loose," he said. "So if you're here about him, I say beat feet, my man."

The woman kept her face turned away from me. She was drinking from a soda can. Lipstick was smeared on the top. She stank of cigarette smoke.

"I need to talk to you," I said to Marcel.

"Talk."

I looked at the back of the woman's head. She wore a frilly white blouse and a bra with black straps that showed through the fabric. Marcel stuck a tightly folded ten-dollar bill between her fingers. "Cloteel, can you get us somet'ing cold?"

"No," she said.

"Somet'ing wrong?" Marcel said.

"If you wit' him, you ain't wit' me," she said.

She dropped the folded bill on the bar and walked to the women's room. Her buttocks were massive, the backs of her thighs printed with the bar stool. Then I remembered her.

"She don't mean anyt'ing by it," Marcel said.

"Right," I said. I leaned in close to him. "The whack you drove on? Was the hit a guy named Gerald Levine, middle name Shondell?"

"Maybe."

"He was Mark Shondell's cousin."

Marcel stared at his food. "I've spent a lot of time with Father Julian. I'm staying off the juice and the spike and weed and everyt'ing else. The way I was before I got turned out."

His Cajun accent had deepened, as though he wanted to regress into childhood. I wanted to be sympathetic to him. But I knew Marcel's history, and I could only guess at the number of people he had killed.

"Is your lady friend part of your new life?"

"I don't judge."

"She sold her infant child for a few bags of brown skag. She cut the skag with insect poison and sold it to some teenagers."

"She's clean now, so you can shut down the sermon."

He was right. My remarks about the woman were a cheap shot. It's easy to be righteous about people at the bottom of the food chain until you spend one day in their shoes.

"Come outside," I said.

"I ain't lost nothing out there."

"Come outside or I'll bust you right here."

"For what?"

"Public stupidity." I removed a pair of cuffs from my coat pocket and held them below the level of the bar where he could see them. I let my voice climb. "I'll bust your friend, too."

"Okay," he said. "You're a hardnose, Dave. You gonna pay for that, you."

We walked through a narrow hall and a storage room full of keg and bottled beer and out into an alley lined with Dumpsters and garbage cans. Two people were copulating vertically behind a Dumpster. They took no notice of us. We walked down the alley to the side street. In the mist I could see the glow of spotlights in the town square. They stayed focused at night on the pillared courthouse and on the church that had been there since 1844 and on the Evangeline Oak and on the graveyard where I first kissed a girl named Bootsie Mouton who later became my wife.

I looked back at the couple behind the Dumpster, then took off my hat and wiped the mist off my face with a handkerchief.

"The fuck is with you, Dave?"

"Nothing."

"You got a look like the whole world is ending."

"Shut up and listen, Marcel. You told me the Shondell vic went out hard. You said he was a marshmallow, that he made baby sounds."

"You get off on this?"

"What'd y'all do to him?"

"I ain't saying. And it wasn't me done it. I tole you I drove, nothing else."

"Clete Purcel said you were in on the Tommy Fig hit. Y'all freeze-wrapped his parts and tied them to the ceiling fan in his shop."

"I was sixteen years old."

"Who did the vic molest, Marcel?"

"I don't know."

"You said y'all took Polaroids for Pietro Balangie?"

"Yeah, he didn't allow molesters in the city or jackrollers in the Quarter."

"I got that. But none of that was personal with Pietro. The whack on Gerald Shondell Levine and the photos were."

"I ain't getting into this, man."

"Who was the molester's victim, Marcel?"

"It was hearsay."

I shoved him against a brick wall. He tried to slap my arm away. I grabbed him by the throat and pinned him hard against the bricks. His whiskers felt like wire. "Was it a child?"

"Who you t'ink molesters molest?"

"Lose the coon-ass pronunciations and theatrics."

"You already know," he replied.

I grabbed his lapels and banged him again and again into the wall. "I want to hear it from you. Say it!"

"The two other guys are dead. That leaves me as probably the only guy who knows who the perv put his hands and mout' on. That's why I'm not a reg'lar visitor to New Orleans. That's why I went nort' and did some work in Camden and Brooklyn. That's why I don't go down Memory Lane with Adonis Balangie. The painter sodomized him for five years. Use my name to Adonis and I'll punch your whole ticket. Now get your fucking hands off me before I forget we go back."

I began to walk away, then stopped. "Where'd y'all dump the body?"

"We put acid on it. It ain't a body no more," Marcel said.

"Where'd you put it?"

"I already tole you. On the nort' side of Pontchartrain Lake."

"The exact spot, Marcel."

"T'ink I'm gonna tell you that?"

"Okay," I said. "I'll just tell Mark Shondell you helped kill his cousin."

"You're a bum, Dave."

"Tell me about it," I said.

Two minutes later, I walked down the alley in the mist, alongside a rivulet of black rainwater, past the two people who had finished their coupling and were now sharing a bottle of synthetic wine. "What's happenin'?" I said.

They looked at me fearfully.

We're supposed to protect and serve. But sometimes we exploit and screw the most helpless of the helpless; in this instance I had used Marcel LaForchette. With no other place to put my anger, I picked up a rock and flung it against a Dumpster. I saw the couple flinch and instinctively grab each other.

I BANGED ON CLETE'S door early the next morning, the air cold and the rain dripping audibly out of the trees where the Teche had overrun its banks. He answered the door in his skivvies. "Why not wake up the whole motor court?" he said.

I stepped inside without being asked. "Get dressed."

"For what?"

"We're going to New Orleans. You need some rubber boots."

"It's Sunday."

"Remember those stories about a place where Pietro Balangie buried his bodies?"

He sighed. "We've got enough problems, noble mon."

I told him everything Marcel had said. When I finished, Clete was sitting on the side of the bed, still undressed, a coffee mug imprinted with the marine globe and anchor balanced on his thigh. "Have you told Dana Magelli about this?"

"No."

"You're protecting LaForchette?"

"He cooperated. He's trying to go straight. Why jam the guy?"

"I think something else is going on here, Dave. You keep putting your necktie in the garbage grinder, starting with the Balangie woman. Now we're about to dig up Adonis's childhood. I think you're on a dry drunk."

"Not true, Cletus."

"You've lost two wives. Either go to more meetings or buy a bottle of Jack. But stop messing with the Balangies."

"Are you in or out?"

He set down his coffee cup on the nightstand and cupped his hands on his knees. "I had a dream last night."

"Forget dreams. That's all they are."

"We were sliding off the edge of the earth, you and me," he said. "I don't know what we're into. I've never felt like this in my life."

CLETE AND I got in my truck and, four hours later, found the spot Marcel had described. The lake was to the south, capping in the wind, the willows bending in the inlets. To the north were warehouses, rusted oil tanks, and an obsolete sewage plant. The sky was gray, the smell of burning garbage in the wind. We stood in a sump that was like a mixture of glue and quicksand and wet cement, and began shoveling and raking and probing for a bottom with a long iron bar that once was part of a school flagpole. We did this for two hours. Our lack of procedure and legality probably seems strange. But anyone who buys in to the average television portrayal of law enforcement deserves any misfortune that happens to him. Most of us give it our best, but a lot don't. So how do we sometimes put away the worst members of the human race? Answer: We salt the mine shaft, lie on the witness stand, conceal exculpatory evidence, and cut deals with jailhouse snitches. We also dig big holes and find nothing and bury something for our colleagues to find two days after we're gone.

We found part of a shoe and pieces of bone that could have belonged to seagulls or small four-footed animals. Maybe some of the bone fragments could have belonged to people, but I doubted it, and the shoe could have washed ashore and been buried by a storm. In effect, the sump seemed bottomless; it would require a large forensic team and many days of labor and a huge amount of tax money to produce anything of evidentiary value.

Clete leaned on his shovel. His clothes and boots were flecked with mud and wet sand. A blister had formed on his right hand. He had not uttered a word of complaint.

"Let's pack it up," I said. "Sorry to get you out for this."

"At least we know LaForchette is probably telling the truth about the hit on the perv. Maybe one day somebody will dig him up. You know anything about him?"

"I heard he was eccentric and moved to New Orleans. That's it."

"There's something I don't get. LaForchette said the perv molested Adonis for five years?"

"Right," I said.

"And in all that time Adonis didn't say anything to his father, or his father didn't know something was going on?"

"Molestation victims blame themselves. Maybe Adonis was afraid of his father."

"There's another possibility," Clete said.

"Don't start thinking too deep on this," I said.

"Fathers rape their daughters, and the daughters are so confused they think they enjoy it. They think it's a natural expression of their father's love. Then when they realize it's not, they get fucked up in the head and feel double the guilt. It's the ultimate mind-fuck."

I looked at the sky. The stench of the burned garbage seemed worse. The clouds over the lake looked like they were weeping. "There's something cursed about this place. Let's get out of here."

"And go where?"

"A diner. Shoot me the next time I drag you out of the sack on a Sunday."

"You got to keep a bright outlook," he said. "Like when my ex dumped me for that phony Buddhist priest in Colorado who made his flock take off their clothes. I told her no hard feelings and gave the two of them my favorite toothbrush. You got to stay on the sunny side, noble mon."

WE ATE HAMBURGERS at a truck stop outside LaPlace, where Kid Ory was born on Christmas Day in 1886. Why did I mention that fact? Because as Mr. Faulkner famously said, the past is always with us, and we can no more deny its presence than we can deny the dead who lie buried under our cane fields and golf courses and interstate highways, their mouths and eye sockets stopped with dirt, their identities and final words still hanging on the wind if we would only hear them.

But Kid Ory was not on my mind. Clete was doing something at our table that I didn't understand; simultaneously, he was receding to a place inside himself that had no sunny side. He had taken from his wallet the photo of the Jewish mother and her children who were walking to a gas chamber at Auschwitz, their shoulders hunched in the cold.

I touched his forearm. "Maybe not dwell on that today, huh?"

"Why not?"

"Because you can't change it."

"What kind of people would put children in a gas chamber?"

I saw the waiter glance at us, then look away. I put down my hamburger and pretended I needed to use the restroom. When I returned to the counter, Clete had refolded the photo and placed it inside its pouch. But the pouch still lay on the counter next to his wallet.

"You know some of Kid Ory's recordings are on the jukebox here?" I said.

"Yeah," he said, looking at nothing.

"What's wrong, Cletus?"

"Sometimes I think Nazis like Goebbels and Mengele are still out there, waiting for their time to come around again. I got this voice in my head that wakes me up in the middle of the night."

"It's not just a bad dream?"

"It tells me we're supposed to stop something that's about go down," he said.

"I think you're flirting with depression," I said. "It peels off a piece of your brain and gets inside you. You got to get outside of yourself, Clete. And don't be telling anybody about voices in your head."

"Why?"

"It's a symptom of schizophrenia," I said.

"I've always had voices in my head," he said.

"So have I. That's why I don't tell anyone. It can get you locked up." He pushed away his plate. "I got to get some air."

"Finish your hamburger. We'll listen to a couple of Kid Ory numbers."

"I feel like the earth is dying," he said. "What's wrong with me, Dave?"

HE TOLD ME to drop him off at the apartment and office he owned in the Quarter. I tried to argue with him, but he said he had work to do for New Orleans's most famous bondsmen, Wee Willie Bimstine and Nig Rosewater, and he would see me in New Iberia during the week.

"What about your Caddy?" I said. It was still in New Iberia.

"I'll get a rental."

Clete's Cadillac convertible and his building in the Quarter were the only two indispensable material possessions in his life; along with his porkpie hat, his personae was incomplete without them. This was the first time I was truly worried about his state of mind.

It was dusk when I drove away from his apartment. In the rear-view mirror, I saw him struggling with the lock on the gate of his courtyard. I braked to the curb and started to back up. He must have seen my brake lights, because he waved me on, almost angrily, then raked the gate loose from the jamb and disappeared inside the shadows.

I drove around the block. By the time I was in front of his building again, the lights were on upstairs. Nonetheless, I pulled to the curb. He opened the French doors onto the balcony and stepped outside. The sky was a deep purple, the Spanish ironwork on his balcony draped with bougainvillea and bugle vine.

"What are you doing, Dave?" he called.

"I'm starting a second career as a voyeur," I replied.

He shut the French doors and turned off the lights. I drove away, my heart sick.

I THOUGHT ABOUT GOING to a meeting of the Work the Steps or Die, Motherfucker group, but the problem on my mind was not booze or dry-drunking; it was Clete Purcel and the wheels that turned inside him.

I had never worried about Clete going up against the Mob or corrupt cops or homicidal meltdowns who sang on their way to the injection table. (Do you know John Wayne Gacy's last words to his executioners? "Kiss my ass.") The real enemy in Clete's life was Clete; his self-destructive powers were far greater than the ones he unleashed on his adversaries.

Someone had figured out a way to get to him. The man in the cowl who had hung him from the wrecker had taken on mythic dimensions. Was he a religious fanatic? A common Sicilian gun-for-hire? Or a man whose progenitor had a triangular-shaped head and could have slithered from a tree in a Mesopotamian garden?

I had no answer. Not about the man in the cowl, not about Clete, not about myself. The loss of a spouse, the depression that follows, the loneliness inside one's home are not easy to bear. Fidelity to the dead is not only onerous; at four in the morning, it can be a bed of iron spikes.

What am I saying? Every cop, either in plainclothes or in uniform, knows that eventually he will meet a vulnerable woman, perhaps a rape victim, a battered wife at a shelter, a survivor of a family catastrophe, a junkie hanging by a thread at the methadone clinic. Maybe the cop is well intentioned and tries to assure himself that he will not cross the line and violate his role as the knight errant in blue. But maybe the woman or girl is too helpless, too warm inside his arms, her face too beautiful to get out of his mind.

I started to take I-10 through Baton Rouge to New Iberia, then swung off the exit into Metairie. A rainstorm had blown in from the Gulf, covering the moon and stars and sprinkling the asphalt with hailstones. By the time I reached Leslie Rosenberg's house, the streets and rain ditches had begun to flood. I parked and ran for her porch, rain blinding me. When she opened the door, her face looked like it was caught in a strobe, bladed and unsure, as though she were entering a crossroads that had no traffic signals.

"What's the haps?" I said.

LESLIE WAS WEARING white shorts and sandals and an olive-green T-shirt and had been doing exercises in front of the television when I rang the bell. *Shane* was playing on the television. I had not realized how tan and long Leslie's legs were. They looked like they never ended.

"I don't want to ask," she said.

"Ask what?" I said.

"Why you're here."

"You told me to drop by sometime. Have you ever been a CI?"

"A what?"

"A confidential informant."

"Maybe my morals are tattered, but I'm not a rat, thank you very much."

Good for you, I thought. I looked at the television. "I love that film. The screenplay was written by A. B. Guthrie. He wrote *The Big Sky.* I met him in Montana."

"Go back to that CI stuff. You thought I'd sell out Adonis?"

"No," I said. "I didn't mean that at all."

She stepped closer to me. "Don't lie."

"I've seen the devotion you have toward your child. You think that's lost on me?"

She seemed to take my measure. "You're a funny guy for a homicide roach."

"Who told you I worked homicide?"

"I asked around."

"Why would you do that?" I asked.

"I don't let everybody in my house. Want to watch *Shane*?"

"Sure," I said.

We sat on the couch. Her daughter was asleep in her bedroom. The rain was thudding on the roof and the windows. The intensity of *Shane* is like no other western I have ever seen, including *My Darling Clementine*. In the last scene, set at dusk, the little boy Joey, played by the child actor Brandon deWilde, runs after Shane, calling his name plaintively. But Shane disappears into the shadows of the Grand Tetons, into an obscurity that makes you want to weep.

"Wow," Leslie said.

"Yeah, there's no film like it," I said. "The story's only historical equivalent is the biblical account of Eden. The sodbuster family builds a log house and a farm in a place that's like the first day of creation. Good vanquishes evil, but you know that valley at the base of the Tetons will never be the same again."

She was looking at me with a strange expression.

"I say something weird?" I asked.

"I don't get you."

"What's to get?"

"You show up in lightning and hail storms, then disappear. I don't know what you want, but it's *something*. You don't want to get into my bread?"

"Where did you get your vocabulary?"

"At the convent. You got something bothering you?"

"I lost my wife a while back."

"How far back?"

"One day or one thousand. There's no difference."

"I'm sorry. How'd she die?"

"Lupus. I lost my previous wife to a pair of killers who used shotguns."

Leslie was quiet a long time. The rain was whipping across the windows. The image made me think of the scene in *Shane* when Alan Ladd is accused of cowardice at a meeting of sodbusters and he goes outside without replying and stands in the rain by himself, but only the little boy sees him.

Leslie got up from the couch and turned off the television. She looked at me with one hand propped on her hip. "You think I'm coarse? Vulgar? Whatever?"

"I think you're admirable and brave. I think Adonis Balangie is a bum and has no business being around you. I'd better go. I've got to be at the department at oh-eight-hundred."

She seemed to study her hands. "You meant that about admirable and brave?"

"You sell yourself short. It'd be an honor to be the lover of a woman like you."

"Say again?"

"You heard me," I said, getting up from the couch. "I've got to boogie."

"Stay for some ice cream."

"I don't know if that's a good idea."

"You called Adonis a bum. I know what Adonis is. The problem is me. I'm his whore."

"Don't talk about yourself like that."

She stepped closer to me, breathing hard. I could feel her breath on my face. "I don't have a way out."

"Just tell him to beat feet."

"And roll the dice with my daughter?" she said.

"Don't give up, Leslie. You're one of the good guys. Do the short version of the Serenity Prayer: Fuck it."

"Yeah?"

"Yeah."

She sank her nails in the back of my neck and pulled my face to hers. But she kissed me only on the cheek, then walked into the kitchen and left me in a male condition I certainly didn't need.

"You coming?" she said from the doorway.

I waited a few moments, then went into the kitchen and sat at the table while she filled two bowls of ice cream and sprinkled cinnamon on them.

"I have a DVD of *The Green Mile*," she said.

"That's a good one," I said.

"Let's go back in the living room."

I cannot be sure of the events that followed. I remember her inserting the DVD into the player, and I remember eating the ice cream, then setting down the dish on the coffee table, the spoon clinking. I felt my head sink on my chest and heard the voices of the actors who played the guards at a Louisiana penitentiary. I heard the voice of the condemned Cajun about to be executed in the electric chair. I felt myself lean over sideways into a pillow, and then I felt Leslie's fingers in my hair and on my neck and brow.

But I was no longer in Louisiana. A dream, a door into a separate reality, or perhaps simply the exhaustion of the day had taken me back to the last scene in *Shane*, except I was the little boy running through the dusk calling Shane's name. The mountaintops were purple, glistening with snow, and made me think of a woman's breasts, and I found myself mounted on a horse that surged rhythmically under me, then a woman's voice whispered wetly in my ear, her tongue touching the skin, *I've waited for you a long time. I was born to be with you. Oh, oh, oh.*

I woke trembling, unsure of where and who I was.

Chapter Nineteen

THE WEEK WENT by without incident. Clete came back to New Iberia and spoke little of the unexplainable experiences we had shared. I said nothing about my visit to the home of Leslie Rosenberg. We were deep down in the fall now, hovering on the edge of winter, our two-lane back roads striped with impacted mud from the cane wagons on their way to the mills, the air cold and dense with an odor like brown sugar spilled on a woodstove.

Late Saturday afternoon I drove to Henderson Swamp with my outboard and fished by myself in lily pads that had already stiffened and turned brown on top of the water. The western sun wobbled like a candle flame in the current flowing between the two willow islands where I was anchored. I was surrounded by miles of water, all of it dotted with flooded cypress trees and duck blinds and the remnants of abandoned oil platforms. There was not another boat in sight. I wore a canvas coat and an old fedora tied under my chin with a scarf, but just the same I could not get warm. Years ago I would have had a bottle of brandy in the bottom of the boat. Now I had a 1911 army-issue .45 in a zippered case tucked in my tackle box. Beside it I also had a drop, a five-shot .22 revolver cast from metal that was one cut above scrap.

Why was I carrying a drop? Because ever since Clete and I had gotten involved with the Shondell and Balangie families, we had been confronted with situations and people and aberrant behavior that made no sense, and I believed that before it was over, we would experience much worse and that no one would ever accept the story we told about it. The oath we took, the laws we upheld, the justice system passed down to us by men such as John Adams and Thomas Jefferson no longer had application in our lives.

I could feel the temperature dropping. I pulled the anchor and set it on the bow, dripping and muddy and tangled with hyacinth roots, and drove my boat deeper into the swamp. When I cut the engine and slung the anchor off the bow, I saw a shack nestled behind a flooded canebrake, the tin roof streaked with moss and eaten with purple rust. The small gallery was supported by wood posts that were half submerged in the water.

Two children of color were standing on the gallery. Both were barefoot and had blue eyes and light skin. The boy wore overalls that had only one strap, the girl a wash-faded dress that was as thin as Kleenex. A fog bank was puffing out of the willows onto the water.

"Want to buy some worms?" the boy said.

"I'm fishing for sacalait," I said. I held up my bait bucket. "That's why I have these shiners."

The faces of both children seemed hollowed out and lifeless, like apparitions in the mist. The interior of the shack was dark. There was no glass in the windows, no outbuilding on the bank, no boat tied to a post or a tree trunk, no parked vehicle nearby.

"Where're your folks?" I asked.

"Out yonder," the girl said.

"Out yonder where?"

She pointed. "Where the fog is at. They gone after a gator."

"The season is long over," I replied. "Where do you keep your worms?"

"Behind the shack," the boy said. "Come see. We got big fat night crawlers."

The fog was wet on my neck, the breeze pushing the water under the shack's gallery. "Aren't y'all cold?"

"No, suh," the boy said.

"Where do you live?"

"Right here," he said.

"I don't believe you," I said. "Tell you what, I'll take a look at those worms."

I used the paddle to push my way through the canebrake until the bow of my boat slid onto the bank. The fog was gray and thicker now and contained a smell like carrion or offal thrown on a fire. Behind me, I heard a splash I normally would associate with a gator slapping its tail on the water or a huge gar rolling in the hyacinths. When I looked back at the shack, the children were gone.

I unzipped the .45 and took it from its case and put it in the right-hand pocket of my canvas coat. I put the drop in the left pocket and stepped onto the bank. The footprints of the children were clearly stenciled in the aggregate of mold and dirt and rainwater on the gallery. As soon as I stepped on it, my foot plunged through the boards as though they were rotted cork.

I went around to the rear of the shack. The back door hung by one hinge. The prints of small bare feet led from the front door out the back, then faded like cat whiskers on the ground. However, other prints were dramatically visible and freshly etched by someone wearing at least size-eleven shoes or boots with lug soles. They led up a broken levee into a clutch of willows and disappeared into a canal lined with cattails and blanketed with lichen as thick as paint. But I could see no muddy clouds in the water, no broken reeds, no imprints of a shoe or boot on top of the stenciled tracks of raccoons and possums and nutrias and deer that crisscrossed the mudbank.

I returned to the shack. The ground under my feet was badly eroded by the runoff from the levee. In a glistening pool I saw three small rough-surfaced tan balls that any kid raised on Bayou Teche would recognize. They were called slave marbles. In antebellum times, black children made them from the clay they dug from the bayou and baked in a tin oven. I picked the balls from the dirt and rolled them in my palm. I wondered how much time had passed since a child had touched them. I wondered what his life had been like, the travail and suffering that had probably been his only legacy.

Out in the fog I heard a clunking sound, like wood on wood. I dropped the slave marbles in my left coat pocket, took out my .45 and eased a copper-jacketed hollow-point into the chamber, then walked to the edge of the swamp. I heard the knocking of wood on wood again.

"Who's out there?" I called. "Tell me who you are!"

My words were lost inside the thickness of the fog, the dripping of trees I could not see.

"I have no doubt that's you, Gideon!" I called. "I wanted to believe you were a misguided guy trying to do a good deed or two! But only a coward would use children to front for him!"

I heard the labored sound of oars. This time I saw no galleon traveling through time. The bow of a wood boat appeared at the edge of the fog bank, a shadowy figure couched in the middle, the oars resting in the locks. The figure was wearing a hooded raincoat. The boat bumped against a cypress stump and drifted sideways. I held my .45 behind my back. "You're Gideon?"

"Correct." He turned his head and I saw his face. It made me swallow.

"What'd you do with those kids?" I said.

"They're safe."

"Are you using a voice box of some kind?"

"You're a stupid man," he said.

"Probably. Why'd you want to hurt Clete Purcel?"

"Mr. Purcel injures himself."

"How about you row up on the bank and we talk about it?"

"I'm a revelator," he said. "You should feel honored. We don't give our time to everyone."

I could feel the pulse beating in my right wrist, the cold steel frame in my hand. "Where are you from, Richetti?"

"Address me as Mr. Richetti or as Gideon."

"Tell me where the children are, partner. I'd owe you a big solid on that."

"You're a simpleton, Mr. Robicheaux. You want the children out of the way so you can do as you will."

I felt like he had stuck a dirty finger inside my brain. "Come a little closer. I can hardly hear you."

"*Idiot,*" he said.

"You got that right. I should have capped your sorry ass as soon as I saw you."

I gripped my .45 with both hands and began firing at the boat's waterline. There were seven rounds in the magazine and one in the chamber. I could see the flash leaping from the muzzle, hear the spent cartridges splashing in the shallows, hear a round go long and hit a tree trunk. I saw wood fly from his boat and float in the water. But Gideon Richetti showed no reaction, not even when a round went high and whanged off an oar lock.

The slide on the .45 locked open on the empty chamber. Richetti and his boat drifted into the mist. I opened and closed my mouth to clear my hearing. I could hear the sound of his oars thinning among the flooded trees. I could not believe what I had just done. I had fired into a fog bank that could have been occupied by hunters or other fishermen or even the children who wanted to sell me night crawlers.

I got into my boat, my hands shaking, and started the engine and drove into the fog. The aluminum hull screeched against the cypress knees protruding from the water, all of them as hard and shiny as wet stone. I saw no sign of Richetti and his boat. Nor did I see any channels in the lichen that floated between the trees.

I killed the engine and drifted in the silence. The water was black, the sun a smudge of egg yolk on the horizon. Inside that soiled piece of Eden, I saw the worst image I could possibly see under the circumstances. There was a patina of blood on a tupelo stump, and a strip of wash-faded cloth that was as thin as Kleenex.

THE NEXT DAY was Saturday. My first stop early that morning was Father Julian's house outside Jeanerette. The sun was just above the trees when he opened the door. He made a pot of coffee while I told him everything that had happened the previous evening at Henderson Swamp. He sat down at the kitchen table, his face empty. He stared through the window at the graveyard. I felt my heart constricting.

"You think a stray bullet hit the little girl?" he said.

"I don't know what to think."

"But you feel you shouldn't have fired at the boat?"

"I should have gotten in my boat and gone after him."

"Why didn't you?"

"I thought he'd get away in the fog."

"That's not convincing, Dave."

"I thought this was my only chance," I said.

"To do what?"

"To prove he was human."

"Because you think that may not be the case?"

"Yes," I said.

He wiped at his chin with his thumb. "I think you did the best you could."

"What are you not saying?" I asked.

"I'm troubled about this hooded man who has shown up in your life and Clete's."

"You think he's actually an evil spirit?"

"I prefer not to," he replied.

"Prefer?"

"Superstition has its origins in fear. Ultimately, all our problems have their origins in fear."

"I saw the guy's face. It looked reptilian."

"I think this man Richetti is linked with evil forces. But they're human, not cartoon characters out of a fable." He held his eyes on mine. But there was a quiver in his throat.

"Thanks for listening to me," I said.

"Don't let them undo you. For the love of God, don't do that."

"Who is 'them'?" I said.

"Take your choice," he replied.

MY NEXT STOP was at a dirt-smudged two-story stucco house with a Spanish-tile roof on the ragged end of West Main, where Carroll LeBlanc lived in solitude except when an occasional woman or two moved in and then moved out. LeBlanc was long removed from his role as an NOPD vice cop, but I always had the sense that he kept one appendage or another in the game. He answered the door bare-chested and barefoot and wearing blue jeans. Behind him, on the sunporch, I could see a young blond woman in tight white shorts and a pink blouse chewing gum and rolling a Ping-Pong ball around on a paddle.

"It's Saturday, Robo," LeBlanc said. "I hope this isn't about work."

"Yeah, it is about work. I'm dropping the dime on myself."

"Great. Write it up. Mail it to me. Or stick it under my office door Monday morning."

"I need to talk to you now."

"I'm in the middle of a Ping-Pong game."

"Yeah, I can see that. You're bridging the generation gap?"

"That's my daughter," he said.

I felt my face flush. "Sorry. I've got to talk to you, Carroll."

"So talk."

"I may have shot a child."

"The fuck you say?" His face had drained. The string of moles under his eye looked as stark as dirt on his skin.

"May I come in?" I said.

"Yeah, just keep it down. I don't believe what you just said."

"Believe it."

He looked sick. I had never seen LeBlanc like this. He talked to his daughter, then motioned me into the kitchen and closed the door behind him. I gave him every detail about my confrontation with Gideon Richetti in the swamp. By the time I was finished, he was trembling.

"Are you all right?" I asked him.

"Yeah, why wouldn't I be all right?"

"You look like you're about to hit the deck."

"I shot a black kid in the Desire Project when I was a rookie," he said. "He was nine years old. That's how I ended up in vice after I made plainclothes. Nobody wanted to partner with me."

I looked away from the shame in his eyes. "Everybody makes mistakes."

"Yeah, try to sell that when you're in the barrel," he said. "So we're talking about blood on a stump and a piece of cloth?"

"That's it."

"What do you mean, 'that's it'? We're going out there."

"What for?"

"Because I don't believe this shit."

"What shit?" I said.

"This fucking guy from outer space or whatever."

"Your agitation isn't about Richetti," I said. "What are you keeping from me, Carroll?"

"Mark Shondell has a hard-on for you. You slapped his face in public."

"What does that have to do with you?"

"I was a juicer and taking freebies and collecting for a shylock and had to find another job. Shondell smoothed the way for me. Here in New Iberia."

"Why the favor?" I said.

He clenched his teeth and breathed through his mouth before he spoke. "The Balangie family was starting to slip. Crack was replacing all the other drugs on the street. A handful of black pukes were taking over the projects. Shondell wanted to make a move. I helped him."

"Shondell is involved with narcotics?" I said.

"I think it was personal with him. He wanted to screw up Adonis Balangie any way he could."

"Why are you telling me this, Carroll?"

"I wanted to help people and be a good cop. I saw a kid on a fire escape with a gun. I swear he pointed it at me. I let off three rounds. One went through a window and hit the nine-year-old in his bed. The kid on the fire escape had a BB gun."

"You want my badge?" I said.

"No, we're going to Henderson Swamp. You weren't drinking, were you?"

"No."

"I want you to UA at Iberia General."

"Okay," I said.

"Know why I'm going along with this stuff you just told me?"

"No."

"I'm a loser. Just like you. Know what losers have in common? They tell the truth because they don't have anything to lose."

I gave a urine specimen to the lab at Iberia General, then hitched up my boat trailer and met Carroll LeBlanc two hours later at the swamp.

THE SKY WAS clear and blue and bright as silk when the bow of my boat clunked against the tupelo stump. The strip of cloth was gone, but the blood had dried in the grainy wood.

"You're sure this is it?" LeBlanc said.

"No doubt about it," I replied.

"There's stumps all over here. A bird could have smacked into this one. The cloth looked like it was from the girl's dress?"

"Yes," I said, my stomach hollow.

"Nope, this is a scam, Robo. Somebody is trying to mess up your head."

"I saw what I saw."

He stood up in the boat and used his pocketknife to cut a piece of the bloodied wood from the stump. He placed it in a Ziploc bag. "We'll check it out at the lab. I could use something to eat. You hungry?"

"You're an okay guy, Carroll," I said.

"Say again?"

"You're on the square."

"If I were, I'd hang Shondell out to dry. But I want my job."

"He'll burn his own kite," I said.

"Good luck on that."

We drove to the levee and ate crab burgers and gumbo on the dock and watched a black kid fly a kite that resembled a quivering drop of bright red blood in an otherwise immaculate sky.

Chapter Twenty

CLETE HAD JUST gotten back from New Orleans and asked me to meet him on Sunday morning by the recreation building in City Park. I went to an early Mass at St. Edward's, then drove across the drawbridge at Burke Street onto the oak-shaded serpentine lane that led to the playground and the swing sets and the jungle gyms in the park.

Clete was sitting at a picnic table, dressed as though for church, his porkpie hat crown down on the table, except he was not headed for church and was drinking from a long-neck, even though it was barely ten A.M. I sat down across from him. There were gin roses in his cheeks.

"Why'd you want to meet me here?" I asked.

"Somebody tried to creep my cottage and my office. I got to do a sweep."

"Who'd want to bug your cottage and office?"

"For openers, that pus head Shondell." His fingers were curled around the label on the beer bottle, his gaze unsteady, his knuckles as rough as barnacles.

"Hitting it pretty early today, aren't you?" I said.

"It's afternoon somewhere. I think you're about to go in the skillet, Streak."

"Not me."

"Adonis Balangie came to my apartment in the Quarter last night. He had two of his gumballs with him. He said either you get your head on straight or you get disappeared, and disappeared will be the least of it."

"Straight about what?"

"Getting into the wrong bread box. I'm not talking about Penelope Balangie, either."

"So who *are* you talking about?" I said, trying not to clear my throat before speaking.

He took a piece of notepaper from his shirt pocket and looked at it. "Leslie Rosenberg, who evidently is his regular punch. He says you not only got it on with her, but you told her to quit the job he gave her. You know this broad?"

"She's not a broad."

"*Excuse* me. Did you pork this lady who probably graduated from Sophie Newcomb?"

"I'm not going to talk to you on this level."

"Answer my question, Dave."

"I don't know. I was at her house. It was raining. I had some kind of blackout."

"That's convenient. I got to try that the next time I get caught milking through the fence."

"Maybe I did."

"Got it on?"

"Yeah," I said. "I remember the rain and a voice that said, 'I've waited for you a long time. I was born to be with you.'"

"Don't do this to me, Dave. One of us has got to stay sane."

"Then the voice said, 'Oh, oh, oh.'"

He looked at me, an alcoholic shine in his eyes. "You mean like—"

"Yeah, a climax."

"I hope she took snapshots. You can send them to Adonis. You know how to do it, big mon."

"I don't care about any of this, Clete. I may have shot a child in Henderson Swamp."

I told him everything. His face drained. His voice sounded like a bucket of rust. His eyes were damp. "That guy Richetti is real, isn't he?"

"Yeah, he is," I said.

"I'm going to bring this shit to an end."

"It's not that easy. You know it, too," I said.

"What if I just take Mark Shondell off at the neck? What if I put his head on a spike?"

"You're serious?"

"You weren't hung upside down from a wrecker hook," he said. "I can't get that out of my head."

"We don't know that Richetti is working for Shondell."

"Mark Shondell is putting the blocks to a teenage girl everybody has deserted, including her mother and stepfather. I say we cap him. I also say we cap anybody who gets in our way, starting with Adonis Balangie. In the meantime, you stay away from his punch, what's-her-name?"

"You shouldn't drink for the rest of the day. Let's hammer down some bacon and eggs."

He threw me his cell phone. "Call Victor's. They'll deliver. I need something from the car." He went to his Caddy and came back with another beer. He twisted off the cap and sat down. "You're not going to say anything?" he said.

"It wouldn't do any good."

"Dave, something political is going on with Shondell and Bobby Earl. Like Father Julian said. Maybe it's like Hitler going into the Rhineland in 1936. Nobody stood up to him, so he decided to take Czechoslovakia and then Poland."

"This is New Iberia."

"Tell Huey Long that. Do you realize you just told me that maybe you shot a little girl? That we're sitting here talking about it? We should have already shoved a twelve-gauge up Shondell's ass."

"I'm with you in whatever you want to do," I said.

"Talk to the Jewish broad. Find out what's going on. And keep your flopper on lockdown."

"You're talking about Leslie Rosenberg?"

His eyes went out of focus. Or maybe he deliberately crossed them. "Duh! What did you tell her that made her quit her job with Adonis?"

"I told her she deserved a better life."

"Then you got it on?"

"I don't remember."

"No clue, huh?" he said. "What was the status of your pole when you got home?"

"Will you—"

"That's what I thought," he said.

I waited for him to start taking me apart again. Instead he poured his beer on the grass and set the bottle on the picnic table and stared at it. "Dave, we've got to get to the bottom of the business at Henderson Swamp. This isn't us. There's got to be an explanation. I'm about to have an aneurism here."

I walked away and got in my truck and drove home, the steel grid on the drawbridge rattling under my tires.

MONDAY AFTERNOON CARROLL LEBLANC came into my office without knocking, a clipboard in one hand. "Reptile blood," he said.

I stood up, a fishhook in my windpipe. "You got the lab report?"

"Yeah," he said. "The tech wasn't real happy. Something about giving lab priority to the death of a snake."

I sat back down and lowered my head into my hands, breathing slowly through my mouth. "Thanks, Carroll."

"No problem. You all right?"

"Sure."

"You don't look like it."

I sat up straight, dizzy, spots before my eyes. "Tell the lab I owe them one."

"The less said about this stuff, the better."

"I saw what I saw out there."

"No, you didn't. Nothing happened."

I opened my desk drawer and took out the three slave marbles I'd found behind the shack. I rolled them on my blotter. "I don't think finding these was a coincidence."

"Don't get back in your spaceship, Robo."

"Can you call me Dave, please?"

"I'll call you crazy if I hear any more of this."

I looked through the glass in my door. A patrolman had hooked up a man with thick salt-and-pepper hair and was walking him down the hall. LeBlanc followed my eyes. "What?"

"That's Marcel LaForchette."

"Yeah, he pulled a knife on a guy in Clementine's."

"What's Marcel doing at Clementine's?" I said.

"Upgrading his lifestyle. How would I know? Stay out of it."

"Nobody was hurt?"

"Ask the chamber of commerce guy he threatened. He dumped in his pants—literally, on his shoes." LeBlanc's eyes lingered on my face. "Why the look?"

"I don't buy it."

"What's with you and LaForchette?"

"I could have been him."

"I know where this is going," LeBlanc said.

"Then you know more than I do."

"You're a laugh a minute, Robo. I mean Dave."

I FOUND MARCEL LAFORCHETTE and the patrolman and a detective in an interview room at the end of the hallway. I talked with the detective outside, then asked if I could have a few minutes with Marcel. After the patrolman and detective were gone, I sat down across from Marcel at a steel table that was bolted to the floor. He was wearing a navy blue sport coat and pressed gray slacks and a red silk shirt and polished needle-nosed Tony Lama boots. His wrists were cuffed behind him, the ratchets hooked too tight, biting into the veins.

"You could be charged with aggravated battery, Marcel," I said.

"Yeah, I deserve it. I don't know what made me do that."

"Neither does anyone else. The detective said you asked for segregation."

"Yeah, I don't like being around amateurs. I need to relax a bit, too, get some shut-eye, watch a little TV."

"I got good news for you," I said.

"Yeah?" He shifted in his chair, a flicker of pain in his face.

"The guy you threatened is a good guy. He figures you were just drunk, which you and I know was not the case."

"What are you saying?" he asked.

"The guy says no harm, no foul."

Marcel's eyes searched in space, then came back to mine. "You getting off on this?"

"We don't like people wasting our time. You want wit pro, talk to the feds."

"Wit pro is for snitches."

"It beats the boneyard."

I got up from my chair and used my handcuff key to unlock the bracelet on his left wrist, then locked it on a table leg.

"What are you trying to do to me?" he said.

"You're afraid of Mark Shondell. The question is why."

"I tried to tell you once before."

"You saw lights flashing in his face during an electrical storm. That doesn't mean he has supernatural powers."

"Two days ago I was working in the garden and he was on the patio when he got a call from Eddy Firpo. Firpo's a lawyer and a music promoter or some shit. Maybe he's mixed up with Nazis, too."

"I know who Firpo is. What about him?"

"He must have told Shondell his nephew and Isolde Balangie are releasing a music album. Shondell went nuts. The girl ain't supposed to get near Johnny. Now they got an album out."

"What does any of this have to do with you?"

"When he got off the phone, he knew I'd heard everyt'ing."

"Heard what? Say it. Specifically."

"He said to Firpo, 'This is on you. I'm sending Gideon.'"

My mouth went dry.

"I've seen this guy. He doesn't look human," Marcel said. He began jerking the bracelet against the table leg. "Put me in lockdown or let me go. You hear me, Dave?"

"You saw Gideon Richetti?"

"I don't know about his last name. But a guy named Gideon was in Shondell's backyard. His skin was green. His neck looked like it was dripping scales into his shirt. I t'ought it was because of the light in the trees. Then I saw his fingers. I never seen fingers that long."

"I'm going to get us a couple of cold drinks from the machine," I said. "I think you need to talk to Father Julian."

"How's Father Julian gonna get rid of a guy like that?" he said. "Dave, I was in lockdown wit' the worst people in the world. What we're looking at now is different. You got to believe me." Both his hands were shaking, the bracelet rattling against the table leg. "I heard somet'ing that don't make sense. About a Jewish woman. Shondell said to the guy on the phone, 'Drown her. Or gut her and weigh her with stones.'"

"I take back what I said about your alcohol content," I said. "I think you left the dock too early today, partner."

But in truth I was unnerved, and my show of incredulity was hypocritical. "What was the woman's name, Marcel?"

"I can't t'ink."

"How do you know she's Jewish?"

He stared as though seeing an image inside his head. "The name was Rosenberg. Leticia Rosenberg."

"Go on," I said.

He blinked. "I take that back. The first name was Leslie. Yeah, that's it. Ever hear of somebody named Leslie Rosenberg?"

Chapter Twenty-one

I COULDN'T SLEEP THAT night. I thought about the late afternoon when I'd stood on the dock not far from the amusement pier and watched the waves swell in the sunset and boom on the beach and fill the air with a spray that was like the healing power of water from a baptismal font. Considering the present gravity of my situation, these were probably foolish thoughts to muse upon. But what recourse did I have in my dealings with either wicked men or unseen forces whose origins I didn't want to think about?

Clete and I had the same problem. Telling others what we had seen or what we knew about the man named Gideon served only one purpose: Our listeners wanted to flee our presence. In effect, we were collaborating with the enemy and destroying ourselves. Somehow we had to turn our situation around.

Stonewall Jackson was an eccentric and improbable military figure, homely and unkempt, simplistic and doctrinaire. He paused to pray before an attack, giving the enemy more time to prepare, and galloped in battle with his right hand in the air because he believed there was an imbalance of blood in his body. He was also one of the greatest tacticians in the history of warfare. His most quoted tactical advice is "Always mystify, mislead, and surprise the enemy."

This was the opposite of everything Clete and I had done in our confrontations with the Shondell and Balangie families. It was not entirely our fault. The events I have described so far were frightening because they seemed born from a separate dimension and, more disturbing, they had no connection to the world as we know it or the physical sciences on which we daily rely to explain our origins. It was like waking up one day and speculating that the spirits haunting the massive forests of pre-Christian Europe were indeed real and the Druids who hung ornaments on trees to seek their favor were not superstitious after all.

I feared for Clete more than for myself. The pain of his childhood, his memories of an accidental killing in Vietnam, the loss of his career as a detective were the invisible crown of thorns that sat always on his forehead. He already had enough weight on his shoulders without having to hump my pack.

Tuesday morning I went into Carroll LeBlanc's office and told him I was going to New Orleans.

"To do what?" he said.

"Investigate the dismemberment of the two guys in the barrel."

"That's Vermilion Parish's case."

"That's where they were dumped," I said. "The homicide started here."

"You don't know that."

"Cut it out, Carroll. Mark Shondell had somebody put a meat saw to those poor bastards, and you know it."

He had both feet on his desk. He picked up the yellow legal tablet from his blotter and stared at it. "I just got a call from Dana Magelli. He said Isolde Balangie showed up in a homeless shelter on Airline Highway, stoned out of her head."

"Where is she now?"

"At her house. With Penelope and Adonis Balangie."

I thought about the implications of that simple statement. LeBlanc caught it. "Yeah, exactly," he said. "Mark Shondell just got his nose rubbed in it. You're not going to New Orleans about the two guys in the barrel, are you?"

"No."

"So why are you going?"

"A woman named Leslie Rosenberg."

"You're kidding," he said.

"You know her?"

"She was a stripper on Bourbon," he said. "I heard she hooked up with Adonis Balangie."

"Past tense," I said.

He let his feet drop to the floor. "What does Leslie Rosenberg have to do with anything?"

"You wouldn't believe me," I said.

"Try."

"Mark Shondell wants her disemboweled."

He rubbed his face.

"What is it?" I said.

"That spot where you found the slave marbles? I heard that was part of a barracoon owned by the Shondell family. You know, one of those slave pens? I heard awful things got done there."

"I didn't know that," I said.

"Probably coincidence?" he said, his face lowered, one hand twitching on his thigh.

"Yeah," I said.

"Like hell," he replied.

I CHECKED OUT A cruiser, turned on the flasher, and drove straight to Adonis Balangie's home on Lake Pontchartrain. Out on the lake, I saw the boat with black sails that I had seen on my last visit to the Balangie home. Its sails were swollen with wind, the nylon shiny and wet from the waves bursting on the bow. I rang the doorbell. When I looked back at the lake, the sailboat was gone.

Adonis pulled open the door. He was wearing brown dress trousers with a stripe in them and thin suspenders and a yellow shirt that looked as soft and smooth as butter. "What do you want, Robicheaux?"

"What's with the sailboat that has black sails?" I replied.

"You're here to ask about sailboats?"

"No, I want to see how your stepdaughter is."

"None of your business."

"You went to Clete Purcel's apartment with a couple of your trained morons and made a threat against me. How about you step outside and repeat your threat to my face?"

He looked over his shoulder, probably to see where Penelope was, then looked back at me. He started to speak, but I cut him off. "I hear Leslie Rosenberg is trying to clean up her life. That means you stay away from her. You copy on that, you fucking greaseball?"

I guess until that point I hadn't realized the degree of animus I bore Adonis. Maybe it was the pride he seemed to take when he inspired fear in others, or the way he posed as a family man while he kept a triad of mistresses, or the fact that he used his stepdaughter as human currency with Mark Shondell. Or maybe I didn't like to visualize his trysts with Leslie Rosenberg. No, this wasn't a time for self-mortification. Adonis was everything I said he was: a bully and a parasite and a narcissist who deserved a .45 hollow-point in the mouth.

Penelope Balangie came through the French doors, a cat as plump as a pumpkin in her arms. "Oh, hello, Mr. Robicheaux. Please come in."

"I understand Isolde is back home," I said. "I just wanted to see how she's doing."

Adonis bit his lip and stared into space. "Mr. Robicheaux is here to cause trouble in any way he can, Penelope. It's time he had a history lesson."

I saw the apprehension in her eyes. "No. Don't do that, Adonis. Please."

"Oh, Detective Robicheaux won't object," he said. "He has all the answers. Some of his friends put my father in Angola. A seventy-two-year-old man working in a soybean field. My father aged a decade in three years."

"Could I speak to your daughter, Miss Penelope?"

"I'm going to show you some film footage," Adonis said. "After we're finished, I think you'll want to be on your way. Or maybe I'm wrong. Maybe you have no interest in Gideon Richetti."

I wanted to believe he was mocking me, that his mouth would twist in a cruel or amused fashion, that in effect he would become a categorical persona I could define and dismiss. But his eyes had darkened with the same cast I had seen in the eyes of men who had witnessed events and deeds that will never leave their dreams.

I followed him and Penelope into a small theater at the back of the house. There was a big screen on one wall and a projector on a platform at the back of the room. The seats were made of deep, soft leather and arranged stadium-style.

"The footage you're going to see has been digitized," Adonis said. "But none of the images or the lighting have been altered."

"So?" I said.

"You've seen Gideon, haven't you?" he said.

"Why would you think that?"

"He broke the neck of a cabbie in the Quarter," Adonis said. "He must have shown up on a security camera in the vicinity or at the guesthouse where he was staying. But I suspect he also came to see you. Am I correct?"

I didn't answer. I didn't want to confirm anything he said and add to his show of superiority. He turned on the projector. "This footage was taken at a fascist rally in Naples in 1927," he said. "That's Mussolini in the jodhpurs and tasseled fez in the midst of his Black Shirts on the platform. Keep your eye on the right-hand side of the screen."

There was no soundtrack, but it wasn't needed to convey the essence of the man and the probable content of his speech. His fists were knotted and propped on his hips, his chin and nose in the air, his rubbery lips moving in a way that made me think of a spastic colon. The faces of his followers were filled with delight. Then I saw, at the edge of the crowd, a tall, lithe, and muscular man wearing a slug cap and a disheveled suit, his nose hardly a bump, a half-grin on his face.

"Look familiar, Mr. Robicheaux?" Adonis said.

"Detective Robicheaux, if you don't mind," I said.

He froze the image on the screen. "Do you know the man in civilian clothes or not?"

"He looks like the guy named Gideon," I said.

"Looks like?"

"Maybe he's a relative of our guy," I said.

"Right, there're lots of people around who resemble pythons," Adonis said. "I've got another question for you. Why is Gideon the only man on the platform who seems unsure if he got on the right bus?"

Again I refused to agree with him. I guess that was a foolish way to be. But I sincerely believed he was an evil man and served no one's interest except his own. "That's the whole show?" I said.

He clicked the control button on the projector several times. "This next one is V-J Day 1945, on Bourbon Street. I wasn't around then, but I hear it was a real blast."

Yes, it was. On the day the Japanese surrendered, America was joyous from the East to the West Coast, and people in the Quarter poured into the streets, Dixieland bands blared on the balconies, and the dancers from the burlesque bars climbed on car tops and stripped off their clothes.

The footage on the screen had been taken at night not far from Tony Bacino's gay joint at Bourbon and Toulouse. Maybe because of the late hour and the amount of alcohol consumed by the revelers, the faces in the crowd were grainy and stark, as though drawn with charcoal, their glee besotted and grotesque, more like a celebration of the fire-bombing of Dresden than the liberation of the earth. I don't know why I felt this way. I know it seems unfair to the poor souls who were happy the war was over and that they or their family members would not have to die in it. All GIs who had seen the tenacity of the Japanese in the Pacific theater had ceased arguing with the doleful projection of "Golden Gate in '48." But the photos and newsreels that showed the aftermath of Hiroshima and Nagasaki were not easy to look at.

Adonis froze the frame again. "What do you see?"

"People getting loaded and having a fine time," I said.

"Check the guy standing in the doorway at Tony Bacino's."

It was Gideon Richetti, if that indeed was his name. Except he had not aged from the 1927 newsreel; nor was he any older than the man I'd encountered at Henderson Swamp.

"How do you explain this, Mr. Robicheaux?" Adonis said.

"I can't."

"Look at his expression."

"I don't need to," I said. "They're all alike."

"Who is?"

"Psychopaths. They're unknowable. It's a mistake to put yourself inside their head. If you do, you might not come back."

"It looks as though the light is trembling on his face."

"Yeah, I know. He looks like a ghoul."

"But he's bothered by something, isn't he?"

"How would I know?" I lied.

"You don't want to believe he's a tormented spirit," Penelope said.

"I'm signing off on this," I said. "I've seen Confederate soldiers in the mist. Maybe they were born out of my imagination, or maybe they have a message for us. But both of you betrayed your daughter. That's real. Playing around with voodoo in your home theater isn't going to change that."

"You'd better leave," Adonis said.

"I want a word with you outside," I said.

"Say it right here."

"Stay away from Leslie Rosenberg," I said. "She's trying to live a decent life. Find another playground."

"You son of a bitch," he said.

His wife seemed in shock. She looked around as though she didn't know where she was. "I put Tabby down," she said. "Where did he go? It's his feeding time."

"I'm going to walk outside with you, Mr. Robicheaux," Adonis said. "There's a door behind the screen. Go through the door and into the yard. Do it now."

"You were molested for years by a member of the Shondell family," I said. "Your father had the molester tortured to death and buried in a bog on the north side of Lake Pontchartrain. That means you couldn't square the situation on your own, maybe not even as an adult. Maybe you dug it."

Adonis pushed me in the chest. "Do that again and I'll break your sticks from the bottom of your feet to your neck bones," I said.

He hit me in the sternum with his fist, twisting the knuckles to ensure pain. I caught him on the nose, splattering blood across the projector, then I got him high on the cheekbone and on the jaw. He tried to get up and fight back, but in seconds the worst in me had its way, and I was stomping the side of his head, aiming for bone or cartilage whenever I could find it. Penelope was crying and beating my back with her fists.

When it was over, I tore the movie screen from the ceiling and went through the back door into the daylight, off balance, the sky and the statuary on the lawn and the lake spinning around me. All the way to the cruiser, I could hear Penelope Balangie weeping, not in a hysterical fashion, not with shock at the level of violence she had just witnessed, but instead in a sustained, repressed, and mournful way, like someone at Golgotha watching a condemned man drag the means of his execution to the crest of the hill.

Chapter Twenty-two

I DROVE TO THE home of Leslie Rosenberg in Metairie and made a fateful decision that had nothing to do with my job as a detective. Or perhaps she had already made the decision for me by quitting her job as a cashier, telling Adonis Balangie she wouldn't be seeing him again, and notifying the bank that she would no longer be making payments on the home for which he had made the down payment.

As she told me these things in her living room, I wondered if I had actually influenced her decision or if she was a player in a drama whose complexities I could only guess at. No one contends with the raison d'être of deathbed conversions, but seldom do people change their entire lives and give up all they own and put themselves and their loved ones—in this case a severely handicapped child—at the mercy of the storm.

"You're sure you're doing the right thing?" I asked her.

"You're the one who said to fuck all my worries."

"That's why I seldom take my own advice."

"I'm moving into a shelter. I need to pack."

"Do you have any relatives in the area?"

"The last people I need to see are my relatives."

"Could I use your phone?"

"Do it before service is cut off. I put the disconnect order in this morning."

I went into the hallway and called New Iberia. Elizabeth was watching me from her wheelchair. When I got off the call, she smiled at me. "It's nice to see you," I said. I had never seen eyes as clear and blue. It was like staring into infinity. "Would you like to go to New Iberia?" I said. Her cheeks were pink, her hair gold like her mother's but with a red tint in it. "I bet you'd like it," I said, and winked at her.

I went back into the living room. I could see Leslie through a bedroom door, pulling the sheets and covers off the bed and stuffing them in a big cardboard box. She was wearing jeans and a tight beige sweater that looked wash-faded and utilitarian. "The shelter is short on linens," she said.

"I just talked with some Catholic nuns in New Iberia," I said. "They have a cottage waiting for you. They'll give you a job at their center. They help people get a second start."

"What about Elizabeth?"

"I think she'll find many kind people there."

"I've never been to New Iberia."

"It's a grand place."

"In what way?"

"We only let the best people in," I said.

IT WAS STRANGE driving back to the city of my birth with Leslie and Elizabeth in the cruiser. In minutes I had effected a geographical change in their lives that might have irreversible consequences. Please don't misunderstand me. The world in which I grew up was a poem. Others might talk of our illiteracy, our lack of education, our racial injustice and insularity and fear of the outside world, and be correct in all their judgments. But those were the shadings in the painting. Bayou Teche was a way of life. Our ancestors brought both Europe and the mysteries of the Caribbean to Louisiana, and among the crypts in our graveyards were the names of families who had fled Robespierre's guillotine or been exiled by the British from Nova Scotia or gone to the gates of Moscow with Napoléon Bonaparte. They also contained the remains of the boys in butternut whose remains were shipped from Shiloh and Port Hudson.

Our culture was an incongruous composite of Spanish and continental French aristocrats and Acadian peasants and Atakapa cannibals and Africans sold into the green hell of the cane fields. Our churches were sometimes more pagan than Judeo-Christian. Hedonism was not only the norm but celebrated as a virtue. The gentry screwed down and married up. But nonetheless Acadiana, as we call it, was a haven, a place where a woman was always addressed as "Miss" coupled with her given name and a man was addressed with the same equal parts courtesy and familiarity. To not shake another man's hand was an insult. To not remove one's glove before shaking hands was a sign of inbreeding, coarseness, and social stupidity.

As we crossed the arched bridge over the Atchafalaya at Morgan City, I could see the wide sweep of the wetlands, the flooded gum trees and the miles of channels and bayous that bled into the Gulf of Mexico. We were entering the heart of Acadian country, where tidal surges and hurricanes could overcome the levees and float coffins from their crypts and shadow the land and leave behind amounts of water that swallowed whole forests, creating bays where the treetops protruded from the surface like patches of deep green watercress, the branches filled with raccoons and rabbits and possums and small deer, all of whom were in danger of drowning or starving to death.

But we always believed that the sun would rise again, and even though another generation might pass away, the earth would abideth forever, even though it was unlikely we would know those biblical terms. Like the Bedouin whose concept of God derives from his experience inside the immensity and great emptiness of the desert, we believed that our marshlands and swamps and rivers and bayous were not only Edenic but somehow created especially for us.

It was a terrible kind of innocence to be possessed by. We began to see, when it was too late, that the earth is not inexhaustible and that it cannot bind its own wounds as fast as we can inflict them. Also, candor requires me to say that these conclusions are not held by everyone, and the revelers whose mantra is "Let the good times roll" often remind me of Irish celebrants trying to put a good hat on the funeral of a loved one.

I did not want to dwell on these unhappy perceptions. It was a glorious day, I told myself. I wanted to bring a degree of happiness to Leslie Rosenberg and her poor afflicted daughter. Outside of Jeanerette, we stopped to eat in a café that smelled of gumbo and po'boy fried oyster sandwiches and dirty rice and crawfish étouffée, and as soon as we sat down, I heard a duet singing on the jukebox like the year was 1955.

Leslie saw the look on my face. She glanced at the jukebox and back at me. "What's going on?" she asked.

"That's Johnny Shondell and Isolde Balangie."

"Adonis's stepdaughter?"

"Do me a favor?" I said, smiling.

"You don't want to hear Adonis's name?"

"I ripped out his spokes this morning."

We were waiting on our food. She had put a cracker in her mouth. "I didn't get that."

"I took him down. In his home theater. In front of his wife or whatever she is."

"Please tell me you didn't do that."

"I have nonchemical blackouts sometimes. This was one of them."

"You should have told me this earlier."

"It's not of consequence," I said.

She was quiet a long time, the jukebox still playing.

"Have you met his employees, the ones from Sicily?" she said. "They never speak. They're like shadows. There's no light in their eyes."

"I hear they're gumballs."

"The guys with smashed noses and emphysema lungs are for show. The Sicilians look like Hollywood body doubles for Pee-wee Herman but will take your soul as well as your life."

I loved Leslie's language. "Let me explain something about Adonis," I said. "He hit me in the chest and twisted the blow so it would bite into bone. He likes to shame and hurt people and make them feel bad about themselves. Only one kind of person does that: a coward and a bully. He got what he deserved. I wish I had busted him up more than I did."

She smoothed her daughter's hair and looked for the waiter. "I think we should go," she said. "Can we take the food with us?"

Another song by Johnny and Isolde began playing. "You know what Swamp Pop is?" I said.

"No," she answered.

"It's called the New Orleans Sound. The melody tinkles like crystal. Ernie Suarez and Warren Storm from Lafayette had a lot to do with it. Fats Domino and Guitar Slim, too. It's like listening to 'Jolie Blon.' You know it's about a lost love of some kind, something you can't tell other people about."

"So why isn't it still around?"

"It takes the listener too deep inside himself."

"That's a strange thing to say."

"Why do you think people live on cell phones? It's because they don't want to live with their own thoughts."

"I want to go, Dave."

"Don't ever be afraid of men like Adonis Balangie," I said.

"Something is happening inside me I don't understand. It has nothing to do with Adonis."

"You feel sick?" I said.

"It has to do with fire. It's been in my dreams every night for a week. Fire on my legs and arms."

Have you known people who stare into space and obviously see a dark place inside themselves rather than the external world? I'd like to say it was that simple with Leslie. But it was not. Her brow was not knitted; her eyes were calm rather than alarmed. I saw certainty in her face that I have seen only in people who are about to accept a terrible fate that has been unfairly imposed on their lives. I witnessed two electrocutions in the old Red Hat House at Angola. The men I watched die had that same look in their eyes.

Her stare broke. "I shouldn't have said anything. You've been very kind. We need to go. Elizabeth needs to take her nap. Did you know that the hum of a car engine through the metal and seats is approximately in B-flat, the same as the hum of blood in the arteries of a pregnant woman? That's why children sleep so easily in the backseat of an automobile."

"I didn't know that," I said, in the way you speak to people with whom you must be very careful.

"Two days ago Adonis called and said the revelator is here. Adonis said a great change is at hand."

I had learned long ago not to engage with either rhetoric or ideas that are dipped in fear, because the result is always the same: You don't lessen the other person's burden by one ounce, but you break your own back. "I'll pay the check and have the waiter wrap our food," I said. "I'll meet you in the car."

"Did I say something to affront you?"

"No, never," I replied. "Look outside. The devil is beating his wife."

"It's raining while the sun is shining?"

"Yeah," I said. "I've never figured out how that expression came about. Do you know?"

But like most people preoccupied with an obsession, she had lost interest in the small talk of the day. I went to the register and waited while the waiter added up our ticket and put our food in Styrofoam boxes. Johnny and Isolde's song ended, and the only sounds I could hear were the very fine chips of hail clicking on the roof and windows and a kitchen helper scraping dirty plates into a garbage pail, scowling at us as though we were directly responsible for his status in the world.

I DROVE UP THE two-lane road that followed Bayou Teche into Iberia Parish. For some reason I felt that the environment around me was changing, the same way the sea can transform itself without explanation, pulling the stars from the sky and lighting a groundswell that makes you feel you're sliding down the shingles of the earth. Outside my windshield, the blend of winter-green trees and the camellia-petal softness of the season and the pink sun hiding behind the smoke from stubble fires had been replaced by a brass-like brilliance as harsh and cold to the eye as wind blowing across fountain water.

Maybe the distortion of the light had to do with the hailstones melting and sliding across my windshield. But that explanation was too simple. I felt as though I were seeing Eden on the first day of creation, before God's hand had finished its work. I felt I was looking at a garden of thorns.

I looked in the rearview mirror. Elizabeth was asleep under a quilt, and Leslie was staring straight ahead as we passed a trailer slum in Jeanerette and rumbled across a drawbridge and passed two antebellum homes that could have been lifted out of *Gone with the Wind.*

"My," she said.

"My what?" I said.

"They're so white and beautiful, with the azaleas and hibiscus and hydrangeas blooming in front."

To our left was Bayou Teche, running fast and flat, swollen with mud and storm debris and dented with raindrops in the sunlight, the glaze of the surface as bright as razors.

"The nuns are just down the road," I said.

"I know what the dream was now. That's how I died in an earlier time."

"Dreams are dreams and should be treated as such," I said.

"This is a haunted place, isn't it? You see things here, things that aren't real, don't you?"

I did not want to talk about the supernatural with Leslie or anyone else. For the first time in my life, I had actually become afraid of it.

"Depends on how much guilt you have," I said.

"I was burned at the stake," she said. "For being a Jew."

"Don't do this," I said.

"I won't say this publicly. I won't be an embarrassment to you, if that's the problem."

"*That* is not the problem," I said.

"Then what is?"

I didn't answer. We passed a small cemetery full of half-sunken crypts set back in a grove of gum and persimmon trees, then drove through the immaculately maintained cane fields owned by LSU. Up ahead I saw the self-help center run by Catholic nuns who had come to South Louisiana to unionize the field workers in the cane fields. Take a guess how that worked out.

"You and Elizabeth will like these ladies," I said.

"He's out there," Leslie said.

"Who's out there?" I asked.

"The man named Gideon. He's come for me."

"I don't want to hear that."

"You shouldn't have attacked Adonis."

I parked in front of the self-help center. It was located inside a lovely old gingerbread house with a wide gallery, surrounded by trees and a velvet-green landscape. "This craziness ends here," I said.

She closed her eyes and hung her head on her chest. "I feel very tired. I have to sleep."

"Take a nap," I said. "I'll go inside. We'll all feel better later. Okay?" I could not hide my irritability.

This time it was she who didn't answer. The only person I wanted to talk to now was Clete Purcel. No one else would understand the madness that had come into our lives, and no one else would have the courage to deal with it. I wondered if I had bought in to folly and superstition or the manipulations of Mark Shondell. Worse, I wondered if the medieval world wasn't indeed much more than a decaying memory—in reality, perhaps it still defined us and had opened its maw and was about to ingest us.

I knocked on the door of the gingerbread house. But the nuns did not answer. Father Julian Hebert did. "Are you here about Marcel LaForchette?" he said, his voice quavering as though he did not want to hear the answer to his own question.

Chapter Twenty-three

I STEPPED INSIDE. "WHAT happened?"

"Marcel went crazy and came through the door and terrified all the personnel," Julian said. "The sisters called me and thought I could settle him down. Fat chance."

"Where is he?" I asked.

"Gone. The sisters went after him. But I don't think there's an answer for Marcel. At least I don't have one."

"Bad message from a man of the cloth," I said.

"He's either afflicted, or what he told the sisters and me is true."

"Told y'all what?" I said.

"This man Gideon gave him a thousand dollars to leave New Iberia. Marcel tried to give the money to the Center. He's afraid of it."

"How did Gideon know Marcel needed to get out of town?" I asked.

"I don't know. The implications of all this business about a green man in a cowl are more than I want to deal with."

"What's our choice?" I said.

"The biggest frailty in our makeup is our willingness to engage evil, Dave. It's always a trap. When you engage it, it becomes part of you. That's the only way I can think about this."

"How do you not engage it?" I said. "Heinrich Himmler viewed the inmates in the camps before they were sent to the gas chamber. They had to look into his face through the wire. I can't imagine what that would be like." I saw the hurt in his eyes. "I'm sorry, Julian."

"Marcel said Gideon pressed the money into his palm. When Marcel tried to resist, Gideon grabbed Marcel's wrist and forced the money on him."

I waited. "What's the rest of it?"

"There was an abrasion around Marcel's wrist. With pustules in it, like tiny pearls."

"I'm not buying in to this, Julian."

"I'm telling you what I saw."

"Marcel must be working a con of some kind," I said.

"Don't be surprised if your best thinking gets you nowhere."

"There's another possibility," I said.

"What?"

"Maybe Adonis Balangie is making a move on the Shondell family," I said. "Maybe all this other stuff is theater. Maybe Penelope Balangie is as greedy as he is." I swallowed when I put Penelope in the same category as Adonis.

"You may be correct about Adonis, but you're mistaken about Penelope," Julian said. "Her problem is she thinks a good cause justifies any means. Did she catch your eye?"

"Pardon?"

"You heard me," he said.

"She's attractive, if that's what you're asking," I said.

"What you mean is she's beautiful and not easy to forget in the middle of the night."

"Speak for yourself," I said dishonestly.

"You're right. I sometimes convince myself that my weaknesses are the weaknesses of everyone."

How had I gotten into this? Here was a man dedicated to God who got credit for nothing and blamed for everything and often lived under the authority of dictatorial men who could make life miserable for a diocesan priest. Now he had me to put up with.

"You're the absolute best of everything that's good in Christianity, Father Julian," I said. "Anyone who says otherwise should have his butt kicked around the block."

I waited for him to speak, but he didn't.

"Julian?" I said.

"What?"

"Are you okay?"

"I'm not important. You are. And so is Clete Purcel and also Marcel LaForchette. One thing, however: I do not fear the green man."

"You don't?"

"The real evil in our community is Mark Shondell."

"I don't get it," I said.

"In one fashion or another, the man in the cowl seems to be a historical figure, a wandering soul, perhaps. He tried to help the prostitute and Marcel. Mark Shondell is homegrown and revered in our culture, a man who has the stench of an incinerator on him."

I walked back to the cruiser. Leslie was sound asleep. Elizabeth peeked at me from under the quilt, her blue eyes as clear as water. They reminded me of the eyes of the mixed-blood children I had encountered in Henderson Swamp. I woke up Leslie and moved her and her daughter into the Center, then drove to the department on East Main, my head throbbing.

I HAD THE DISPATCHER put out an APB on Marcel LaForchette. It was 4:46 P.M. The grotto next to our building was deep in shadow, the sun a red spark in the live oaks overhead.

"Armed and dangerous?" the dispatcher asked.

"No."

"Then why are we picking him up?" he said.

I had to think about it. "For his own safety."

The dispatcher's name was Wally. He was a big fat man who ate candy bars and fried pies all day and seldom missed an opportunity to make a sardonic comment. "You moved a stripper into the nuns' place?"

"Who told you that?"

"You left the door to LeBlanc's office open."

"Thanks for eavesdropping, Wally."

"What's your secret wit' the ladies?"

"Maybe if you took the peach pie out of your mouth, I could understand what you're saying."

"The woman in the waiting room," he said. "I'd go on a diet for something like that. Scout's honor." He spread his fingers on his heart.

I walked to the door of the waiting room. I couldn't believe it. Penelope Balangie was sitting stiffly in a folding metal chair at the back of the room, her knees crossed, wearing a lavender suit and hose and a pillbox hat with a veil, like a woman out of the 1940s.

"That's who I t'ink it is, right?" Wally said behind me. "Adonis Balangie's old lady?"

"No, that's Mother Teresa." I walked to the back of the room and sat down next to Penelope. She was breathing as though she had run up stairs, which she had not. "If you or Adonis want to file charges against me, do it," I said. "Then leave me alone."

"Someone has to help me," she said.

"I'm not the man for it. I showed that this morning."

She leaned close to my face, her eyes riveted on mine, her face bloodless. "You're not understanding me. This is about a man who is going to be killed. Am I supposed to say nothing?"

"Who's going to be killed?"

"I don't know his name. People who work for Adonis told him there's an open something-or-other on this man."

"An open contract?"

"Yes, that's what he called it. Does that mean what I think it does?"

"The target has a DOA tag on his big toe. Adonis didn't explain any of this to you?"

"Mark Shondell is the one ordering the man's death. I don't want to talk any more about Adonis. You brought his mistress to New Iberia?"

"She doesn't think of herself as a mistress."

"I don't want to talk in here. Where can we go?"

"I'm very tired, Miss Penelope. Don't tell me you don't like to be called 'Miss,' either. I'm going home now. I'm going to politely ask that you not come here again."

"You're supposed to be a man of conscience. I'm trying to warn you about a man's impending death."

"Is the target Marcel LaForchette?"

"I told you, I don't know the person's name," she said.

"Goodbye, madam."

I walked out of the building. A storm front had moved in from the Gulf, shadowing the bayou and City Park and East Main, blowing leaves and pine needles into the circular driveway where the grotto stood, candles flickering in the votive glasses at the foot of the statue. Then the clouds burst, and the rain pounded on my head and shoulders and ran down inside my shirt. I went back into the building. Wally was at the candy machine.

"Did you hear anything on LaForchette?" I said.

"Nutting, Dave."

I waited for him to make another sarcastic or cynical remark.

"No comment?" I said.

"You want some paper towels? You look like a drowned cat."

"No, thanks."

Wally looked into space.

"You want to tell me something?" I asked.

"I always felt sorry about LaForchette," he said. "I t'ought he got a bad deal, going to jail as a kid and all. What's wit' that woman?"

"Penelope Balangie?" I said.

"She was crying. You said somet'ing bad to her? That ain't like you, Dave."

THE EVENTS THAT followed are hard to put into words. They're the kind that make you wonder how you could have prevented a serious blot on your soul or changed a life or lifted someone from his despair with a gift as small as a smile, a gentle word, a touch on the cheek. Or, in my case, simply ignoring a bothersome knock on the door.

The sky remained dark that evening, the rain unrelenting, the oaks and pecan trees in the yard quaking like apparitions when lightning rippled through the clouds. I was eating a frozen dinner in the kitchen when I saw a vehicle turn off East Main and bounce into my driveway, the high beams on. I put aside my food and went into the living room. Someone's pickup was parked behind mine, the windshield wipers slapping, the engine running. I opened the front door but could not see who was behind the wheel.

"Who's that?" I hollered.

I waited, but there was no answer. It wasn't unusual for lost tourists to pull into my driveway. I closed the door and went back into the kitchen and sat down at the table. The headlights in the driveway continued to burn through the front windows. Then I saw someone in a slicker and a flop hat run for the front steps; a moment later, a fist pounded violently on the door. I removed a five-round titanium .38 Special snub from the cutlery drawer and stuck it in the back of my belt, then went into the living room again and unbolted and opened the front door.

Marcel LaForchette glared at me from under his hat. "I need to confess."

"See Father Julian."

"This is about you, motherfucker."

"I don't like people swearing on my property or in my home. I'm also out of Purple Hearts. I'll see you at the department tomorrow."

"That's what you t'ink."

He stiff-armed me backward and stepped into the room. I had not realized how strong and solid his body was. His face was beaded with water and twisted in an angry knot. He smelled like leaves and earth and the sulfur of the storm.

"You're a pro, Marcel," I said. "Eighty-six the melodrama, will you?"

"Maybe I'll bust your jaw."

"I never jammed you." I said. "I never ran you in with the low-lifes."

"You always talked down to me. Just like you're doing now."

"Has Mark Shondell got a contract on you?"

"Open hit. I say fuck it. I been there before. You heard of Sammy the Bull?"

"Sure."

"Sammy tole me I was the best."

"But you got straight and you're on the square now. I'll fix us some coffee and you can tell me what's on your mind. Okay?"

"No, not okay," he said. He reached inside his raincoat and removed a Magnum-22 Ruger single-action revolver with white handles. He let it hang from his right hand, his slicker dripping on the rug. He tilted his head and grinned.

"Private joke?" I said.

"You ain't never put it together, have you?"

"You lost me, podna."

"I'm talking about you and me. You don't see it? Look close. The hair, the eyes, maybe the nose a li'l bit."

"We're coon-asses," I said. "Maybe distant cousins."

"My mother tole me she got it on wit' your old man, Big Aldous."

"I don't believe you."

"Big Aldous didn't stick it to every woman on the bayou?"

"That was later in his life. When my mother was unfaithful."

"You lying son of a bitch. He kept a whore in Abbeville. They had a son named Jimmie."

"Why drag up all this grief? You were always stand-up. Are you going to let a bum like Shondell screw up your head?"

"It ain't Shondell done it. It's you. I didn't have a father or mother. When you were seventeen, you went to SLI. When I was seventeen, I got my rectum tore out in St. John the Baptist Parish prison." He shoved me again. "I want to hurt you, Dave. I want to kill your animals and burn your house. I want to do t'ings I ain't never done to nobody else."

"Your anger is with yourself, bub. Run your shuck on somebody else."

"Big Aldous come to my house once. He was drunk. He had a Christmas tree tied on the roof of his car. He was taking it to y'all's house. He didn't bring nutting to mine."

"I'm sorry all that happened, Marcel. But I can't change it. Neither can you."

"You got a gun on you, ain't you?"

"No," I said.

"You didn't answer somebody beating on your door wit'out your piece? You're a cop. Don't be putting your hand behind you. I'll dust you right here."

"I've had a good life," I said. "Do whatever you're going to do."

"Know why I use a twenty-two?"

"The round bounces around inside the skull. Unless you're using hollow-points. Then it doesn't matter."

He lifted the barrel so it was pointed at my sternum. I had never seen his eyes so bright. They seemed about to shatter in the sockets. "You made fun of me when I said I might become a PI. 'Member that?"

"When I visited you at Huntsville? Yeah, I was kidding."

"I ain't," he said.

He pressed the muzzle of the .22 into the soft flesh under his chin, pushing it deep as though he wanted to do double injury to himself. Then he pulled the trigger.

Close up, the report of a .22 Magnum is almost as loud as a .45 auto. It's deafening. The round drove up through the roof of his mouth and into the brain, splattering my face with his blood. He collapsed under his hat and slicker as though he were dissolving into a pool of black ink, one hand locked on my shoe.

Chapter Twenty-four

THE CORONER, PARAMEDICS, uniformed deputies, and Carroll LeBlanc and another detective did not finish their work until almost two A.M. Most of the time I sat in the kitchen, watching each person methodically do his job so there would be no doubt about the integrity of the investigation. The blood on my hair and face was photographed before I was allowed to wash it off. I also had to give up my shirt in case it contained powder burns. I knew the questions that would be asked of me, but I did not fear them. The questions I had to ask myself were another matter.

Could I have twisted the pistol from Marcel's hand when he pressed the muzzle under his chin? Maybe. What if I had distracted him and lied and told him my father had spoken fondly of him? What if I had told him I had some juice in Baton Rouge and could get him a pardon so he could work as a PI?

But the greater concern I had, the one that left me feeling empty and weak at heart and unable to think, was my attitude when I'd visited Marcel in Huntsville Prison. I'd treated him as I would have a gerbil, a genetic accident, a slug lifted from under a rock, at best a spiritually impaired man whose soul had been stolen at age seventeen. I'd treated him with the dignity I would have shown a germ.

How is it I never thought he could be my half brother? Did I deliberately ignore the possibility because I didn't want to share my father, who was the only person in my life after my mother deserted us? The answer was probably yes.

"We're pretty much done here," LeBlanc said. He was wearing a sport coat and slacks and a tie. He screwed a filter-tip cigarette in his mouth. "Mind if I light up?"

"I'd appreciate it."

"No problem." He dropped his cigarette back in the pack, then scratched his cheek. "LaForchette had his piece inside the raincoat?"

"Yep."

"You thought he was gonna smoke you?"

"For a moment or two."

"What'd he say before he went out?"

"He said 'I ain't.'"

"I ain't what?"

"When I visited him in Huntsville, he said he'd like to be a PI in New Iberia. I made a joke about him working at a car wash. Then I told him I was only kidding. So now he was proving he didn't kid. Big triumph, huh?"

"Then he shot himself? For no reason you know about?"

"The guy had a miserable life."

LeBlanc wrote in his notepad. "Took his secrets to the grave?" he said, not looking up. "Why is it I don't believe you, Robo?"

"He said there was an open hit on him."

"Ordered by who?"

"Probably Mark Shondell or Adonis Balangie or both of them," I said.

"You have evidence of that?"

"No."

LeBlanc huffed something out of his nose, his eyes receded deep inside the thickness of his skin as though he lived inside a husk. "You keep giving me about half the story, Robo. I can't say as I like it."

"The man came here and killed himself in my living room. I'll live with this the rest of my life. Now get off my back, Carroll."

"Has this got something to do with the voodoo guy or whatever he is at Henderson Swamp?"

"Could be."

He closed his notebook. "I was afraid you'd say that. Here's what's going in my report: LaForchette was born to lose and wanted an audience when he shuffled off to wherever guys like him go. Merry Christmas."

"He thought I was his half brother and I got all the breaks."

"Is that true?"

"Probably."

"Go take a shower. You look like you just got out of Auschwitz."

"Why do you use that as a comparison?" I said.

"What, that's not politically correct?"

"Just don't do it."

"Got to tell you this, Dave," he said, "you're one crazy son of a bitch. Whatever you suffer from, I hope it's not contagious."

"I wish you wouldn't use profanity in my house."

I WENT DEEPER INTO my funk and knew I would not sleep until the next night, and until then I would have no rest, no peace, no respite from the voices and people and sometimes monstrous shapes that dwelled inside my head.

How do depression and obsession work? I'll try to explain. The rain made me think of knives in the glow of the streetlamps along East Main. But the rain or my associating it with knives was not the problem. It was the key that opened the lockbox on places I didn't want to revisit: a nineteen-year-old kid mowing down a birthday party with Ma Deuce in a free-fire zone; digging up bodies buried by a serial killer who kept human trophies; opening the back of a moving van stuffed with illegals in hundred-degree heat; swimming across a bayou at night, trying to get to my house and stop a man who murdered my wife, Annie, with a shotgun while I watched.

This is not a complaint. It's just the way it is, and to pretend otherwise only intensifies the neurosis. The daylight is not necessarily a cure, either. The same images can hit you at a traffic light, or at your workplace, or when you're making love, or when you're getting swacked out of your head in a bar that has no clocks.

Call it PTSD or agitated depression or psychoneurotic anxiety or all three in one package. The unconscious or the memory bank finds images that fit the emotion, and all of them are obscene or depraved or unbearably cruel. If you have a history as a juicer or as a user of army-hospital dope or as a romancer of barmaids who look like Elizabeth Taylor under the glow of a Dos Equis sign, you can find yourself not only back on the full-tilt boogie but inside a straitjacket, maybe sedated into the fourth dimension, no extra charge.

If you are very unlucky and talk to untrained or inexperienced people about this syndrome, people who perhaps mean well but tell you to toughen up or to control your thoughts, you will probably enter a place that is the psychological equivalent of the Iron Maiden. In other words, as a black kid who'd had both arms blown off said to me on a hospital ship, "Welcome to Shitsville, Loot. Come on in, the water is fine. Just a little dirty."

I felt overcome with sorrow about Marcel's death. I had thought him a psychopath and hence someone who, of his own volition, had murdered the light in his soul. But he had tried to go straight, had sought out Father Julian's help, and had trusted me with many of his private thoughts, admitting in the last moments of his life his envy of me.

I had identified him with the forces of cruelty, but in reality he was more a victim than a perpetrator, and my experience in the world, for what it was worth, had brought me no closer to an understanding of man's predilection for inhumanity. No matter the society or the historical era, the succubus and the incubus seemed to work their way into our midst, or were latent or embryonic in us from the jump.

Both Catholics and Protestants burned tens of thousands of women as witches. When the Puritans finished exterminating the Indians, they turned their talents on their neighbors and hanged nineteen of them and took three days in pressing one to death. In Europe, drawing and quartering, mass hangings, public emboweling, and death by fire—including the burning of Joan of Arc at age nineteen—were the message of the elite to those who had no power. Serfs impaled noblemen and raped their wives in front of them; they skinned bishops as well. Martin Luther despised Jews and was often quoted by the Nazis in their defense of the Final Solution. Hiroshima, Nanking, My Lai, their legacy is always there, their exponents and justifiers at the ready, the banner of heaven or nation flapping above their heads.

By five A.M. I was shaking and wanted desperately to talk to Clete Purcel. But my calls went straight to voicemail. I also wanted to drive to St. Martinville and start drinking at sunrise in a dark brass-railed saloon with slow-moving ceiling fans not far from the Evangeline Oak where I had first kissed my wife, Bootsie. No, I didn't want to simply drink. I wanted to swallow pitchers of Jack Daniel's and soda and shaved ice and bruised mint, and chase them with frosted-mug beer and keep the snakes under control with vodka and Collins mix and cherries and orange slices, until my rockets had a three-day supply of fuel and I was on the far side of the moon.

But I was about to learn that I didn't need to drive to St. Martinville to blow out my doors. My deliverer from the sauce pulled into my driveway just as the rain stopped and the stars and moon went out of the sky and a fog bank forty feet high and as white and dense as cotton rolled off the bayou and swallowed my house. Talk about frying your own grits. I was just getting started.

Chapter Twenty-five

Penelope balangie didn't knock on the door. She clicked on the glass with her nails as though afraid she would wake me up. I took the chain off the door and opened it. She was holding a lemon meringue pie in a covered pie pan. "I thought you'd need something to eat."

"Where'd you get the pie?"

"At the bakery."

I looked at my watch. It was 6:23 A.M. "The bakery is closed."

"I woke them up."

"You know what happened here?" I said.

"The whole city knows."

Behind her, the fog was so thick I could hardly see the yard or trees or streetlamps. "Come in."

I had thrown out the rug Marcel died on and had cleaned the blood from the floor. I had also showered and shaved and changed clothes, and hoped I did not look like I felt. She walked past me into the kitchen and began making coffee without asking permission.

"I don't know if you should be here, Miss Penelope," I said.

She was no longer wearing the lavender suit and pillbox hat but a baby-blue cashmere suit with a white blouse and white hose, which meant she had come to New Iberia with luggage. "Sit down," she said.

"Kind of you to ask me," I replied, and remained standing.

"The man who died here? He was the one the killers were after?"

"He may have been my half brother. At least that's what he said before he shot himself."

"I'm very sorry, Mr. Robicheaux."

"You have to forgive me, but I don't understand you. In fact, nothing about you makes sense."

She took the plastic cover off the pie and got cups from the cabinet. "No one will believe my story. Nor will they believe yours or Mr. Purcel's. That means we're members of a very lonely club."

"So tell me the story."

"Maybe later. Eat first. Please. I want to explain something you're probably experiencing now or will experience later."

"Oh, really?"

"Don't be sarcastic." She placed her hand on my chest. I could feel my heart beating against it. I sat down.

"Start eating," she said.

I didn't argue.

"People who commit suicide in a dramatic fashion often have an agenda and are involved in a fantasy that leads to their death. They're filled with rage and seek revenge against those who have hurt them. They slash their wrists or jump from buildings or fire bullets into their brain. In their fantasy, they witness the discovery of their body by people they hate. In that way, they leave behind a legacy of guilt and sorrow. Don't let this happen to you, Mr. Robicheaux."

I put a teaspoon of pie in my mouth and drank from the coffee cup she had placed by my elbow. But neither would go down. I choked and held a napkin to my mouth. She was standing behind me now. She spread her hand across my back. It felt as warm as an iron on cloth. "You're shaking," she said.

"I have malaria."

"From where?"

"Vietnam or the Philippines. Who cares where you get it?"

"After all these years?"

"Give it a break, Ms. Balangie," I said.

"You're one of us now."

I stopped trying to eat. "One of what?"

"The people who have to see into the other world, the one we try to deny in modern times."

"Sorry, I'm not up to listening to any more craziness, Italian or otherwise."

"Did the man who died see Gideon Richetti?"

"Yeah," I said.

"What does that tell you?"

"The price of knowing the Balangie and Shondell families is too expensive."

"Your wife died recently?"

"I've lost two wives."

"I didn't know."

My hand was trembling on the teaspoon. "You need to leave."

"Walk me to the door."

"You can find your way."

"No. Get up."

I wiped my mouth with a paper napkin and rose from the table. I looked straight into her eyes.

"Well?" she said.

"You're a big girl. You need an escort to leave someone's house?"

"I want you to do just that. I mean, escort me."

My eyes lingered on hers. I felt a longing I couldn't explain, as though I had never smelled a woman, or kissed one, or slept with one. I felt as I did when my mother abandoned her family. I felt as though I were on the edge of a grave, that the only light in the world was trapped inside my home, inside the fog, and the rest of the earth was disappearing.

I put my arms around her and lifted her against my chest and put my mouth on hers. I felt her feet barely touching the tops of my shoes, her breasts against me, her fingernails digging into my back, her auburn hair warm and clean-smelling in my face, the ache in my loins unbearable.

Then we were in my bed, and I went beneath a harbor off Bimini, the sunlight shattering on the surface, a coral cave inviting me deep into its recesses, its walls covered with pink lichen and the gossamer threads of sea life that had no name. Some believed this was the eastern edge of ancient Atlantis, a suboceanic kingdom where spring was eternal and mermaids wore flowers in their hair and where each morning one could cup water from the fountain of youth.

But I could no longer control the images in my head, and I felt them slipping like confetti from my body into hers, and I buried my face in her hair and bit her shoulder and heard myself saying, "Pen . . . Pen . . . Pen," as though it were the only word I knew.

I DIDN'T GO TO work that day. At six P.M. I bought a bucket of fried chicken and biscuits and a sealed cup of gravy at Popeyes, then took them to Clete's cottage in the motor court on East Main. The rain had flooded the tree trunks along the banks of the Teche and quit at sunset. The sky was magenta and looked as soft as velvet, the bayou swirling with organic debris and yellow froth and dimpled with the water dripping from the trees. Clete saw me through his window and opened the door. "I've been calling you all day," he said. "Where have you been?"

I walked past him into his small living room. "I had my phone turned off. I was asleep."

"The whole day?"

"Why not?" I said.

He closed the door. "Did you ever figure LaForchette for a suicide?"

"I had him figured wrong on several levels. You want to eat?" I put the Popeyes sack on the breakfast table.

"Yeah, sure," Clete said. He gave me a look. "I got a feeling more is on your mind than LaForchette going off-planet."

I told him how I'd busted up Adonis Balangie in his home theater, and how I'd moved Leslie Rosenberg and her daughter from Metairie to New Iberia, and finally, how I'd ended up under the waves off Bimini with Penelope Balangie at my side. He listened without interrupting, his hands like big animal paws on the breakfast table, his gaze focused on empty space.

After I finished, he continued to stare without speaking.

"Hello?" I said.

"Let's see if I have this straight," he said. "You start the day by beating the shit out of Adonis in his home, in front of his wife, then motor on over to the house of his regular punch and move her to New Iberia. His wife drops by your house after a guy blows out his brains in your living room, and to celebrate the occasion you put the blocks to her?"

"Lay off it, Cletus."

"Excuse me, I left something out. You also put in some boom-boom time with what's-her-name, the stripper and regular pump for Adonis?"

"Leslie Rosenberg."

"Right," Clete said. "So you think Adonis might be a little upset? A guy who thinks women are property?"

"He dealt the play," I said.

"No, Penelope Balangie did."

"Wrong."

"Keep telling yourself that. She'll have you mumbling to yourself."

"She swears she's not married to Adonis."

"You believe her?" he said.

"Yeah, I do." But I stumbled on my words.

"Why would a broad with her kind of class use up her life as a house ornament for a greaseball? Ask yourself another question: Why would a guy like Adonis not try to nail her? How would you like to look at those knockers every morning and say, 'Nope, not for me. Hands off.'"

"Can you stop thinking in those terms?"

"You know I'm telling the truth."

"You don't know her."

"And you do?"

This time I didn't try to answer. "I'll see you later."

"You didn't ask why I was calling you all day. Li'l Face Dautrieve came to my office. She's still living in the Loreauville quarters and hooking halftime. A piece of shit named Jess Bottoms fixed her up with some of his friends and paid her with bills that were marked with purple dye."

"Like the bills given to the hooker in New Orleans by Gideon Richetti?"

"That was my first thought," he said. "I called Dana Magelli and got him to run the serial numbers. Bingo. Li'l Face's bills are part of the same series."

"Who is Jess Bottoms?"

"He manages pit bull fights."

"Why did Li'l Face bring the bills to you?"

"She thinks there's a gris-gris on them," he said. "Bottoms says he'll give her fresh bills, but he's got to get the marked ones back. She already spent some of them."

"So you think Richetti tried to buy another prostitute out of the life, and instead the money got spread around to her friends?"

"Something like that," Clete said. "Li'l Face is scared of Bottoms. He's big on beating up women."

"Where's Bottoms now?" I asked.

"Sunset," he said. "Once known as the nigger-knocking capital of Louisiana."

WE DROVE IN Clete's Caddy to a paintless farmhouse south of Opelousas. It was surrounded by burning sugarcane stubble that glowed alight whenever the wind gusted. There was no grass in the yard, no livestock in the pens. I could see the silhouette of a two-story barn in back, and hear dogs barking.

"How do you want to play it?" I said.

Clete cut the engine and killed the headlights. "He was a deputy sheriff in Mississippi."

"So?"

"Don't be subtle," Clete replied.

We walked up on the gallery and knocked on the door. The sky was an ink wash, the smoke from the stubble eye-watering. Through the glass in the door, I saw a man rise from the kitchen table and walk through a hallway into the living room. I have been in law enforcement a long time. In the American South, there is a kind of lawman every decent cop instantly recognizes. His uniform is usually soiled and wrinkled, more like army fatigues or marine utilities, as though he has worked long hours in it. If allowed, he wears a coned cowboy hat. His posture and physicality exude a quiet sense of confidence, whether he's leaning against a rail or gazing idly at something he doesn't like. There is no moral light in his eyes. For reasons you cannot explain, he bears an animus toward the world, particularly toward people of color, no matter how poor or powerless they are.

Jess Bottoms opened the wood door but left the screen latched. His head had the shape of a smoked ham, his shoulders thick and humped like football pads. He wore khaki trousers and suspenders, half-top slip-on boots, and a long-sleeve snap-button white shirt with silver stripes in it. His stomach hung over his belt like thirty pounds of bread dough. He glared at Clete, then at me.

I opened my badge holder. "Dave Robicheaux, Iberia Parish Sheriff's Department, Mr. Bottoms. I'd like to get some information from you regarding a prostitute named Li'l Face Dautrieve."

"Nigger works out of the quarters in Loreauville?" he said.

"Can we come in?" I asked.

"I'm eating."

"It's in your interest," I said.

"What is this, Purcel?" he said.

"It's like he says, Jess. We think you might be in danger."

Bottoms unlatched the screen. "I got people coming over. They arrive, you leave."

He pushed the screen open with his foot and then walked back into the kitchen. The interior of the house looked worn and old, the wallpaper water-stained; the lamps barely gave light. But the kitchen had obviously been refurbished, as though it were the only part of the home that had a purpose. The appliances were new; a flat-screen television was playing on the wall. I heard dogs barking again. Bottoms sat down and dug into a T-bone, chasing it with sips from a bottle of beer.

"You have a kennel?" I said.

His eyes were on the TV. "What's this danger I'm in?"

"Can we turn off the television?" I asked.

"I'm watching a show," he said, his eyes not leaving the screen.

"Li'l Face says you paid her three hundred dollars to pull a train," Clete said.

"I never knew a nigger who didn't lie," he said.

"This is part of a homicide investigation, Mr. Bottoms," I said. "We're not interested in the sex life of your friends. You gave Li'l Face some marked bills. We'd appreciate your telling us where those bills came from."

"I dug them out of your mother's maggoty, insignificant cunt," he said. "Does that answer your question?"

"That's a mouthful," I said.

Clete walked to the television and hit the off switch with the flat of his fist. "What's with those dogs?"

"They're dogs," Bottoms said. "Turn the set on."

"What time do you feed them?" Clete said. "You feed them after you fight them?"

Bottoms cut a piece of steak and lifted it to his mouth and chewed thoughtfully. "How about you suck my dick, Purcel? When you finish, you can tell the Dautrieve girl her black ass is grass."

"I'll be right back, Dave," Clete said. He went out the back door, letting it slam.

"What's he doing?" Bottoms said.

"Search me."

Bottoms looked out the screen at the darkness and the sparks twirling into the sky. "Maybe I can share some information with you," he said.

"If I share some with you?"

"My enterprises tend to be cash-only. I made a mistake giving marked bills to a hooker. I was treating some businessmen. There's nothing illegal in what I was doing."

"Solicitation is not illegal?"

"I gave her money to be an escort. Her and maybe some of her friends. Both white and black ladies. It wasn't a big deal. It's part of the business. Where you been?"

"That remark you made about my mother? I let it pass because you're dealing with an individual who *is* a big deal. I think you know it, too."

"I got to piss. Get yourself a beer out of the refrigerator."

He went into a hallway bathroom and closed the door. I heard him flush the toilet but heard no water run from the faucet. He came back in the kitchen and upended his beer bottle, the foam bubbling inside the neck. I heard a metallic clanking sound out in the dark. He stared at the screen door. "What's he doing out there?"

I didn't have a chance to reply. Clete came through the door with an aluminum boat paddle and slammed it across Bottoms's head, knocking him sideways out of the chair.

"What are you doing?" I said.

"Go see what's in that barn," Clete said. "There's one dog dead in the straw. The others got sores all over them. The stink is awful. Get up, Jess."

"No," Bottoms said, holding his face.

Clete lifted Bottoms to his feet, then drove his head into the counter and beat it on the rim of the sink. Bottoms fell in a heap on the floor, his eyes crossed, his forehead laid open.

"Ease up, Clete," I said.

"Stay out of it, Dave."

Clete picked up the beer bottle and shoved it in the garbage disposal and flipped on the switch. The glass clanked and splintered and screeched and rumbled through the drainpipe. Clete hauled up Bottoms by his belt and wrapped one of his suspender straps around the faucet, then shoved Bottoms's right hand into the disposal unit and rested his thumb on the wall switch. "Try taking out your big boy without fingers, Jess. Where'd the marked money come from?"

"A robbery," Bottoms said, his face the color and texture of someone slipping into shock.

"Not good enough, Jess," Clete said.

"The strap's around my throat. I cain't breathe."

"Try."

Bottoms was crying. I rested my hand on Clete's shoulder. "It's not worth it," I said.

"Back off, Streak."

"I will not," I said, easing myself between him and Bottoms. I slipped the suspender strap from the faucet and lowered Bottoms to the floor.

"Don't mess this up," Clete said.

I squatted down next to Bottoms. "Jess is going to help us. We're also going to have the Humane Society out here. Right, Jess? Are we on the same wavelength?"

But he couldn't answer. He had obviously suffered a concussion or maybe a skull fracture.

"Take your time, partner," I said. "Look on the bright side."

He coughed and spat in a handkerchief, then wiped his face with it. "The guy who did the robbery gave it to a whore. To give her a better life or some bullshit. I took it from the whore and gave some of it to Dautrieve. The guy came in my yard and said I either get every dollar back and give it to him or I'm going somewhere I cain't imagine. But that bitch Dautrieve had already spent some of it."

"What did the guy look like?"

"He was wearing a hood. I couldn't see his face. Except for his eyes. They looked like slits."

I glanced at Clete. "Richetti," he said.

"Who's Richetti?" Bottoms said.

"A guy you want to run from," I said, getting to my feet.

"Don't leave me screwed up in the head like this," Bottoms said. "I got a weak heart. You got to tell me who this guy is. That money is from the Mob? The guy is an assassin? Why you looking at me like that?"

"I hate people who hurt animals," Clete said.

"Pit bulls are made to fight," Bottoms said. "An animal has to earn its keep. It's the law of nature."

Clete slipped his .38 snub-nose from his shoulder holster, flipped out the cylinder, and dumped the rounds into his palm. I knew what he was going to do next. "Let it go, Cletus," I said.

"Wait in the Caddy."

"No."

"I mean it, Dave."

"No," I repeated.

"You're making me angry, big mon."

I looked down at Bottoms. His face was white with blood loss. "What's the last thing the guy in the hood said to you, Mr. Bottoms?"

He had to think. He looked up at me. " 'No matter what you do, you'll eventually be mine.' What's that mean?"

"You don't want to know," Clete said.

He snicked the cylinder back inside the frame of his pistol, then replaced the pistol in his shoulder holster and dropped the loose rounds in his coat pocket. He took out his cell phone and dialed 911 as we went out the door.

"You need to get the Humane Society out to the home of Jess Bottoms in Sunset," he said. "I'm going to call the Associated Press in New Orleans about what I saw here. My name is Clete Purcel. Bring an ambulance for Mr. Bottoms. Out."

Chapter Twenty-six

Friday evening clete and I headed to Baton Rouge to hear Johnny Shondell and Isolde Balangie play and sing at a club by the LSU campus. The drive on the elevated highway across the Atchafalaya Basin is spectacular, particularly when a yellow moon is rising above the miles of black-water bays and flooded trees draped with Spanish moss. But I could not clear my head of the moral conflict I had brought into my life, namely my relationships with Leslie Rosenberg and Penelope Balangie. I was also worried about the degree of damage Clete had done to Jess Bottoms. Felony assault was felony assault.

"You think Bottoms will file charges?" I said.

"No, he'd have to explain too many things. Prostitutes, money laundering, illegal gambling. Plus, he's afraid of Gideon. You shouldn't have stopped me, Dave."

"From forcing him to play Russian roulette?"

"You turned soft on me. You do that with these guys."

"You don't see it, Clete," I said. "We're becoming somebody else. It's like catching a disease."

He swerved in the middle of the causeway to miss a possum. "Wrong. We'll never be like these guys. The Hillside Strangler, the Menendez brothers, Ted Bundy, that's the kind of people you're putting on the same level as us?"

"No," I said, too tired to argue.

"Look at the books on the backseat I got from the library on the Renaissance and the Middle Ages. I just figured out something."

He had changed the subject, as he always did when he felt he had hurt me. "Figured out what?"

"Nothing has changed since back then," he said. "Rich families still use their children to forge alliances. How about the Kennedys auctioning off Jackie to that Greek, the one without a neck. He looked like a frog wearing sunglasses. I heard when he died, it took two months to bury his dong." He took a hit from his flask, then another. "Dave, I've been thinking. As far as Richetti is concerned, I think he's a defective. What's the population of any prison like? Most of the inmates were probably beat on with an ugly stick when they were children."

"Who were the two black kids with blue eyes that I saw with him in Henderson Swamp?"

Clete took another hit from the flask, the cap tinkling against the side. "He probably gave them five bucks to jerk your chain."

The late sun had turned the trees red in the bays. Herons were standing in the shallows, their long legs as slender as soda straws. Clete was driving with one hand, the whiskey having its way, his face warm and serene in the dashboard's glow.

"You still here?" he said.

"The blue in their eyes was just like the blue in the eyes of Leslie Rosenberg's invalid daughter," I said.

"See? There you go. You let your imagination loose. That's what these guys want us to do."

"Which guys?"

"Mark Shondell and the people he's a hump for. A guy like that doesn't have the smarts to amass all that money on his own. I bet that money with the dye on it was his."

"I saw Richetti in a newsreel with Benito Mussolini."

"You saw a guy who looked like him. Here's a more serious subject. What about the Balangie woman? You got feelings for her? You had a weak moment and wanted to get your ashes hauled? What are we talking about here?"

"Guess."

"Okay, so you were on the square. But it's got to end, noble mon. If she's done it with you, she's done it with others. I got a feeling those 'others' are in a landfill or a swamp courtesy of her husband. Sorry, I forgot. He's not her husband."

I stared out the passenger window at the miles of wetlands slipping past us into the darkness, a solitary ember of sunlight dying on the horizon.

"Come in, Earth," he said.

"Leslie has dreams about flames crawling on her skin."

"That's what nightmares are," he said. "Falling from cliffs, mountains crashing on our head, getting buried alive, stuff that early man was afraid of."

"You saw Richetti, Clete. He hung you upside down. That wasn't a dream. Stop lying to yourself."

He put both hands on the wheel. I could see him breathing, his knuckles ridging.

"What are you hiding?" I said.

"One of those books talks about an infamous executioner in the sixteenth century. He burned a lot of Jews. His name was used to scare children. It was Gideon Richetti."

THE CLUB WAS overflowing, strung with Christmas lights, the dance floor packed with young people. Johnny and Isolde were on the stage and having a love affair with the crowd. She looked like a mermaid in her white strapless dress plated with sequins, a nimbus surrounding her hair, her mouth small and red, her tattooed bouquet dry and cool and pale on her shoulder. Johnny was equally radiant, without a line in his face. Who would believe he had recently been in rehab, doubling over with cramps during withdrawal and thinking of life in terms of one minute at a time?

Clete and I had to stand against the back wall. He went to the bar and brought back a whiskey sour for himself and a Dr Pepper with cherries and ice for me. "Do I feel old," he said.

"That's because we're old," I said.

He sipped from his drink, his brow furrowed, and I knew something other than our age was on his mind.

"Guess who's over there in the corner," he said.

I looked through the crowd but couldn't see anyone I knew.

"Mark Shondell and Eddy Firpo," Clete said. "I need to get Firpo alone."

"Bad idea."

"Firpo set me up with Richetti in Key West," he said. "If it hadn't been for Johnny, I would have died in a fire an inch at a time. I still have nightmares."

"What's Firpo going to tell you?"

"Maybe we'll get the gen on Richetti," he said.

"I think you know what Richetti is. You just won't accept what your mind tells you."

"So what is he?" Clete said.

"Maybe he's like a hologram. Maybe all of us are."

"Dave, that's the dumbest thing you've ever said."

He was probably right. But I could already see the lights of regret and pity in his eyes. "Hey, what do I know?" he said. "That's why I don't argue. Remember what Dale Carnegie said? The only argument you win is the one you don't have."

"You know who else said that?"

"No."

"Charlie Manson."

"You're kidding."

"It was one of his come-on lines."

"There goes my whole evening," he said.

I took a drink from my Dr Pepper. It felt cold and bright inside my mouth, the cherries sliding sweet down my throat. But the fact that it tasted good wasn't enough. I could smell the alcohol in the drinks of other people, and feel it reach out and lay its old claim on my soul, as though all the pain I had gone through and all the meetings I had attended meant nothing. But the mysterious and glorious elixir-like smell of alcohol, and the transformative effect it had on my nervous system, and the near-erotic relationship I had with it, were not my only problems. Three men had just come in the side door and taken a table in back. Two of them were not taller than five-six and had the determined, vaguely irritable faces of South European peasants and wore suits that had a shine like Vaseline. I was surprised at how good the third man looked in spite of the beating I had given him in his home theater. He was dressed in a tailored gray suit with thin stripes and a crimson handkerchief folded in the breast pocket and an open-necked purple shirt. He looked straight at me as though I were the only person in the club. I felt my heart drop. It was not out of fear. My guilt about Penelope was like a hot coal in my stomach.

"You sick?" Clete said.

"You and I weren't meant for this kind of life," I said.

"When did you decide that?" he said.

"Just now."

He followed my eyes. "Is that Adonis?" he said.

"In the flesh. Who are the guys with him?"

"I don't know. He imports his hitters. I think we ought to leave."

"No."

"Are you trying to commit suicide?"

"I have to get on the square about this stuff," I said.

"And tell him you bagged his old lady?"

"Don't talk about her like that," I said.

"You know what I'd do if I got hooked up with a woman that beautiful and with that amount of class?"

"No, what?"

"I don't know. I never had the chance."

Which wasn't true. But Clete was Clete, always humble, always protecting my feelings. He took another sip from his whiskey sour, holding it in his mouth so he could savor the taste and let it slide slowly down his throat. I could smell the lemon juice and Jack Daniel's and syrup and maraschino cherry and orange slices on his breath, like a warm gift from the heavens. I felt I was two seconds from ordering one. I coughed slightly and cleared my throat. Before I could speak, Clete said, "Check it out."

Father Julian Hebert was in the midst of the line dancers, his arms spread on the shoulders of two fat women. But I could not keep my eyes off the rows of liquor bottles behind the bar.

"You got that look, Dave," Clete said.

"What look?"

"The one that means you should go to a meeting. I'll go with you."

"I don't know what you're talking about."

He looked at the remainder of his whiskey sour and called the bartender over. "I'm done with this. Give me a glass of milk, will you? My ulcers are on fire."

THE BAND TOOK a break, and I caught Father Julian at the bar. "What are you doing here, partner?" I said.

"What I always do," he said. "Dance."

"Have you seen a few people we've crossed paths with?"

A bartender squirted Coca-Cola in a cup full of ice and handed it to him. Julian waited until the bartender was gone. "You mean Mark Shondell?"

"Yeah. And Adonis Balangie. With his hired help."

"I didn't see Adonis. Is Penelope with him?"

"She's staying at a hotel in New Iberia, out by the four-lane," I said. I felt my heart swelling, my collar shrinking on my throat. "I've gotten involved with her."

Julian looked out at the dance floor, his egg-shaped face composed, every hair on his head in place. He was wearing jeans and loafers and a long-sleeve workout shirt. I tried not to think about the loneliness and the longings that must live inside him.

"Marcel LaForchette took his life in your living room," he said. "I know the kind of man you are, Dave. You blame yourself for what others do. But this time maybe you reached out to the wrong party."

"You said Penelope was a good woman."

"Some historians say Lucrezia Borgia was charitable to a fault."

"That just sent a shudder through me," I said.

But I had lost his attention. He was staring at Mark Shondell's table.

"What is it?" I said.

"Shondell bothers me. The people he brings to New Iberia bother me. What he has probably done bothers me." His face looked as though the oxygen and the netlike reflections of the disco ball had been sucked from the room.

"What has Shondell done?" I asked.

His jaw flexed. "I don't have the evidence. It involves the very innocent. I've already said more than I should. I don't have my glasses. Who's that man with him?"

"Eddy Firpo. He's Johnny Shondell's manager."

"He's a lawyer?"

"How'd you know?" I said.

"I've seen him in New Orleans. He's an anti-Semite. He also represents child porn vendors."

"Mark Shondell is a child molester?"

"I don't know what he is. I'd hate to find out."

"I need your help, Julian. Everybody in Iberia Parish is afraid of Mark Shondell, no matter what they pretend. Tell me what you know."

The expression on his mouth was bitter. "Get away from the Balangie family. Spend time with your daughter. Isn't she coming home for Christmas?"

"She's on a school trip to Paris."

"Join her," he said.

Johnny and Isolde had gone back onstage. Julian was staring across the dance floor at Mark Shondell and Eddy Firpo's table, his eyelids fluttering.

"What are you thinking?" I said.

"I'd like to tear them both apart. Limb and joint." He walked away from the bar, swaying slightly, as though his gyroscope had stopped working.

Isolde and Johnny went into Dale and Grace's version of "I'm Leaving It All Up to You." When they finished, the crowd went wild.

I couldn't find Clete. I looked in the restroom and checked the Caddy. It was parked just where we had left it. My mouth was dry, my hands stiff when I tried to close them, my heart racing for no reason; a pressure band was tightening around the right side of my head, a prelude to hitting the deck, getting sloshed, or bursting a vessel in the brain.

Then I saw Clete smoking a cigarette by the side of the club. He was grinning, his teeth as big as tombstones, his porkpie hat slanted on his forehead, the Clete Purcel of old—unafraid, irreverent, always slipping the punch and shining on the worst the world could throw at him.

My cell phone throbbed in my pants pocket. I put it to my ear. "Hello?" I said.

Clete saw my expression when I heard the voice on the other end. The joy went out of his face as though someone had clicked off a light.

"DO YOU KNOW who this is?" the voice said.

"Your voice is not one people forget," I replied.

"Are you mocking me?"

"No, sir, I know better than that."

Clete flipped away his cigarette and began walking toward me. The front door of the bar was open, and I could hear Johnny and Isolde singing "Red Sails in the Sunset."

"Look, Mr. Richetti—" I began.

"Be quiet," he said. "I need to ask a favor of you."

"Sir?"

"Tell the Jewish girl I'm sorry."

"Which Jewish girl?"

"Her child is crippled."

"You're sorry about what?"

"She'll know," he said.

"Why don't you tell her yourself?"

"I'm ashamed. I would frighten her also."

"Buddy, you're one for the books."

"You and your friend Mr. Purcel must leave the nightclub."

"Why?"

"Evil men are there."

"*You're* talking about evil? The guy who tried to light up my best friend?"

Suddenly, the transmission was filled with static. "You're breaking up," I said.

"Don't underestimate what you're dealing with, Mr. Robicheaux."

"You mean you or these evil guys you're talking about?"

"It's not my choice to be what I am," he said.

"That's a hard sell. You have free will, right?" All I could hear was the wind in my other ear. "Still there?" I said.

"Yes, I have free will, and I misused it."

"That takes us to the heart of the matter. What exactly are you, sir?"

He cleared his throat with a sound like scrofulous matter breaking loose inside a clogged sewer pipe. Then Clete grabbed the cell phone out of my hand and put it to his ear. "If this is who I think it is, be advised that I'm going to kick a telephone pole up your ass." Clete waited for a response, his eyes on mine. He took the phone away from his ear and looked at it. "He must have hung up."

"Do you realize what you just did?" I said.

A vein was pulsing in his temple; his eyes were cups of sorrow. "I want to blow up somebody's shit."

Chapter Twenty-seven

WE WENT BACK inside and stood at the bar. Clete ordered a lemonade. Johnny and Isolde were singing "The Wild Side of Life." It wasn't Swamp Pop, but nonetheless it was the flagship of every honky-tonk ballad ever written.

Clete drank half his lemonade in one long tilt of the glass. I had the feeling he had spiked it with his flask. "Sorry I blew it with Richetti," he said.

"He'll be back."

"Think so?"

"Unto the grave, if he has his way."

Clete gazed at the bandstand and the multicolored lights playing on Isolde's sequined dress. "Jesus, I love that song. It's like a hymn."

"It was. The melody is from 'The Great Speckled Bird.'"

He finished his drink and this time ordered a whiskey sour; he gazed across the dance floor. "Adonis is pinning us."

"Let him."

"I don't know how I defended that guy," Clete said. "Maybe because he was in the 173rd. How could he sell out his stepdaughter like that?"

"A fraud is a fraud, a bum is a bum. There's no mystery about human behavior."

"I'm going to have a talk with Adonis."

"I thought you wanted to leave him alone," I said.

"That was before Richetti called. Something's about to go down. I think Adonis knows what it is. Otherwise he wouldn't have those two button men with him."

"It's your call," I said.

I followed him across the dance floor to Adonis's table. Both his people had the dark, lean faces of men who work in extreme heat; neither one looked directly at us.

"How's it going, Adonis?" I said.

His hands formed a pyramid; he tapped the ends of his fingers together. I realized his face was heavily made up. I knew that at some point I would pay a price for the beating I had given him.

"Fine, Mr. Robicheaux," he said. "And you? Seen my wife lately?"

"Cut the cutesy routine, Adonis," Clete said. "We just had Gideon Richetti on the phone. I think you and him and Mark Shondell and Eddy Firpo are all hooked up. I also think Richetti is just a guy, a world-class creep but flesh and blood, not some evil spirit delivering telegrams from a pizza parlor run by Leonardo da Vinci or whoever."

The eyes of the two bodyguards took on a muddy, troubled look, as though an element had entered the situation that they were not prepared to deal with. "How about it, fellas?" Clete said. "You *capisci* who Gideon Richetti is?"

Both men looked at Adonis like sentinels waiting for the go-ahead.

"My employees aren't part of this, Mr. Purcel," Adonis said.

"You pimped out your stepdaughter," Clete said. "Do these guys know that? How do you say 'pimp' in greaseball?"

"Time for you to leave our table, sir," Adonis said.

"You tell Eddy Firpo I'll be dialing him up," Clete said.

"I have nothing to do with Firpo, and neither do Isolde and Johnny Shondell," Adonis said. "They got out of their contract with him."

"So that puts you in control?" I said.

"I own restaurants and fisheries and an olive oil company in Italy," Adonis said. "Ta-ta, gentlemen." He jiggled his fingers at us.

I cupped my hand around Clete's bicep. It felt like concrete. "I talked with Richetti tonight, Adonis," I said. "He showed concern for our safety. That means his alliances have changed. I don't know if that's of interest to you or not."

A single strand of oily mahogany-dark hair hung on his forehead. He touched a place on his cheekbone where I had kicked him. "Would you repeat that, please?"

"I like your threads," I said. "Keep fighting the good fight." I gave him a thumbs-up and went back to the bar.

Clete joined me seconds later. He was wheezing with laughter. "You pissed in his brain. The guy won't sleep for a week." He kept laughing and snorting at the same time.

"You want some gumbo?" I said.

"These guys got gumbo?"

"You bet," I said.

"Maybe there's some sunshine in all this."

That was Clete.

TEN MINUTES LATER, Clete finished his gumbo and washed it down with a Bud and wiped his mouth with a paper napkin. "Do you know Louisiana has the highest rate of heart and vascular disease in the country?"

"You're carrying on the tradition?"

"It beats a bowl of cornflakes in North Dakota."

Isolde and Johnny invited people from the dance floor and tables to come up on the bandstand and join them in singing Danny & the Juniors' signature song, "Rock 'n Roll Is Here to Stay." Isolde danced with a former governor. A black man with taps on his shoes walked on his hands across the bandstand. Someone in back climbed on a table and let go with his own tenor sax. The entire building was shaking. But inside all the celebration and the innocence and happiness of the crowd, I saw the players in our medieval tale moving about like characters marked for death, distracted by a tolling of bells that only they heard.

I saw Mark Shondell and Eddy Firpo go to the men's room; Father Julian disappeared in back also; then Adonis's two men left their table and walked through the crowd as though searching for someone.

"I got to hit the head," Clete said.

"I just saw Firpo and Mark Shondell go in there."

"That's got nothing to do with my kidneys," he said. "I'll be right back."

"Give it a few minutes, Clete. Don't crowd the batter on this one."

"You worry too much. The Bobbsey Twins from Homicide are back in town. Wish I was thirty years younger. Look at the women in this place." He pulled on his dong. "Go, Tigers."

Then he was gone. I looked at my watch. It was 10:17. I saw Gideon Richetti standing to the left of the bandstand, and at first I thought I was having a hallucination. But he had the same height and athletic physique as Gideon and was wearing a hooded Tulane jacket and tight leather gloves, the kind a race-car driver or a speed-bag boxer might wear, his head and face buried inside the bowl of shadow created by his hood.

I headed for him, knocking through a couple of tables. People in silvery conical hats were forming a bunny-hop line. The man with the tenor sax had climbed up on the bandstand and was blasting out Harry James's "Back Beat Boogie," the drummer tearing the seams in the shoulders of his jacket, his drumsticks a blur.

"Gideon!" I yelled above the heads of the dancers.

He turned his back and began working his way to the fire exit. He was no doubt a powerful man, one that made you think of a primitive creature lifting stones into place on a medieval structure.

"Richetti! It's Dave Robicheaux!" I shouted. "I just want to talk."

I almost knocked a young woman to the floor and had to grab her and apologize to both her and her boyfriend. They were kind and full of smiles, and I felt like a fool. Gideon was almost to the fire exit. I had a .22 auto Velcro-wrapped to my right ankle. If I got a clear shot in the parking lot, I was going to drop him and worry about legalities later. Not rational? Neither were any of the things that had happened to Clete Purcel, Marcel LaForchette, and me.

Gideon crashed out the door. I followed him into an alley that stank of garbage and out to the parking lot of a loan company. I stopped long enough to pull my .22 auto from my ankle holster. He ran under a streetlamp and looked over his shoulder. This time there was no mistaking his identity. I could even make out his bump of a nose and eyes that were like watermelon seeds.

I could have fired justifiably somewhere below his waist. It would have not been legally justified, but morally, I thought I had the right. We needed Richetti strapped in custody. Or strapped to a table in a medical lab. If I missed, the round would probably hit concrete and ricochet against the front of a building. However, here's the problem in that kind of situation: You have somewhere between one and two seconds to make a judgment. The wrong choice can kill an innocent person. The wrong choice can also ruin your life. Ask a cop who has stacked time in a mainline joint. You do not have to die to go to hell.

I aimed the .22 auto at his buttocks, then lowered it and let it hang from my hand. Gideon Richetti disappeared into the darkness. I put away the .22 and walked back to the fire exit, which was still open, then heard a woman scream inside. The music stopped, and the entire building became quiet. Coincidentally, the woman I had almost knocked down was the first out of the exit, her face dilated, her hands waving meaninglessly at the air as though she couldn't breathe. Her mouth was an oval, but no sound came out.

"What is it?" I asked.

"That poor man," she said, a tear slipping from each eye. She tried to speak again but began hiccupping and couldn't stop.

I TOOK OUT MY badge and held it over my head and worked my way through the huge half-circle of people around the entrance to the men's room. Eddy Firpo had made it out of the toilet stall and fallen through the doorway onto the floor, where he now lay on his back, his trousers and belt and jockey shorts around his ankles, his shirtfront soaked in blood. The wound across his throat was the kind usually inflicted by an instrument such as a box cutter or a barber's razor. A rubber tourniquet was tied on his upper left arm. The syringe was still in the vein, gray sediment and backed-up blood inside the barrel.

I asked everyone to move back, then knelt by the body. There were no defensive wounds that I could see. His pigtail had been sawed from his scalp and stuffed in his mouth; his gold cross and chain were gone. Three vintage postage stamps inside a mashed cellophane container were pasted to the sole of one shoe. I knew nothing about stamp collecting, but these stamps were crisp and delicate and lovely in design and must have been expensive. What were the odds of their ending up next to a public toilet bowl where Firpo happened to step on them?

Two cops, a medic, and a fireman were trying to get through the crowd as gently as they could. Father Julian, Clete, and Adonis and his button men were nowhere in sight. Mark Shondell was comforting a woman who had almost been knocked down by Firpo when he burst out the door.

Somebody dropped a raincoat on Firpo's body. Shondell patted the young woman's back. He had become the protector, the man above the fray, the man of all seasons. Her hair was inches from his face. I saw his nostrils swell, his lips press together. Then he twisted his wrist so he could see the time on his watch. I wondered how one man could fool so many people for so many years.

Chapter Twenty-eight

THERE WERE NO witnesses to the murder. Firpo must have been seated in a stall shooting up when his executioner entered the room. What happened after that was a matter of speculation. The stall door was neither locked nor broken. Would Firpo sit on a commode and shoot up without sliding the bolt? That made no sense. Which meant he probably knew the killer and opened the door of his own volition.

Several people in the nightclub had motivation to punch Firpo's ticket. Maybe financial need had forced Adonis Balangie to pimp out his stepdaughter to Firpo and Mark Shondell, and Adonis had sent one of his Sicilian gumballs into the stall to even the score. The vicious nature of the killing, the sawed-off pigtail stuffed in the mouth, had the ritualistic overtones of the traditional Black Hand—also known as the Mafia—which had been in New Orleans since 1890, the year they murdered the police commissioner.

Mark Shondell was another candidate. Firpo was a hype. Shondell probably blamed him for getting Johnny on the spike and for Johnny running off with Isolde. Also, Shondell was probably Firpo's silent business partner, and perhaps Firpo's company assets would transfer automatically to Shondell, who would have no trouble finding a psychopath with a box cutter.

Then there was Gideon Richetti. There seemed to be no end to his potential. Unfortunately, we had no idea who or even *what* he was. I wanted to dismiss him as a meltdown. But like all categorizations, that didn't slide down the pipe. Truth be known, I wondered if I was having a nervous collapse.

As I sorted through all the people who might want to take Firpo off the board, I couldn't exclude Clete. There had been slips in Clete's life. He had taken ten grand from the Mob and killed a federal witness, although the shooting was an accident. More significantly, he experienced psychotic episodes that could visit unimaginable levels of rage on a misogynist or predator or an abuser of the elderly or someone who was cruel to animals. Plus, he daily nursed his hatred of neo-Nazis and was convinced they were going to have at one least one more historical grab at the brass ring.

Earlier in the evening he'd said he wanted to blow up someone's shit. His favorite banzai cocktail was a jigger of Jack lowered into a mug of cold beer. I could imagine Clete throwing a couple in the tank and going after the man who had arranged for him to be tortured to death by Gideon. In fact, I wondered why he hadn't already done it.

The last name on the list was the one I hated to think about, not because I believed he was guilty but because he was too honest, the kind of man the system can grind into pulp.

Look, this is how the system works. Or, rather, how it doesn't work. The law is usually enforced only upon the people who are available. The members of the Pool are always close by. The Pool consists of recidivists and dysfunctional people who skipped toilet training and couldn't discuss the recipe for ice water. The recidivists think their rap sheets have the historical importance of the Magna Carta; their jailhouse tats are the equivalent of military citations. They take pride in their first-name relationship with cops. If they aren't guests of the gray-bar hotel chain or at the least don't have a sheet, no one would know they ever existed.

What's the point? The system was created to handle only certain kinds of people. If you are on the square and wander into it, chances are it will cannibalize you.

Excuse my digression. My real problem was the postage stamps on Firpo's shoe. I would have to show them to the locals. I would also have to tell them where I thought they came from.

Just as the first homicide detective arrived, I saw Father Julian standing by the front entrance and walked over to him. "Let's go outside," I said.

"Why?" he said, looking at the paramedics bringing in the gurney.

"It's important."

"Who was hurt?"

"Eddy Firpo. He wasn't hurt. He was murdered."

"The lawyer with Mark Shondell?"

"Come outside. Don't argue. We don't have much time."

Naturally, he resisted. I took him by the arm and walked him through the door. The wind was cold and damp and smelled of the chain of lakes north of the campus. "Were you carrying some collectible postage stamps tonight?" I said.

"No."

"You didn't buy some in Baton Rouge for your collection?"

"Why are you asking me this?"

"There were three stamps stuck to Firpo's shoe."

"What does that have to do with me?"

"How many people in Baton Rouge bring valuable historical postage stamps into a nightclub?"

"Are you saying I'm involved with this man's death?"

"My opinion is irrelevant," I said. "It's those cops in there we need to worry about. If there's anything you need to tell me, now's the time."

"What did the stamps look like?"

"I saw some Latin or Italian words on them. One stamp was postmarked 1891."

The crow's-feet at the corners of his eyes drained of color. "I didn't bring any stamps into this club."

"Okay," I said.

"Okay, what?" he said.

"I believe you. If the cops question you, tell them what you just said. Then say nothing else. If they press you, tell them you want a lawyer."

"I don't need one," he said. "I didn't do anything wrong."

"Why did you react when I mentioned the 1891 stamp?"

He paused. "I have an 1891 Monaco stamp at home."

"Get in your car and drive back to New Iberia," I said. "Don't talk to anyone until I call you."

"What's happening here, Dave?"

"Everything will be fine," I replied. "I promise."

Want to know what a pompous jerk sounds like? I had just out-done myself.

Chapter Twenty-nine

I TOLD THE BATON Rouge homicide detectives what I had seen but left out any mention of Julian. The next morning, which was Saturday, I drove to the hotel where Penelope was staying. I used the lobby phone and asked her to have breakfast with me in the dining room.

"Your voice," she said.

"What about it?"

"You sound tense."

"It's a lovely day," I said. "Toggle on down."

"Toggle?" she said.

Fifteen minutes later, she walked into the dining room. She had on a pink sundress and a broad straw hat, the kind Scarlett O'Hara might have worn. "Why the flowers?" she said.

I handed her the bouquet of roses I had just bought at the florist not far from the Shadows. "Let's order, then talk," I said.

The waitress came to our table and wrote down our order, then smiled at the roses and left.

"So tell me," Penelope said.

"Would you like to get married?"

"With whom?"

I looked out the window at the cars entering and leaving the four-lane. "Take a guess."

"You?"

"I've never had to seek humility," I said. "It always finds me."

"You're asking me to marry you?"

I watched the waitress filling our coffeepot at the service counter.

She had auburn hair and the strong young body of a working-class Cajun girl.

"Unless you're thinking of doing something this weekend," I said.

"Because your conscience bothers you?"

"Good enough for a romance, good enough for a ring," I said.

"I appreciate what you're doing, Dave, but we may not be right for each other."

"It was just a thought."

"I don't think I've ever known anyone like you."

"You've probably been lucky," I replied. I put a twenty-dollar bill on the tablecloth.

"You're leaving?"

"Yep, see you around."

I walked through the revolving glass door and out into the sunshine. But not fast enough.

"You're not going to just walk away from me like that," she said at my back.

"No offense intended," I said.

"No offense? You drop flowers in a woman's face, then give her five seconds to decide if she wants to live a lifetime with you?"

"Maybe I'll have a short lifespan."

"You're doing this to get rid of me, aren't you?"

"No, but I wonder why you've lived all these years with a Mafia gutter rat. An uptown one, but still a gutter rat."

"I've told you. Others are dependent upon our families."

"I think that's pure rot. You're a grand and charitable woman who befriended a man in a time of need. It was an honor to be part of your life."

"Don't go."

"Got to do it. You deserve a better man than the likes of me."

But I couldn't move, and I didn't know why.

"Second thoughts?"

"You're one of the most beautiful women I've ever seen. I'd like to kill Adonis Balangie. Know why?"

"No."

"I know he's had you. I also know you've lied about it. It's not the man, it's the lie that killed us, Penelope."

I got in my truck and dropped the keys. I couldn't put the key in the ignition. When I finally drove away, I looked in the rearview mirror. She was still standing in front of the hotel, the brim of her hat wilted on either side of her face. I don't think I ever felt worse in my life.

CHRISTMAS CAME AND went. The days were warm and cool at the same time, and at night, electrified white clouds of smoke billowed from the stacks on the sugar mill. The weather seemed more a harbinger of spring than the real Louisiana winter that awaited us, one of dreary rain-darkened days that can seep into the soul.

My adopted daughter, Alafair, came home from France, then returned early to her part-time job in the bookstore at Reed. Penelope did not call. I grieved that I'd hurt her. The breakup was about Adonis, not Pen. No matter what she claimed about her marital status, she had lived with him for years. Furthermore, he was a dangerous and, I think, jealous man, and if he thought another man was taking her away, I believed he might kill her.

But my concerns with the Balangie family were about to fade quickly and be replaced by others. In mid-January, Father Julian called me at the office. "There're two homicide detectives from Baton Rouge here. They say they have a search warrant."

"For what?"

"It's about my stamps."

"Put one of the detectives on."

The man who took the phone breathed heavily into the mouthpiece, like a heavy smoker or a consumptive. "Detective Niles," he said. "What can I h'ep you with?"

The accent was North Louisiana or perhaps Mississippi.

"This is Detective Robicheaux," I said. "Did you guys check in with us before you executed the search warrant?"

"We're not required to do that."

"Most law enforcement people consider it a professional courtesy."

"That's why you blew the Firpo homicide scene before I could interview you?" he said.

He had me. "I'm on my way, and I'll be at your disposal."

"Noted," he said. "And not needed."

He broke the connection.

I checked out a cruiser and was at Julian's house in fifteen minutes. The screen door hung open. I stepped up on the gallery. The living room was a wreck. Through the hallway, I saw a big man in a brown suit leaning into the refrigerator, rattling things inside. His head looked as hard and large as a bowling ball. He held his fedora in one hand. His partner was flipping the mattress off Julian's bed. Julian was watching both detectives at the same time, his face tight with anger.

"What's with you guys?" I said to the detective in the brown suit.

He turned around, holding a saucer with four sugar cubes on it. "What's this look like?" he said.

"Sugar cubes?" I replied.

He tilted them off the saucer into a Ziploc. "We'll take them to the lab."

"You're talking about acid? In the refrigerator of a priest?"

"I know your reputation, Robicheaux," he said. "I used to have a drinking problem myself. I know you just got reinstated. Leave us alone and we'll leave you alone."

"Why the search warrant on Father Julian?" I asked, hoping they had nothing of evidentiary consequence.

"There were some postage stamps stuck on Firpo's shoe," he said. "The stamps had the good father's prints on them. His prints were also on file with the NCIC. Two federal busts for trespassing at the School of the Americas."

Julian took a step toward the detective. "Those stamps were stolen from my house. Those sugar cubes aren't mine, either."

"You're sure, Julian?" I said.

"I saw the other detective open the refrigerator earlier," he said. "It looked like he put something inside."

"How about it?" I said to Niles.

"Maybe the maid left the cubes in there," Niles said. "But tell me this: Why didn't the good father report the theft of the stamps?"

Julian started to speak, but I lifted my hand. "Father Julian gives odd jobs to people who have been in the system. He figures they've got enough grief without his adding to it."

Niles didn't answer. He was a hard man to read. Were he and his partner on a pad? Or was he just a burnt-out old-time flatfoot who had smoked too many cigarettes?

"What's your opinion, Detective Niles?" I said.

"Firpo was mixed up with child porn," he said. "Maybe Father Hebert did everybody a good deed. Maybe he's like us. He's tired of the degenerates running society. Maybe he decided to put his thumb on the scale."

I glanced through the front door. An Iberia Parish cruiser was pulling onto the grass. Two people were in front, one a blond woman. She got out of the cruiser and stretched her arms. She was wearing navy blue slacks and a starched white shirt; her gold badge hung from a lanyard on her chest. I stepped out on the gallery.

Carroll LeBlanc, the pro tem sheriff, got out from behind the wheel and gazed at me over the top of the cruiser.

"Why the grin?" I said.

"Guess who your new boss is," he replied.

Helen Soileau, my old Homicide partner, walked up the steps. She opened the screen and let it slam behind her. "What's this crap about two Baton Rouge homicide roaches who didn't check in?" she said.

"Long time no see, Soileau," Niles said.

"Not long enough," she replied. "And it's Sheriff Soileau to you."

Niles's partner came out of the bedroom. He had a hooked nose and a head that looked like it had been squeezed inside a waffle iron. "I'll be," he said.

"Pardon?" she said.

"Weren't you a meter maid at NOPD?" he said.

She looked at the disarray in the living room, then at Niles. "Y'all want to explain this?"

"Nothing to explain," Niles said. "Father Hebert fled a homicide scene in Baton Rouge. Some collectible stamps belonging to him were on the vic's body."

"So you came down here and tore up his house?"

"No, we searched it," Niles said. He held up the Ziploc. "This was in the refrigerator. There's discoloration in each cube."

"Get out of here," she said. "Take your shit with you."

My cell phone vibrated in my pocket. As I answered, Helen went to her cruiser, slid her baton from the front seat, and smashed out a side window in the unmarked car driven by the two detectives.

Niles stared through the screen door. "Are you drunk?" he said.

She walked back inside and tapped him with the baton in the middle of his forehead, hard enough to leave a white spot. "File a complaint with the DA. I'll give you his private number."

But I was no longer paying attention to Helen and her behavior. I had seen her take down too many bad guys, some of them cops, some of then psychotic, and I knew how it would end. I was listening to Leslie Rosenberg on my cell phone.

"I had a nightmare and was burning to death," she said. "When I woke up, there was ash in my hair. A green man was in the yard."

"Start over," I said.

"I'm not crazy. I could smell smoke in my clothes. I know him. From long ago."

"Where are you?"

"In my cottage."

"I'll be there in a few minutes," I said.

"I didn't tell you the rest of it. I confronted him. He tried to touch me."

"Where is he now?"

"Looking at me. Through the screen."

I took the cell phone from my ear. "Helen, I want you to listen to this."

"I'm a little busy right now."

I walked down on the grass and shoved the detective named Niles.

"Do what you're told and haul your worthless ass out of here," I said. Then I gave Helen my cell phone. "Now listen."

I HEADED UP OLD Jeanerette Road to the self-help center run by the activist nuns and the cottage where Leslie and her daughter were now living. Leslie was on the gallery when I arrived. The tide was in, and the bayou was high and dark and running through the cane-brakes on the bank. I wondered if Gideon had hidden somewhere along the bank or escaped in a boat. That he had appeared at the cottage in broad daylight indicated that he had become bolder and perhaps more dangerous.

I got out of the cruiser. "Is your daughter all right?"

"She's sleeping," Leslie said. "The man just left." She looked at her watch. "He said he'll call you on my phone in approximately seven minutes. He said you left your cell phone with the sheriff. How could he know that?"

"I have no idea."

"Who is he, Dave?"

"Gideon Richetti."

"I don't mean his name. Who is he? *What* is he?"

"He didn't try to explain himself?"

"He cried."

"Cried? With tears?"

"He said he could never make up for what he did to me. That was when he reached out his hand. It looked like a claw. It had scales on it. The nails were pointed. I could smell him. The odor was like mold."

"Did anyone else see him?"

"No one. You don't believe me?"

"You bet I do."

"He said something that's really crazy—that I'm already part of his world. He said I leave my body in the dark hours, but I have no memory of the deeds I do. He said eventually, my body will go with my spirit, and then I'll be gone entirely."

"What did you tell him?"

"That I can't leave. That I have Elizabeth to take care of. That's when I called you."

Her cell phone chimed inside her wash-faded jeans. She worked it out of her pocket and opened it. "You want to take it or not?" she said.

I WALKED DOWN TO the water with the phone to my ear. "Is that you, Mr. Robicheaux?" Gideon said.

"You're scaring the hell out of a nice lady, bud."

"That's not my intention."

"My friend Clete Purcel may be in a lot of trouble for busting up a guy you dragged into our lives."

"Mr. Bottoms?"

"Correct," I said.

"He's no longer a problem for either you or Mr. Purcel."

"What did you do to him?"

"He's not your business any longer. The Jewish woman is. She's halfway between my world and yours. It was she who saved Mr. Purcel's life."

"You cut this stuff out. I don't want to hear it anymore. Father Julian may have had LSD in his icebox. Did you have anything to do with that?"

"I'm his friend."

"I don't think he would see it that way."

"The problem you have, Mr. Robicheaux, is your lack of belief. You do not trust your eyes or ears. That's going to change."

"How?" I said.

"I will prove to you how all this is real. On Bayou Teche there is a special place where an event occurred with your father and you many years ago. You have never told anyone else about either the place or the event, have you?"

"No."

"Go there at eleven o'clock tonight."

"Hold on."

"What is it?"

"Are you from hell?"

"Those definitions are relative."

"How so?"

"In Vietnam, after you called upon Puff the Magic Dragon, did you feel pride as flames leaped from the straw homes of peasants who harvested rice with their hands? Did their screams fill you with glee? Did you smile upon your work to see?"

I dropped the phone and lost my balance and fell on one knee when I tried to pick it up.

Chapter Thirty

AT ELEVEN THAT night I walked along the edge of the Teche to a live oak that was over two hundred years old, not far from the old Burke home. It was here, on V-J Day in 1945, that I first fished with my father. He was a huge, illiterate man who fought in saloons for fun and racked pipe on the monkey board high above a drilling rig on the Gulf of Mexico, under the stars, the wind in his face, the waves crashing below, fearless unto the day the drill punched into an early pay sand and the casing blew out of the hole and Big Aldous Robicheaux clipped his safety belt onto the Geronimo line and leaped into the dark, never to be seen again.

But I no longer dwelled on the tragedy of my father and mother, and the deprivation and violence and loneliness that defined their lives. Rather than thinking of Big Aldous's last moments sliding down the guy wire as the rig melted and toppled with him, I thought of this spot on the bayou where he taught me how to fish. He had bought me a cane pole and a balsa-wood bobber and a weight fashioned out of a perforated .36-caliber lead ball he bought from a colored man for twenty cents. It was a fine gift to receive, but I could catch no fish with it, although I baited the hook first with crickets, then night crawlers, and finally red wigglers.

In my disgust, I swung the weight, the hook, and the bobber out in the center of the lily pads and fouled the hook in the roots below. I was ready to throw my pole in the water. Big Aldous was smoking a hand-rolled cigarette, blowing the smoke into the wind. He flicked the cigarette in the bayou. "Don't be getting mad, no," he said. "You got to outt'ink the fish, you."

I was lost.

"See, you done put your hands on the bait, Davie," he said. "The fish can smell you. So you got to change the smell."

"How do I do that?" I said.

"Spit on your bait. What you t'ink?"

I lifted the poor drowned worm on my hook from the water and spat on it, then swung over the current. The bobber floated downstream about one foot and plunged out of sight. I pulled up the cane pole with such violence that I broke it in half and flung a goggle-eye perch into a limb above my head. My father had to borrow a rake from the Burke home and comb the fish out of the tree.

I don't mean to tire others with this account. But everyone has a private cathedral that he earns, a special place to which he returns when the world is too much late and soon, and loss and despair come with the rising of the sun. For me it was the little dry mudbank on which I now stood, the tide rippling past me, the ducks murmuring and ruffling their wings among the cattails and flooded bamboo.

Then a giant wobbling soap bubble of incandescence descended on the bayou, bent and distorted, metamorphic, its colors changing from pink to yellow and red and pink again, as though it were swirling with fire that contained no heat. In the center was the galleon Clete and I had seen before, the oars dipping into the Teche, but this time Gideon was standing in the bow, beckoning. "Don't be afraid," he called.

"No, I will not board your ship, sir," I said.

"You must."

"I came as you asked," I said. "Please do not act in an authoritarian fashion."

A boarding hatch opened on the gunwale, and a ramp slid from the deck to the bank. I found myself drawn up the ramp, inside the bubble, the light as tangible as tentacles on my skin.

Gideon was not wearing a cowl. His tiny ears and nose and the reptilian tightness of the skin on his face and skull were frightening.

Down below, between the hull and the deck on both sides of the ship, were row after row of men chained to their benches and oars, some dozing with their heads on their chests, others with the expressions you would associate with infants ripped from their mothers' grasp.

In the midst of the oarsmen sat Jess Bottoms, his feet bare, chains attached to his wrists and ankles. His hair was barbered and his clothes were clean. His face was stupefied. He was examining his chains as though he could not understand their presence on his body.

"Sometimes decades pass before these fellows know where they are," Gideon said. "In reality, all of us are outside of time. There is no past, present, or future. The future you and Mr. Purcel have is already taking place. It will just take a little while for you to find your way to it."

"I don't wish to talk about the future," I said. "I don't want to be on board your ship, either."

"You're just a visitor, Mr. Robicheaux. People such as you don't make the cut."

"Then why am I here?"

"I need you to help me."

"Sir?"

"I was used to kill many people. I have no peace. The one I grieve over most is Leslie Rosenberg. She was totally innocent of any crime. I hate what I have done."

"Any crimes you have committed were done with your own consent. I suggest you lose the ashes-and-sackcloth routine."

"You won't help me?"

"I'm not a theologian. Call up Father Julian."

"Evil people are about to hurt him."

"Mark Shondell?" I said.

"Don't speak to me about the Shondells."

"You were at his house," I said. "Marcel LaForchette saw you there."

"I will not discuss this."

"You worked for him. Why denounce him now?"

"Don't tempt me, Mr. Robicheaux."

"Then don't be a hypocrite."

"Be gone with you," he said.

"Did you kill Firpo?"

"I kill no one. They kill themselves."

"That's a lie," I said.

"I can do you great injury."

"The words of a bully," I said. "I thought better of you."

His skin and the scales on it were luminous with an oily sweat. He raised his hand as though to strike me. I knew I was in mortal danger but could not move. Suddenly, Gideon and the galleon and the poor devils on it disappeared, and I was on the bank, deep in the shadow of the live oak, the air dank and cold and throbbing with frogs.

I walked home like a drunk man and woke in the morning face-down on the couch, my clothes on, the soles of my shoes rimmed with mud.

IT WASN'T EASY to tell Helen Soileau all this, but I did. As she listened, she flicked a ballpoint pen in a circle on her ink blotter. She had started her career as a meter maid at NOPD and had ended up my partner in Homicide in New Iberia. I believed several people lived inside Helen, both male and female, all of them complex. She was a good cop and a brave and loyal friend but also mercurial and sometimes violent.

After I finished, she propped her cheek and chin at an angle on her palm, as a teenager might. "There are a couple of things that bother me about your account, bwana. Number one, you said this character Gideon mentioned Vietnam and calling for air support."

"That's right. He knew things about me he could have no knowledge of."

"But he used a phrase I've heard you use before: 'Did he smile upon his work to see?' Where's that from?"

"William Blake's poem about the nature of evil."

"You and Gideon read the same books?"

"That's a possibility," I said.

"The other part that bothers me is you say you walked home like a drunk man."

"I haven't been drinking, Helen."

"When was your last drink?"

"Nineteen months ago."

She dropped her ballpoint in a drawer. "This story doesn't just sound crazy, it scares the shit out of me," she said. "I have to be honest, Streak. I think you're having a nervous breakdown."

"Is Clete having one? Is Leslie Rosenberg having one?"

"Ever hear of mass hysteria? How about Salem, 1692?"

"I told you what I saw and heard," I said. "Do with it as you wish. I'll see you later."

"This morning I heard from Baton Rouge PD," she said. "The sugar cubes from Father Julian's refrigerator contained LSD. Second item: A friend of mine who works in the diocesan office says two anonymous callers have accused Father Julian of child molestation. A third caller said he tried to rape her."

"That's ridiculous," I said.

"They have to deal with it. Father Julian has pissed off a lot of people, particularly these right-to-life fanatics."

"I think this is Mark Shondell at work," I said.

"Let Father Julian fight his own battles, bwana."

"Great attitude," I said.

"Have you ever considered the possibility Julian may not be innocent?"

"He killed Eddy Firpo? Stop it."

"How did his stamps end up on Firpo's shoe?" she said.

"They were planted."

"You don't know that."

"Glad I'm on the side of the good guys," I said.

I walked out of the office. She wadded up a piece of paper and threw it at my back. I walked back inside and picked it up and placed it on her desk. "Shame on you, Helen," I said.

THAT NIGHT I ate by myself at Clementine's. Outside, dust was swirling out of the streets, paper boxes and pieces of newspaper bouncing down the asphalt and the sidewalks. The light was strange, too, as though it were draining from the western sky into the earth, not to be seen again, robbing us of not only the day but the morrow as well. Of course, these feelings and perceptions are not uncommon in people my age. This was different. As I mentioned earlier, I have long believed that my generation is a transitional one and will be the last to remember what we refer to as traditional America. But somehow the fading of this particular evening seemed a harbinger of a sea change, perhaps a tectonic shift in the plates on which our civilization stood.

Vanity? That could be. But how do you just say fuck you to the culture and the people who kept Hitler and Tojo from shaking hands across the Mississippi?

The front door opened, and with a gust of rain-peppered wind at his back, Johnny Shondell walked past the bar and sat down across from me in the dining room, the candle on my table flickering on his white sport coat. "What's happenin', Mr. Dave?" he said.

"No haps, Johnny," I said.

He looked his old youthful self, his system free of skag and tobacco and booze. His dark blue silk shirt was unbuttoned at the top, exposing his tan chest.

"Where's Isolde?" I said. I didn't know whether they were still on the run from Mark Shondell. I assumed they were not, since the uncle had been at the nightclub in Baton Rouge to hear Johnny and Isolde play when Eddy Firpo was slashed to death.

Johnny's gaze roamed around the room. "She's at the motel. We're flying out to Nashville in the morning for a session at Martina and John McBride's Blackbird Studios. It's an album tribute to Hank Williams. Did you know he was the crossover guy to rock and roll, not Elvis? Listen to 'My Bucket's Got a Hole in It.' Your neighbor told me you were probably here."

"Can I help you with something?"

He looked over his shoulder and back at me. "Mr. Dave, you're the only person who came to see me in rehab. I won't ever forget that. So I thought maybe I could tell you about something that's tearing me up, that I don't understand, and that I can't talk to other people about."

"Does this have to do with your uncle Mark?"

"He wants me and Isolde to get involved with some of these college kids who want to take down the Confederate flag and the statues of the generals or some shit like that." His eyes went away from mine as though he had said something obscene.

"When did your uncle become the John Brown of New Iberia?" I said.

"You mean the guy who tried to set the slaves free?"

"Yeah, *that* John Brown."

"Uncle Mark has always treated black people okay. Right?"

Because to him, they're not important enough to think about one way or another, I thought. "How do you feel about the issue?"

"A lot of our fans carry Styrofoam spit cups. Plus, they don't come to a concert to beat each other up."

"I'm not objective about your uncle," I said. "But everyone in this town knows he does nothing that is not in his interest. They also know he will destroy anyone who gets in his way. Why would he want to help college kids tear down statues of people who have been dead for over a hundred years?"

"You got me," he said.

"If you really want to make people mad, tell them you've decided which flags they can fly and which icons they can see in public places," I said. "You're a smart kid, Johnny. Whom do you think this benefits?"

"Right-wing dipshits in general?"

"That says it all, partner."

He looked wanly at the ceiling. It was plated with stamped tin and had been there since the nineteenth century. "Can I say something else?" he asked.

"I'm listening."

"Isolde's mother has got it in for you. The only thing stopping Adonis Balangie from hurting you has been Miss Penelope."

"I hope you and Isolde have great careers," I said.

"Don't shine me on, Mr. Dave. You've seen Gideon recently, haven't you? Up so close you couldn't lie to yourself about who or what he is?"

I felt the air go out of my lungs. "How do you know that?"

"It's in your eyes. You've seen things other people won't believe. So you've stopped talking about them."

"I stopped talking about them after I came back from Vietnam, Johnny."

"Yeah? Well, the Shondells and the Balangies stopped jerking themselves around over four hundred years ago. That's why Adonis Balangie's eyes are dead. That's why I accept the fact that my uncle Mark might be a monster. The world is a fucking zoo."

"Don't use language of that kind, Johnny," I said.

"I got to ask you something."

"What?" I said, knowing what was coming next.

"Did you sleep with Miss Penelope?"

I crimped my lips and didn't answer.

"I didn't think you were that kind of guy, Mr. Dave," he replied. "She's a sweet lady. I think that blows."

Try going home and falling asleep with words like those in your head.

Chapter Thirty-one

THAT NIGHT THE sky was sealed with clouds that resembled the swollen bellies of whales, and when lightning split the heavens, hailstones thundered down all over Iberia Parish, particularly out on the four-lane, where a slender man wearing a tall-crown hat and a three-piece suit and spit-shined pointy-nose cowboy boots entered a truck stop café and sat down in a booth and ordered a piece of pecan pie and a glass of chocolate milk.

The storm was so severe that most truckers traveling the four-lane had parked under the overpasses to protect their windshields and windows. As a consequence, the man in the Stetson was the only customer in the café. The only waitress on duty, Emily Thibodaux, said she never believed that one day a man in a café would cause her to lose control of her bladder and pee a pool of urine around her shoes.

Carroll LeBlanc and I arrived at the café at a quarter past midnight, just after the first ambulance and fire truck had gotten there. The Thibodaux woman was sitting at a table, smoking a cigarette, her lipstick smeared on the cigarette butt, her hand shaking as violently as her teeth were chattering. A blanket was wrapped around her. She looked like a frightened Eskimo.

"He had silver hair?" Carroll said.

"Yeah," she said. "Wit' yellow in it, like dirty soap was ironed into it. His voice was way down inside himself. I don't t'ink he's from around here."

"He had a foreign accent?" I said.

"No, suh. Maybe Texas or Mississippi." She looked toward the service window in the kitchen. There was a sorrow in her face that

I've seen only among civilians in war zones or in the aftermath of fatal accidents or natural catastrophes.

"Start over," Carroll said.

"He come in and sat down and left his hat on. His eyes didn't have no color."

"What do you mean, no color?" Carroll said.

"Like cataracts. I brought him his pie and chocolate milk, and he called me back and said did I know Clete Purcel. I tole him Mr. Clete comes in late at night, but he ain't come in tonight, maybe 'cause of the storm and all. He axed me what time he comes in when he comes in. I tole him I wasn't sure."

"That's what got him jacked up?" Carroll said.

"No, suh," she said. "I was walking away and he said, 'This pie tastes like dog turds.' I tole him that wasn't a nice way to talk. He said, 'Talk to me like that again, you cunt, and I'll put somet'ing in your mout' ain't gonna be pie.'"

She sniffed and wiped her nose with the back of her wrist.

"Go on," I said.

"I went in the kitchen and got a fresh piece of apple pie and give it to him." She drew in on her cigarette and exhaled slowly, staring into the smoke as though she wanted to hide in it.

"Tell us about the homeless man," Carroll said.

"He come in off the road dragging a suitcase, wit' ice in his hair, coughing in his hand somet'ing awful. He wanted a cup of coffee, but he only had fifty cents. I tole him I'd make up the difference, me, but I couldn't give him no food. Troot' is, I'd get in trouble for letting him stay inside."

"Go on," I said.

"The man in the hat tole me I'd better get that pile of stink away from him. I went into the kitchen and got the homeless man a piece of apple pie and tole Tee Boy, that's the cook, I knowed I was stealing from the café, but I cain't let nobody starve. I said, 'At least I'm serving him pie ain't got no germs on it.' Tee Boy axed what I meant, and I tole him I spit in the apple pie I give Mr. White Trash for calling other people names."

She looked for a place to put her cigarette. Carroll took it from her and got up from his chair and flicked it out the door. I waited for him to come back. "What's the rest of it, Miss Emily?" I said.

"The service window was open," she said. She looked into space, as though her words were written on air and she would have to look at them the rest of her life. She started to cry.

"This isn't your fault, Miss Emily," I said. "This man who came in here is evil. Don't let him hurt you any more than he has."

"Tee Boy got seven children."

Tee Boy was black and must have been six and a half feet tall. I had not looked at the body yet. And I didn't want to. Through the window, I could see uniformed deputies stringing crime-scene tape around the parking lot and the building. More emergency vehicles were coming down the four-lane, flashers rippling in the rain.

"What happened then?" Carroll said.

"I went back out and started wiping off the tables, like we do before we close, even though we wasn't closing. I seen a shadow cover my shoulder and arm and hand and then the table, like the shadow was alive. I turned around and he was standing right behind me."

"How was he dressed?" Carroll said.

"He had on a blue suit and a gray vest that didn't look like they belonged together. Everyt'ing about him was like that. He had a funny smell, like bedclothes when a man and woman has been lying on them and doing t'ings."

"Where was the homeless man all this time?" I said.

"In the bat'room," she said. "If Mr. Fontenot finds out he was in there, I'm gonna lose my job."

"I'll talk to your boss," Carroll said. "Just tell us what happened, Miss Emily."

"The man said—"

"Said what?" I asked.

"I don't like using these words. I know his kind. They beat up on women, yeah."

"What did he say, Miss Emily?" I asked.

"He said, 'I want you to sit down and watch this, bitch. Then I'm gonna light you up. Oh, am I gonna light you up.' That's when I wet myself. The homeless man come out the bat'room door, and the man in the suit shot him t'rew the face. Then he went after Tee Boy."

"That's when you hid in the freeze locker?" I said.

"I couldn't go out the front 'cause he could see me, so I run down the hallway to go out the back, where my car is at. But the Dumpster guy moved the Dumpster and blocked the door."

"You could hear from inside the locker?" I said.

"Yes, suh," she said. "Tee Boy couldn't understand why the man was mad at him. He kept saying, 'I ain't got no truck wit' you.' Then there was five or six shots. The man said, 'How you like that, nigger?'"

I saw Helen's cruiser pull up in front. I patted Emily Thibodaux on the back and went into the kitchen. Tee Boy was lying on his side, his face in the shadow of the stove. The wounds were tightly grouped in the center of his chest. The brass on the floor was probably nine-millimeter. The closest shell to the body was six feet away. I realized Helen was standing behind me. "What's your witness say?" she asked.

"The shooter was asking about Clete," I said. "He insulted her. She spat in his pie and bragged to the cook about it. Our guy overheard the conversation and went nuts and started shooting."

"He shot the surveillance cameras, too," Helen said. She looked at the grouping of the wounds in Tee Boy's chest and the distance of the shells from the victim. "Think we have a pro?"

"I'm not sure," I said. "He doesn't seem to fit."

"Did you talk to Clete yet?"

"Haven't had time."

"This is his late-night hangout when he's not in the slop chute. That means our guy knows Clete's routine. Get on it. I'll do the notification."

"You know Tee Boy's family?"

"For twenty years. Tell Clete we want this guy alive."

I WENT TO CLETE'S cottage at the motor court. It was still raining, the oak trees dripping with it, the bayou high and yellow, the surface lighted by an arc lamp on the opposite shore. There was a boom of thunder that shook the water out of the trees. I wondered if, out in the darkness, Gideon was on his galleon, waiting to come back into our lives, adding more souls to his vessel of pain and despair.

I banged on Clete's door. He answered in his boxer shorts and a strap undershirt. "Why don't you wake me up in the middle of night?" he said.

I stepped inside and shut the door behind me. "I would have waited till morning, but I thought you might be in danger."

"How?" he said.

I told him every detail of the shooting: the terrorization of the waitress, the homeless man walking into a bullet that blew his brains on the restroom door, the five rounds pumped methodically into Tee Boy's chest, the colorless eyes of the shooter, the ill-matched three-piece suit, the spit-shined boots, the language the shooter used to degrade Emily Thibodaux. I also told him about Mark Shondell's attempt to involve his nephew Johnny with the people who wanted to undo nineteenth-century history.

"I can't process all this," Clete said. He was sitting on the bed, still in his underwear. "What does Shondell have to do with the Civil War, and how is that connected with the shooting at the café?"

"I don't know."

"Okay, forget Shondell for a minute. The shooter sounds like a guy named Delmer Pickins. He works out of Amarillo and Dallas and beats up hookers and does hits most pros won't deal with. I saw him at Benny Binion's World Series of Poker a couple of times. But I never talked to him, and he's got no reason to be looking for me."

"What do you mean by 'hits most pros won't deal with'?"

"He'll cowboy anyone for five grand. He does revenge hits and takes pictures for the client."

"Can you get in touch with him?"

"A guy who wants to kill me?"

"How about cooling it on the irritability?" I said.

"Dave, you're not hearing me. Pickins is the bottom of the septic tank. Whoever hired him did it because he's a sadist and bat-shit crazy. He's also disposable. Know what I think?"

"No."

"If Delmer Pickins is our guy, he's after both of us. Or the guy who hired him is."

I knew where Clete was going, but I didn't say anything.

"I know Adonis Balangie and Mark Shondell would like to take you off at the neck," he said. "You got it on with Adonis's wife— sorry, his companion he never sleeps with—and with his regular punch who he bought a house for. You also took time out to slap Mark Shondell's face in public."

"So I'm the one to blame?"

"You didn't let me finish. I think this is about money. Or power. Adonis isn't going to hire an ignorant peckerwood like Pickins. This Confederate-statue stuff is the issue. Look, Eddy Firpo had neo-Nazis in his house. Mark Shondell is an elitist and closet racist if I ever saw one. We're living in weird times, Streak. I bet forty percent of the country wouldn't mind firing up the ovens as long as the smokestacks are blowing downwind."

"I don't believe that."

"What, about the Herd?"

"Yeah. People are better than that."

"Keep telling yourself that," he said.

He got up from the bed and opened the icebox. He pulled out two cans and threw one to me. It was a Diet Dr Pepper. He popped his can and drank from it. "You know how many times you've said maybe the South should have won the Civil War?"

"I wasn't serious."

"You fooled me. Come on, noble mon. You hate political correctness as much as I do. How about the poor fuck who lost his job because of affirmative action? Here's a guy who gets a bolt of lightning in the head because of somebody else's mistakes."

"I'm the target because of my influence on Johnny Shondell?" I replied.

"No, because you're intelligent and you'll give Shondell a hard time politically. Not many people can do that. Plus, he's a scorpion."

I sat down next to Clete on the bed. I hadn't opened my cold drink, and I set it on the night table. I feared for Clete. I was protected by the culture of law enforcement, one that is ferociously tribal in nature. Clete was a disgraced cop, a lone soul sowing destruction and chaos everywhere he went, and hated by the Mob and NOPD. I felt his eyes on the side of my face.

"So why would Shondell send a hitter after you?" I said.

"To get me out of the way so they can go after you unhampered."

"I think it's more complicated than that," I said. "Gideon was sent to burn you alive, Clete. Now this creep Pickins is in town. It's you they're after. There's something in you that's a threat to them. We just don't know what it is."

"Yeah, they're jealous of my waistline. Where do you dig up this stuff, Dave?"

That was Clete, never able to understand the repository of virtue that lived inside him. He went to the sink and poured his Dr Pepper down the drain. "I'll get some sheets and a blanket for the couch. You need to get some rest, noble mon. We'll watch a film. I just rented *The Passion of Joan of Arc,* made in 1928. I've seen it three times. God, that girl was brave."

MOST NEUROSCIENTISTS BELIEVE that 95 percent of the human mind is governed by the unconscious. I believe them, because that is the only way I have ever been able to understand the behavior of my fellow man. Jonathan Swift said man was a creature "capable" of reason. I think he had it right. I believe that most human activity is not rational and is often aimed at self-destruction. I also believe that ordinary human beings will participate in horrific deeds if they are provided a ritual that will allow them to put their conscience in abeyance.

I have many memories I can suppress during daylight but which come aborning at night: a battalion aid station in a tropical country, helicopter blades thropping overhead, the raw smell of blood and feces, a man calling for his mother, his entrails blooming from his stomach as though it had been unzipped. The garish images from the aid station are to be expected. But I have another kind of dream, one that frightens and depresses me far more than my experiences in Vietnam.

I witnessed two electrocutions in the Red Hat House at Angola Prison, in both cases at the request of the condemned. The building was constructed in the 1930s to house the most dangerous convicts on the farm. They wore filthy black-and-white-striped uniforms and red straw hats and worked double time on the levee under a boiling sun from first bell count until lockup. More than a hundred convicts were buried in that levee, some of them shot just for the amusement of a notorious gun bull.

Later, the Red Hat House became the home of Angola's electric chair, known as Gruesome Gertie. The fact that I'd watched passively while a man was cooked alive had a peculiar effect on my life. It did not fit with my perception of the supposed democracy in which I lived. A man wearing waist and leg chains was delivered to the unit by the same people who had fed and cared for him for years on death row. The warden, a rotund man with a hush-puppy accent, oversaw the ritual; also in attendance were the prison chaplain, a physician, two journalists, and what was called "the team," employees of the state who wore charcoal-gray uniforms and red "boot" patches on their shirtsleeves, the boot appellation derived from Louisiana's geographic shape.

The executioner, a man I knew for many years, was called "the electrician." Of all the people in the room, only he showed any emotion, and it was pure hatred for the men he launched into eternity. Not the kind of hatred that flared or the kind that caused people to rage or get drunk or strike others. His anger never left his eyes; there was never more of it and never less of it, as though he nursed it the way a professional drunkard nurses alcohol, the way a man can love a vice so much he dare not abuse it lest it be taken from him.

The preparation of the condemned by the team was methodical. The condemned man's head was shaved, his rectum packed with cotton, an adult diaper wrapped around his buttocks and genitals, a gown dropped over his body, slippers placed on his feet.

The skin of both men was as gray as shirt board. Their glands seemed no longer able to secrete the juices that kept the tissue on their bones. There was dried mucus on their lips, dirt under their fingernails, razor scrapes in their stubble, and a sheen of fear in their eyes that was luminous. As I watched the preparations taking place a few feet away from the chair in which the condemned sat, I tried to keep in mind the severity of the crimes he had committed. But I couldn't. I was consumed by the process, the detachment of the team, the specificity of each man's work, all of it aimed at a pitiful wretch who watched their hands touching his skin, buckling the straps on his body, placing a saline-soaked sponge and caplike electrode on his shaved head, putting a lubricant and electrodes on his ankles, and finally, dropping a black cloth over his face so none of us would have to see its reconfiguration when the first jolt hit him.

Each man's body stiffened against the straps with such force I thought the oak in the chair would burst apart.

The odor made me think of the laundry where my mother ironed clothes with women of color, inside a building that had no ventilation and no fans. I had a hard time swallowing and had to look at the floor a full minute before I stood up.

I left both executions without speaking to anyone else in the room. On both occasions I rumbled across the cattle guard at the main gate and drove straight to a bar one mile down the two-lane and got swacked out of my mind. In twelve-step programs, pathetic drunkards such as I end up trying to figure out the nature of God, no matter how unknowledgeable we may be about such subjects. But the real mystery for me is not in the unseen but in the one at our fingertips: How is it we can do so much harm to one another as long as we are provided sanction? How is it we make marionettes of ourselves and give all power to those who have never heard a shot fired in anger or had even a glimpse of life at the bottom of the food chain?

The day after the killings on the four-lane was Saturday. I woke up on Clete's couch at ten A.M. Clete had left me a note that read, "Coffee on the stove, beignets in icebox. I'll see if I can get a lead on Pickins. Don't let those motherfuckers get behind you."

Chapter Thirty-two

THE TREES WERE still dripping, but the skies had cleared and the wind was cool and flowers were blooming in the yards along East Main. I showered and shaved and put on fresh clothes and checked in with Helen at the department and ate lunch at Victor's, then returned home and called Alafair at Reed College in Portland.

It's hard to tell your child that you're lonely and the child's absence is a large part of the problem. In fact, I believe the inculcation of guilt in a child is a terrible thing. So I said nothing about my state of mind or the murders out on the highway, or the likelihood that either Clete or I would pay a price for our involvement in the feud between the Shondell and Balangie families.

I had pulled Alafair from a downed plane out on the salt when she was five years old. Technically, she was an illegal, a refugee flown with her mother out of El Sal by a Maryknoll priest who died with the mother in the crash. I nicknamed her Baby Squanto for the Baby Squanto Indian books she read, and I watched her grow into a beautiful young woman who earned an academic scholarship to Reed but whose dreams still took her back to the day an army patrol came into her village and decided to create an example.

I was about to end our conversation when she said, "Is everything okay, Dave? You sound funny."

"We had a double homicide out on the four-lane last night," I said. "The shooter may have been after Clete."

"You need me there? I can get a flight this afternoon."

"We're fine here."

"No, there's something else wrong, isn't there?"

How do you tell your daughter about multiple encounters with a time traveler who was an executioner in the year 1600 and perhaps an adherent of Mussolini in the 1920s?

"Dave, you tell me the truth or I'm coming home," she said.

"I've met someone," I said to avoid opening a subject I would not be able to shut down.

"Good. Who?"

"It didn't work out."

"Who, Dave?"

"The wife of Adonis Balangie, although she says she's not his wife."

"I don't believe this."

"I asked her to marry me. She didn't seem in the mood. So I said adios."

"You're making this up."

"You miss Paris?"

"I was only there a week. Don't change the subject."

"We've got some bad stuff going on here, Alf," I said. "I think it may involve evil entities. It's hard to explain. I think Mark Shondell wants to kill Clete. I believe Shondell might be in league with the devil."

I don't think I ever heard a longer silence in my life.

FATHER JULIAN WOKE almost every morning before dawn and jogged three miles along Ole Jeanerette Road, which paralleled Bayou Teche and traversed the emerald-green pastures of the LSU experimental farm. He had been an only child, and solitude had been a natural way of life for him long before his ordination. But rather than simplifying his life, ordination brought him complexities he had never envisioned. Early on he realized he would always be addressed by others as a condition, a cutout, an asexual waxwork standing at the church entrance, hands folded in piety as he welcomed his parishioners to morning Mass.

He also learned that offending the hierarchy could get him buried in western Kansas. Among his superiors, compliance and sycophancy were often lauded, and mediocrity was rewarded. Father Julian Hebert was known as a "Vatican Two priest," a liberal left over from the tenure of Pope John XXIII, which for many in his culture was like being known as Martin Luther.

But he couldn't blame all his problems on the authoritarian nature of the institution he served. In his private hours or in the middle of the night, he had to concede that many of the passions burning in him were not those of a spiritual man: the flashes of anger that left his face mottled; the bitterness he felt when he accepted injury or insult; the twitch in his right hand when he saw a child abused or heard a racist remark or watched a chain-saw crew mow down an oak grove in order to build another Walmart. Sometimes his efforts at self-control were not successful. Two years ago he had lost it.

A large, sweaty off-duty policeman at a Lafayette health club was punching the heavy bag while he told a story to two other cops. Julian was hitting the speed bag and at first paid no attention to the story, then realized what he was hearing. "He took his dick out and rubbed it all over her," the man said, steadying the bag, laughing so hard he was wheezing. "From top to bottom, I mean it, in her hair, everywhere."

Julian let his hands hang at his sides and stared at the floor. Finally, in the silence, the teller of the story looked at him and smiled crookedly. "Hey," he said.

"You're a police officer?" Julian said.

"Yeah, what's up?"

"I'm Father Hebert. I'm okay at the speed bag. But I don't have the moves for the ring. You look like you do."

"You're a padre?"

"I was when I woke up this morning."

"Sorry about the language."

"Can you show me?"

"The moves?"

"Yes," Julian said. He opened his mouth to clear his eardrums;

they were creaking, as though he were sinking to the bottom of a deep pool.

"Rotate in a circle, see," the man said. "Never lead with your right except in a body attack, then hook your opponent under the heart. Catch him with your left, then chop him with a right cross. It's easy. Where'd you learn the speed bag?"

Julian didn't answer.

"You hearing me?" the policeman said.

"Yes," Julian said.

The policeman's forearms were thick and wrapped with black hair, a fog of body odor wafting off his skin. "You really want me to show you?"

"Yes."

"Don't deck me, now, Father," the man said, grinning.

Julian slipped on a pair of padded ring gloves, his eyes veiled.

"Good. Let's dance," the man said.

Julian had to breathe through his nose to slow down his heart. His skull felt as though it were in a vise. "Who was the woman?"

"Woman?" the man said. "What woman?"

"The one who was sexually abused."

"I was talking about something that happened in a case."

"You said circle to the left? Or lead with the left?"

"Forget about that. What's this with the woman?"

"Is this how to do it?" Julian said. He flicked his left into the man's face. Then again.

"You're trying to fuck with me? Why you looking at me like that? You want to get serious here?"

"Hit me."

"You got a crucifixion complex?"

"Is the woman in an asylum?"

"You fucking with me? Big mistake, Father."

The man forgot his own admonition and led with his right, then discovered he had just swung at empty space. Julian's blows were a blur, landing with such force and ferocity that the larger man couldn't raise his arms. He went down on the floor mat, but Julian went down on one knee with him, beating his face as though hammering a nail. "Don't you ever harm a woman again," he said through his teeth. "You got that? Shake your head if you hear me!"

But neither the man nor his friends could speak or move. Julian pulled off his gloves and slung them aside and got his gym bag out of his locker. He walked outside without showering or changing clothes. Then he put his vehicle into reverse and bounced over the curb into a fireplug.

NOW, AS HE pounded down Old Jeanerette Road in the sweetness of the morning in his cheap running shoes, past plantation homes strung with fog from the bayou, he wondered if he was a failure both as a priest and as a man, one who had lied to himself about his secret obsessions and his constant unfulfilled sexual yearning.

He had become a priest after reading Ammon Hennacy's *Autobiography of a Catholic Anarchist,* then had lived at the Catholic Worker farm in Marlboro, New York, and been a missionary in El Salvador, jailed five times in civil protests.

In reality, who was he? Perhaps a closet sybarite. The idea was not untenable. He could not deny that he was attracted to women. Actually, "attracted" was not an adequate word. They were the most beautiful and intelligent creatures in God's holy creation, and so superior to their male counterparts that the comparison was laughable. He literally burned for them, not just in his sleep but throughout the day. His desires were oral, penile, glandular, olfactory, auditory, infantile, protective, lustful, spiritual, and ultimately, torturous when he woke early in the morning and sat throbbing in his underwear on the side of his bed, asking God for an exemption to let him have a woman's love and the love of the children that would come from their union. Then he despised himself for his self-pity.

As he jogged down the road, he could not keep his mind off the three or four women who, as always, would be at Saturday afternoon Mass, a distraction he could not get out of his head until Mass was over and they were gone. One had thick blond hair and a complexion that looked as smooth as an orchid's petal; another one was buxom and jolly with a small Irish mouth and mischievous eyes and freshly air-blown red hair and perfume strong enough to get drunk on; another was tall and part black/part Indian and wore purple and scarlet dresses she must have gotten into with a shoehorn; and number four always managed to have the top of her blouse unbuttoned, a gold chain and cross hanging inside her cleavage, her hand warm and fleshy when she squeezed his.

Now he was the subject of a homicide investigation. Hallucinogens had been planted in his refrigerator, and stamps from his collection stolen and glued on the shoe of the murder victim. His name was sullied by charges of child molestation, the one sin Jesus denounced so vehemently that he warned the perpetrators they would be better off not born or fastening millstones about their necks and casting themselves into the sea.

When he got back from his run, sweating and out of breath, he went straight to the kitchen and took a bottle of brandy from the cupboard and poured three inches into a jelly glass. Then he poured the brandy back into the bottle and stared listlessly out the window, wondering if a day of deliverance would ever be his.

THAT EVENING, AT sunset, he locked the church and returned to his small house and tried to keep his mind clear of negative thoughts. Fifteen minutes later, hail began bouncing like mothballs on the roof and the lawn, followed by a steady rain and a wind that thrashed the trees and bamboo along the bayou. A bolt of lightning struck the water just beyond the drawbridge, and he thought he saw a man running along the road with a raincoat over his head. When he looked again, the man was gone.

He fixed a fried-egg sandwich and a slice of chocolate cake and poured a glass of milk, then sat down at the table and began to eat. He would work on his stamp collection that night and go to bed early, then rise in the morning with gratitude for the life and the opportunities that had been given him. Or at least he would try to do these things, he told himself, knowing the weakness that seemed to live in his soul.

A car came around a bend in the road, its headlights on, and Julian saw the man with the raincoat standing among the crypts by the bayou. He put down his sandwich and opened the back door. A mist blew through the screen, touching his skin. "Can I help you?" he called.

"My dog jumped out of my car!" the man said over the sound of the rain on the roof. "You seen a yellow Lab? He's just a pup."

"No, I haven't."

"I saw him run into the graveyard."

"Come in," Julian said. "I'll get an umbrella and a flashlight."

"That's mighty kind of you."

The man approached the kitchen door, hunched under the raincoat, his face turned up toward the light, as twisted as a squash. Then he was inside the kitchen, dripping on the linoleum.

"What's that in your hand?" Julian said.

"This?"

"Yes, what is it?"

"I'll show you." The man stuck a stun gun into the side of Julian's neck and knocked him across the kitchen, then stunned him twice more and pressed him to the floor with a pointy-toed, spit-shined cowboy boot. With his free hand, he clicked off the overhead lights.

"Due to my upbringing, I never cottoned to the ministry," he said. "By the way, my name is Delmer Pickins. I give you my name 'cause you won't be passing it on."

He lit a cigar and puffed it alight, then blew off the ash until the tip glowed like a hot coal. "Time to get on it, boy."

JULIAN COULD NOT tell what the man named Pickins did to him. An eye mask had rendered him blind, and his wrists had been pulled behind him and cinched with ligatures. He knew he had passed out at least once. The greatest pain was in his fingers and feet and his genitals. He could control the nausea and his sphincter but not his fear, because he had no way of knowing where the next blow or mutilation would come from. He tried to call upon Joan of Arc for her strength, she who at nineteen was burned at the stake, a peasant girl who couldn't read or write yet had accepted death by fire rather than renounce the voices she believed came from God.

Julian thought of the three Catholic nuns Maura Clarke and Ita Ford and Dorothy Kazel and the lay missionary Jean Donovan, who were beaten and raped and murdered by El Salvadoran soldiers at the orders of higher-ups and deserted by their own government. He thought of Saints Perpetua and Felicity and their agony as they awaited decapitation in the Carthaginian arena as part of a birthday celebration for the emperor Geta, brother of Caracalla. And he thought of Jesus, mocked and flagellated and left to slow suffocation on the cross. How did they get through it? How could anyone be so alone and so defenseless and so betrayed and yet be so brave?

Julian tried to think of green pastures and a hole in the sky through which he could escape the fate that had been imposed on him. But he knew no angel was about to descend through the roof and carry him into the coolness of a starry night; nor would there be a friend to bind his wounds, no maternal figure to hold his hand and dispel his fears.

Hell was not a furnace in the afterlife. It was right here and, in this instance, controlled by a degenerate whose tools were fire and a pair of pliers and a screwdriver.

Then he heard the kitchen door open and felt the rain and wind crawl across the floor and press against the walls and windows.

"Who are you?" Pickins said.

"I'm Mr. Richetti. How do you do, sir?" said a voice that sounded like it rose from a stone well.

"You walked in on a private situation. This here is a child molester."

"Liar."

"How'd you like a bullet in the mouth? Who the fuck are you, anyway? Take that hood off your head."

"Gladly. Get on your knees."

"What happened to your nose? What *are* you?"

"You have approximately one minute to live."

Julian rubbed the side of his face against the floor until the eye mask slipped partially onto his forehead. He could see a large figure silhouetted against the window. The figure's shoulders were square, his chest flat, the thickness of his upper arms pushed out from his torso.

"Do you wish to say anything by way of apology?" the figure said.

Pickins squeezed the trigger four times on a snub-nosed, chrome-plated .357 Magnum, the sparks streaking into the darkness. Then he lowered the revolver and stared dumbfounded at the silhouette. He raised the revolver and fired the two remaining rounds. "What the fuck."

"Now you will come with me," the figure said. "Some of your old companions await you."

"I ain't going nowhere."

The figure walked to Julian and leaned over and pulled the eye mask gently from his head, then melted the ligatures with one touch of his finger. "Stay here, Father. What is about to happen has nothing to do with you; hence, you should not be witness to it. I admire you, sir."

Julian pushed himself against the wall on the heels of his hands. The figure lifted Pickins by his throat and carried him out to the two-lane as though he were as light as straw. Julian wished he had not limped into the living room and watched through the window the scene taking place on the two-lane while nests of electricity bloomed silently in the clouds and the wind ripped limbs from the trees.

Chapter Thirty-three

Helen Soileau picked me up at my house in a cruiser, and the two of us rolled down Old Jeanerette Road in the rain. Julian had called in the 911. A fire truck and an ambulance and paramedics were already at the scene. A short, square-bodied fireman in a yellow slicker and a fire helmet who wore a handlebar mustache met us by the roadside. "Daigle" was painted in black letters on the back of his slicker. Emergency flares were burning along the edges of the road.

"Is that what I think it is?" Helen said.

"Watch where you step," Daigle said. "One of the medics puked."

"Where's Father Julian?" I said.

"They're packing him up," Daigle said.

"What do you mean, pack—" I began.

"Bad choice of words," Daigle said. "His fingers and privates got worked over pretty bad. There were pliers and a metal file on the floor. The file had scorch marks on it. The burner on the stove was lit. Whoever done that is a real piece of shit."

"He's going to make it, right?" I said.

"Yeah," he said. "If somebody can clean what happened out of his head."

I clicked on my flashlight and walked down the roadside. There were no skid marks on the asphalt or tire indentations by the rain ditches. A human arm lay in the middle of the two-lane, and a leg farther on, the foot sheathed in a pointy-nose Tony Lama. Farther on I saw the torso of a man, most of the clothes gone, one arm and one leg attached, the knee snapped backward. I shined my flashlight on the rain ditch. The head of a man with silver hair bobbed among the cattails.

"Mother of God," Helen said.

I shone the light up and down the road. Blood was splattered all over the asphalt. But there were no drag marks, no spot that showed impact with a vehicle, no tire print in the blood, no streaks of grease or rust or tissue of the victim.

Helen was breathing audibly through her nose, her hands on her hips. "How do you read this shit?"

"Gideon Richetti."

"Goddamm it, don't say that."

"Let's talk to Julian."

"You know what will happen around here if this gets out? 'Sheriff's department opens investigation into ghost from the seventeenth century.'"

"Gideon is a revelator."

She stuck her fingers in both ears. "I'm not going to listen to this. This is a hit-and-run, probably by a big truck. The body got snagged in the undercarriage. Does bwana copy?"

"That's crap and you know it," I said. I clicked off my light.

"Where do you think you're going?" she said at my back.

"The medics drove away with Julian while we were jacking off. I'll be at Iberia General. I'll bum a ride."

She grabbed me by the arm and spun me around. "Outside of Clete Purcel, I'm the best friend you ever had, Dave. Don't talk like that to me again."

"Wake up, Helen. We're dealing with the supernatural. We just can't tell anybody. Sometimes the truth isn't an easy burden to bear."

SHE TOLD ME to take the cruiser while she waited for the coroner. On the way to the hospital, I called Clete and told him Julian was being admitted and asked him to meet me there. "I think Delmer Pickins tortured him." I said. "There're body parts scattered all over the road in front of Julian's house. I suspect they belong to Pickins."

"I had a few drinks before I went to bed," Clete said. "I'm having a little trouble following this."

"It's Gideon."

"I knew that was coming."

"In or out?" I said.

"Let me brush my teeth. We ROA at the ER."

He was there in fifteen minutes. His face looked poached. I could still smell liquor on him. I put a roll of mints in his hand.

"My liver feels like an anvil," he said. "Where's Father Julian?"

"Behind the curtain," I said.

Clete had seen the worst of the worst in free-fire zones. But this was different. The wounds were inflicted systemically, engineered to draw the maximum in pain and humiliation. Clete's face was bloodless and as tight as a drumhead, his green eyes shiny. "Hey, Father," he said, his voice hoarse. "I thought I'd better come down here and make sure you didn't run off with one of the nurses. Like the Blue Nun running off with the Christian Brothers or something. That was in a poem I read by a Catholic nun."

"Call me Julian."

"We're going to get you well," Clete said. "Dave and me and the docs and the nurses. We'll be going out on the salt and catching us some white trout."

"I have to say something," Julian said. His voice was weak, the corner of his mouth puffed, three inches of stitches in one cheek, one eye swollen shut, both hands wrapped with bandages.

"Go ahead," Clete said.

"I watched my tormentor die. I took pleasure in his suffering."

"You got it all wrong," Clete said. "What you were watching was justice being done. You paid the cost for getting this guy off the planet. The pain you suffered made sure this cocksucker will never hurt anyone again. End of story."

I had to hand it to Cletus. I had never thought of it that way, and I suspect Julian hadn't, either.

"It was Gideon who ripped Pickins apart?" Clete said.

"Who?" Julian said.

"Delmer Pickins. The guy who tortured you. Gideon tore him up?"

"Yes," Julian said.

"Who would send a guy like that after you?" Clete said.

Julian fixed his unclosed eye on the ceiling. "I don't know."

"You're not being on the square, Father," Clete said. "Mark Shondell put a hit on both of us and, I suspect, on Dave, too. He's going to send somebody else after us."

"Don't do what you're thinking," Julian said, his voice barely audible.

"I don't *know* what I'm thinking," Clete said. "See, my own thoughts scare me, so I don't allow myself to think. That's how I keep control of myself."

Under other circumstances, we would have laughed. But there was a great evil in our midst, and it was of our own creation and had nothing to do with a time traveler from the year 1600. The evil I'm talking about was incarnate in a Sorbonne-educated man whose family had lived among us for generations. He had vowed to destroy Hollywood and the Jews in it and was probably a molester and had ordered the murder of his enemies. We feared his power and his name, and lied to ourselves and doffed our hats and pretended we were simply adhering to a genteel culture passed on to us from an earlier time. In the meantime Mark Shondell was kindling the fires of racism and the resurgence of nativism and division, all of it inside his headquarters on the banks of Bayou Teche, the place I loved more than any other on earth.

Clete and I left the hospital together. The rain had stopped, and the constellations were cold and bright, and great plumes of white smoke were rising from the lighted stacks of the sugar mill. Clete had not spoken since we had left the ER. An unlit cigarette hung from his mouth. He opened the door of his Caddy; the interior light reflected on his face. His eyes were pools of darkness. I pulled the cigarette from his mouth and tossed it over my shoulder.

"Don't try to stop me, Streak."

I shoved him in the chest.

"What the hell are you doing?" he said.

I shoved him again. Hard.

"Cut it out, big mon."

"You're not going to do this, Clete."

"I've done worse and you didn't say anything about it. Now get away from me."

"You'll end up in Angola and give the high ground to Shondell."

"The only ground he's going to get is a shovel full of dirt in the face."

"I'll hook you up and put you in a cage if I have to," I said.

He got in his pink Caddy and slammed the door, then started the engine and rolled down the window. "Mark Shondell turns people against each other. You're falling into his trap, Streak. Now step back."

He put his vehicle in reverse and almost drove over my foot, then floored the accelerator and bent down on the wheel like an albino ape. As I watched him drive away in the darkness, the blue-dot brake lights coming on at the drawbridge, I felt I was witnessing the end of an era or perhaps the end of innocence in our lives. For the first time, I truly understood why the music of Johnny Shondell and Isolde Balangie laid such a large claim on our souls.

ON SUNDAY HELEN told reporters from *The Daily Iberian, The Daily Advertiser,* and The Associated Press that the death of Delmer Pickins was being investigated as a hit-and-run homicide and that Pickins, a former inmate of Huntsville Penitentiary, was in all probability fleeing the scene of an assault on a local priest when he was struck by a vehicle traveling at high speed. The violence of the impact indicated the vehicle was a large one, perhaps a truck.

Two days later, Mark Shondell and a houseguest, a Central American army general who may have been involved in the murder of Archbishop Óscar Romero, were having breakfast by the pool when a sniper locked down on them from across the bayou and let off three rounds. The first splattered a decanter of tomato juice on the white tablecloth; the second clipped off the general's right index finger; and the third popped through Shondell's blue silk kimono as he was racing for the safety of the house, with no injury to Shondell.

As soon as we got the 911, I called Clete's cell phone, which went immediately to voicemail. I also called his office in New Iberia and his office in the French Quarter. Both receptionists told me he was out of town, perhaps fishing in the Florida Keys. Or Biloxi. Or Kemah over in Texas. "You know how Mr. Clete is," the receptionist in New Iberia said.

"No, I don't know how Mr. Clete is," I said. "Can you tell me?"

"He goes here, he goes there. You never know where he's at. Want to leave a message?"

There is nothing like life in southern Louisiana.

At noon I called Penelope Balangie at her home on Lake Pontchartrain. That probably does not seem a wise thing to have done. But I had no doubt about the identity of the shooter on the bayou. Clete was a dead shot. That the shooter had fired three times without mortally wounding his target suggested either an amateur or a pro. I believed it was the latter. My only doubt had to do with Clete's intention.

"Is that you, Dave?" Penelope said.

Her voice had an effect on me I wasn't expecting. You remember what it was like after you had a fling or a romance or even a marriage and you thought it was over, that it was better for both of you to part, that after a kiss or a handshake or even a last go-round in the sack you'd say goodbye and remain friends, then you'd see her or him walking down a street or getting on the elevator unexpectedly with you, and your heart would drop and your mouth would go dry and you knew that in fifteen minutes you were going to be out of breath and pawing at her or his clothes as well as yours, knowing you were back on the dirty boogie and about to get it on in serious fashion.

"How you doin', Pen?" I said.

"Not bad. How about you?"

"We've had a few troubles over here," I said. "Somebody shot at Mark Shondell this morning. That means he's going to go full out in his war against us."

"Who is 'us'?"

"That depends. I'm wondering if Adonis might help Shondell by parking one between my shoulder blades."

"Adonis wouldn't do that."

"Yeah? Johnny Shondell said you bear me ill will."

"That isn't true. Do you know where Johnny is?" she said.

"He said he and Isolde were going to Nashville to cut a Hank Williams tribute record."

"They left Nashville on a rented plane. Johnny has a pilot's license. No one knows where they are. I'm very worried. Mark Shondell won't rest until he ruins Isolde's life."

"Why did you ever turn her over to him?" I asked.

"Because I was a fool," she said.

"Maybe she'll call. She and Johnny are kids. They don't know what parental worry is like."

There was a silence. Then she said, "There's still a chance for us, Dave."

I had to get out of my discussion with her. She was beautiful and educated and smelled like the ocean or perhaps a mermaid and a garden full of flowers when she made love. "Is Mark Shondell mixed up with white supremacists?"

"He's an elitist. He looks down on them."

"That doesn't answer the question," I said.

"He uses them."

"Gideon saved the life of Father Julian."

"What?"

I told her what had happened at Julian's house.

"I'm glad he helped Father Hebert, but that will not free Gideon of his burden," she said.

"I don't understand."

"To reclaim his soul, he has to be forgiven by someone he has injured. Gideon has the intellect of a peasant. He's dull-witted and heavy-handed, and he often hurts rather than helps people. That's why he's so dangerous. He hurt your friend Mr. Purcel. If I were you, I would be protective of my friend."

"Are you trying to mess me up, Penelope?"

"I don't think this conversation is serving any purpose."

"Put Adonis on," I said.

"I loved you," she said. "I thought you were the one."

She hung up slowly, so the receiver would rattle in the phone cradle.

CLETE CALLED ME on my cell that night. I had just spread newspaper on the floor and fed my cats and my pet raccoon Tripod. One of the cats believed Tripod was hogging the food and bit him in the tail. "Where are you?" I said to Clete, trying to distribute a can of sardines with one hand.

"In Texas. My receptionist says you were looking for me."

"Big surprise?"

"Johnny and Isolde might have gotten abducted in Nashville. I think I got a lead on them."

"Did you finally embalm your brain?"

"Do you want to know what I found out about Johnny and Isolde or not?"

"No, I don't. You shot off an El Salvadoran general's finger. You just missed blowing one of Mark Shondell's kidneys out of his side."

"Says who?"

"There's only one person I know who's that crazy."

"Gee, I'm really sorry to hear that a pair of great guys like Shondell and the greaser had their breakfast disturbed," he said.

"I didn't say it happened at breakfast."

He didn't reply.

"I talked with Penelope Balangie today," I said. "Gideon Richetti can't redeem himself until he's forgiven by someone he has hurt. She thinks he may unintentionally do harm to you."

"You called Penelope Balangie?"

"Yes."

"And I'm the guy with bad judgment? Tell me who's sticking his dork in the light socket." He waited. "You there?"

"Yeah."

"I can't blame you," he said. "That broad is every guy's wet dream. She might even be on the square. Look, I've been checking out some ties Mark Shondell has in Miami and Jersey, Fat Tony Salerno's crowd, mostly. There's this rich-boy gutter rat that's about to make some political moves. The gutter rat is also mixed up with the Russian mafia."

"What's that got to do with us?"

"I don't know," he said. "But Shondell is a big player. This is how one guy close to the gutter rat put it: Working-class people think liberals look down on them, and they think the black people and Hispanics want to take away everything they've worked for. Shondell thinks the gutter rat is headed for the White House."

"Are you in the slop chute?"

"One other thing. Remember when we saw a boat with black sails out on Lake Pontchartrain, in front of the Balangie compound? I saw one yesterday."

"Talk to you later, Clete."

"Don't hang up on me. This Gideon stuff is tearing me apart. I see that guy in my sleep. I see the fire he was building under my head."

"You know how I feel when you say that?"

"No."

"I wish you'd parked one in Shondell's face."

BUT SYMPATHIZING WITH Clete's irrational behavior brought me no solace. I woke each day with the sense that time was ending. This was a phenomenon I had carried with me since childhood, when an evil man named Mack seduced my mother and made her a whore and destroyed our family. After Mack came into our lives, I had nightmares about the sun turning black in the sky and dipping over the edge of the earth, never to return.

The dream followed me to the Central Highlands of Vietnam and the bars of Saigon and Hong Kong and Manila and the drunk tank in the New Orleans French Quarter. But now the dream was no longer a dream. The feeling of loss didn't end with the dawn; I carried it throughout the day. The season did not follow its own rules. At the end of the day, the moon was orange and low in the sky, the dust rising like ash from the fields, as though autumn were upon us rather than the end of winter and the advent of spring.

I felt as though I had stepped inside a place that was outside time, a place where reason and the laws of cause and effect held no sway, where the fears we inherit from our simian forebears flare in the unconscious and lead us back to the monsters we thought we had left behind.

Helen Soileau assigned Carroll LeBlanc and me to the assault on Father Julian and what she called the "hit-and-run." One of the first people we questioned was Leslie Rosenberg. In my case the reason was not entirely professional, either. I had the same inclinations toward her as I did Penelope Balangie. This does not speak well for me. A psychiatrist would probably say the loss of my mother at an early age was responsible for my absorption with women, but I cannot imagine any man not being absorbed with them. If you live long enough, you eventually learn that almost every aspect of the universe is a mystery, no more understandable by the scientist than by the metaphysician. And the greatest mystery in creation is the spiritual and healing transformation of a woman when she gives herself to you. It's a gift you cannot repay, a memory that never dies. That was the way I felt about Leslie. She had another quality, one possessed by almost every badass biker girl. They may pop chewing gum and have a pout on their face and eyes that say "Wanna fuck," but I've yet to see one who wasn't a closet flower child.

I say "we" questioned Leslie. That's not quite right. When Carroll and I went to her cottage, he didn't get out of the cruiser.

"What's wrong?" I said.

"My stomach," he said. "You mind going in by yourself?"

"No problem."

I knocked on the door. Leslie opened the screen and let me in but continued to stare at the cruiser. "Who's that with you?"

"Carroll LeBlanc."

"A vice cop?"

"No, he's Homicide. He was a vice cop at NOPD."

"I remember him. He tried to grab my ass."

"He's a different guy today," I said.

"I'll send a few bucks to Franklin Graham. I got to pick up the sitter and get to work. Is this about Father Julian and the guy who got splattered on the two-lane?"

"Yeah, we've had a hard time catching up with you."

"I don't like to be used," she said.

"Pardon?"

"I talked with Father Julian. You already know what happened. Nobody is going to believe any of us. Why be a pincushion?"

"Did you see Gideon Richetti?"

"I saw him last night. Outside my window."

"Not the night of the assault? Last night?"

"That's what I said. He's changing."

I was afraid to ask what she meant.

"His skin, his pigmentation," she said. "He has hands, not claws."

"I'd like for LeBlanc to hear this."

"He's not coming in this house."

"What does Richetti want from you?"

"Nothing. He says I'm already a spirit, so his apology to me is too late. He wants your friend."

"Clete Purcel?"

"You said it, not me."

"You have to talk to this guy, Leslie."

"My ass."

"Don't talk like that."

"God, are you weird," she said.

"I thought you might think better of me."

She stepped closer to me, her eyes six inches from mine. Her face was unlined, her teeth white. Her breath smelled like marinated strawberries. "Maybe I do. But I'm bad news."

"In what way?"

"I wasn't burned because I was a Jew. I was burned because I was a witch. I didn't get on a pole on Bourbon Street because a bunch of drunk dimwits raped me; I loved every minute of it. I got high watching those fat shits drool on the bar."

"Yesterday's box score," I said.

"Great metaphor. I'm fucked up, honey-bunny. I always will be. Spirit or not, that's why I'm attracted to guys like you."

I could not believe I had just had a conversation of this kind. Who needs hooch and dope? I'll take the natural world anytime.

CARROLL LEBLANC AND I headed back toward New Iberia. The tide was coming in on the Teche, and the wind was pushing waves up on the banks. There had been tornado warnings before sunrise.

"I really don't feel good, Dave," Carroll said.

"Want to go to the ER?"

"Maybe to City Park for a few minutes. They got a Coca-Cola machine in the rec hall."

"Sure."

"What'd Rosenberg tell you?"

"Don't worry about it," I said. "We can talk later."

"I got a problem."

I looked at the side of his face. His eyes were half-lidded, as though he were nodding off or on downers. "You got a daughter," he said. "You know how they get in trouble."

Alafair didn't get in trouble. Or at least she didn't look for it. But I didn't correct him. "She's at Reed in Portland."

"I let my daughter talk me into sending her to the University of Texas. I had to borrow the out-of-state tuition."

I didn't want to talk about money and college debt. You borrow it for your kids or you don't. As I mentioned, Alafair had an academic scholarship. "You sure about the ER, Carroll?"

"Yeah, just get us to the park. I got to tell you something."

"What?"

"I don't know, man. I can't think straight."

I was becoming more and more uncomfortable with Carroll's behavior. We drove down East Main, through the tunnel of oaks that ends at the Shadows, and crossed the drawbridge and pulled under the shade trees by the rec building in the park. Carroll opened the passenger door and vomited. I went inside and bought an ice-cold Coke from the soda machine and handed it to him. He drank from the can, then wiped his mouth with a handkerchief.

"I don't want to hear about people's finances," I said. "Mine are bad enough."

"A masseur knocked up my daughter and gave her herpes. She had an abortion. Now she's using cocaine. How can this much shit happen in six months?"

"I'm sorry."

"I'm broke and I got to get her in rehab."

I didn't know where the conversation was going or why Carroll had chosen me to unload on. "Can I do anything?"

"I think maybe this is punishment for all the things I did in vice at NOPD. That kid I killed, the freebies from the hookers, all the flake I packed up my nose."

"You're not being punished for anything, Carroll. A bad guy hurt your daughter. He's the issue, not you, not her. Tell the Man on High you're sorry for your mistakes and you need some help down here. One day your daughter will be all right."

He blew his nose. "Sorry I got to talking so personal."

"I don't think you heard me."

"About what?"

"Talking to the Man."

"You're probably right, but how do you handle all this stuff in the meanwhile? Anyway, thanks for the Coke. You didn't tell me what Rosenberg said back there?"

"Gideon Richetti is at the center of all this."

His face turned the color of a toadstool.

Chapter Thirty-four

CLETE CALLED ME on my landline that night. The moon was up, the clouds torn like strips of black cotton, leaves and broken tree limbs floating in the Teche. A tornado had touched down outside Lake Charles. I had brought in the cats and my raccoon, Tripod. All of them were lying down on the throw rug, tails flipping, as though they were observing the events of the evening. When Alafair was home, they got on the furniture, including the breakfast table, which they covered with seat smears. Why do I mention these little guys at this juncture? Because at that moment they were the only aspects of normalcy in my life.

I picked up the phone on the third ring. "What's the haps, Cletus?"

"I'm on the bottom of Terrebonne Parish. I could use some backup in the next twelve hours or so. I think a pile of shit is about to go down."

"What kind of shit?"

"Adonis and his old lady are over here. I saw them at a restaurant in Houma. Mark Shondell has a house on stilts south of here. This insider guy I know says Johnny and Isolde got kidnapped by some dickheads, guys who used to run with Delmer Perkins. Guys who carry blowtorches and pliers."

"Mark Shondell is behind the kidnapping?"

"He wants to control their careers and screw up the Balangies. But the bigger deal is political. All these cocksuckers are. They've been with us since the German Bund. They've just been waiting for their time in history."

"Who is 'they'?"

"The cocksuckers I was just talking about."

A conversation with Clete could be the equivalent of driving a nail into your skull. "Where are you staying?"

He gave me the name of a motel in a small settlement on the south end of Terrebonne Parish, almost to the salt water.

"There's something I need to tell you," I said.

"It better not be about Lizard Man."

"He may be looking for you, Leslie Rosenberg says."

"If you see him before I do, tell him to get lost."

"Maybe he wants your forgiveness."

"Tell him I'll meet him on Mars in about five hundred years or so. Dave, I still feel like we're inside a nightmare of some kind."

"How's your weather?" I said.

"What's the name of that song you like by John Fogerty?"

"'Bad Moon Rising'?"

"That's the weather in Terrebonne Parish."

THE FIRST PERSON I saw the next morning at the department was Carroll LeBlanc. "Where you going in such a hurry, Robo?"

"Taking a ride over to Terrebonne."

"Need some help?"

I waited while two uniformed deputies walked past us, then said, "Mark Shondell is making a move."

"Yeah?" LeBlanc said.

"Yeah," I replied.

"How do you know?"

"Clete Purcel told me."

"Purcel should know."

"Say again?"

"He's paid a lot of dues. He's been around."

I started to walk away.

"A move how?" Carroll said.

"I'm not sure."

"I do something wrong?" he asked.

"No."

"Because you don't sound eager to have me along."

"I'm going to talk to Helen right now. Why don't you join us?"

"Thanks," he said. "Sorry again for yesterday. I mean that pity-pot stuff. You know how—"

We were at the stairwell. "After you," I said.

We went into Helen's office. She was looking out the window. The sky had turned yellow, and birds were rising from the trees in the park. I told her about Clete's phone call and his belief that Mark Shondell might be holding Johnny and Isolde.

"That's for the FBI, Pops," she said.

"I bet they'd love getting in on this," I replied. "Want me to tell them we're dealing with a guy from the year 1600? Or the possibility that Mark Shondell is in league with evil forces?"

"You lay off that voodoo dog shit, Dave," she said.

"Helen, we can't rule anything out," Carroll said. "There's something weird going on. Look at the sky. It's like hurricane season in August."

"End of discussion," she said. "How long do you need to be in Terrebonne?"

"Two or three days, maybe," I said.

"The media better not hear any of this," she said. "You copy?"

I didn't reply.

"Yes, ma'am, we copy," Carroll said.

She waited for me to answer. "Dave?"

"Yeah?" I said.

She was fiddling with some papers on her desk, her head down. She looked up, obviously tired. "I get on your case because I can't begin to guess what we're dealing with. Don't get mad at me. And don't get hurt in Terrebonne."

"Yes, ma'am," I said.

I HAVE TO PAUSE at this juncture and say something of a personal nature. Death's a motherfucker. We already know that. However, I was about to learn it comes in many forms, and that one's own transition might not happen at a specific time but instead may take place at several different stops on one's journey; in effect, there are no parallel lines, only the swirling vortex of which we're a tiny part. I was also about to learn that time and historical sequence are relative, and that those who deny the existence of an aperture in the dimension are a fond and foolish group. Call it madness, but I believe the sulfurous sky we witnessed that day was the backdrop of a drama about good and evil, just as the wine-dark waves at the amusement pier in Texas were the same as those Homer described three thousand years ago.

The rain began falling as I turned south at Houma and drove down to the salt. Carroll had dozed off, his head on his chest. He looked older, tired, the line of moles blacker under his left eye. His body shook suddenly, and he made a sound down in his throat but didn't open his eyes. In my career I've known three cops who ate their gun. Others did it a day at a time with pills and booze. Carroll had all the signs of a cop about to burn his kite.

We drove down a cracked stretch of asphalt road through miles of wetlands and sawgrass and palmettos and a swamp in which the algae was so thick it undulated with the tide like a milky-green blanket. In the distance I could see a crossroads and a small motel and a café and slips that had been cut for both sailboats and cabin cruisers, but much of the coastline had been eroded by saline intrusion, and the docks and shelters and wooden walks had been abandoned.

I went over a rise in the road and hit a pothole. Carroll's head jerked up. "We there?"

"This is it," I said.

He rubbed his face. "I had a dream. Did I say something?"

"No."

"I was climbing this ladder up to a real high place. I had my daughter with me and a dog I had when I was a kid. I had to drop one of them."

"Your daughter is going to be okay, Carroll."

"She never had a mother. That's the problem."

"There's Clete's motel," I said.

"He's quite a guy, huh? The Navy Cross and two Purple Hearts in Vietnam?"

"Something like that. He doesn't talk about it."

"Be honest with me on something. Were you or Purcel ever tempted to take juice at NOPD?"

"I'm going to let that one slide, Carroll."

"I didn't mean to rumple your threads. Geez."

I could see a few houses on stilts out on the bay. Waves full of sand were sliding into the sawgrass. In a few years most of this area would be washed away.

"When we get back to New Iberia, you and I need to have a talk," I said.

I pulled up to the motel just as Clete stepped out of a room, his Caddy parked by the door. He was wearing a suit and tie and his porkpie hat. "Big mon," he said.

THE THREE OF us sat in an isolated booth at the back of the motel café. Clete and I ordered coffee. Carroll ordered a beer. Clete's eyes met mine, then he looked out the window at four brown pelicans flying in formation just above the surf.

"Here's what I got," Clete said. "Shondell has a fuck pad on stilts about a mile down the levee. A pontoon plane has been there a couple of times. Shondell has some muscle on a tugboat close by. My insider guy thinks he saw Johnny Shondell."

"Who's your insider guy?" I asked.

Clete glanced at Carroll. "A guy who owes me some favors."

Carroll caught it. "You don't trust me?" he said, trying to smile.

"A guy who does airboat rides," Clete said.

"You saw Adonis and Penelope in a restaurant in Houma?" I said.

"They ignored me. Maybe they didn't even notice me," Clete said. He scratched his forehead and looked around. "I mentioned the muscle on the tugboat. I had my binoculars on it. I saw a couple of women. I also saw a guy who worked with Delmer Pickins. The guy's a sadist. Maybe that fuck pad is more than just a fuck pad."

"Maybe your imagination is running away with you," Carroll said. Clete's eyes locked on Carroll's. "Could be."

"You think Isolde is in there?" I said.

"I don't know," Clete said.

"How long you been scoping the place?" Carroll said. He took a sip from his beer.

"What difference does it make?" Clete said.

"I was just asking," Carroll said.

"I got to take a drain," Clete said. He looked at me. "See you outside, Dave."

A FEW MINUTES LATER, I asked Carroll to take our unmarked car up the road, where he could get cell phone service, and check in with Helen. "Sure," he said. "Sorry about ordering that beer. It helps calm my stomach."

"It's all right," I said.

"You're stand-up, Robo."

No, just dumb, I thought.

Carroll drove away. Clete and I walked along a partially destroyed levee. The sawgrass was flattening in the wind, the sky yellow, the air filled with salt spray. "LeBlanc's dirty," Clete said.

"His daughter is messed up. He's going through a bad time."

"Quit looking for good in people when it's not there, Dave."

Maybe he was right. Anyway, I knew better than to argue with Clete. We walked in silence until the levee made a bend and we could see a large house on stilts out in deep water. A tug and a pontoon plane were anchored by the pilings. Clete looked through his binoculars. "I can't believe it."

"What?" I said.

"Shondell is on the deck with Adonis and Penelope Balangie. They've been jerking us around from the jump."

"Maybe they're negotiating."

"They're scum, Dave, including Penelope Balangie. She's taken you over the hurdles six ways from breakfast."

"You shot at Shondell and the El Salvadoran, didn't you?" I said.

"So what?"

"I didn't get on your case, did I?"

"Of course you did. You're always on my case."

"Clete, no one is ever going to believe the events you and I have been privy to except Father Julian and Leslie Rosenberg. We can't be fighting with each other."

"Tell me about it."

"No, you're not hearing me. Maybe it's all going to end here."

His green eyes looked as hard as glass, unblinking even in the wind. "What do you mean 'it's all going to end'?"

"I think we're outside of time now. I think the big secrets aren't secrets at all. We turn them into secrets by denying their reality. Shondell is one of those guys who will destroy the earth. He's the essence of evil. I wish you had smoked both him and the general."

"This isn't like you, noble mon."

"Explain Gideon to me."

"I think LSD is involved," he said.

"You're taking yourself over the hurdles, Clete."

He put the binoculars in my hands. "You call the play. I say bust 'em or dust 'em."

"There is no busting Mark Shondell."

"Maybe you're finally seeing the light."

"No cowboy stuff. Got it?"

Clete began tapping the air. "I'm the one got hung upside down over a fire at Shondell's orders. That guy is going to have dinner with the crabs."

I looked through the binoculars. Penelope and Adonis and Shondell were talking on the deck. Penelope's expression had the melancholy solemnity of the women in Botticelli's paintings. I wanted to travel across the water and put my mouth on hers. I wanted to touch her breasts and hair and put myself inside her. Clete was right. Her presence in my life wasn't nearly over.

I handed Clete the binoculars. "Carroll and I will knock on the door of the stilt house tonight."

"Y'all will knock on the door?"

"We have to do it by the numbers, Clete. We don't have a warrant or probable cause."

"Why at night?"

"Some of his men will be high. They'll also feel safe."

"At night they feel safe?" he said.

"They go back to the womb."

"No matter what you say, this is about Penelope Balangie," Clete said. "You think you still have a chance with her."

"Wrong," I said. "Wrong, wrong, wrong."

He walked toward the motel, his coat blowing, one hand clamped on his porkpie hat. I had treated him in a moralistic fashion and had indicated that his lack of a policeman's badge made him secondary to a deeply flawed lawman like Carroll LeBlanc. But Clete was wired and determined to have justice for the psychological damage done to him in the Keys; he was also extremely dangerous when he took revenge on misogynists and child abusers. Plus, we didn't know where Johnny and Isolde were, and bullets don't care about the targets they find.

Chapter Thirty-five

BY MID-AFTERNOON CLETE was out of his funk and concentrated on our objective. He called the airboat pilot who had given him information about Shondell and asked him to meet us in a café ten miles up the road. I told Carroll to keep his eyes on Shondell's stilt house. The airboat pilot was a Cajun from Houma who had lost a leg in the propeller of his father's airboat when he was twelve. He had intense brown eyes and a narrow unshaved face that made me think of an unhusked coconut. His name was Dallas Landry. He said he had seen no sign of a young couple matching the description of Johnny and Isolde.

"How about the guys on the tug?" I said. "You talk to them at all?"

"They ain't the kind of guys you talk to," he said.

"How many guys are there?" Clete asked.

"Four or five. Lots of ink on both arms. They got women wit' 'em, too."

"Hookers?" Clete said.

"They ain't from the convent."

"You've been very helpful, Dallas," I said. "Is there anything else you can tell us?"

"Mr. Mark had a guy there a couple of times. A lawyer, maybe. They was laughing about Adonis Balangie. They said they was gonna take everyt'ing he's got. I pretended I didn't hear nothing. He's got a five-hundred-foot yacht about two miles out in the Gulf. He's got sailboats on it."

There was another question I wanted to ask him. He wasn't the kind of man we euphemistically call a "confidential informant," many of whom are motivated by aggrandizement or fear or a desire to be accepted or to feel important. He was taking considerable risk, the least of which was loss of his job.

"Why'd you come forward, Dallas?" I said.

He stared at his coffee cup. "Mr. Mark bothers me."

"In what way?" I said.

"I ain't got a way of putting it. It's the way he looks at them young girls. I ain't seen him put a hand on them. But I seen the way he looks. Somet'ing else, too." He knotted his fingers.

"Go on," I said.

"He got somet'ing dark in him, Mr. Robicheaux."

Just then Carroll LeBlanc came through the café entrance. "What's going on with you guys?" he said.

"You're supposed to be watching the stilt house," Clete said.

"I didn't know where y'all were," Carroll said. He glanced at Dallas Landry. "Who are you?"

"I run an airboat service," Dallas said.

"Oh yeah, Clete told me."

"Walk outside with me," Clete said to Carroll.

"I'm not going anywhere," Carroll said. "What the hell is going on?"

Clete went outside by himself and got in his Caddy.

"See you around, Mr. Robicheaux," Dallas said.

"You, too," I said.

Carroll sat down at the table. I wanted to take him apart.

"I saw Johnny Shondell, so cool your jets, Dave," he said. "I couldn't get cell service, so I motored on up the road."

"You're sure it was Johnny?"

"He was standing on Shondell's deck, wearing shades and a Hawaiian shirt. He looked pretty relaxed."

"You've got beer on your breath," I said.

"You want me to bag ass, I'll understand."

"Get your act together, Carroll," I said. "I'll see you at the motel."

"You trying to hurt me?" he said.

I went outside and got in the Caddy. The top was up, the hand-waxed pink paint job sprinkled with leaves from the oak tree overhead.

"You don't look too hot," Clete said.

"You're the best guy I've ever known, Clete," I replied.

He started the engine, an unlit Lucky Strike hanging from his mouth. "Sometimes you truly perplex me, noble mon."

THERE ARE EPIPHANIES most of us do not share with others. Among them is the hour when you make your peace with death. You don't plan the moment; you do not acquire it by study. Most likely, you stumble upon it. It's a revelatory moment, a recognition that death is simply another player in our midst, a fellow actor on Shakespeare's grand stage, perhaps one even more vulnerable than we are, one who is unloved, excoriated, condemned to the shadows, and denied either rest or joy. John Donne went so far as to refer to this sad figure as "Poor Death."

That evening I saw a transformation in the heavens that to this day I cannot explain. As I stood on a sand spit and watched the lights come on in the Shondell stilt house, the tide washing through miles of sawgrass, I realized the sky had turned a gaseous green, and the air had become as heavy and dense as a barrel of wet salt, the sun buried in a solitary cloud on the horizon, blood-red and flaming orange, like the inside of a torn peach.

As if on a panoramic movie screen, I saw Vikings slaying villagers with their axes, Richard the Lionheart's Crusaders beheading Muslims on their knees, Buonaparte setting fire to a Russian village in the snow, the boys in butternut dropping like wheat on Cemetery Ridge, Comanche Indians dragging children with ropes through cactus, British tanks crashing down on a German trench at the Somme.

I saw the slaughter of the innocents at Nanking, Ernest Hemingway blown to shit in an Italian field hospital, Audie Murphy firing a fifty-caliber on top of a tank that was burning, James Bowie tossed on bayonets in the chapel at the Alamo, a navy corpsman pulling Clete down a napalm-scorched hillside on a poncho liner, and I saw myself calling in Puff the Magic Dragon on an Asian village, and maybe for the first time in my life, I realized the insignificance of my own death.

I also realized that the re-creation of my generation and era in the form of Isolde Balangie and Johnny Shondell was an innocent fantasy and a fitting tribute to the New Orleans Sound. The piano keys tinkling with a fragility like crystal, the throaty resonance of the saxophone, the muffled rolling of the drums, the coon-ass and Irish Channel accents of the vocalists, all of it echoing as though recorded in an empty college gym, all of it leading one day into Phil Spector's Wall of Sound—this was the era that I always believed was the best in our history. But it was gone, and to mourn its passing was to demean it. The ethereal moment lives on in the heart, so what is there to fear?

I heard Clete behind me. "Ready to boogie?" he said.

"When you are," I replied.

He was wearing his porkpie hat and a raincoat, his hands in the pockets. He looked at the waves sliding in with the tide; they were dark, laced with foam, filled with shell life. "Smell that air."

"Yeah," I said.

"I got a feeling about something. We're standing on the edge of creation. Or maybe the end of it."

"Could be."

"Dallas is putting his airboat in the water," he said.

"What's under your coat?"

He opened the flap. A cut-down sawed-off Remington twelve-gauge pump hung under his armpit.

"I hope we don't have to use that," I said.

"Shondell could grind us into fish chum and nobody would miss a beat, Dave."

I let my eyes go flat.

"Not in front of Penelope Balangie?" he said.

"Something like that."

"Dave, your learning curve never ceases to surprise me."

DALLAS LANDRY HAD pulled the airboat up to the dock. I knocked on Carroll's door at the motel. He pulled it open so quickly that my hand fell into empty space. "It's time?" he said.

"Yeah, what do you think?" I said.

He had showered and changed into elastic-waist slacks, boat shoes, a long-sleeve jersey, and a sport coat. He was wearing a shoulder holster, his badge hanging from his neck. "What are you carrying?" he said.

"Snub thirty-eight."

"You got an ankle rig?"

"Dial it down, Carroll."

"What do we do about the guys on the tug?"

"That's up to them," I said.

"You're not talking about blowing up anybody's shit?"

"No."

"Because that sounds like Purcel. Are there twelve-step programs for brain disease? That guy doesn't understand boundaries."

"Is there anything you want to tell me, Carroll?"

"Like confess something?"

"Call it what you will."

"I already told you. My daughter needs my help."

"Time to rock, partner," I said.

We walked outside, into the wind and salt spray and the smell of shellfish stranded in the sawgrass by receding waves. Carroll was breathing heavily, his mouth tight, his nostrils swelling. "I'm with you, Robo. If we got to put hair on the walls, that's the way it is. Right? Fucking A. We got to keep the lines simple."

This was the guy afraid of blowing up people's shit?

WE RODE ON the airboat to the stilt house and got out on a floating dock that was fastened to the pilings. Dallas Landry cut the propeller just as a big man exited the cabin on the tug and shone a flashlight on us. Carroll lifted his badge from his chest so it caught the flashlight's beam. "Get back in the cabin, asshole," he said.

I could hear waves slapping against the pontoons on the airboat. The man went back in the cabin. I told Dallas to come back in one hour.

"I t'ought you wanted me to wait," he said.

"We'd rather have you in a safe place," I said. "If we're not standing outside in one hour, call for the cavalry."

"Yes, suh, I got it," he said.

He clamped on his ear protectors and restarted the propeller, then drove away, the backdraft flattening the water. I started to mount the steel steps that led to the deck above us, then I heard a sound I had heard before: wood stroking against wood, oars lifting and dropping back into the waves, perhaps a taskmaster drumming cadence on a forecastle. Clete heard it, too. I searched the horizon in all four directions but saw only the black-green curl of the waves and a lighted ship on the southern horizon.

"That bastard is out there, isn't he?" Clete said.

I nodded but didn't answer. Carroll looked at me and at Clete and then at me again. "What are y'all talking about?"

"You didn't hear anything?" I said.

"No, nothing. Something's going on?"

"It's probably a buoy," I said.

Carroll's eyeballs were clicking back and forth. "You're not talking about this ghoul or whatever?"

"Stay behind me," I said.

I climbed the stairs, my shoes ringing on the steel steps, then crossed the deck in the wind and knocked on the door. The waves below were gaining strength, pitching against the tugboat and smacking the floating dock against the pilings. I wondered about the tolerance of Dallas Landry's airboat.

Mark Shondell answered the door in a red smoking jacket like Hugh Hefner might wear. "Why, Dave, how good of you to come see us. And Mr. LeBlanc and Mr. Purcel. We were just discussing the possibility that the Aryan race might not be the most intelligent after all, and then in you walk."

The interior of the living room was exotic, the walls covered with bookshelves and leopard and zebra skins, the furniture made of African blackwood and ivory and glass, the carpet an inch thick, swirling with color. A chandelier burned with the warm radiance of candles.

Adonis and Penelope and Johnny Shondell were standing at the mantel below a brass clock. They stared at us like people who had suffered a heart attack. But I was no longer looking at them or the decor in the living room or even Mark Shondell. Through the window, I could see waves bursting on the bow of a double-decked galleon, its long oars dripping green fire.

"We were in the neighborhood," I said. "Is Isolde home?"

Chapter Thirty-six

JOHNNY WAS FROZEN at the mantel, his face sick. "Dave, you're such a fool," Penelope said. "And damn you to hell for it."

"Where's your daughter, Penelope?" I said.

"Don't address my wife by her first name," Adonis said.

"Hey, Adonis, time to keep your mouth shut," Clete said.

"Let's not have unpleasant words," Shondell said. "Do you have a warrant of some kind, Dave?"

"We don't need one," I said. "We're not here to arrest anyone or to search your dwelling."

"Dave, I don't appreciate your being here," Shondell said. "You struck me in the face. In an earlier era, you would have been called out. Under the Dueling Oaks. Do you understand what I am saying to you?"

"I'm trying to grab a noun or adverb here and there," I replied.

"Our situation is not a humorous one, sir," he said. "You are meddling in things you know nothing about. I am going to ask you once, and once only, to leave the premises."

"Listen to him, Dave," Penelope said.

"Where's your daughter?" I said.

"She'll be here soon," Penelope said.

"Good. We'll wait," Clete said.

"Did y'all see the galleon?" I asked.

"What?" Shondell said.

"I just saw Gideon's galleon," I said. I pointed at the window. "Take a look. To the southeast, perhaps fifty yards from where we're standing."

Shondell walked to the window. "The wind and the waves have played a trick on you."

"Dave?" Carroll said behind me.

I did not want to hear any more from Carroll LeBlanc. "What is it?"

"I've really messed up."

"In what way?" I said.

He looked deathly ill. "I didn't pass on some information I got from Helen."

"What information?"

"Somebody scooped up Father Julian from the hospital," he said.

I turned around. "Say that again?"

"People went into Iberia General and grabbed him."

"Why didn't you tell me?"

"Because he's on a pad," Clete said.

"Dave, I've been trying to tell you," Carroll said. "My daughter was gonna be on the street. I didn't know Shondell was gonna do all this."

"You didn't have a clue, huh?" I said.

"You wouldn't listen to anyone, Dave," Adonis said. "You were too busy bedding my wife."

Clete stuck his finger in Adonis's face. "You open your mouth one more time, and I'll paste you all over this room."

"Apparently, we have a little problem," Shondell said. "Mr. Bell, would you step out here, please?"

A large man in a fedora and a rumpled suit came out of the kitchen. He had a dissolute, fleshy face, small eyes, and bad teeth. He was holding a pistol-grip AK-47 with a thirty-round banana magazine. He grinned, exposing the gaps in his teeth. "Put your hands on your heads or we'll have a great deal of mop-and-bucket work to do."

"Dave, this is the cocksucker who sapped me in Key West," Clete said.

"Pleased to meet you," Bell said.

"Take their weapons, Adonis," Shondell said.

Adonis didn't move. "Did you hear me?" Shondell said to him.

"You don't take out cops," Adonis said.

"Do you want to see black or white sails tonight?" Shondell said. Clete and I didn't know the significance of the black sails we had seen, but obviously, Adonis did. He peeled back Clete's raincoat and pulled the cut-down twelve-gauge from his shoulder, then disarmed both me and Carroll. Penelope's eyes were shiny with shame.

"How about you, Johnny?" I said. "Whose side are you on? Where is Isolde?"

He stared at the floor. Carroll could not look me in the face.

"People know where we are," I said.

"Afraid not," Shondell said. "Your airboat pilot no longer exists. Your colleagues have no idea where you are, courtesy of Detective LeBlanc. You slapped me in public, Mr. Robicheaux. You cannot imagine the ordeal that awaits you and Mr. Purcel."

"What about LeBlanc?" Clete said.

Shondell studied Carroll's face. "Maybe we'll make up some games. A behavioral study of sorts."

Two men from the tugboat came heavily up the steps and hooked up our wrists behind our backs with plastic ligatures, then pulled black cloth bags with drawstrings over our heads. One of the men soaked our faces with a spray can. I smelled an odor like ether, then my knees caved as though I had been dropped through the trapdoor on a scaffold.

I WOKE ON A hard surface, wrists bound, hood secured tightly under my chin, surrounded by a humming sound like a ship's engine. I realized my ankles were bound as well, and my Velcro-strapped hideaway was gone. I felt a pain like I had been kicked in the back, and I groaned when I moved.

"Is that you, Dave?" I heard Clete say.

"Yeah."

"Glad you're awake," he said, perhaps three feet from me. "I can't see anything."

"Where's Carroll?"

"There's a third guy in here. I can hear him breathing. Maybe that's him."

"Where are we?"

"I think next to the engine room. I heard somebody slamming a hatch and clanging down a ladder."

"I can't remember what happened," I said.

"No mystery. Carroll LeBlanc is a Judas. If we get out of this, I'm feeding him to the shrimp."

I tried to twist the ligatures off my wrists. Instead, they cut into my veins. "Did you tell your receptionist where you were going?"

"No. After I fired those rounds at Shondell, I thought I'd keep my location unknown."

"Tell me the truth, Cletus. Did you try to take Shondell out?"

"Yeah," he said. "I still had a buzz on from the night before."

"Maybe you'll get him next time," I said. But I knew there would be no next time, and so did he.

"I think we're fucked, Streak," he said. "Shondell is nuts, isn't he?"

"I don't think he's crazy at all. I think he has evil powers."

"Don't talk like that. We've had these shitheads around us all our lives. They're just coming out of the woodwork now."

I heard a groan. "Is that you, Carroll?"

"Yeah," he answered, his voice thin, hardly more than a gasp. "That's you, Dave?"

"Sure," I said. "Clete is here, too."

"I'm sorry," he said.

"Yeah, you're always sorry," Clete said. "Where are we?"

"Probably on his yacht," Carroll said.

"What's this ordeal he's got planned for us?" Clete said.

"I heard something once. From a pimp Shondell uses. He's got a collection."

"A collection of what?" Clete said.

"Shit from the Middle Ages. I don't want to talk about it."

"What kind of shit?" Clete said.

"Sick stuff, man," Carroll said.

We heard people coming down a ladder and someone opening the hatch on the compartment we were in. The person stepped inside but didn't speak. I was breathing through my mouth, sucking in the cloth of the hood, my heart thudding; I could hear the welt on my shoe scrape the deck when I moved. My breath was foul, my face itching and sweating as though it were encased in dried mud. "Who are you?" I said.

"Having fears in the silence?" Shondell said. "The imagination is a powerful engine, isn't it?"

He went silent again. I tried to measure time by counting the seconds. But I couldn't concentrate and I lost count, and I desperately needed to go to the head. Five minutes must have passed. I tried to pretend he was no longer in the compartment. I also tried to convince myself that the coolness in the steel deck was absorbing me into its molecular protection, taking me somewhere else in the universe, freeing me from the impotence and vulnerability that now constituted my life. I was totally under the control of an evil and sadistic man. What a fool I had been.

"Would you like to go to the bathroom?" Shondell said. "Just say so."

"Yeah, we would!" Carroll said.

"Good boy. See what can happen when you're under the right discipline?"

"What are you getting out of this, Shondell?" I said.

"Everything," he said. "The reconstruction of the republic. A new era is beginning, and it's based on the purity of the Nordic race."

"There's no such thing as a Nordic race," I said.

I heard Shondell squat down close to me. I could feel his presence like an obscene hand hovering above an unguarded part of my body. I could see nothing through the hood. He touched my forehead with the tip of his finger. "Scared?"

"I'll make you a promise," I said. "If I ever get loose, I'm going to twist off your head and piss on it and flush it down a toilet."

"Let's see how you feel by this time tomorrow." He got to his feet again. "I need you in here, fellows."

I heard other men coming through the hatchway.

"Get our friends to the bathroom and make sure all their needs are met," Shondell said.

The ligatures were taken from my ankles, and a man held me by each arm and led me to a toilet; one of them freed my wrists and let me relieve myself, the hood still on my head. "You guys know I'm a cop, right?" I said. "You know what happens when you kill a cop in Louisiana."

"We *are* cops," one of them said.

They led me back to the compartment, then took Clete and Carroll LeBlanc to the head and brought them back.

"I want to show you my collection," Shondell said.

"Is Penelope in on this?" I said.

"How stupid can you be, Dave? Would she be with Adonis if he were not a rich and powerful man?"

"Fuck your collection," I said.

"You're an educated man. Profanity is the tool early man used to ward off situations he couldn't change—in other words, a confession of inadequacy. Does it bother you that you're such a predictable fellow?"

Chapter Thirty-seven

THE HOODS WERE removed from our heads, and we were marched down a passageway to a forecastle that had leather-padded bulkheads and blue plastic tarps spread on the deck. There were no portholes, and I had no way to get a bearing. Chains with sheep-lined leather cuffs hung from the bulkheads.

"How do you like my arrangement?" Shondell said. "Roomy, soundproof, and with an array of items that go back perhaps five hundred years."

At the far end of the compartment were primitive machines and worktables covered with metal instruments. The machines were constructed of brass and iron and oak and heavy bolts and spikes and pulleys and cogged wheels with long wood handles attached to them.

"Anything to say, Mr. Purcel?" Shondell said.

"Eat shit," Clete said.

"When it's your turn, the man whose finger you shot off will be here to cheer you along," Shondell said. "You don't mind, do you?"

"What are you going to tell Johnny about all this?" Clete said.

"He'll know you went away. He's a good boy. He'll stay that way."

"What about Isolde?" I said.

"Believe me, these are not your concerns. In the next twenty-four hours, you're going to be extremely preoccupied." Shondell gazed at the machines and instruments that represented the darkness I had tried to plumb in Marcel LaForchette. How could I have mistaken the torment in poor Marcel for the disease that lived inside Mark Shondell?

"I love the names of these things," he said. "The scold's bridle for loquacious housewives, the choke pear for expansion of the mouth and other places, the iron maiden, the scavenger's daughter for compressing people who need size reduction, the rack, and the thumbscrew. How about my favorite, the brazen bull? The victim is inserted inside and slowly boiled. There're pipes inside that make his screams sound like the roaring of a bull."

Carroll LeBlanc was crying.

"Nothing to say, Dave?" Shondell said.

"It looks like a junk pile that your average pervert would probably appreciate," I said.

"I think you'll change your tune." Shondell looked at the brazen bull and grinned. "That's a hint."

"Here's one thing that won't change, Shondell," I said. "No matter what happens to us, you'll remain the same. You're trash, your family is trash, and your ancestors were trash. I think God keeps a few people like you around to remind the white race we've got some serious problems. I heard the Shondells worked as pubic-latrine cleaners for Robespierre during the Reign of Terror. Is that true?"

Maybe it was the light or my imagination, but the creases in his face seemed to deepen, with an effect like soil erosion, the blood leaving his lips. He exuded an odor that smelled like an unchanged bandage. There were whiskers showing above his collar, the way they do when an old man cannot shave adequately.

Then he seemed to collect himself. "A young woman awaits me now," he said. "After a nap and a shower and a fine breakfast, I'll return, and we'll continue our talk. General Mendoza will be accompanying me."

"Mr. Shondell, you promised you'd get my daughter into a hospital," Carroll said.

"Oh, yes," Shondell said. "Thank you for reminding me. A lovely girl."

WE WERE TAKEN back to the compartment where we had woken up, the ligatures on our wrists. Bell locked us in. We sat on the deck in the white bareness of the compartment, hands bound behind us, the engines humming through the bulkhead. I was reminded of the play *No Exit* by Jean-Paul Sartre. The characters find themselves in a windowless room and discover they are not only dead but in hell.

"Hey, you guys, I know this won't mean much, but I'm sorry I sold you out," Carroll said.

Neither Clete nor I could bring ourselves to look at him.

"Y'all hear me?" he said.

"Yeah, we heard you," Clete said. "That means you don't need to say any more."

"We saw all their faces," Carroll said.

"Yeah," Clete said.

"That means we got no chance, huh?" Carroll said.

"No one is putting the glide on you, LeBlanc," Clete said. "Now shut up."

"I don't want to go out like this," Carroll said. "With you guys hating me. My daughter never had a mother. I tried my best. I didn't think all this would happen."

"I'm going to come over there and kick the shit out of you," Clete said.

"Listen to me, Carroll," I said. "You owned up. You're genuinely sorry. We accept that. Now we're going to do everything we can to get out of here. Shondell has a weakness."

"What?" Carroll said.

"He's vain and afraid," Clete said. "He knows what's waiting for him down the track."

"What's waiting for him?" Carroll said.

"Probably everything he's done to other people," Clete said.

"Yeah?" Carroll said. "What good does that do us?"

Clete struggled to his feet. "There is no us. There is me and there is Dave. Then there is you. There is no *us*. Do you have that straight, you pinhead?"

It would have been funny in any other circumstances. But we were inside a nightmare, perhaps an atavistic memory of real events passed down through the eons, like dreams of falling or burning or being buried alive. We had no place to hide, no mother to wake us, no descent from the heavens by a winged spirit with a shining broadsword.

Then we got a visitor I didn't expect.

ADONIS STEPPED INTO the compartment and shut the hatch behind him. He wore floppy white slacks and a purple corduroy shirt with a chain and cross around his neck, as though affecting a man of leisure who was at peace with both heaven and earth. His hair was freshly barbered, lightly oiled and combed back on the sides. If a mirror had been available, I'm sure he would have been looking at his reflection.

He carried a small tin box in his palms as though it were a sacred object. It was painted with purple roses and green vines. "Hello, fellows," he said.

"Lose the guise, Adonis," Clete said. "You're working with that perv."

"I'm the only person on this yacht who will tell you the truth about your situation. I'm also the only one who might help you."

"Help yourself by dropping the dime on the perv while you have time," Clete said.

Adonis turned toward me. Considering the circumstances, his lidless eyes and swarthy good looks and calm demeanor were impressive and not to be taken lightly. However, if I hadn't known better, I would have believed that Shakespeare had Adonis in mind when he said the prince of darkness was always a gentleman.

"You realize you will not leave this place?" he said.

"So?" I said.

"I can make your ordeal easier, or I can end it now."

He opened the tin box. It contained a syringe and two glass ampoules of liquid.

"I think I'll pass," I said.

He ticked one fingernail on the box. "This is as good as it's going to get."

"You're offering us a hotshot?" Clete said.

"Morphine," Adonis said.

"What are you giving up in exchange for Isolde?" I said.

"Almost everything we have."

"How do you know a greaseball is lying?" Clete said. "His lips are moving."

"Clete's right, Adonis. You're a bum. I think you're about to become Shondell's silent partner."

"Penelope loves you," he said. "If she goes to the authorities, her daughter will be killed. Any power I have cannot stop Mark Shondell."

"He's not of this earth?" I said.

"That's right," Adonis replied.

"Wonder why he hauled butt when I shot at him," Clete said.

"You shot at Mark?"

"You got to do something for kicks."

"The three of you are going to die a horrible death," Adonis said. "Take the morphine."

"If we go through trial by ordeal, that's the way it is," I said. "Now get out of here. You're stinking up the compartment."

I was surprised at his reaction, because I had not expected one. He blinked, and his lips parted as a child's might if an adult pinched his cheek and shamed him in public.

"Something else you can take with you," Clete said. "I hear Gideon Richetti wants to do me a solid. Guess what that means for you, dick-wipe."

LATER SOMEONE TURNED off the overhead light, and immediately, the compartment was plunged into darkness. I lost track of time. An hour could have been a day, and a day could have been an hour. I wasn't sure when I was awake or when I was dreaming. After a while the two states of mind became interchangeable, one no more rational or irrational than the other. I tried to think of the sun bursting on the horizon, splintering the blue sky with a gold radiance that reached into infinity. I also envisioned a full moon rising with the wispy, cold fragility of a communion wafer.

Whatever my fate was, I wanted it over. I wished I had not witnessed the executions in the Red Hat House at Angola. I don't know how the condemned men didn't go mad anticipating a death that by anyone's measure is grotesque and cruel. Long ago I came to believe that these criminals were far braver men than I. Now I was confirmed in that belief. I had spoken with bravado to Adonis. But my words did not reflect what I felt. My breath was rank, my armpits reeking with a vinegar-like stench, my hair damp with sweat, even though the compartment was frigid.

We were given a bucket to use as a latrine. Carroll LeBlanc soiled himself. Clete snored. We felt like animals. Then, inside a deep sleep, I heard Clete call my name.

"What's the haps, Cletus?" I said.

"I dreamed you and I were at an LSU–Ole Miss game. It was raining down whiskey. We stomped Ole Miss's ass."

"Fuck these guys, Clete."

"You got it, big mon. We've got to get our hands on a weapon."

The hatch opened and Bell stepped into the compartment. "If you got to relieve yourselves, now's the time," he said.

Chapter Thirty-eight

ASIDE FROM BELL, our escorts wore zip-front silver overalls and goggles and plastic covers on their hair and plastic booties on their shoes and latex on their hands; they looked more like space aliens than medieval torturers.

I know the presence of men like these in our tale might test the limits of one's credulity. But let me tell you of my first visit to Angola Prison. I have never told this to others because my account, if believed at all, would change nothing in the system, do no good for the victims, and depress people of goodwill who want to believe in their government, their media, and their fellow man. Since then I have never doubted that there are people in our midst, significant numbers of them, who would have worked at Auschwitz in the time it took to sign their names on the job application.

Angola was a convict-lease prison founded during Reconstruction by an odious man named Samuel James. Under his tutelage, thousands of convicts, mostly black, died of sickness, malnutrition, and physical abuse. The favorite instrument was the Black Betty. More than one hundred convicts still lie in the levee along the Mississippi River. In the second half of the twentieth century, inmates were put in narrow, perpendicular iron sweatboxes set in concrete in the middle of summer, with no space to sit down, a bucket between their legs. One man was kept there nineteen days. His body was molded to the shape of the box.

While I was a visitor, a convict who fell out on work detail was placed on an anthill. A convict who sassed a gun bull was taken to the hole and whipped with a three-foot chunk of garden hose; the man who beat him called the process "making a Christian out of a nigger."

What kind of men were these? Uneducated peckerwoods with a jaw full of Red Man? That's not even close. Sexual nightmares and psychopaths and the cruelest people on earth? Don't doubt it for a minute.

Just before we reached the compartment where Shondell kept his collectibles, Clete leaned close to Carroll LeBlanc. "It's never as bad as you think," he said. "You fucked up, but you did it for your daughter. Streak and I don't hold it against you."

That was Clete Purcel.

The hatch was closed. Bell looked at his watch.

"How much is Shondell paying you for this?" I said.

"You don't get it, do you?" he said.

"What's to get?" I said. "You have a black soul. I hope you enjoy your shuffleboard retirement in St. Petersburg before you cash in."

"I'm already on the other side," he replied.

"I didn't catch that."

"I'm already across the Big Divide. You're sure a dumb son of a bitch, aren't you?"

I heard feet walking fast behind us. "Sorry I'm late," Shondell said. He was wearing a suit and tie. "Please forgive me if I don't stay around for all the festivities. I have some business to do, but I'll have everything on film and I can look at it later. Ready to get started?"

He opened the hatch. At first I couldn't see clearly past the hatch-way. But obviously, Shondell was stunned. I stepped sideways so I could see past him. The inside of the compartment had been torn apart, the chains and leather padding ripped from the bulkheads, the machines of torment thrown about like toys, the oak levers snapped off, the steel shafts doubled over, the cogged wheels twisted out of shape, the Brazen Bull pulled inside out.

"Must be the maid's day off," Clete said.

Shondell's face looked maniacal. "Secure the yacht," he said to Bell.

"We're at sea, sir," Bell said. "We're secured already."

"Get Adonis Balangie down here."

"Yes, sir. Should I tell him about this?"

"I told you to get him down here. So go do it."

Shondell's rage and indignation were feigned. I've seen fear in men's faces when the 105s were coming in short, and I've seen the desperation in the eyes of men who knew the dust-off wasn't coming and the Great Shade was about to pass over their faces; but I had never seen terror greater than I saw in Shondell's eyes during that moment. It was my belief then, and my belief now, that he saw the future and was terrified and would have traded his soul to avoid it.

Unfortunately for him, he had probably bartered away his soul many years ago.

BELL TOOK US back to our compartment. He didn't turn out the light. "This doesn't change anything. You guys know that, don't you?"

Surprisingly, Carroll LeBlanc spoke up. "Adonis Balangie wanted to cut us a break. I want to take him up on it. I can't go through this shit again."

"What break?" Bell said.

"A break. What do you care?" Carroll said. "Show some mercy."

Bell closed and locked down the hatch.

"What are you doing, Carroll?" I said.

"You said we needed a weapon," he replied.

FIFTEEN MINUTES LATER, Adonis opened the hatch and stepped into the compartment. One of the men in silver overalls stayed outside. Adonis was wearing a light overcoat, damp with sea spray. "What's this about a break?"

Clete and I lowered our heads. Our hands were still bound behind us.

"You said you'd shoot us up," Carroll said. "I got no illusions. I'd like to take you up on that."

"You're not out for the Medal of Honor?" Adonis said.

"Don't make fun of the guy, Adonis," I said.

He reached into his coat pocket and removed the tin box that contained the syringe and the ampoules of morphine.

"Before you give him that, can you answer a question?" I said.

"What's the question?"

"I don't get this stuff about a black sail and a white sail."

"If this deal is worked out and most of what we own is transferred to a bank in Malta, Isolde will be on her way to us in a boat with white sails. If not, the sails will be black."

"Why not use a radio?" Clete said.

"Because other people can pull the transmission out of the air," Adonis said. "Because Mark Shondell likes to pretend he's a man for the ages."

Clete's green eyes were half-lidded, his shoulders humped; he resembled a contemporary Quasimodo brought down from the bell tower. But as always, Clete's externals were misleading, his intelligence and complexity silently at work in a gargantuan body he had spent a lifetime abusing with weed, pills, cigarettes, trough-loads of deep-fried food, and oceans of booze. Put more simply, Clete Purcel was the human equivalent of an M-1 tank plowing through a stucco building.

I could see his upper arms expanding like a firehose swelling with pressurized water. In the corner of my eye, I saw him twisting the ligatures on his wrists, working them over the heels of his hands, ignoring the broken vessels and torn flesh, blood slipping off the ends of his fingers, all of this with his eyes straight ahead, like a brain-dead man gazing at empty space.

Suddenly, his hands were free. He clamped one on Adonis's mouth and the other on the back of his neck and drove his skull into the bulkhead, then dropped him to the deck as though he were a rag doll. He opened the tin box and removed the syringe. It was already loaded.

"Hey, guy out there!" he called through the hatchway. "Balangie is having a seizure! Get him out of here! We got enough problems!"

The man in overalls came through the hatch. "Seizure?"

Clete hooked his arm under the man's chin and peeled it back, then jabbed the needle into the carotid and plunged down the piston with his thumb. "How you like it, shit breath?"

The man's mouth fell open and his eyes rolled. Clete eased him to the deck and went through his pockets. He found a box cutter but no firearm. He sliced the ligatures on my wrists, then Carroll's.

"We've got to get a gun," he said.

I went through Adonis's pockets while Clete stood by the hatchway. "Nothing," I said.

"Got any idea what time of day it is?" Clete said.

"No," I said.

Clete chewed his lip. "You call it, Streak."

"When we were up the passageway, I thought I could feel the screws behind us," I said. "If there's an armory, it's probably aft."

"What about these two guys?" he said.

"What about them?" I said.

"What if they wake up?"

I knew what he was thinking. "Lock them in and leave them alone."

"Okie-dokie, big mon," he replied. "How you feeling, LeBlanc?"

"No matter how this comes out, I think you're a righteous dude, Purcel," he said.

"Don't tell anybody," Clete said.

I SUSPECTED WE WERE two decks down. We walked in the direction opposite the torture compartment and could hear the screws turning louder and louder under the hull. We found no armory, only a refrigerator unit and two compartments full of canned goods and a ladder at the end of the passageway. I went up first. As I got to the top, I saw a man twenty yards away, his back to me. He was dressed like a ship's officer and seemed to be guarding the entrance to a cabin. I ducked down below the level of the deck.

What? Clete mouthed.

Bogey at twelve o'clock, I answered.

He hooked his hand in the back of my belt and tugged gently, then squeezed past me up the ladder, the syringe clenched in his right hand. He paused briefly, then sprang down the passageway, garroted the sentinel, and jabbed him in the throat with the needle. I motioned for Carroll to follow me.

Clete opened the hatch to the cabin the ship's officer had been guarding. Father Julian was sitting on one bunk and Leslie Rosenberg on another. Elizabeth lay on a third. The word "angelic" would probably apply to Elizabeth, with her blue eyes and golden hair, but I don't like to think in those terms. We dragged the unconscious sentinel inside the cabin and closed the hatch behind him.

"Y'all doin' all right?" I said.

"What the fuck does it look like?" Leslie said.

"You know how to say it, Leslie," I replied. "How about you, Julian?"

"I think Leslie put it well," he replied. The purple and yellow bruises and lesions and burns patterned on his face by Delmer Pickins were still there, but he actually managed to laugh. I take back my comment about the use of words such as "angelic." I think there are people who have auras that could light the darkest dungeon on earth.

"No one saw y'all kidnapped?" I said. "You didn't get a message out?"

"You think we'd be here now?" Leslie said.

"Bingo!" Carroll said. He was squatted down next to the ship's officer. He held up a .25-caliber semi-auto, then eased back the slide to confirm that a round was in the chamber. He felt in the officer's other coat pocket and found two spare magazines, both loaded.

"How many people are on board?" Clete said.

"We were blindfolded," Leslie said.

"Why does Shondell want y'all?" he said.

"Tell him," Julian said.

"He believes I'm growing in power," she said. "He thinks I'm working in concert with Father Julian to ruin his name."

"How are you going to acquire more power?" I said.

"I've already explained that, but you refused to hear," she said.

"Don't start that stuff again," Clete said. "We keep it simple. We take it to them with tongs. Right, Dave?"

But Clete was fooling himself. He knew we had little control of our fate. And he did not want to accept that we were dealing with preternatural forces.

"There's something we haven't told y'all," I said. "About Shondell's collectibles."

"What collectibles?" Julian said.

"Instruments of torture," I said. "He was about to put us through the grinder. Except someone tore his machinery apart—someone who could twist iron wheels like licorice."

Leslie looked into Clete's face. "Do you remember me, Mr. Purcel?"

"What, from the Quarter?" he said.

"During your torment in the Keys. I saved you."

"No, no, no," he said. "No thanks, no help wanted, no more green monsters in my life or archangels flying around."

Leslie sat down by her daughter and stroked her hair. "If you can be kind to Gideon, you will change American history."

"I don't want any of that crap," Clete said. "I'm going to cool out as many of these guys as I can and worry about the other stuff later on. Like after I've been dead a few hundred years."

Carroll had gone into the head. He came back out, his face white. "There's a porthole in there. Take a look."

"What is it?" Clete said.

"See for yourself," Carroll said. "I don't want to believe in stuff like this. My head is coming off my shoulders. It's some kind of mind-fuck. Sorry, Father."

"I think I'll survive," Julian said. He went into the head, then came back out, pinching the bridge of his nose and widening his eyes, as though arranging words in his head before he spoke them. He looked at Clete. "Did you kill someone today?"

"No," Clete said. "I ran Adonis's head into the bulkhead and put a hypodermic needle in a guy's neck."

"The man you injected, what was he wearing?"

"Silver overalls."

"He's tied to the mast of Gideon's prison ship. His entrails have been pulled out."

"I didn't do anything like that," Clete said.

"I didn't say you did," Julian replied.

"What time of day is it out there?" Clete asked.

"You tell me," Julian said. "The sky is purple and green and full of electricity."

"Dave, we've got to make a move," Clete said.

Just then the yacht pitched, then seemed to mount a swell and dip forward and slip down a deep trough. It smacked bottom with such force that it jarred out teeth and splashed seawater through the port-hole in the head.

"Come on, Dave, don't just stand there," Clete said.

I looked at Leslie and her daughter. I had the feeling I would never see them again.

"Do you hear me, Dave?" Clete said.

"Let's go," I said.

"What about me?" Carroll said.

"Give me the piece and stay here," Clete said.

"I'm not up to it?" Carroll said.

"It's me that green bastard is after," Clete said. "You may be the guy who has to get everybody home, Carroll. Do us a solid."

"Yeah, no problem," Carroll said, handing the .25 semi-auto and spare magazines to Clete. "Yeah, we're gonna get through this. Right? Somebody knows we're here. We just got to hold on."

Have you ever seen someone rolled up in an embryonic ball at the bottom of a foxhole, his eyes squeezed tightly shut, his forearms clamped on his ears, while an artillery barrage marches through his position? That's what Carroll LeBlanc made me think of.

Chapter Thirty-nine

CLETE AND I went into the passageway. The yacht pitched again, almost knocking both of us down. The only time I had been in seas this violent was during Hurricane Audrey in 1957, when I was on board a drilling rig. As then, I felt as though we were inside a maelstrom, one in which the physical laws of the universe had been suspended. I heard dishware crashing, furniture turning over. I felt a wave hit the gunwale and the side of a hull with the density and power of wet cement.

Behind me, someone opened the hatch on the cabin and stepped outside. It was Leslie.

"What is it?" I said.

She moved close to me so Clete couldn't hear. "Maybe I'll see you in another time."

I looked up and down the passageway. We were totally vulnerable. "Leslie, this isn't the time for it."

"I know." Paradoxically, she stood on the tops of my shoes and put her arms around me and pressed her chest and head against me. I could feel her heart beating and her breath on my skin.

"You're a good man," she said. "So is Clete. No evil can ever destroy you."

Then she was gone. She didn't walk away. She was just gone.

"Dave, don't just stand there," Clete said. "Haul ass."

"I was talking to Leslie."

"Leslie? There's nobody else here. Come on, big mon. We've got to get out of Crazy Town."

THE ELECTRIC LIGHTS began flittering as we worked our way forward. Then they went out altogether and came back on. Two popped, the glass tinkling on the deck. A tall figure came down the ladder from the main deck. He was wearing flip-flops, his face in shadow, his hands tanned, his midnight-blue silk shirt unbuttoned on his chest and stomach, his tight white bell-bottoms hanging below his navel. He looked high.

"What are you doing here, Johnny?" I said.

"Trying to save you from getting killed," he replied. "I saw you on the surveillance camera."

"Who else saw us?" Clete said.

"Nobody," he said. "It's chaos up there. Half of the electrical system is down. Uncle Mark is going apeshit."

"You don't look like you're about to lose the love of your life," I said.

"My uncle shot me up."

"You let him?" Clete said.

"I was asleep. That tin box Adonis had, those were my works. I put a hotshot in there. I was gonna use it on myself if I didn't get Isolde back."

Clete looked at me. If Johnny was telling the truth, Clete had jabbed the hotshot into the neck of the man in the silver overalls and killed him. "What's going on with the green monster out there?" Clete said.

"He wants to talk with you," Johnny said.

"Don't tell me that," Clete said.

"He said it over our radio. Just before it went dead."

"Can you get us some heavy firepower?" I said.

"Bell has all that stuff," Johnny said.

"Where does he store it?" I said.

"I don't know."

"You're not being helpful," Clete said. "You've got to get out a Mayday."

"There's some kind of shield around the yacht," Johnny said.

Clete looked at me again, then at Johnny. "Go back down the passageway to the cabin where Father Julian is and stay there."

"No."

"*No?*" I said.

"Isolde is on her way here," Johnny said.

"From where?" I said.

"Another ship. I'm going now. I don't like the way y'all are talking to me."

"Then hoof it, kid," Clete said.

Johnny went back up the ladder. He glanced back once, his face twisted with either hurt or anger, before disappearing.

"Think he'll rat us out?" Clete said.

"Let's get on the starboard side," I said. "At least he won't know our whereabouts."

"I got to face this guy Gideon, Dave. That doesn't sit easy."

"Let him come to you."

"My stomach is flopping," he said. "Jesus Christ, we did it this time, didn't we?"

WE FOUND A ladder to the top deck on the starboard side of the yacht. The air was cold, clouds of fog as white as cotton scudding across the water, the morning sun just breaking on the horizon, its rosy hue dissolving inside the fog. Flying fish skimmed the waves like bronze darts.

"Got any idea how far from shore we are?" I said.

"I don't hear any buoys," Clete said. "There's no sand in the waves."

"I wish I had a coat."

"Dave, if I don't come back from this, kill Shondell."

"You'll piss on his grave."

He started to say something, then looked past me into the fog. "Oh, shit," he said.

The prison galleon was no more than forty feet away, rising with the swells, the planks in the hull and gunwales and the quarterdeck bright with spray. Then it drifted closer, perhaps ten feet from the railing on the yacht, the oars receding inside the loopholes. Gideon Richetti descended from the quarterdeck. I didn't say "walked," he descended. He was wearing a long overcoat made of leather, the collar up, a floppy hat on his head. But he was not the same creature I had seen before. His scales were hardly visible, his face lean rather than triangular in shape. I wondered if I was looking at the same man.

"I want to speak to you, Mr. Purcel," he said.

The voice, however, was the same; it echoed, or rumbled, as though trapped in a stone cistern.

"You'll speak to us both, Mr. Richetti," I said.

"Stay out of it, Dave," Clete said.

"That's a very good suggestion," Gideon said.

"Say what you got to say," Clete said. "Yeah, I'm talking to you. You hung me upside down and were going to boil my brains in my skull. You were a loser four hundred years ago, and you're a loser now."

"I wish to ask your forgiveness."

"FTS on that, Jack," Clete replied.

"I don't know what that means."

"Fuck. That. Shit. You burned Leslie Rosenberg to death. You know where that puts you? With the Nazis. I've got a picture in my wallet I'd like to show you. A Jewish mother and her kids going to the ovens. Were you there?"

"I'm sorry for all the suffering I imposed on other people, Mr. Purcel. If you can't forgive me, then don't. But I had to try."

"Clete?" I said.

"Shut up, Dave."

"You forgave LeBlanc."

"Hey," Clete said to Gideon. "Why'd you tie a dead guy to the mast and tear out his guts?"

"I was angry. He was going to torture you and your friends to death. Sometimes I lose control."

"*Sometimes?*" Clete said.

Gideon was silent. I could hear waves hitting against both vessels, and feel the deck rising and falling under my feet. "Do it, Clete," I said.

"I don't usually listen to Dave's advice, but I owe him a solid or two," he said. "You reading me on this? Look at me. I'm talking to you, asshole."

"There's a sailboat in the distance," Gideon said.

"Screw the sailboat," Clete said. "I forgive you. That means get out of our lives. Freshen up, take a shower, get yourself some breath mints and industrial-strength deodorant, haunt a house, find a girl-friend who's not choosy, get your ashes hauled, but leave us the fuck alone."

"You have to stop Mark Shondell," Gideon said. "He is about to bring a great evil upon the earth."

The clouds of fog billowed across the deck, as cold as ice water, so white and thick I could not see my hands. I clenched Clete's upper arm to make sure he was there. It was as hard as a chunk of curb stone. "Can you see anything?" I said.

"No, nothing," he replied.

I wiped my face with my hand. It was as slick as rainwater. "Where's the sun?"

"I don't know," he said.

The fog broke into dirty wisps, like smoke from a garbage incin-erator. I could see the water now. It was dark green and streaked with froth and lapping against the hull. As the fog thinned, I thought I saw baitfish in the waves or perhaps seaweed or flotsam from a wreck. Then I saw pieces of cloth, what looked like sweaters and stocking caps and primitive tunics made of coarse wool, shoes that were hardly more than leather wrapped around the foot, glimpses of bone and a hank of hair, faces that were as gray as soaked parch-ment, arms and naked legs and bloated stomachs roiling with a wave, then sinking into the depths.

"What happened to the galleon?" I said.

Clete shook his head. "I need a drink. I'd settle for a quart of gasoline." Then he looked at me blankly, as though reviewing a video in his head.

"What is it?" I said.

"The storage compartment down below. One of them had emer-gency flares and two gasoline cans in it."

I heard footsteps approaching us. Clete took the .25 semi-auto from his pocket.

"It's me. Johnny," a voice said. "Everything is down. The whole electrical system. Even the batteries are dead. Did you guys see anything?"

Neither of us answered, because neither of us trusted Johnny anymore. I had also lost faith in Penelope. Perhaps they were simply people who represented an idea or a cause that was greater than themselves, and as for all surrogates, the burden was greater than they could bear. I wanted also to believe that Penelope was not married to Adonis, and I wanted to believe this namely because, even with all my faults, I had never slept with another man's wife.

What was the shorter truth? The woman I wanted with me was Leslie Rosenberg, and I knew that she and her daughter, Elizabeth, whose blue eyes were like looking into the face of God, were about to be taken from me forever.

I looked down at the flotsam in the water. I had no doubt it contained the clothing and shoes and remains of people who lived hundreds of years ago. "Did you see that down there?" I said to Johnny.

"Yeah, Gideon turned his rowers loose," he replied. "That's what he's supposed to do."

"Would you explain that, please?" I said.

"He's a revelator. He makes people reveal who they are. Then they're free. Leslie changed, too. She became an angel."

I didn't want to hear any more theology from Johnny Shondell.

"Sooner or later Shondell is going to search the ship," Clete said. "Are you our friend or foe, Johnny?"

"I got to get Isolde back," he said.

"Get out of my sight," Clete said.

Chapter Forty

WHEN JOHNNY WAS gone, we worked our way back to the storage compartments. We found a case of wine and poured out three bottles and refilled them with gasoline and recorked the necks, then taped cotton pads from a first-aid kit to the bottoms and wet the pads with gas and put the bottles in a duffel bag with four emergency flares.

I suspect our behavior seemed grandiose. We were certainly out-numbered and outgunned. We were also physically exhausted and emotionally burnt out, the way you feel coming off a three-day whiskey drunk, lights flickering behind your eyelids, a bilious taste in your mouth, a clammy smell like a field mortuary on your skin. I tried to keep in mind the admonition of Stonewall Jackson I quoted earlier: Always mystify, mislead, and surprise.

I also believed we had another weapon on our side: Shondell was a bully, and like all bullies, he was probably a coward. The electrical system was still down, and the ship surrounded by fog, which gave us an appreciable degree of cover. The downside: We could not be certain of our environment. We seemed to be in a vortex, one similar to the eye of a storm. Even though the sun had risen, the skies were dark again, the waves filled with the same black luminosity I had seen when I stood on the dock by the amusement pier, wondering if Homer was still with us, his sirens winking at us, lifting their wet hair off their breasts, guiding us onto the rocks.

The truth is, I wanted the world to be enchanted, hung with mysteries and flights of the imagination. Why? Because with that belief, we become subsumed by creation and a participant in it, a living particle inside infinity. We abide in the presence of Charlemagne's knights jingling up the road to Roncesvalles; we flee mediocrity and predictability, and we delight in the rising and setting of the sun and no longer fear death because indeed the earth abideth forever. I wanted Gideon to be real; I wanted to hear the clash of shields and Arthur pulling his sword from the rock and see Guinevere waiting on the parapet of the castle in the dawn, shrouded with a golden nimbus.

Why not? It beats dining out at Chuck E. Cheese.

WE SOAKED THE compartment with gasoline, and Clete lit a piece of paper and set the deck ablaze with his Zippo. In minutes flames were curling outside the hatch, flattening on the passageway ceiling. We worked our way forward again and started a fire among Shondell's collection of torture instruments. The padding on the bulkheads burst alight and, in the heat, seemed to blacken and split instantly into lesions. The smoke was thick and black and noxious, like the odor that comes from the stack on a rendering plant.

Clete gagged. "What is that?"

"Blood," I said.

"Shondell is going down for the count, right? We're agreed on that?"

"We don't know the politician he's working for, the rich-kid gutter rat."

"It doesn't matter," Clete said. "Shondell is joining the Hallelujah Chorus? We're copacetic on that?"

"What do I know?"

"Don't get in my way, Streak."

Twice we encountered Shondell's employees or acolytes, all of them carrying either flashlights or fire extinguishers. Only one had a firearm. Clete threw him overboard before he could use it, cracked another man's skull against the bulkhead, and caused the others to melt back into the darkness. I began to feel there were different levels of people who worked for Mark Shondell. Louisiana's economy is based on the oil industry. If you're in, you're fine. If you're out, you might have to close one eye. Babylon might be a real fling with Beat-My-Daddy Slack, but you don't have a lot of selections when you're in the mop-and-pail brigade. It's hard to be proud of your spendolies when you're working in a porn shop or in a drive-through daiquiri window.

I thought I saw women in the shadows, perhaps the prostitutes I believed were on board the tugboat anchored by Shondell's stilt house. Shondell was the light inside the lantern. The candle moths swirling around him would always be there, and if they were singed and killed by his flame, others would replace them. Bell was one of them, although more intelligent and experienced in the ways of the underworld. There must have been others on board like him, but we didn't know where they were. Rats abandon sinking ships. I hoped that was the case.

Clete opened the valve on a propane tank in a compartment behind the galley, flung an emergency flare inside, and locked down the hatch. The aftermath of the explosion sounded like a junkyard falling off a truck.

Up ahead I could see flashlights inside the bridge, the beams crisscrossing and bouncing off the panoramic windows and consoles and panel monitors and chart tables and myriad dials that had been rendered inoperable by a force outside the yacht. The sky was now sealed with purplish-black clouds, except in the south, where a vaporous green ribbon of light stretched across the horizon and a solitary boat was pitching toward the yacht, its white sails swollen with wind.

Then I saw Johnny coming toward us, below the bridge, his clothes sculpted against his body, his hands held up as though he were trying to stop traffic on a street. "Don't go up there, Mr. Dave," he said. "Y'all don't know what you're doing."

"How many people are up there?" Clete said.

"I don't know," he said. "Y'all and Gideon are messing up the deal."

"Messing up what deal?" Clete said.

"Isolde is on her way. Everything is set up. Gideon shut down the power. Fire is coming out of the portholes on the stern. Uncle Mark is backing out of the deal."

"How many guns are up there, Johnny?" I said.

"That's all you got on your mind?" he said.

"Where's Bell?" I said.

"I don't know. Belowdecks, maybe."

"Does he still have the Kalashnikov?"

"The what?" he said.

"The AK-47," I said.

"You're going to get Isolde killed."

"*We* are?" Clete said, touching his chest. "I feel like flinging you over the rail, Johnny."

"Then do it," Johnny said. "If I lose Isolde, I lose everything."

"Where's Penelope?" I said.

"On the bridge," he said. "With Adonis."

I rested my hand on his shoulder. "Take care of Father Julian and Leslie and Elizabeth and Detective LeBlanc. We'll do everything we can to protect Isolde."

"I already went down there," he said. "Leslie and her daughter are gone. So is that LeBlanc guy. Father Julian is real sick."

"Leslie is gone?" I said.

"Yeah, what did I just say?"

"You're really starting to piss me off, Johnny," Clete said. "How would you like me to dribble your head on the deck?"

"I said she's gone. Maybe with Gideon. Now Gideon is screwing up everything, and y'all are doing everything you can to help him."

"Get lost," Clete said, and shoved him in the back.

"Don't do that," Johnny said.

Clete shoved him again, this time along the rail. "I'll count to three, then you're going over the rail."

"Fuck you, Mr. Clete."

"'Fuck you, Mr. Clete'? I just love that," Clete said. "I'm about to knock you down."

"Johnny, there are lifeboats on both sides of the ship," I said. "Get one ready and put Father Julian in it. We're not going to let your uncle destroy us."

"What are you going to do about Gideon?" he said.

"The enemy of my enemy is my friend," I said.

"Sell that when Uncle Mark's yacht blows up and Isolde is dead," he said.

IN JOHNNY'S WAY, he was right. In my vanity, I had thought I could find the origins of human cruelty. The upshot was the discovery of a time dimension that perhaps existed simultaneously with our own. I knew no more about the nature of man than when I'd visited Marcel LaForchette in Huntsville Pen, a man who turned out to be my half brother and who killed himself in my living room. In my search for the origins of human cruelty, I had come to the same dead end as the psychiatrists who look into the heart of darkness and are so frightened they thank God for the clinical term "pathological," because it allows them to cleanse the images planted in their minds by the patients they tried to cure.

What's the lesson? That's another easy one: Don't be taken in by bullshit from people who have no idea what evil is about.

JOHNNY LEFT US, perhaps to launch a lifeboat, perhaps to help Father Julian, perhaps to betray us. Clete and I had few choices. We had the .25 semi-auto and the duffel bag and the Molotov cocktails and the emergency flares. We could try to take the bridge or launch a lifeboat with Johnny and Julian. If we chose the latter without putting Shondell out of business, we would probably be machine-gunned in the water. Clete seemed to read my mind. "Worried about Penelope?"

"What do you think?"

"She dealt the play."

"Maybe, maybe not."

"Make up your mind, Dave. We don't have much time."

"If we had the AK—"

"We don't."

My throat was dry, my face small and tight in the wind. "Light it up."

Inside my head, as though watching a movie, I saw a young United States Army second lieutenant talking into a radio, an Asian village and rice paddy in the background, tracer rounds streaking out of the hooches, flying like segments of yellow-and-red neon above the paddy.

"You're sure?" Clete said.

I lifted a Molotov cocktail from the bag. The bottle felt cold and heavy in my hand. "Give me your Zippo."

Clete ran his hand down my arm and pulled the bottle from me. "You won't be able to live with yourself, Streak."

"Watch," I said. I took the bottle back.

But my bravado was soon upstaged. I heard a sound behind me and turned around. I did not know where Carroll LeBlanc had come from other than the darkness. But his sudden reappearance was not the issue. His expression was lunatical, inhuman, his eyes devoid of conscience or reason, his clothes slick with blood, one hand clenched on a dripping butcher knife. "I do'ed it, Robo. I mean I piled up those motherfuckers all over the place, with their guts in their laps, like Gideon. It actually gave me a hard-on. What's happening, Purcel? You don't look too good."

Then he laughed until he was hardly able to breathe or stand, his mouth a round black hole, as though he had accidentally swallowed a spirit hidden inside the wind.

I CLIMBED THE LADDER to the bridge with Clete behind me. I stopped while he flicked the Zippo and held the flame to the cotton pad on the bottom of the wine bottle. Then I tossed it through a side window on the bridge and watched it break on a hard surface and fill the bridge with light. I threw the remaining two bottles into the flames.

I took no pride in what I did. Nor did I want to see the images that danced before my eyes. I had replicated a scene from Dante's *Inferno*. The flames looked liquid, the players made of wax, frozen in time and space as though carved out of the heat, the surprise in their faces like that of children. Was I filled with pity? Did I abhor the incubus in me that could set afire his fellow creatures? I cannot answer any of these questions. I wanted to be a million miles away.

"Get down!" Clete said.

"What?"

"Bell!" he said.

As fast as the bottles had exploded, the flames had shrunk into strips of fire that were rapidly dying for want of fuel. Oh, yes, the damage was there. I saw two burned men crawl from the hatch, and one man shivering with pain and shock, his teeth chattering, and Mark Shondell in a corner, his hair curled from the heat, his face misshapen and painted with blisters, part of his lip gone, probably bitten off. I saw Penelope in the background, on the deck, under a raincoat. Adonis was gone. But Bell was not.

He opened up with the AK-47, blowing out glass, whanging rounds all over the superstructure. Clete jerked me back down the ladder, firing blindly at Bell, his eyes wide with adrenalin, as though he were looking into an artic wind.

Bell stopped shooting and ducked below the bridge window, but I knew we were in trouble. He had the high ground and we didn't. He also possessed the best infantry assault rifle in the world. And Mark Shondell, the brains behind Bell and his fellow troglodytes, was still alive. Curds of black smoke were rising from the stern, and the gallery was burning with such ferocity that the portholes on two adjacent compartments were filled with yellow flame that was as bright as a searchlight.

In the distance I could see the sailboat pitching in the waves, throwing ropes of foam over the deck. The white sails had been taken from the masts and replaced with black ones.

"Look what you did, Mr. Dave," a voice said behind me.

It was Johnny. He had his arm around Father Julian. Carroll LeBlanc was staring at them with an idiotic grin.

"Shut up, kid," Clete said.

"Black sails mean she's dead," Johnny said. "I can't believe we've done this."

He had said "we," not "you." But that was poor consolation. Clete was right. I would find no solace for my part in what we had done.

Know why war sucks? We usually kill the wrong people.

Chapter Forty-one

Clete pulled me aside. He had taken Carroll's butcher knife from him. He put a fresh magazine in the semi-auto and pulled and released the slide and clicked on the safety and placed the gun in my hand. "I got to get to Bell. You keep him busy until I can get behind him."

"That's a bad idea," I said.

"No arguments, big mon."

"Where's Adonis?" I said.

"Who cares?"

"He's a survivor," I said. "He'll cut a deal. Maybe he can get us some serious weapons."

"Adonis may also be rallying the troops. I can't believe I ever stood up for that guy. Come on, we got to put it in gear. Hey, I got one for you."

"What?"

"Know what Ambrose Bierce called a pacifist?"

"Wrong time for it, Cletus."

"A dead Quaker." He hit me on the arm. "Stomp ass and take names, noble mon. The Bobbsey Twins from Homicide are forever."

Then he was gone.

The only other time I had ever been in such close proximity to a murderous enemy was in Vietnam. We got into night-trail firefights when Sir Charles was no more than five feet from us. Oddly, we had come to respect Sir Charles and his ability to live inside the greenery of a rain forest and suddenly materialize out of the mists, his uniform little more than black pajamas, his sandals cut from an automobile tire, his day's ration a rice ball tied inside a sash around his hips.

Sir Charles could be incredibly cruel, as the VC demonstrated in the capture of Hué when they buried alive both civilians and prisoners of war. But Sir Charles was brave and had a cause, one that he saw as noble. Mark Shondell could lay no such claim. He sought revenge on others for his own failure, and helped inculcate racial hatred and fear in the electorate to divide us against ourselves. I had known his kind all my life. Except Shondell was not an ordinary man. Marcel LaForchette believed Shondell may have been in league with diabolical powers. I don't know if there is any such thing. But I do believe there are people in our midst who wish to make a graveyard of the world, and their motivation may be no more complex than that of an angry child flinging scat because he was left with regularity in a dirty diaper.

The ribbon of green light on the southern horizon was creeping higher into the sky, the waves subsiding, the sailboat rising and falling with the rhythm of a rocking horse. I felt a drop of rain on the back of my neck, like a reminder of the earth's resilience. Then I looked at Father Julian and felt the same sense about him. There are those among us who can walk through cannon smoke and grin about it while everyone else is going insane. That was Father Julian Hebert.

We were in the lee of the superstructure of which the bridge was part, but not at an angle where Bell could fire upon us. "How you doin', Julian?" I said.

"Not bad," he replied.

"You're not a very good liar."

"I'll practice."

"I've got to entertain Bell," I said. "I hope to come back. If I don't, try to get on board a lifeboat. Penelope is on the bridge. Maybe she can go with you."

"You still have feelings for her?"

"None that are good."

"Who's the liar?" he said. But at least he smiled.

I WENT UP THE ladder. The bridge windows were broken, the jagged and burnt frames like empty eye sockets against the watery greenish band of light in the south. I saw no sign of Bell. He had told Clete he was in the First Cav. I suspected he was telling the truth. He didn't silhouette, he didn't give away his position; he made no sound at all.

"Dave Robicheaux here, Mr. Bell," I said.

No answer.

"Is Penelope okay?"

"Go away, Dave," she said.

"Mr. Bell, how about we drink mash and talk trash? You can drink the mash, I'll talk the trash." I had the semi-auto in my right hand. "Hey, I'm lonely out here," I said.

No response.

"You doing all right, Mr. Shondell?" I said.

The entire yacht was quiet. The sailboat was closer, its black sails taut with wind, flecked with foam. I thought I could see someone in the wheelhouse. I also thought I saw a swimmer knifing through the waves, headed for the sailboat. I wiped my eyes and looked again. The swimmer had no flotation equipment, wore no shoes, and took long, even strokes, twisting his head sideways to breathe, like a long-distance pro. I couldn't see the swimmer's face, but I was almost certain I was looking at Adonis Balangie.

I was crouched on the ladder, just below the bridge. "Hey, Mr. Bell!" I said. "You were in the First Cav? That's righteous, brother. Central Highlands, right? I was there. Came home alive in '65. Sorry for the incoming. Let's start over."

Still no response. Bell was hard-core, the kind of cynic who concludes he's going to hell the day he's born.

"Did you hear me, Mr. Bell?"

"Yeah, I got the message. Come on in. Have some coffee."

If he wasn't a cop now, he had probably been one in the past. He knew what waited for him if he got locked up in a mainline joint. A cop in the shower is a bar of soap; on the yard, he can be shanked in the time it takes for a guard to turn his back; in the mess hall, his food is a cuspidor. In a joint like Angola, multiply everything I said by ten. But I thought I'd give it a try anyway.

"I can guarantee you friend-of-the-court status," I lied. "Maximum bounce, three to five. With luck, fifteen months. You can do it on your hands."

"No kidding?" he said. "Come a little closer. My hearing aid isn't working."

"Sure," I said. "If you guys can get a Mayday out, we'll have the chopper on the way."

"Can't hear you, sweetheart."

A bucket lay on its side between the ladder and the bridge. I picked it up and threw it across the deck. Bell tilted the Kalashnikov out the window and began firing, the ejected shells bouncing on the console and the deck. He had jungle-clipped a second thirty-round magazine to the one inserted in the magazine well. With a flick of his wrist, he could reverse an empty magazine and replace it with a fresh one and be back on rock and roll in less than three seconds.

Then I saw Clete's silhouette looming behind him.

Bell had just eased off the trigger and was probably trying to see if he had ricocheted a couple of rounds into me. For just a second I looked straight into his face. He seemed to realize he had blown it and that Clete was standing behind him. I even thought I saw him smile as he would at a fellow traveler, one who poses as a servant of the people or the nation but secretly knows he's a mercenary. Any way you cut it, I think he knew he was about to do the Big Exit and was trying to sign off with a measure of good cheer, perhaps with a few words such as "Way to go, laddie. Kiss the ladies for me and pour a toddy in my coffin."

A bit romantic? Yeah, probably. But watching a violent death can eat your lunch, particularly when you're a participant.

Clete formed his left arm into a hook and wrapped it under Bell's chin and jerked back his head, curving the butcher knife into his heart. Bell's lips pursed silently like the mouth of a fish out of water. It should have been over. Bell went straight down, his arms flopping at his sides, the Kalashnikov dropping out of view. I heard the steel butt strike the deck. In my mind's eye, I saw myself running into the bridge, finding Penelope all right, looking at Clete with relief, convinced we were about to reenter the rational world and flee forever the web in which we had entangled ourselves, not unlike Stephen Crane's soldier returning from the war and rediscovering the beauty in a buttermilk sky and green pastures blooming with wildflowers.

Alas, there is always the canker in the rose, the shaved dice in the cup, the loss of the nail in a horse's shoe that brings down a kingdom. Clete could not believe his eyes. The Kalashnikov bounced once off the deck and landed in the lap of Mark Shondell.

"Oh, my, isn't this a gift?" he said. "Thank you so much, Mr. Purcel."

Clete barely got through the hatch before Shondell lifted the muzzle and opened up.

THE FIRE WAS spreading through the ship. I could see other people on the stern, but I didn't know if they were crew members or prostitutes or Shondell's goons. If the latter, I suspected they were calculating the risk of deserting Shondell by going over the side or getting into a firefight on the bridge. The half-clothed body parts of the two private investigators stuffed in an oil barrel and dropped in Vermilion Bay had been a reminder of Shondell's policy regarding employee disloyalty or failure. Someone had tried to launch a lifeboat but had made a mess of the pulleys and tipped the boat over. Two people were trying to hold on to the sides. They wore life jackets and one of them may have been the man Clete threw overboard. If the yacht went down, the hull or the screws might take them with it.

Then I saw three men working their way forward. They stayed in the lee of the superstructure and were crouched in the manner of infantry approaching an objective. We were running out of time, and I saw no solutions to our problems. Johnny and Father Julian and Carroll LeBlanc and Clete and I were huddled in the shadows perhaps twenty yards aft of the bridge. We were a sorry-looking bunch, I'm sure. My system could no longer produce adrenalin, and Clete was in the same shape. We were hungry and cold and probably on the edge of physical and nervous collapse, unable to think clearly or distinguish the tricks of the mind from Gideon's supernatural manifestations and the very real possibility that we were about to die.

Johnny was sitting on the deck, his knees pulled up before him, his head down.

Clete shook him gently by the shoulder. "Get out of it, kid. Slip the punch and swallow your blood. Don't let your enemy know you're hurt."

"Isolde is dead," Johnny said.

"You don't know that," I said.

"These things have happened before, Mr. Dave," he said. "My uncle always wins. I have to stop him."

"What are you doing, Johnny?" Father Julian asked.

"Getting up," Johnny said. "Ending this."

"Your uncle is going to kill anyone who comes through that hatch," Clete said.

"That's the point," Johnny said. "Then you can shoot him."

Julian stepped in front of him. "It's time I have a talk with your uncle."

"No, he hates you, Father," Johnny said.

"Then I must have done something right in my life," Julian said. He looked at me. "Keep Johnny here, Dave."

I knew we had only minutes, if that. Shondell's people would soon have us surrounded. Julian was about to give his life so I could get a clear shot at Shondell. Arguing with him would not change his mind. If I didn't act, his sacrifice would be for nothing. "I'll be behind you," I said.

But I had forgotten about Carroll LeBlanc. "Give me back the knife," he said to Clete.

"What for?" Clete said.

"It's my knife."

I looked at Clete and shook my head. But he ignored me. "It's LeBlanc's decision," he said. He let Carroll take the knife from his hand.

Carroll grinned at me, his face sweaty and bloodless, looking like a deathly ill man burning with fever, the string of moles below his eye as dry as baked dirt. "Let's do it, Robo."

He went up the ladder, his grin like a half-moon slit in a musk-melon. Clete and I went behind him. I had the .25 semi-auto in my right hand. Then Carroll turned briefly and stared into my face. "Sorry I let you guys down. I hope this makes it right." "It's okay," I said. Then I stumbled. The semi-auto caught on the rail and fell from my hand and tumbled into the darkness. Carroll never faltered. He went through the hatch and took a burst from the Kalashnikov in the chest and the face. Shondell was sitting down, his back propped against the console; his mouth resembled a horizontal keyhole where he had bitten off half of his upper lip, exposing his teeth. Carroll went down on his face and I knew I was next. I saw the glee in Shondell's eyes as he raised the muzzle of his weapon. I had no defense, no moat or castle behind which to hide. This time it was for real: In two seconds I would be spaghetti on the bulkhead, and Clete would catch the next burst and tumble on top of me, and the weapon that couldn't get us in Vietnam would have gotten even at last.

But that's not what happened. Shondell pulled the trigger and the firing pin snapped on a dud. I had never seen a man look so surprised and so afraid. In the corner of my eye, I saw Penelope getting to her feet. "Run, Dave," she said.

I didn't have time. Clete almost knocked me down. He kicked the Kalashnikov from Shondell's hands and pulled him to his feet and slammed his face on a glass-covered chart table. I had not seen the emergency flare he was carrying in his side pocket, but there it was. He tore off the cap and banged the striker on the tip. There was a spark, then the flare was aflame, hissing like a snake. Clete shoved it over Shondell's teeth and down his throat.

I tried to pull Clete away from Shondell but to no avail. I knew he had gone back in time and was walking with the Jewish woman and her three daughters to a gas chamber at Auschwitz. I stepped back and did not try to intervene.

He grabbed Shondell by the neck and began beating his head on the chart table. The glass did not break, but Shondell's head did. It broke the way a flower pot full of dirt does, and then it came apart, a sanguine mist rising from Shondell's hair. Clete couldn't or wouldn't stop. He knotted the neck of Shondell's shirt and coat in his fists and hammered the remnants of Shondell's head against the edge of the glass until Clete's hands slipped loose and Shondell slid to the deck, his neck a stump.

Clete stared down at Shondell's body as though he did not know where it had come from. Penelope was pressed against the bulkhead, her skin and purple dress freckled with blood and brain matter. There was no fear in her face, only dismay and perhaps disappointment.

"What did you expect, Penelope?" I said. "Where did you think this would end?"

"Look!" she said, pointing at the sailboat as it crossed in front of the yacht. "There's Isolde on the deck with Adonis. If you had just listened to me and waited."

"Can I ask you a question, Miss Penelope?" Clete said.

"*What?*"

"Do you know where I could put together a pitcher of Jack on shaved ice with a few mint leaves on top and a lime slice or two? I'd be in your debt."

Small hailstones began clicking on the ceiling of the bridge, then grew in size and volume and velocity until they were bouncing like Ping-Pong balls all over our ship, their cool white purity shutting out the world, chastening the wind, denting the waves and swells, creating an operatic clanging of ice and steel that Beethoven's Fifth couldn't match.

But it wasn't over. I'll try to explain. See, it's got everything to do with Clete Purcel. As Clete would say, I'll give you the straight gen, Ben. I wouldn't give you a shuck, Chuck.

Epilogue

HERE'S THE MINUTIAE of the situation, although Clete and Father Julian and I don't wish to visit it anymore, and when we go out for dinner, we talk about the world that others see and live in and pretend their vision of things is the correct one.

Johnny fired up the pontoon plane anchored at the stilt house and flew himself and Isolde into Mexico, and for many years their music was a doorway into the past for those of us who wanted to hold on to what was best in our youthful days. Penelope and Adonis grew prematurely old, as though they had outlived their time. I saw her on occasion at the racetrack in New Orleans or in a restaurant in the Quarter, and she was always polite and demure, but for just a second her eyes would linger on mine and her face would become warm and contemplative, and whether imaginary or not, I would smell her perfume, even feel it wrapping around me, like the heavy odor of magnolia on a cool spring night, and I would hear a warning bell at a train crossing and make an excuse and get out of New Orleans as quickly as I could.

But this is not what I wanted to tell you about. I have learned little in life, acquired no wisdom, and given up dealing with the great mysteries. Stonewall Jackson talked about mystifying the enemy. I've got news for the general. You don't need to mystify anyone. On balance, our best thinking has been a disaster from birth to the grave.

What happened to Shondell's yacht? We don't know. It disappeared, with his body and the bodies of his employees. I saw it go under from the deck of the sailboat, the keel rolling out of the waves, black smoke gushing from the portholes and open hatches.

Maybe it slipped off the continental shelf. Why not? There's a German submarine down there, its crew still on board. Maybe Mark Shondell found the company he deserved.

But let's look again at the larger story. Leslie and her daughter also disappeared, probably forever, at least in tangible form. However, I see her and Elizabeth with Gideon in my sleep. I even feel her fingers touch my brow, and I know I'm not alone. Clete says he saw them inside a white fog off Key West. He takes the tale a step farther. He says Gideon has come twice in the early A.M to his apartment on St. Ann Street, like a brother-in-arms who cannot let go of shared memories.

Clete has always been a closet bibliophile. For years, in a small room overlooking his courtyard, he stored hundreds of paperback books he bought in secondhand stores and yard sales, most of them about American history and the War Between the States. He read and reread James Street's *Tap Roots* and *By Valour and Arms,* Margaret Mitchell's *Gone With the Wind,* MacKinlay Kantor's *Andersonville,* Bruce Catton's *A Stillness at Appomattox,* and all the works of Shelby Foote.

He also loved to visit Civil War battlefields. Not long ago Clete was visiting a site near the place where Grant had begun his Wilderness Campaign, which would eventually culminate at Appomattox Courthouse. Coincidentally, that same weekend, a collection of neo-Nazis and Klansmen had assembled in a city park, supposedly to oppose the removal of Confederate statuary. In a torchlight march, they chanted an anti-Semitic mantra of hatred and paranoia and carried the battle flag of Robert Lee and the Army of Northern Virginia next to Hitler's swastika. The next day one of their members plowed his car into a crowd, injuring many and killing a young woman.

Clete left town, sickened by what he saw.

Late at night, back in New Orleans in the midst of an electric storm, Clete said Gideon sat down with him at the back of a poolroom. But he no longer resembled the reptilian figure who had haunted our lives. He was clean-shaven and clear-skinned and dressed in a corduroy coat and work pants and suspenders and a floppy hat an Italian vineyard owner might wear.

"The man Shondell served is in your midst, Mr. Purcel," Gideon said. "But you should not worry about him. He will be destroyed by his own machinations."

"Who's the guy?" Clete asked.

"You already know."

"I don't want to believe that. I don't want to hear it, either."

Gideon squeezed Clete's arm. *"Arrivederci."*

I didn't want to hear any more of the story. I had already put aside the unhappiness of the past and no longer wanted to probe the shadows of the heart or the evil that men do. It was time to lay down my sword and shield and study war no more. It's odd, but just at dawn the other day, I saw a narrow boat with a hand-carved dragon's head on the bow floating down Bayou Teche. On the boat I saw a woman reclining on her side, smiling at me, her lips parting, pulling me once again into the mists of ancient Avalon. Her hair was golden, her skin as pale as milk, a necklace of flowers hung on her breasts, and this is what she said:

May the road rise up to meet you.

May the wind be always at your back.

May the sun shine warm upon your face,

the rains fall soft upon your fields, and until we meet again,

may God hold you in the palm of His hand.

Acknowledgments

A writer's life can be a grand one, but the success she or he experiences involves many other people, most of whom receive little or no credit for their contributions to the work of the writer. In my case, I owe a debt to large numbers of people who have been at my side in one fashion or another for the many years I have been a published writer.

The meek and humble reference librarians are at the top of the list. I'm convinced that if Western civilization collapses, the reference librarian will be there to save us from ourselves. Book vendors are in the same category. So are the book reps at the publishing company. So are the publicists and editors and copyreaders who go beyond duty and call to get it right. If a writer can say his or her life has been a grand one, as mine has, the debt is enormous, and it would take hours to thank all the people who have been so loyal to both me and my work.

I wish to thank my daughter Pamala and my wife, Pearl, for their encouragement and editorial suggestions, and for all the marketing help given to me by Erin Mitchell. My thanks go also to my publishers, Carolyn Reidy and Jonathan Karp, and also Richard Rhorer and Stephen Bedford and Elizabeth Breeden and Sarah Lieberman and Jonathan Evans and all the other fine people at Simon & Schuster, particularly my editor, Sean Manning, and his team, Lake Bunkley and Tzipora Baitch, and also Jackie Seow, whose book jackets are always engaging and in some lovely way encapsulating of the book, and artworks in themselves.

A special thanks to E. Beth Thomas, who is one of the best copy and literary editors I've ever worked with.

Also, my undying appreciation to Philip and Mary and Anne-Lise Spitzer and Kim Lombardini and Lukas Ortiz and the Spitzer Agency.

Thanks to my children, Jim, Andree, Pamala, and Alafair, for being there.

And lastly, thanks to all my readers. You're a grand bunch, and it's an honor to be among you.

About the Author

James Lee Burke is a *New York Times* bestselling author, two-time winner of the Edgar Award for Best Novel, and the recipient of a Guggenheim Fellowship for Creative Arts in Fiction. He has authored thirty-nine novels and two short story collections. He lives in Missoula, Montana.